# RECKLESS ROAD

# RECKLESS ROAD

## CHRISTINE FEEHAN

**THORNDIKE PRESS**
A part of Gale, a Cengage Company

LIBRARY OF CONGRESS CIP DATA ON FILE.
CATALOGUING IN PUBLICATION FOR THIS BOOK
IS AVAILABLE FROM THE LIBRARY OF CONGRESS.

ISBN-13: 978-1-4328-8373-7 (hardcover alk. paper)

Published in 2021 by arrangement with Berkley, an imprint of Penguin
Publishing Group, a division of Penguin Random House, LLC.

Printed in Mexico
Print Number: 01     Print Year: 2021

For Khloe Wren —
thanks for being such an inspiration
in the trenches.

Special thanks to Adaiah La Vonda
for naming Hannah's shop the
Floating Hat and inspiring me to write
the scene with Hannah and the
mischievous little boys!

# FOR MY READERS

Be sure to go to christinefeehan.com/ members/ to sign up for my private book announcement list and download the free ebook of *Dark Desserts*. Join my community and get firsthand news, enter the book discussions, ask your questions and chat with me. Please feel free to email me at Christine@ christinefeehan.com. I would love to hear from you.

# ACKNOWLEDGMENTS

As in any book, there are others to thank. Brian for competing with me during power hours for top word count, when I wanted to move fast on this one because I kept insisting on writing it over and over. Domini for always editing, no matter how many times I ask you to go over the same book before we send it for additional editing. Sheila for your help with all the notes. Denise for always finding ways to keep us going no matter how difficult the circumstances.

Special thanks to Susan Cordeiro, who first suggested using 287 for the name of the restaurant, "for all the children who were taken into the school . . . to show none of them were forgotten." I loved this suggestion so much!

Special thanks to Amy Sutcliffe Pierce, who first suggested Crow, but in Russian. She said to name it ворона to honor their crow tattoos and colors. I decided to go with the English version, but I loved the suggestion of

9

using it in Russian.

I decided to combine both of these suggestions together for Crow 287. To me this sounded simple but meaningful and very much like Alena.

# TORPEDO INK MEMBERS

Viktor Prakenskii aka *Czar* — President
Lyov Russak aka *Steele* — Vice President
Savva Pajari aka *Reaper* — Sergeant at Arms
Savin Pajari aka *Savage* — Sergeant at Arms
Isaak Koval aka *Ice* — Secretary
Dmitry Koval aka *Storm*
Alena Koval aka *Torch*
Luca Litvin aka *Code* — Treasurer
Maksimos Korsak aka *Ink*
Kasimir Popov aka *Preacher*
Lana Popov aka *Widow*
Nikolaos Bolotan aka *Mechanic*
Pytor Bolotan aka *Transporter*
Andrii Federoff aka *Maestro*
Gedeon Lazaroff aka *Player*
Kir Vasiliev aka *Master*
Lazar Alexeev aka *Keys*
Aleksei Solokov aka *Absinthe*

**Newer Patched Members**
Gavriil Prakenskii
Casimir Prakenskii

11

**Prospects**
Fatei
Glitch
Hyde

# ONE

Fog churned over the ocean, the wind blowing the roiling mass over the highway, turning the silvery night a dark, angry gray. Wisps curled around the truck as Gedeon "Player" Lazaroff maneuvered one of the severely tight curves on Highway 1 along the Northern California coast. He was familiar with the highway, but most of the time he rode his Harley and had his brothers riding with him. In some ways he was thankful they weren't with him, but he would have welcomed the comfort of their company.

The dark gray mist thickened so it seemed an impenetrable wall, and he slowed down, although he was so close to home his inclination was to step on the gas to get there faster. He was nearly desperate to make it back to the Torpedo Ink clubhouse and the solace of the room he used there. He owned a house and normally would have gone there, but at this point, he didn't have the time. The clubhouse was much closer, and the longer he was out in public, even in the seclusion of the truck, the more dangerous it was. He knew that, and he had vowed never to take chances with anyone's life again.

The cell played Master's short tune announcing a call, and Player hesitated, swearing under his breath. Sweat beaded on his forehead and trickled down his face. He wiped at it with his palm before hitting the Bluetooth. Cell phone service was spotty at best on Highway 1, and he hoped it wouldn't work. Naturally, he wasn't that lucky.

"Yeah?" He was abrupt. Off-putting. Hoping Master would get the hint.

"You okay? Where are you?"

"About four miles from home." Deliberately, he hadn't distinguished between the clubhouse and his residence.

There was a small silence. Four miles from home meant Player had been pushing hard. Far too hard. Risking trouble. Already, they'd broken the rules by separating. Torpedo Ink members stayed close. When running a mission, they paired up, eyes on each other at all times. They'd gotten into unforeseen trouble, and Player needed to get home fast. Master wasn't able to drive as fast. He carried an unexpected passenger with him, and Player couldn't risk being in close proximity with her, not in his present state of mind, although he'd only told Master he was feeling very sick and needed to get home.

14

Master had to drive the passenger's vehicle home anyway, so it had all worked out for the best. They'd reported to Czar and let him know Player was coming in early without Master, and Master was bringing in "baggage."

"Tell me," Master insisted.

"Fog rolled in."

"Pull over. I'll send someone to you."

"I'm close. I can make it. Just one of my damn headaches." Player poured confidence into his voice, ignoring the way the road seemed to be coming alive with the fog wrapping it in loops and whorls like smoke from a pipe. "Less than four miles now." He shook his head trying to clear it. All that did was rattle his already hurting brain. He clenched his teeth against the pain.

"You sure? Go to the clubhouse — it's closer."

"Yeah. Good idea. I can make it." He could. There was no one with him. He was good. Just make it into the yard. Park the truck. Get to his room and lie down. His head was pounding. It felt like his brain was coming apart. He had made it home a day early, so that was a good thing. "I can make it, no problem," he reiterated, trying to sound unaffected.

Blue and red cut through the gray veil of fog in the rearview mirror, and he cursed silently as he looked down at the speedometer. Shit. Speeding. He could have sworn he'd slowed down. Hadn't he? He couldn't remember now. He was sweating bullets.

"Gotta go, Master, you're breaking up anyway." He needed to concentrate. He dropped the connection before Master could protest.

They had run what was supposed to be an easy assignment, trailing a couple of Ghosts that Code, their computer genius, had uncovered. Find out where the two were going, which motorcycle clubs they were targeting next. Easy, right? Torpedo Ink wanted to know who they were.

The Ghosts turned out to be businessmen who had been preying on weaker members of the various outlaw motorcycle clubs, specifically those members who gambled, getting them in deep and then making certain that they gave up information on the clubs running drugs or guns or trafficking in return for getting out of debt. The Ghosts wanted cuts into those particular businesses.

When a club reacted negatively, they had the president's old lady kidnapped, raped and tortured until the club complied or she was returned dead and another woman was taken. The Ghosts had a particularly vicious group of hit men doing their dirty work for them.

Player's club, Torpedo Ink, had rescued two women belonging to separate MCs from the hit men the Ghosts kept on retainer. In both

16

cases, Torpedo Ink had been hired secretly so no one associated them with the rescues. The larger clubs didn't want it known that they had gone outside their club looking for help. Torpedo Ink didn't want it known that they had helped. They were a small club, and they wanted to stay under the radar — from law enforcement, other clubs and definitely the Ghosts.

The very fact that the Ghosts kept themselves out of the line of fire by hiring hit men to do their dirty work for them was why they called themselves Ghosts. They believed no one could ever trace them. They didn't know about men like Code, who were that good with computers and could track just about anyone.

Player took his foot off the gas and eased the truck to the side of the road, watching the deputy pull in behind him. He was two lousy miles from the Caspar turnoff and the clubhouse. Two miles. In his present state, it was dangerous to have any interaction with any other human being. That had been the reason he'd separated himself from Master. Being safe. Making certain everyone was safe. Now this, all because he hadn't been paying attention. He knew better.

He hit the back of his head against the seat twice in recrimination and fished his license out of his wallet. Transporter and Mechanic, fellow members of the Torpedo Ink club,

17

always kept the vehicles in the best of shape, the paperwork up to date and in the glove compartments. He had no doubt everything was in order, but he was so tired he wasn't certain if the truck was clean of any weapons. He just couldn't remember if he'd given everything to Master or if he'd kept guns with him.

He was exhausted, seventy-two hours without sleep and he'd used his psychic gift for far too long, something he knew better than to do. It not only drained him and took a huge toll physically and mentally on him, but if he used it for too long, it began to spill over into his reality. That was the main reason he had pushed so hard to make it back to his room at the clubhouse. He needed to be where he was surrounded by familiar things and he could replenish his strength and allow his fractured brain time to recover.

He'd always kept that side effect from his fellow Torpedo Ink members. They thought he would get a migraine and *Alice's Adventures in Wonderland* characters would appear. It would be funny, and they would all get a laugh. They had no idea how truly serious and fucked up that reality could get, or how it could really morph into something far, far more dangerous.

He buzzed down his window and shut off the truck as the deputy walked up to his vehicle. He recognized him right away. Jackson Deveau was a good cop, but one difficult, if not impossible, to misdirect. Just his luck. Player's head was pounding so bad his stomach began to twist into knots. He glanced around the truck, hoping like hell everything was in place and there were no weapons in sight. He had a carry permit, but it was best to not make any waves — especially with Jackson.

"Player," Jackson greeted as he took the license, his dark eyes moving over Player's face, seeing too much like he always did. "You all right?"

It was never good to try to deceive Jackson if you didn't have to. The members of Torpedo Ink suspected he was a human lie detector. He just seemed too good at figuring everything out.

"Feel like shit. Was trying to get home and didn't realize I was speeding until I saw your lights. Sorry, man." He resisted rubbing his pounding temples. "Do you need the registration and insurance? The truck is registered to Torpedo Ink, and the insurance is up to date. Czar's going to kick my ass for this."

Jackson handed him back his license. "I have to see the papers, Player."

Player reached over and opened the glove compartment, noting that Jackson's gaze followed the movement, one hand out of sight, probably near his weapon. Jackson didn't take chances, not even with the people he knew and actually liked. It was always difficult to tell with Jackson whether or not Torpedo Ink was included with those he liked. The cop's expression gave very little away.

Player handed over the registration and insurance and gave in to rubbing his temples. He didn't want to look too long at Jackson or the fog that was drifting in off the ocean. He'd been creating illusions longer than he should have been, and now those edges were blurring with reality. More than once, when he was tired, his mind played tricks on him and he couldn't separate reality from the worlds he created. People had gotten hurt. Several had died. He didn't take chances. He worked on that all the time, and he knew when he needed to shut it down, which was more than twenty-four hours ago.

"Thought you always ran with a partner." Jackson said it casually as he carefully inspected the paperwork.

Player cursed silently. His heart was beating too fast. Behind the deputy, a large caterpillar floated in the air, smoking a giant blue-green hookah. Big rings of smoke curled around the truck. Around Jackson. Player began to count in his head. Numbers. Repeating them over and over. The caterpillar began to puff in time to his counting, the smoke coming out in the shapes of his numbers at first, then morphing into letters of the alphabet.

"Master picked up a passenger in New Mexico. I got sick and couldn't wait for them, so I hit it for home."

Little beads of sweat trickled down his face. There was no stopping it. The smoke letters tilted first one way and then the other, rocking as if in tune to music. He realized he was tapping a beat on the steering wheel as he often did, in keeping with the counting in his head.

"Really sorry about speeding, Jackson, must have started inchin' up on the gas when I got closer to the turnoff without realizing it."

The letters drifted by Jackson's head. Spelling words. *Death to the guards. Off with his head.* Player closed his eyes, but the vision stayed in his mind, refusing to leave, the fog becoming smoke swirling around the truck and closing off the road so that even when he opened his eyes, it was difficult to see anything but the smoking caterpillar, Jackson, the wall of gray and those taunting letters that grew in length and width, filling the sky above the deputy as if condemning him.

Player forced air through his lungs as the smoke from the hookah began to swirl in time to his tapping fingers, the fog rings dropping like nooses around the deputy's neck. Abruptly, he forced his hands away from the steering wheel. He used music to soothe his brain, but it was all part of the fracturing now. He had to get out of there before he hurt Jackson.

"I don't think a few miles over the speed limit is worth Czar kicking the crap out of you. I think we can let it slide this time." Jackson handed back the registration and insurance, watching with his cool, dark eyes as Player put the papers back in the glove compartment. "Make it home safe."

"Will do. Thanks for the break. Nasty weather tonight. You be safe as well."

Player didn't wait for Jackson to get back to his SUV, nor did he look to see if the caterpillar had disappeared. He started the truck and eased it back onto the highway, concentrating on getting back up to speed, wanting to make those two miles as quickly as he could without further mishap. He just had to get to the clubhouse and into his room without any further contact with anyone.

The fog kept curling into shapes — hearts and diamonds, spades and clovers. They floated against the backdrop of the gray wall. The road wrinkled and moved, but he drove doggedly on, knowing the way, forcing his mind to work in spite of the images that had been familiar to him since his childhood.

He turned off the highway and drove toward the ocean, where the fog rose up like a large fountain off the churning waves, spouting into cyclones that danced toward the bluffs. Player tore his gaze from the waves and drove straight to the clubhouse, counting over and over to one hundred in his mind to keep his brain occupied so it wouldn't build stories or shape those cyclones into anything monstrous in the foggy weather.

He drove through the open gates into the parking lot, and to his dismay, the lot was filled with Harleys, trucks and a few random cars. His heart sank. Music blasted out of the clubhouse. Two fires roared in the pits on the side overlooking the ocean, where men and women danced and partied in the fog. He could make out their eerie shapes gyrating even as their laughter was muffled by the heavy mist.

A fucking party. He was a day early, and the club was having a party. He'd forgotten it was on the schedule to meet with another club whose members had come, like them, from one of the four Sorbacov training schools in Russia. The club, calling themselves Rampage, wanted to join Torpedo Ink.

Player didn't dare be around anyone in his present state. He was too worn, his brain fractured, the migraine too severe. He needed time to heal. To rest. A party with lots of people attending was the last place he needed to be. He forced his brain to keep counting, refusing to look at the grayish figures looking like silhouettes in the fog.

He pulled the keys out of the ignition and sat there for a moment, trying to clear his mind, eyes closed tight, breathing deep, counting in his head in the hopes that just by being in a familiar place, surrounded by his brothers, he would be okay. He opened his eyes slowly, reluctantly.

At once he saw the ocean, waves crashing against the bluffs — white foam rising in the air. The beat in his head became lobsters clacking claws together as they danced in the spinning cyclones rushing toward the bluffs, where the eerie shapes in the fog danced with that same beat. The lobsters called to the sea creatures to rise up, and they did, their forms growing in those whirling columns of mist as the beat accelerated, the drumming going faster and faster to match the crazy, gyrating twisters dancing over the wild waves.

The dancers around the firepit moved with the beat, just as out of control, turning toward the turbulent sea and the wall of fog and the strange unnerving cyclones heading for the bluffs. One dancer stumbled backward, nearly falling into the firepit. Several men grabbed for her, pulling her to safety as she screamed and laughed hysterically.

Player saw three men turn to look toward the truck. One sprinted toward him. He let out his breath and closed his eyes. He just had to get into the clubhouse and away from everyone. Maestro, one of his brothers, took the keys from him and wrapped his arm around him. "You should have called ahead. Recognized your *Alice's Adventures in Wonder-*

*land* calling card." There was a hint of laughter in his voice. "How bad is it?"

"My fucking head is about to explode." Player dared to open his eyes, trying to squint, seeing Maestro through the shimmering fog with the strange backdrop of lobsters riding spinning waterspouts in the ocean over his shoulder.

Maestro was a big man with wide shoulders and vivid gray eyes that could look like liquid silver when he became intense. His hair was dark, streaked with silver, and like Player, he wore it longer. He appeared to be very gentle and soft-spoken, but that hid a very dominant personality. Right now, he urged Player out of the truck into the curling fog, where his free hand held the truck keys — but the keys were already morphing into a pocket watch. For a moment, a White Rabbit appeared behind Maestro, looking over his shoulder at the watch and shaking his head, those long ears flopping as he did so. His nose wrinkled, and worry gathered in his eyes. Then the rabbit began to morph into someone else altogether, and Player's breath hitched. He hastily concentrated on the watch.

The watch was intricate. Made of gold. He would never forget that particular watch. He fixated on it. He remembered every detail of it. The way it worked so precisely. The elaborate transparent design. The two covers. The golden chain and swivel fob. As he looked at it lying in Maestro's hand, it grew in size so he could see the images imprinted in the cover. He could hear the seventeen ruby jewels working to ensure perfect precision. He had to stop. He couldn't look at that watch or think about it.

"My head hurts like a mother, Maestro, I've got to close my eyes. Get me inside, will you?" He tried to keep his voice as even as possible, tried to convey that he was really shaky from a migraine, not that his brain was fractured and that any minute he could royally fuck everyone up.

"Sure, Player," Maestro said. "Keep your head down. I'll get you inside. The place is packed," he warned. "A lot of noise."

Player squeezed his eyes closed tight. He couldn't afford to make the pocket watch part of any of this scenario. He was already skating too close to being out of control. "Can't look at anyone," he admitted — and it was a hard admission. He didn't like any of his brothers to know how truly fucked up he was. "Get me to a bathroom. Need a shower to clear my head. I'll go to bed and be fine. Throat's sore. Need water and some Tylenol."

"I'll get you there and bring some water and Tylenol to the bathroom. Let's go."

Player stayed right in step with him, his eyes on the ground. The cement he'd helped pour moved, narrowing, rippling under their feet. Once he took his gaze from the sidewalk, but

26

then he saw the monstrous pocket watch and heard the ticking in time to the lobsters' clacking, and he preferred the strange dipping and wheeling pathway. He just kept pace with Maestro, trusting his brother, not the images in his head.

The common room was overflowing with partiers. Player tried not to look at them as he and Maestro waded through the half-drunk dancers as they gyrated around one another and the bodies pressing close. He did his best not to inhale as they hurried across the room toward the door that led to the back rooms. He couldn't take in the scent of sex. Several girls were going down on men, and two were already on their hands and knees calling out for more. He jerked his gaze from the sight, counting over and over in his head. Drinks were on tables, filled to the brim, and they rose in the air and tipped liquid onto the floor and the backs of men and women as Player and Maestro rushed toward the back.

"Shit, brother," Maestro hissed as laughter erupted all around them. "*Alice's Adventures in Wonderland* strikes again."

Player's stomach lurched. He had deliberately cultivated his fellow club members to see the humor in the crazy things that happened when his "migraines" occurred after he went too far using his psychic talent. He couldn't fault them when they laughed or made light of it. They had no idea how dangerous he was or how much he truly despised the mere mention of that story and every damn memory it dredged up. None of it good. Maestro pulled open the door to the back rooms.

The moment Maestro opened the door, Player could hear women moaning. A few of his brothers were using the rooms, and doors had been left open, something not all that uncommon during a party. The smell of sex was heavy in the confined space of the hall. As they passed an open door, a woman's voice called out, begging for the queen's maids to join them for sex. Her partner answered her, "What the hell are you going on about? What queen? What maids?"

Maestro kicked the door closed as they hurried past. "We never should have shown you that old *Alice's Adventures in Wonderland* porn, Player," he said, laughter in his voice. "You gotta stop thinking about that movie."

Player could have told him it had nothing whatsoever to do with thinking and everything to do with smells, association and his fucked-up, fragmented brain playing tricks. Every open door they passed, Maestro slammed closed with his boot until they were all but sprinting down the rippling floor to the bathroom at the very end of the hallway.

This particular bathroom was considered off-limits during parties to outsiders, and the brothers kept to the rule. Lana and Alena, their sisters, both fully patched members of Torpedo Ink, used that room exclusively, although now they shared it with some of the other members' wives. Maestro yanked open the door and practically shoved Player inside.

"I'll be right back with a bottle of water and Tylenol," Maestro promised and closed the door, leaving Player alone.

The scent of fresh lavender immediately washed the smell of sex away, giving Player a bit of a reprieve. He let himself take a deep breath, inhaling the lavender, taking the scent into his lungs, hoping to chase some of his terrible tension away. Perched on the sink and continuously breathing deeply, he texted Master to tell him he'd made it home safely while he waited for Maestro to return.

Maestro was fast, handing him the water and pills. He also brought him a clean pair of jeans and shirt. "You need me to wait and get you back to your room?"

"Naw, I'm good now. I can make it, no problem. I'll lock up for the night and just sleep it off. You know I'm good once I'm down," Player assured, pouring confidence into his voice. He detested that he'd taken Maestro from the party. Worse, it was dangerous for Maestro to spend too much time with him.

"If you're certain." Maestro dangled the keys to the truck from his fingers.

At once, Player's gaze caught and held there, unable to stop, no matter how much he willed his mind to pull away. The keys morphed into the dreaded gold pocket watch, the case swiveling back and forth, nearly mesmerizing Player. The timepiece began to grow in front of his eyes again. He counted faster, forcing himself to turn his entire body away.

Player tossed back the Tylenol and chased it with water. "Absolutely. The shower will help, and then I'm sleeping as long as possible." By some miracle, he kept from yelling at Maestro to get the fuck out. He kept his voice even and calm.

He didn't look at Maestro, still counting in his head, hoping his brother would take the hint and get out of there fast. He didn't trust himself. No one was safe. No one, not even those he loved. Not when he was this bad. He was fortunate in that he had deceived his brothers for so long into thinking he got vicious migraines and nothing was really wrong with him. No one really ever questioned him, and Maestro wanted to get back to the party.

The moment the door was closed, Player stripped and stepped under the hot water to wash off the road and to try to let the clean scent the women kept in the bathroom clear his fragmented mind. His head was pounding, the roaring so terrible he could barely stand it. Truthfully, he'd only experienced pain this bad once before. That was the time he'd lost total control, and his entire world had come apart when he realized what could happen. He was scared for everyone there in the clubhouse, and if necessary, he was going to bunk right there on the bathroom floor.

He took his time letting the hot water pour over him until he began to hallucinate that the shower floor was beginning to fill up like a pool. He had to blink rapidly, call the numbers aloud to himself as he dried off and dressed. There was no staying in the bathroom. He had to get to his private room, put in earplugs, turn off the lights and go to sleep. The more he slept, the faster his brain healed.

He took several deep breaths of the lavender, deliberately dragging the scent into his lungs, flung the door open, and planted his gaze on the door to his room. It seemed a very long distance away. He sprinted. He was normally fast. Very fast. He had long legs, and he could cover the distance with ease, but the floor undulated like a massive snake, threatening to throw him off balance.

Music played in his head. *Will you, won't you. Will you? Won't you?* He tried to shut it off. Lobsters clacked their claws while snails shook heads and tortoises asked them to dance. He leapt over the wood rising like waves, the creatures looking at him with wide, knowing eyes. He kept his desperate gaze glued to his door. It appeared to be moving as well, growing smaller and smaller, as if he had been dropped into an alternate world. He shook his head hard, drops of sweat hitting the floor. He began to count aloud, uncaring if anyone in any of the rooms heard him. It was the only way he wasn't going to suck them into his reality.

Doggedly, sweat dripping off him, ignoring the seriously pitching floor and the diminishing door, he kept running. He knew this universe, the one that sucked him in and became a nightmare version of reality. Everything in it was too dangerous for words. His fractured mind changed the world around him into a dark, sinister place where torture, murder and vicious cruelty lurked around every corner.

He refused to acknowledge the whispers growing loud enough to interfere with his counting. He lost track for a moment but immediately started over again. Then, thankfully, his hand was on the doorknob, and he shoved the heavy oak door to his room open, all but fell inside, slammed the door closed and leaned against it, breathing hard.

The music changed from lobsters clacking their pinchers together and singing about turtles joining them in a dance to a distinctly Middle Eastern beat. The tinkle of little bells caught at his mind, pulling him out of his head. Lighting in his room was dim. Candles were scattered around, flickering gently. A mixture of essential oils gave off the fragrance of pink plumeria, Egyptian musk and ginger, bathing his senses in the exotic flavors. Instantly his mind filled in all the details of a stormy night, so far from the nightmare images of his childhood and the night they'd accidentally consumed mushrooms.

Player flattened his palms against the door and stared in shock at the most gorgeous woman he'd ever seen in his life, dancing just a few feet away, staring back at him with enormous, startling chocolate eyes, framed with dark lashes. Her hair was dark and extremely thick, still moving with her body to the music, falling past her shoulders in luscious waves. This definitely wasn't part of the familiar nightmare world his fucked-up brain conjured when it was fractured and he needed to be alone and just let it heal.

Soft washed-out blue jeans rode low on her generous hips, and a rose-colored tee was knotted under her equally generous breasts. Her abdominal muscles had been undulating to the music as her hips performed intricate movements and her curvy buttocks and very high rounded tits shook to the music. Coins and bells hung from a wide golden belt wrapped around her hips, and bells swung from an ankle bracelet with every movement she made. She came to an abrupt halt when his shocked gaze hit hers.

"What are you doing in here?" Player man-

33

aged to find his voice. It came out rougher and far more gravelly than he intended, maybe even a snarl. He had a lower register, one that tended to intimidate easily.

He was a big man with wide shoulders, a thick chest, muscular arms and narrow hips. His hair was brown with streaks of blond. It fell a few inches beyond his shoulders, a thick wild mass that made the vivid blue of his eyes only more piercing and direct. He kept a short, trimmed dark beard and moustache that also added to the effect his eyes had on others. He was very aware she might find him extremely intimidating, especially alone in the room with him, but he couldn't move away from the door no matter how much he told himself to step away.

"I'm so sorry."

Her voice was musical. Soft and gentle. Like a cooling breeze sweeping through the room . . . or his mind. She looked genuinely distressed, her amazing eyes expressive, the long lashes sweeping down as color flooded her face.

"One of the Torpedo Ink members told me to come into this room. That I should dance in here." Her explanation came out fast, the words tumbling over one another, and yet at the same time, her tone was lyrical, as if she'd blended the notes with the universe, unlocking some secret formula that set everything right.

Player could see letters floating in the air, but they were moving away from him. Away from her. The eastern-themed music didn't fit at all with the down-the-rabbit-hole nightmare world his mind created when he was so far gone like this. He pressed his palms harder into the door, standing firmly in front of it, more to keep her in now than to keep everyone else out. He recognized that in some way, she was soothing to his fragmented brain, and that was a puzzle he needed to solve. Now he just wanted her to stay and talk.

Her body had been moving when he'd entered, and the rhythm of her bare feet, ball to heel, hip dipping low, swaying gently, hands flowing so gracefully, all kept time with the earth itself. She seemed to flow gracefully, in harmony with the music, with the earth.

He was a woodworker. A musician. Everything about him had to do with nature and rhythm. At the moment, he was so out of sync with nature, so completely out of tune, but he recognized that she was the most naturally gifted woman — make that "naturally gifted person" — he'd ever met. He hadn't known anyone like her actually existed. She could have been born of the earth itself.

It wasn't just that incredible voice of hers, but her body as well, every movement, no matter how small, flowing and soft. He was

35

mesmerized just by the way, when she spoke to him and she shifted her weight from one foot to the other, he felt the heartbeat of the earth, like the beat of the Arabic music playing so softly in the background.

"What are you doing?" He made every effort to gentle his voice. It still came out with his rougher rasp, but he didn't sound like he was going to kill her. That was a plus. "Before I came in. What were you doing?"

The color sweeping up her neck and into her face deepened. "Practicing dancing. They said it would be all right to wait in here."

Player dared to bring one hand up to his neck to massage the tight knots. He tried to breathe through the pain in his head, making it difficult to think straight. His brothers. They must have sent an exotic dancer to his room, thinking he would need some relaxing fun after his long drive. They had no idea the mission had gone to hell and things had taken a turn for the worst. This woman, with her beautiful bedroom eyes and thick pelt of glossy hair, practicing her craft while she waited for him, shouldn't be wasted. He took another deep breath to try to get on top of the crushing pain.

"Your name?" He managed to bite out the question without sounding like he was going to take a bite out of her — at least, he thought he did. She still hadn't moved. The little ankle bells were very still, as were the ones dripping beneath the golden coins around her hips.

"Zyah."

She whispered it, and her name sounded so lyrical to him that already his mind was working on role-playing with her. How could he not? The setting was perfection. She was a gorgeous belly dancer hired by his brothers. They'd known he would come in tired from the long drive and tense after the mission. She was just perfect to relax him. Where had they found her?

"You're practicing your dancing?" He encouraged her to talk to him, needing to hear the sound of that musical voice. The tone seemed to find a way into his fractured mind. Each note, each way she framed the pure pitches, along with the movements of her body, seemed to connect, to transfer nutrients to his starved brain cells.

She nodded, and again the small movement was accompanied by the shifting of her feet, the ball of her foot to her heel and then the sway of her hips. The little bells at her ankles and hips jingled, blending with the beating of the *dumbek,* the Arabic drum that accompanied the music playing. She had such a natural rhythm to her, and he felt it from the bare soles of his feet to the already quieting thunder in his head.

"I don't mind. I didn't realize you were in here. It startled me is all. It's crazy out there."

He gestured toward the hallway, hoping she'd choose to stay. To encourage her, he kept his large frame draped against the door.

"Is this your room?"

He wanted to savor the cadence of her voice, that soft lyrical sound that moved around the broken pieces in his head and knitted them back together. With every word she uttered, the terrible pounding lessened. "Yes, but it feels like an Egyptian oasis out under the stars in here. I wouldn't mind playing your prince. I like role-playing." He flashed her a smile. He'd been told more than once he had a "killer" smile and could melt the panties off a woman if he tried. He was trying now. "My brothers call me Player."

Her laughter was a soft melody, playing over his body like the touch of fingers. A slow burn started out of nowhere, a kind of molten lava moving through his veins as if she'd woken a long-forgotten part of him he hadn't experienced naturally since he was a boy.

"Of course they do. Why aren't you at the party like everyone else?" She tilted her head to one side, but as she did, the thick fall of her hair swayed, her abdomen undulated, hips dipping and shifting in a figure eight, bare feet rising and falling, unaware that she had found the perfect heartbeat with her music, the drum and her enticing laughter.

"I'm more of a solitary man. What about you?"

"My dancing isn't going to work in that crowd." She laughed again, low and musical, her arms moving gracefully out from her body, a sensuous invitation as she began to dance around the room. "I dance only for my prince, remember?"

Her voice was a blend of smoke, sin and sex. That slow burn in his veins became hotter, the fire pooling in his groin, shocking the hell out of him. He didn't have natural erections. He was always in control of his body, commanding his own erections. The nearly violent reaction to the sultry tone of her voice was without comprehension. None. He couldn't conceive of the hot blood pouring into his cock being real. None of this could be real, not if his cock was involved, and there was no denying the enormous and urgent reaction to her.

"You have gorgeous eyes." She did. He doubted if he could make up those eyes of hers. He had a vivid imagination, but her eyes were unusual. They were large, a deep, deep startling color surrounded by dark lashes. He could drown in her eyes, never a good thing for a man like him. He found himself trying to choose the exact color of brown. They were a dark chocolate, almost a near black. "Are you wearing colored contacts?" He knew it wasn't just the deep rich color, but the shape and size of her eyes and the heavy dark lashes surrounding them.

She shook her head, and the action set the dark mass of hair flowing in waves around her face and shoulders and down her back. The lights from the candles caught in the glossy strands, highlighting the sheen, allowing him to see the various shades before the silky mass settled, framing her face and that exquisite bone structure.

"No, I inherited my eyes from my grandmother. I was very lucky to get her coloring."

There was love in her voice when she said *grandmother.* Her voice had gone even softer. She was capable of wrapping a man in real love, the lasting kind. Where that thought came from, he didn't know, since he wasn't altogether certain he believed in love.

"You have unusual eyes as well," Zyah pointed out. "You have dark hair, maybe not as dark as mine, but your eyes are an unusual shade of blue. Almost like an icy blue."

When she spoke, her body moved. The movements were subtle, but his mind was so tuned to her, not even the smallest detail escaped him. It was as if those soft, sensual notes were grounded in the earth the way her body movements were. It was true that he had blue eyes, but his hair was light brown with streaks of blond while hers was a rich chestnut color, a glossy, dark mass that added to her exotic dancer appearance.

"You look like you stepped right out of Egypt or Persia. I've traveled to several of the

Middle Eastern countries and found them quite beautiful."

Zyah smiled. It was slow in coming, but well worth the wait. He found himself holding his breath in anticipation, watching her mouth. She had a generous mouth, just like her breasts and hips. Like her large eyes. Her lips were full and curved perfectly, like a bow, her lower lip bitable. Her mouth was a shade of red without lipstick, although he thought she wore a gloss, and he already had fantasies about having those lips stretched around his cock. When she smiled, he could see her straight white teeth, although there was one little crooked tooth on her bottom row just to the right that set his pulse pounding. She was not only gorgeous but sexy beyond imagining.

"Did you have your own private dancer when you traveled to the various countries?"

That voice of hers, so sultry, curled around him like the sounds of the various instruments playing the Arabic music so softly in the background.

"No, I wasn't there for the beautiful women, although honestly, I never saw anyone who looked like you." He had been an instrument of death each time he'd been there. He was an assassin, trained from the time he was a child. He'd seen the dancers, beautiful women, but he hadn't managed to stay and listen to the music or watch the dancers after he'd killed his intended targets. He couldn't very well tell her that.

"Are you going to come all the way into the room or just stay leaning against the door?"

Her gaze drifted over him, and everywhere she looked it felt as if she touched him, caressed him with her fingers. His cock pulsed. Throbbed. Ached. He wanted to fist it right there while she danced for him. "I don't know. If I move, are you going to leave me?"

She tilted her head to one side, and again, when she moved, her hair swung around her in a sexy slide, setting her body into motion as well. Those small, subtle moves added to the pull on every one of his senses. He found himself totally unable to look away from her. He'd never been so wrapped up in someone so fast. So completely.

"Not if you really want me to stay." Her lashes swept down and back up, almost demurely. A look of innocence clashed with her sensual body movements and the sound of her voice.

"I want you to stay and dance for me. I want you to talk to me. You're the best surprise I've had in years." That was the absolute truth, and he hoped she believed him.

Her smile came again, and more hot blood raged through his veins and pounded through his cock. All on its own. His body actually

42

worked. It was a fucking miracle. *She* was the fucking miracle. He had no idea where his brothers had found her, but whatever they'd paid her to be here in his room waiting for him, it wasn't nearly enough. They couldn't have known she held some kind of elemental magic in her that worked itself into his body, into his brain, repairing all the damage and making him whole again.

She held out her hand to him, and when she did, her arm movements were graceful and flowing, as if she were dancing already for him. He wrapped his fingers around her hand, touching her for the first time. Skin to skin. His cock nearly exploded right along with his heart. She led him to the bed, her hips dipping with every heel-to-toe movement. The gold coins on her hips shimmied and shook, causing the bells to jingle on the belt as well as the bracelet around her ankle. He'd had no idea he could find ankle jewelry so sexy, but he did.

He settled on the bed, pulling off his shirt, barefoot, with only his jeans on, the room lit only with those scented candles. The music started again. He felt the difference in the music this time. It was highly sensuous. He was a musician and very familiar with instruments. His ear was finely tuned to pitches. He recognized the distinctive percussion of the goblet-shaped drum, the *dumbek.* The *kanun* was a stringed instrument that produced beautiful sounds much like a harp. There was a *ney,* a flute that had an amazing tone to it.

Zyah seemed to become one with the harmonious rhythms of the music, her arms gracefully flowing, almost mesmerizing. She moved in a circle, hips swaying, the bells calling to him. When she faced him, her abdomen was completely isolated, undulating, while her arms were moving over her head, hands telling a story. Flowing. Spellbinding. A seductress all his. He was utterly captivated by her. Zyah. His private dancer.

# Two

Player woke slowly, shades of Arabic music running through his mind. He kept his eyes closed, savoring the dream. He didn't have good dreams often and never after a bad experience like he'd had last night. Zyah. He let out a soft sigh, remembering her eyes, the way she'd looked at him while he moved in her. She was scorching hot. So fucking tight he thought she might strangle his cock with her sheath of silk.

He'd never had sex like that in his life. Not in real life and certainly not in his dreams. He had no idea how many times they'd had sex, but he'd taken her over and over, in the bed, on the floor, against the wall, on her hands and knees, any way he could get her. She was the most sensual creature and so damn hot he couldn't get enough of her. He loved the way she responded to him every single time.

He would never be able to conjure up eyes like hers. Large. That particular shade of dark, melting chocolate no one else had. Those long, dark lashes, thick, framing her eyes, drawing him in so he could drown in her when he took her slow.

Then there was her mouth. That fantasy mouth with her perfect lips. If he were a painter, he would paint those lips. The sight of them stretched around his cock while he disappeared into the hot haven of her mouth was so sexy, he'd barely kept it together long enough to enjoy himself. Especially with her eyes looking up at him.

He should have kept his dancer with him. If he had, even though it was a dream, maybe he would have made something good a reality instead of something bad. Instead, when he'd stretched out on his bed, exhausted, and she'd tried to lie down with him, he'd given her a swat on her very beautiful ass and told her he was done with her, to go home.

In his defense, when she'd looked at him with her big brown eyes, he *had* explained he didn't sleep with anyone but that he believed she'd earned every penny the brothers paid her and then some. He'd dug out every hundred-dollar bill he had transferred from his old jeans and shoved it into her hand. He'd been more than generous to his private dancer — he'd given her at least a thousand dollars, and she'd earned every penny.

Why the hell hadn't he kept her in his dream? That would have been the intelligent thing to do, so he could have her night after night. He groaned, his cock hard as a rock all over again. He went still. That was fucking impossible. His cock didn't react to anything without his express permission. He controlled his body at all times. He didn't have dreams, certainly not wet dreams.

Hating to face the day and give up on his private dancer dream, knowing he'd never get that one back, he forced his body to move, to turn over. The first thing that came into his view when he opened his eyes was his nightstand and the wad of money on it. He froze. Staring — just staring. He didn't leave money around. Not when there was a party. Okay, never. He stashed cash in a drawer for easy access, but he never left it out in the open.

Keeping his eyes on it, afraid it might come alive and bite him, he sat up slowly, the sheet tangling the one leg he still had covered. Kicking, he reached for the cash and peeled back the bills. Yeah. Over a thousand. His mythical tip. His dream had been so real, not only was her fragrance — pink plumeria, Egyptian musk and ginger — lingering in the room, but he had her money right there in the palm of his hand.

Player forced himself to look around. Candles burned all the way to nothing were scattered on every surface. He suddenly had a vision of dancing lights flickering over

47

Zyah's undulating abdomen, her swaying hips and graceful arms. The flames had projected her figure onto the wall so that her moving hands were mesmerizing. He'd had not only his private dancer, but a shadow dancer as well. The moment had been beautiful, unique and all for him. She had smiled, her face lighting up, and his entire body had come to life all on its own.

He shook his head, not daring to believe she was real, even with the money in his hand. Zyah was a dream. Women like her didn't exist. An exotic dancer, mysterious and beautiful, giving herself to him so completely, surrendering everything. Her mouth. Pure fire. Her tight pussy, hot as hell, a fucking inferno surrounding his cock and squeezing like a vise, milking him dry. Those eyes of hers staring into his as if he were someone real to her, someone worthwhile.

"No, this can't be happening. Tell me I didn't blow it this big." He whispered his plea to the universe and then forced himself to look down at the floor, because if he actually stuck his dick in a woman, he wouldn't do it without wearing a glove. Not ever. He would protect her and himself.

He groaned again, and this time not in a good way. The evidence lay everywhere. Filled condoms tied with knots scattered all over the floor as if he'd carelessly dropped them and grabbed the next one. They were everywhere, like the candles, condemning him. One by the wall. He remembered pushing her up against the wall, unable to wait to get into her, although he'd had her so many times. He couldn't get enough of her — or her him.

The chemistry between them was explosive. Crazy hot. Off the charts. No wonder he'd thought it was a fucking dream. It was too good to be true. He was so stupid, he hadn't even gotten her number. He pushed his palm against his forehead hard, trying to think what to do. He wasn't about to give her up, not when his body genuinely reacted to her. Not when she made him laugh the way she did. Not when just her voice and the movements of her body could heal his fragmented brain. He'd been handed a miracle, and he'd carelessly thrown it away. Not thrown it away — *driven* it away.

He just had to think. Breathe. Get oxygen to his brain and stop panicking. She was out there somewhere. She wasn't a myth. He hadn't made her up. The brothers had to have hired her. She didn't come out of nowhere. She was in his room for a reason — to entertain him. She'd been a gift to him. His fellow Torpedo Ink brothers had to have her name and number. He breathed a sigh of relief. Of course they would know how to contact her. How else had they gotten her for him?

49

Player took another slow look around the room, this time with satisfaction, letting every detail sink in. He wanted to remember every aspect of the night. Everything, down to the smallest detail, about his private dancer. She'd left behind the remnants of the candles, although he recalled the two of them blowing out the flames over what remained of the dwindling wax. They'd laughed together when they'd nearly hit foreheads. She had such a beautiful, captivating laugh.

They'd sat on the floor together drinking from a bottle of water as if they were sharing the best of wines. They'd had their backs to the bed and their knees drawn up, thighs and hips touching, while in the background, music played softly. His headache was gone. He remembered that distinctly. It was gone at that moment, and it was gone now. She smelled like heaven. Her skin was so soft that he couldn't stop running his palm up and down her arm. After five minutes of talking about nothing and everything, his cock was raging at him *all on its own.* He had pulled her under him right there on the floor and taken her hard and fast, looking right into her eyes, falling into all that deep, beautiful dark chocolate.

He groaned again as more memories crowded in. Eventually, inevitably, between the seventy-two hours without sleep, his fragmented brain — which, granted, she had somehow glued back together — and all the wild, hot sex, he had become so exhausted he could barely keep his eyes open. He'd crawled onto the bed and stretched out. She'd tried to cuddle up next to him. He'd given her what he thought was a playful little swat and a bit of a shove. Maybe the shove had been a little harder than he'd thought.

The smile had faded from her lips. He remembered that now, very distinctly. That mouth of hers. So beautiful. He'd used it more than once, stretching her lips around his thick girth. He would never forget that sensation, or the sight.

*Sorry, don't ever let babes sleep in my bed. You gotta go, honey.* He rolled over, yanked his jeans to him. *Whatever the brothers paid you wasn't nearly enough.* He'd given her everything he had in his wallet. Shoved it into her hand.

Zyah stood there beside the bed, completely naked, his marks all over her soft skin, her every curve, making his body react all over again. Making him hard as a rock just looking at her, knowing he'd put those marks on her. She stared down at the money for a brief moment and then looked at him. Instead of a smile in her eyes, a dark flame burned.

*What is this?* Her voice was low. Soft. The earth seemed to move, to murmur, just for the briefest of moments.

Had he been aware, as he was now, he

51

would have shut his mouth or tried to back-track. But he was too far gone, high on sex and delirious from lack of sleep.

*Seriously, just consider it your tip. Leave your number. Definitely be calling to use your services again.*

*My services?* That same low tone.

*No judgment, babe. Really, you gotta go. I'm done with you for now. I need to sleep.*

He'd watched her pull on her jeans and T-shirt, stuff her underwear into the pocket of her sweater and toss the money onto the nightstand.

His gaze dropped to the end table again and the money there. She hadn't taken it. He closed his eyes again and heard her voice as clear as day.

*Fuck you, Player. I should have known, just by your name. You're damn good at what you do.*

What had she meant? What did any of it mean? She'd left the money he'd given her. He'd thought he was complimenting her. He searched the top of the nightstand. She hadn't left her number. No way to get ahold of her. The brothers had to have it. They'd hired her.

He jumped up and pulled on his jeans, his gaze once more sweeping around the room, taking in everything. Her laughter was still lingering, taunting him. Her exotic fragrance now mixed with the scent of sex and sin. He wanted it to stay that way. He cleaned up, reluctantly tossing the burned candles with the spent condoms into the trash.

Had she left anything else behind? She'd brought her equipment with her to dance, her belt of coins and bells. That was gone, along with her ankle bracelet. He'd tried to steal that ankle bracelet, but she wouldn't let him have it. That had been a gift from her grandmother, she'd said. Every time she spoke of her grandmother, her voice had gone soft and loving. That much had been real about her. He'd loved that tone and the little tidbits she'd dropped about her grandmother.

Player made for the bathroom, took a long shower and felt much better when he emerged. It was late afternoon. That didn't surprise him. What did was that he didn't have the slightest remnant of his migraine. Always in the past, when he had a reaction from building and holding illusions too long, he was sick with blinding headaches for days afterward. He didn't feel energized and happy like he did now. He didn't feel like he was a real human being and not a walking zombie pretending to have feelings.

Just to prove again to himself he wasn't out of his mind, he went back to his room and cautiously opened the door, just enough for him to slip through. He knew he was acting a little insane, even though he was trying to prove he wasn't. He didn't want to let any of her scent escape, whether she was real or a fantasy. No, she was there, all over his room. He inhaled her and carefully closed the door again, locking her fragrance inside.

Three of his brothers were in the common room. All traces of a wild party had been removed. He was grateful he had slept through the cleanup. Too many people could have thrown his brain right back into a meltdown. Code, Maestro and Preacher sat at the bar, and all three swiveled around to face him.

"What are you doing up?" Maestro demanded. "You had a bad migraine last night. Steele is coming in to check on you in another hour or so."

Steele was their resident doctor. Player didn't want him disturbed, not when he was feeling fine. Steele had a wife and child to look after, and Breezy, his wife, was about to get a surprise when Master drove up, bringing the woman with him from New Mexico. She'd been a friend of Breezy's. Hopefully, she still was.

"You can tell Steele I'm feeling fine. I don't even have a headache, but I could use coffee."

Preacher went behind the bar and poured coffee into a mug, shoving it across the thick oak surface of the bar to Player. "You didn't look so good last night. Master called in an SOS."

"Yeah, the migraine was pretty bad, but the dancer you lined up for me managed to turn everything around." Player tried to sound casual. "Thanks for that, by the way. She was a pretty phenomenal gift."

The three men exchanged long puzzled looks while Player took a sip of coffee. Maestro shook his head. "Don't know what you're talking about, bro."

Player set the mug down on the bar. "The dancer. In my room. The belly dancer. You had to have paid her to be there, right?" He was beginning to feel a little desperate. They were staring at him with blank faces, like he was a little crazy. He was beginning to think maybe he was. She had to be real. There were the candles. The condoms. Her scent lingering. No, damn it, she was real. "You knew I couldn't be at the party, so you got me the dancer." He sounded alarmed even to his own ears. Maybe he had finally gone insane.

"Player." Maestro waved toward a chair, as if he were worried Player might fall on his face. "You came in a day early. No one expected you. We don't pay women to come here. You know that. If women come to party, they come with friends or another club. We never pay women. What's this about?"

Player ran his fingers through his hair several times in agitation, walking away from the sharp, focused eyes of his brothers to stare out the window into the parking lot. It was mostly empty of the vehicles that had been there the night before.

"I took a shower last night and went straight to my room," he said. "My head was killing me. I intended to go to bed and sleep as long as I could. I knew I had to avoid everyone. The migraine was bad. I was pretty fucked up," he admitted. He had to admit that. He wasn't going to lie to them. If he was going insane, he needed to know.

He turned to face them. He had their complete attention. "My head was pounding like a mother. I barely made it to the room, slammed the door and leaned against it. The nightmare world my fucked-up brain creates had been busy working the entire time until I closed the door. Suddenly, I was in a completely different world and there was a dancer in my room."

"Player," Code said cautiously.

Player held up his hand. "Hear me out. This wasn't some twisted version from *Alice's Adventures in Wonderland* from eating Alena's hallucinogenic mushrooms when I was a kid with a warped imagination. The music, the bells, the candles, the condoms — *hell,* all of it was real. When she talked or laughed, her body moved at the same time. It was subtle, but when she did, she had some kind of connection with the earth, the way I have.

Whatever it was, she managed to take away my headache completely."

He sounded crazy even to himself. His brothers exchanged long looks while he hung his head, breathing hard.

"I stood in front of the door because I could feel the way she was helping but I didn't know how. I just knew she couldn't leave. When I asked her why she was there, she was told by someone that she could use the room . . ." He trailed off, raking both hands through his hair. What *had* she said? "No one sent her to my room?"

The silence stretched out until Player wanted to scream. He didn't know what to think. She had to be real. What had she said when he first came into the room? She was practicing her dancing. Practicing. She hadn't been expecting him. Maybe he had conjured her up.

Preacher snapped his fingers. "There was a woman. She came with someone else. She didn't want to party, but her friend didn't want to leave. The friend kept whining that this girl promised to be her designated driver. You weren't supposed to come back, so Breezy said she could use your room as long as she didn't touch anything. Breezy left right after that. I heard her but thought she left. In any case, you never stay here anymore, you're always at your house, which was why Breezy said she could use the room and no one would bother her."

Code shrugged. "We have cameras everywhere. She should be easy enough to spot if she was here. Did she take something from you?"

He was already slipping off the bar stool and heading toward the back hallway leading to the control room. The others followed him. Player took up the rear. He had great faith in Code. If anyone could find out the truth, Player was certain Code could. He was their resident genius. Without him, they wouldn't have the money they had, or be able to find the children in need. They would all be in the dark ages. He provided their security. All of them depended on Code, and he always came through, no matter how dark the hour got — like now. This was for Player's sanity.

Code called up the security footage from the night before. "She had to have come in early if Breezy was here," he muttered to himself, flashing forward with blurring speed until he got to the moment when Steele, the vice president of Torpedo Ink, had come in with his old lady, Breezy.

Code followed Breezy's progress through the party, since Preacher remembered it was Breezy giving the woman permission to use Player's room to wait for her friend. Steele greeted the newcomers, members of the new Torpedo Ink chapter that had come in from Trinity and then another club, Rampage, wanting to be patched over. During that time, Breezy was in the kitchen overseeing the food preparation. The club members had brought their women with them, and Breezy came from the kitchen to welcome them when her husband stepped outside with the men. The clubhouse had filled up fast.

Player didn't know how Code could keep his eyes on Breezy with so many bodies crushed together and spilling outside, where the large grills were set up, but he kept the footage rolling fast. Suddenly, he stopped it. "She's talking to two women here, Player. Is either of these the one you're looking for?"

Player found himself frozen, unable to move a single muscle in his body. His heart pounded so hard in his chest, he was afraid it might explode. His mouth went dry. This was too important. If he was wrong, if she wasn't real, and his brain was that fucked up . . . If he was living in some alternate reality and he couldn't get out of it . . .

Code turned and looked at him over his shoulder. "Player? One of these women has to be her. Come look. I've frozen them both on the screen."

Player didn't move. All three of his brothers stared at him as if he'd grown another head. Code calmly printed out the screen capture and brought it to him.

"You're going to have to look. Breezy definitely talked to two women. And you don't have a headache. In fact, you look good. I'm betting my money that she's real, Player. Take a look." Code sounded certain.

Player dropped his gaze to the photograph. Full color. Code always had the best equipment. His dancer was unmistakable. She was talking with Breezy, those exotic eyes of hers looking right at her. She wore the same light jeans and top, although the top covered her beautiful abs, so no one could see how delicious her belly was when she moved, and she wasn't wearing the belt made of layers of golden coins.

"That's for certain her," Maestro said, looking at Player's face. "You've got the look. You're gone, man. Totally gone on her."

"She said her name was Zyah. That's all I know. I gave her money. Over a thousand dollars. She left it on my nightstand. I keep remembering her face now. At the time, I thought I was complimenting her, but I think she was pissed. Hurt. I don't know. I was so damn tired, and by that time I didn't know what the hell I was doing," Player admitted. "Or saying."

Preacher shook his head, smirking a little. "What you're saying is you totally made an ass out of yourself."

"You blew the real thing?" Code asked, sympathy in his voice.

Maestro burst out laughing. "You are so insane, Player. You're always the calm one.

You think things through before you make a move. You rarely party. You don't bother much with the girls who come to play and yet you've got the hots for this girl and now you've screwed things up."

That was all true. He was always careful, especially when there was a party. "She's different. I was pretty far gone, and maybe I've got it all wrong and things didn't happen the way I remember, but if they did, I've got to find her. I can't let her go without trying to fix things."

The grin faded from Maestro's face. "You really did fuck this up bad?"

Player nodded slowly. "I was so tired. I pretty much shoved her on the floor and told her to leave and then made things worse by trying to give her money. I was so confused and tired. You know how I can get, mixing reality and nightmares up, although she was a thing of fantasies, not nightmares. We went at it all night, and I don't recall, not once, telling my body to cooperate. I couldn't stop wanting that woman. I was like some kind of crazy sex machine."

Preacher shook his head. "You definitely made that part up."

"Condoms all over the damn room," Player said. "At least I protected her."

"Holy shit, brother," Maestro breathed. "I'd say that was the real deal."

Code glanced down at his watch. "Steele

61

should be here any minute. You hadn't moved all day, and we were getting worried. He was on his way over to check on you. We can ask him about the girl. He can ask Breezy."

For the first time since he'd woken up, Player found himself relaxing. "I knew you would come through for me, Code. She said her name was Zyah. I'm pretty certain that's her dancing name. You know, when she dances for customers."

Preacher frowned. "You're really convinced this girl is a dancer?"

"You should have seen her. She's definitely a professional belly dancer. No one is that good. She told me she was practicing, but she didn't need to practice. She had to have been dancing since she was a little kid. She did say she was from the Middle East, at least I think she said it. At the time I thought it was part of the role-playing we were doing. The act. She had to have left early in the morning, Code. Can you pull up the video where she leaves? Maybe we can see what she's driving, get the license on her car."

"Good idea, Player," Maestro approved.

Code swung around and immediately fast-forwarded to the early morning hours. He caught sight of Player's private dancer coming out of the back room and into the front, where most of the partiers were sound asleep. She picked her way through the bodies sleeping on the floor and in chairs, making her way toward the exit.

Zyah wore her blue jeans and top, and as she walked, Player could see the little golden bells around her ankle, but the coins were gone from her hips. The camera was directly on her face as she approached the exit, and she lifted a hand toward her eyes. Her fingers brushed first her left eye and then her right.

A man wearing Torpedo Ink colors came up on her right, blocking her exit. Player immediately recognized Destroyer, one of his brothers. He was a big man with very muscular arms covered in prison tattoos. His hair was long, falling nearly to his waist, pulled back in a braid segmented by bands every few inches. He leaned down and spoke to her. She shook her head and dashed at her face again, right under her eyes, giving the man her smile, but Player could tell it wasn't real. His heart had nearly stopped when he saw what were obvious tears on her face.

Code, Maestro and Preacher fell silent. Player looked at them. "I really screwed up. She's fuckin' cryin'. I did that. Shit." He pressed his fingers hard into the back of his neck, tension gathering there. For the first time in his life, he'd had real hope that he had a chance with a woman he could respond to. One he genuinely liked. She'd made him laugh. She'd made his body actually work when he'd thought himself long dead. "She didn't do one damn thing wrong, and I made her cry."

"I see you're already up," Steele said from behind them. "Master texted yesterday and said you were coming in early in bad shape. Maestro confirmed your migraine was particularly bad. I didn't expect to see you up at all, let alone walking around." There was a question in his voice.

Player spun around to face him. "That's the thing, Doc, there was this woman last night, in my room. I don't know what kind of ability she had, but when she spoke to me, the tone of her voice, the way she moved, she took away the migraine." He shrugged. "I know it sounds crazy. You don't have to look at me like that."

"There *was* a woman in his room," Code said, taking the screen capture he'd printed out from Player and handing it to Steele. "And he doesn't have any headache."

"Not only that, but he's functioning," Preacher added.

"I was with him last night," Maestro said. "He was worse than I've ever seen him."

Steele glanced down at the photograph and then at the frozen picture of the woman with Destroyer standing over her. "Tell me about her. And how did she get into your room?"

Player tried not to look at the tears on Zyah's face. That just plain undid him. "At first, I thought she was part of my crazy alternate reality, although it wasn't my normal fucked-up version of *Alice's Adventures in Wonderland.* There was Middle Eastern music playing in my room. I recognized the instruments. Candles were lit with very distinctive essential oils burning. She was in the middle of my floor, belly dancing. She wore a belt with layers of coins and tiny bells around her hips over her blue jeans, and an ankle bracelet with bells. God, she was gorgeous. Every movement was flowing and graceful."

Steele took another look at the picture in his hand. "I want you to go sit down, Player. You look good, but that doesn't mean you shouldn't take it easy. When you use your psychic ability, you actually can injure your brain, which is why you get such horrendous headaches. I'm not saying this woman doesn't have the capacity to heal you. Obviously, something happened, but I still want you to take it easy." He gestured back toward the common room.

Player and the others made their way from the control room to the comfortable chairs. Player found he was grateful to sit down. He wasn't nearly as steady on his feet as he thought he was.

"Tell me about her. What's her name? Where is she from?" Steele demanded.

Player sighed. "She said her name was Zyah, but I think that's the name she uses when she's dancing. I didn't get her last name or a number. I was hoping Breezy did. Preacher remembered that Breezy talked to her last night. She let her into the room."

Steele nodded. "I remember. Breezy texted me and asked me if it would be okay if she used one of the empty rooms to study. She had two job interviews this morning and had promised her grandmother she would help out a friend's granddaughter by being a designated driver. She was with another woman. Winters. Francine Winters. Heidi vouched for her. Your Zyah was Francine's designated driver. Breezy told Zyah she could use the room."

"Did Breezy get a last name?"

"No, it was Francine Winters that Heidi knew. But I can text Heidi." Steele pulled out his cell phone immediately and texted the waitress from their bar. Heidi was completely loyal to their club.

"While you're waiting for Heidi to get back to you, I'll just run the rest of the security tape and see if I can get the car she's driving and maybe a license plate," Code said.

Player tapped out a beat on his thigh before realizing it was an Arabic rhythm from the night before. He dropped his palm on his leg and rubbed, missing her. Needing to feel her skin against his. He kept from rubbing his temple by sheer will. When he looked up, Steele was watching him closely. It was tap out beats on his thigh, count in his head or

66

build bombs in his head to keep himself sane. He had bad habits. Anything he did in his head was better than these outward "tells" that his fellow Torpedo Ink brethren could see.

"She got in your head."

There wasn't much use in denying it. "Yeah. She did. I need to find out how real it all was." He rubbed his thigh again to keep from pressing his fingers to his temples. The headache was coming back, just there, beyond his reach. He didn't want to know it was close.

"Czar drilled it into us never to sleep with one of our marks. Or someone we were just getting some relief from. I didn't feel that way about her, but I'd gone so many hours without sleep and my mind couldn't tell what was real anymore. I kicked her out, said some things maybe I can't take back. I don't know, Steele, but she was crying when she left. There was a thousand dollars on my nightstand, and she just left it there."

Steele sighed. "You tried to give that girl a thousand dollars?"

"I'm afraid so. And I told her to leave. Thought the brothers paid her to be with me. Said that too. The look on her face, man, that wasn't good. Didn't remember it until I woke up this afternoon and realized it was the best dream I'd ever had in my life — except it wasn't a dream."

"When you decide to fuck things up, you're right up there with me, brother," Steele said. He glanced down at his cell phone. "This isn't good. Heidi says Francine Winters is a bitch from hell and that unfortunately, Heidi owed her a favor. Francine insisted she wanted to come to a Torpedo Ink party, and Czar okayed it even after Heidi warned him Francine was out to hook up with a member any way she could. Heidi doesn't know Zyah, but says she seemed way too nice to be friends with Francine. Heidi said she'll ask Francine for Zyah's last name, number and address."

Code returned shaking his head. "She must have parked off the lot and down the street somewhere out of sight. She walked outside the gates and disappeared."

"Great. It just can't be simple," Preacher said.

Player couldn't help himself. He texted Destroyer to ask him if he'd gotten Zyah's last name and what they'd talked about. He added that he'd explain why he needed the information when he saw him in person.

"Listen to this bullshit," Steele said just as Destroyer shoved open the door from outside and strode in. "Heidi says Francine says Zyah is a first-class stuck-up bitch with some kind of hoity-toity job that pays really well. She turns her nose up to everyone just because she has her master's in something. No one

68

likes her, and don't get involved with her. She's very judgy. She wouldn't have brought her, but she needed someone sober to drive her, although it turns out she didn't after all. A Torpedo Ink member, Axle, from the Trinity chapter, apparently gave her his cell number, but she lost it. Heidi says Francine will trade Zyah's information for Axle's. Heidi doesn't believe her. Says no way would Francine ever lose Axle's number if he gave it to her."

"What's going on?" Destroyer asked.

Maestro filled him in while Steele texted Axle asking if he had given Francine his cell number and apprising him of the situation.

"What did you say to her this morning?" Player asked, trying not to sound jealous. Or guilty.

Destroyer had eyes that could look right through a man. He shrugged. "Didn't like to see her cryin'. If someone hurt her, I wanted to know who. She said she was just tired and afraid she'd blow her interview and she couldn't find her friend she was supposed to take home. I didn't believe her, but I let her walk out."

"At least we know her real name is Zyah," Code said. "It's an unusual name. I can work with that. It's a starting point."

That didn't make Player feel much better. He thought of Zyah as his private dancer because he was certain she was an exotic dancer and Zyah was her stage name. That gave him a little bit of an excuse for his bad behavior — at least he told himself it did, even though he knew it was bullshit.

"Axle says Francine is a fuckin' nightmare and no one should go near her. Thinks she should be blacklisted from any club event, but that's just his opinion. He didn't give her his number and hopes he never has to see her again, but he'll take the hit for his brother if Player needs him to. He can always change his number later," Steele translated the text.

Player shook his head. "Tell him thanks, but no. We'll find her another way. There's got to be another way."

Destroyer shrugged his massive shoulders. "I can have a word with this bitch Francine. She'll talk."

Steele shook his head. "We're nowhere near that solution yet."

"Damn, Destroyer, you're a little bloodthirsty," Preacher said with a smirk. "I think you've been hanging around Savage too long."

"I don't hurt women," he denied. "They're afraid of me. She won't be any different. I question her, she'll answer. I should say, most women are afraid of me. Not the one last night. She wasn't afraid at all. Looked me right in the eye. She had something about her."

Player's head jerked up. "What do you

70

mean by that?"

The others all looked at Destroyer. He had a way of seeing into people immediately.

Destroyer shrugged again. "She's gentle inside, but steel at the same time. She's someone who will stand when you need her to. She really feels things, unlike most people, deep down, and once you're in, you're there. I felt bad for her. Whatever hurt her, cut deep."

"Great. That was me," Player admitted. "I was so gone last night I didn't know what I was sayin' or doin' and I threw her out."

Destroyer raised his eyebrow. "You had that woman in your room and you told her to leave? You really were all kinds of fucked up." As always, when he spoke, his voice was mild, a low tone, a bit menacing.

"In his defense," Maestro said, "Czar drilled it into us never to go to sleep with someone in the room with us. That was how you got killed."

Destroyer nodded. "Good advice most of the time. Not so much this time. Came in lookin' for food. Alena didn't cook this afternoon, did she?" he asked, a hopeful note in his usual expressionless voice.

"She's at her restaurant," Maestro said. "She'll feed you. Anything on the menu. She never charges. The money's all the same."

Destroyer shook his head. "I make her uncomfortable. Don't want to do that in her own place. She loves that restaurant. Sometimes she leaves food in the fridge here."

"Might be leftovers from last night," Preacher pointed out.

"Not anything Alena made, though," Maestro said. "Everyone goes back for seconds."

"What else do you know about Zyah, Player?" Code asked.

"She loves her grandmother. I got the feeling her grandmother raised her and that she lives close by. Maybe in Sea Haven. She's definitely from the Middle East."

"Can you narrow it down a bit?" Code persisted. "Which country?"

Player shook his head. "I'm sorry. She didn't talk much about her family dynamic. I didn't either, so I felt like I couldn't pry. After a while we weren't talking all that much."

"Master said he was coming in tonight and wanted me here," Steele said, looking at his watch. "I don't like being away from home all that long. Did something happen that I should know about? He didn't want me to bring Breezy."

"Yeah, we ran into some trouble. We'll fill in everyone at the meeting, but Master has a passenger with him; that's why we were separated. We followed the Ghosts to New Mexico, straight to the diner where Breezy used to work."

Steele's head jerked up. "Is she in some kind of trouble again? Are they coming for her? Czar called me, left me a message and said it was important and to call him back, but I wanted to check on you first. Is this about Breezy? Is she in trouble, Player?"

"No. But the two we were following met up with four members of the Swords club in the diner. I had to work hard to build an illusion fast to keep them from recognizing us. They were very close to us. They were there to make a deal with the Ghosts. But more to the point, they found out Breezy worked there before she disappeared. They were trying to track her down. Delia Swanson, her former boss, told them she didn't know anything more, but the apartment Breezy had stayed in was rented in Delia's name. They didn't believe her."

Steele stood up and paced across the floor. "Please tell me they didn't kill her boss. She loves that woman. And I owe her everything for taking care of Breezy and my boy."

"She was selling the diner. Had a buyer. The fuckin' Swords burned it down that night and made a try for her. We were waiting for them. Master and I took them out and had her throw a few things together. Master has her with him in her vehicle. We thought she could take the empty apartment over the bar next to Bannister's apartment until she decides what she wants to do. She'll be safe with us here. She has her retirement money, and Code and Absinthe can deal with the insurance company for her on the diner," Player said. "At least that was what we thought. We couldn't just leave her there. The Swords would have killed her."

"No, no, you did the right thing by bringing her. We'll talk to Czar. The club can protect her. The Swords don't have a clue you have her?" Steele asked.

"No, they didn't ever see us. Neither did the Ghosts. I held the illusion for over forty-eight hours. That's the longest I've ever managed. I didn't have a choice. We couldn't afford anyone to identify us as being Torpedo Ink. We told her Breezy was with you and we would take her to you and Breezy. She wanted to come. She's not without her own money, so she won't be a burden."

"You're absolutely certain this isn't a setup?" Code asked the question that Czar had already asked when they called him to report everything and ask him what he wanted them to do. "You're sure you weren't made and this woman isn't here to kill Breezy?"

# THREE

"Men are assholes, Mama Anat," Zyah said. "In case you aren't aware."

"Zyah, language." Anat had a small smile on her face when she looked up at her granddaughter. Although she was in her sixties, she didn't look it. There were no wrinkles on her face, only a few crow's-feet around her eyes and laugh lines around her mouth. "Although, I must say, there are times when I might agree with you."

Zyah couldn't help laughing. There was no way to be in the same room with her grandmother and not laugh. It had always been that way throughout the years, when her grandmother had raised her. She felt love welling up the way it always did when she looked at Anat — or even just thought about her.

"It is simply impossible not to love you. I can't imagine a man being an ass . . . a jerk to you. Every man who has ever met you has fallen permanently in love with you. I know because I've seen them come around for years, courting you." Zyah tucked a stray strand of her grandmother's hair behind her ear. The hair, although streaked with gray, was still dark and thick, adding to her youthful appearance.

Anat laughed again and made a trilling sound through her pursed lips. She could make that vibration so many different ways. Throughout her childhood, Anat comforted Zyah or chided her or assured her using several different melodic pitches. Her grandmother portrayed dozens of emotions by using different melodic tones when warbling at her. She still did it in everyday conversation, and each time the habit warmed Zyah as nothing else could.

"You silly child."

"You know it's the truth. Who sent the roses in that blue vase right there on the bedside table?" Zyah asked wickedly.

Anat pressed her lips together, or tried to, in order to look stern. She'd never perfected the look, as hard as she'd tried. "Dwayne River is far too young for me. That would make me a cat woman or whatever you young people call an old woman who goes after a younger man."

"He's six years younger than you. That hardly qualifies you as a cougar, Mama Anat," Zyah pointed out, turning away so her grandmother wouldn't see her laughing.

Anat knew the term *cougar.* She'd called herself that more than once when they watched a movie and she saw her favorite movie star. For her movie star, she would forget her vow of living her life free of men and become a cougar. She'd made that statement each time she watched one of his films.

"I think both interviews went well today," Zyah ventured, changing the subject. She sank into the armchair closest to her grandmother's bed. "Your friend, Inez Nelson, was really nice. I think she's going to put in a good word for me. There were three people sitting in on the interview for the grocery store manager position: Inez, a man they called Czar, and another one they called Absinthe. I think Absinthe could have been a lawyer."

"I thought the position was a grocery store clerk." Anat eased her body carefully to another position. "Why would they need a lawyer, and what kind of name is Czar? Or Absinthe, for that matter."

Immediately, Zyah caught up the pillows that had been scattered around the bed and pushed them behind her grandmother's back. "Czar and Absinthe belong to a club called Torpedo Ink. They own the grocery store with Inez. She wants to get back to her store in Sea Haven, and they need a manager to run the one in Caspar. I'm hoping they hire me so I can stay close to you. The pay is all right, nothing to get super excited about, but it really is the best for around here. I'm kind of looking forward to working there, so I really hope I get the job."

Anat made another little trilling sound, but this time it signaled she thought her granddaughter wasn't telling her the truth, and she wasn't going to put up with it despite the fact that Zyah was all grown up. "You loved your job, Zyah. You traveled all over, which you love to do. You made good money, and you were very respected. Managing a grocery store in a little town is a far cry from what you went to school for," she chided.

"I came home because I wanted to come home, Mama Anat," Zyah said quietly and slipped back into the chair, crossing her arms and leveling her gaze at her grandmother.

"I love you, child, more than anything on this earth. You checked on me, and I appreciate that, but now you can go. I'm fine. I've got my friends here, and they'll look after me. You may as well get that stubborn look off your face, Zyah."

"I am telling the truth, whether you want to believe me or not. I've wanted an excuse to come and live with you for a long time, but how do I give up a job like that one and tell you I was lonely for you and wanted to stay here? Someone breaking in and . . ." Just trying to say it made her choke up.

She could barely look at her grandmother's

fading bruises. Some *monsters* had broken into Anat's home — her sanctuary — and beaten her so that she fell and broke her leg and arm and cracked some ribs. They stole her husband's jewelry and beat her more, trying to make her reveal where her hidden safe was. She told them she had no safe, but they didn't believe her. Fortunately, hearing screams, neighbors called the sheriff, and the robbers had been run off before they killed her. They had threatened her with a knife and told her they were going to "string her up" if she didn't tell them.

Zyah detested leaving her grandmother alone for even a few minutes, but Anat's care cost money, and Zyah was determined that she was going to receive the best care possible. That meant she was getting a job or two jobs while she lived with her grandmother so she could keep an eye on her and oversee her recovery.

She shrugged her shoulders and looked her grandmother straight in the eye, bearing up under that scrutiny, refusing to look away. "I wasn't happy with what happened to you, but I wanted to come. I gave my notice. I didn't take a leave or vacation, both of which I could have done. I left because I wanted to come home and stay with you. If you don't want me to live with you, I can rent my own place, but I'm staying close. I understand if, when you're better, you prefer me to leave so you can be alone to entertain Dwayne." She kept a straight face.

Anat feigned shock. "*Zyah.* That is not funny." But she looked pleased. "Of course I want you to stay with me." She paused a moment, her fingers plucking at the beautiful comforter that she had quilted. "Are you going to tell me about the man who upset you? He caused real unhappiness. You let him in."

Her grandmother hadn't changed in the time she'd been gone. That was a comfort too. She'd always been a good listener, and she'd never been judgmental. She'd taught Zyah to be the same way.

"I brought it on myself. I can't even blame him as much as I want to. Your friend Lizz Johnson? Her lovely granddaughter, Francine Winters, the one you asked me as a favor to be the designated driver for, that granddaughter? You know, that one who has despised me my entire life?"

"That bad?"

"Francine Winters is a shark in the water, Mama Anat, circling men all the time. I don't understand why she manages to get men to fall at her feet, but she does. She lies and cheats and wouldn't be loyal to a man if his life depended on it. She's ending marriage three, and she was bragging that she dated several married men while she was married. She wanted to sleep her way to the top of the Torpedo Ink club so she could be the 'old lady' to the president. She knew two chapters were going to be at the party, and she had her eyes on the president of the new chapter. I guess right away she zeroed in on some poor man she was going to seduce to start her journey upward."

"Oh, dear, Zyah. I'm so sorry for putting you in such a position," Anat said. She eased her body to the side again, running her hand gently over her thigh.

Zyah frowned. "Did you take your pain pills tonight like you were supposed to? The doctor said not to wait. You're supposed to take them every six hours."

Anat waved her hand. "We'll discuss my problems *after.* You went with Francine, the shark, to the party. What happened?"

Zyah couldn't help laughing. "There is no derailing the conversation, is there? The party definitely didn't look like anything I was ready for, so I explained to one of the women that I needed to study for the interviews, and she seemed to understand and told me I could wait in a back room that was supposed to be empty for the night. I wanted to practice belly dancing. I haven't done it for some time, although I was always very good at it."

Anat nodded. "You've been excellent at belly dancing since you were a little girl. The job at the restaurant in Healdsburg?"

Zyah nodded. "Yes. All the waitresses know how to belly dance — it's part of the entertainment there. It's not that far to drive, and I can supplement my income if I get that job as well. I know I have an excellent education . . ."

"I loved that you spent so much time abroad at school and then working," Anat said proudly. "But if you're telling me the truth and you are really finished with traveling, I'm very glad to have you home. Please do get to the part where you meet your young man."

"He's definitely *not* my man, Mama Anat," Zyah said, jumping up and pacing across the bedroom floor to the window to stare out, suddenly feeling like a caged tiger.

She was barefoot as usual. She always felt trapped in shoes. With the soles of her feet pressed to the floor, she felt like she was connected to the earth. She could feel its vibrations. She'd felt connected to Player. She should have known, just by the name he'd given her, but that connection to him had been so strong, and now she wasn't sure she could ever trust her gift again.

"Zyah. Child."

Her grandmother's voice was very soft. Very loving. Zyah didn't dare turn around, not with tears burning behind her eyes. She wasn't shedding them, but her grandmother knew her too well, and she would know. This had cut deep, and it was silly when she didn't even know his real name. He hadn't told her.

He'd given her the truth of him. Player. He played women, and he'd played her for an absolute fool.

"You don't have to tell me if it hurts too much, but sometimes it feels better to share. I'm always here for you. Always on your side."

"I don't know why I liked him so fast. I just gave myself to him, Mama Anat. All in. Everything. I danced for him. Laughed with him. I felt as if I'd known him my entire life. Being with him was magical. I thought he felt the same way. From the moment he walked through the door, he took my breath away. I never got it back. I still can't breathe when I think about him." She couldn't.

She tried not to let her mind go back to that night of pure bliss, of perfection. Everything about Player had been exactly what she'd wanted it to be. Her complete fantasy man. Their connection had been so strong, on such an intimate level, she hadn't even considered holding back. She'd surrendered everything she was to him.

Zyah's hand crept to her throat. She could barely admit the truth to herself let alone to her grandmother. She whispered it, stroking the faint marks of possession he'd left on her body. She had them everywhere. She'd thought they'd meant something to him when he put them there. He'd acted like they did, but she knew better now.

"Can you come and sit with me, child?"

Anat patted the bed beside her.

Zyah's heart clenched. "I might cry, and I cried so much after the interviews, I thought my eyes would burn out of my head. At least I had enough discipline to get through both before I broke down. He isn't worth more tears." But she knew she would shed more. When she was alone in her bed, craving him. He'd set up some kind of terrible addiction.

"Tell me about him."

Zyah closed her eyes against the sudden wash of sensation pouring over her skin. She wrapped her arms around herself and rubbed at her skin as if she could rid herself of his touch. "He felt like fire every time he touched me. He could be so gentle and then turn rough and wild, like he couldn't get close enough to me or get enough of me. I couldn't get enough of him." She made her confession in an even lower tone.

Her grandmother remained silent, something she often did to encourage Zyah to continue telling her something important. Zyah swung around to face her, a little defiantly, this time deliberately looking her straight in the eye. She knew there was no getting around what she was revealing. Anat would understand that she was talking about having been with her partner sexually when she barely knew him. There was no judgment, but then her grandmother wasn't a judgmental person. Throughout her childhood and

84

teenage years, that had always remained a constant trait in her — one Zyah counted on now.

"He was so beautiful. Everything about him was beautiful to me, Mama Anat. His body was covered in scars. So many they made me want to weep. I didn't ask him about them, or the tattoos he had, which covered quite a few. The tattoos were intricate and intriguing. I just talked with him because he seemed to need to hear the sound of my voice. We laughed so much. He loves music the way I do. He loves working with wood. His voice . . ." She broke off again, waving her hands in the air in despair.

Looking straight into her grandmother's eyes, she asked the question that mattered the most, the one that nagged at her continually. "How could I have been so wrong?"

Anat regarded her just as carefully, never breaking eye contact. "You were so certain he was the one for you?"

Zyah nodded without hesitation. There hadn't been any doubt in her mind or heart. Player had connected with her on such a level she felt complete. Soul to soul. She'd been that certain of him.

"I felt his heartbeat. When I danced. I was barefoot. He was barefoot. Something was wrong with him when he came into the room. His heart was straining. His mind was chaotic. His rhythm was off, but we were in perfect harmony. Movements, and the pitch of my voice — we connected, I know we did." She faltered. "I was wrong. I connected with him, but he failed to connect with me. He didn't. Not at all."

"Tell me about him before you tell me what happened." Again, Anat patted the bed beside her.

Zyah couldn't help herself. She accepted her grandmother's comfort. Her grandmother had been through hell, beaten and then robbed by intruders, but it was so like her to think only of Zyah and her anguish over losing what really had only been in her mind — an illusion caused by her reckless behavior. She wasn't like that with men. She was cautious as a rule. Her last relationship had been two years earlier, and it had been a disaster in spite of the fact that she'd entered into it very slowly, taking her time, waiting to be physical with her partner for weeks. She hadn't been with another man since — until Player.

She eased her hips and legs onto the bed, careful not to bump her grandmother's fragile body. She curled onto the bed like a child, her grandmother's hand stroking her hair just the way she had when Zyah was a little girl. It felt the same, like love.

"I came home to take care of you, Mama Anat, but really, I think I came home because I needed this. You loving me. I needed to feel loved. Maybe I thought he was someone special because I needed him to be."

Anat continued to gently stroke her granddaughter's hair, humming softly, the sound filling the room. Zyah closed her eyes and allowed herself to feel her grandmother's comfort surrounding her, holding her close, enfolding her in loving arms.

"I love you so much, Mama Anat," she murmured. "I hope you always know that. I hope when I was away working, you always knew it."

The gentle, loving strokes in her hair never stopped. "Of course I knew, Zyah. You sent me letters every week and far too much money every month."

"I was so homesick. I wanted desperately to come home, but I wanted to make you proud of me. You were such a strong woman, and I wanted to be strong like you. You came here alone after you lost everyone, with me to raise. I didn't want to let you down."

"You could never let me down, Zyah," Anat chided, making her little trilling noise, this time definitely a small but loving reprimand. "You should know that by now."

"What's wrong with me that I can't find the right man? I was so certain. I felt him touch me inside, soul to soul, just the way you said would happen when I listened to the earth. I heard her talking to me. I felt her move through me to him."

Anat continued to stroke Zyah's hair gently. "Gifts are strange things, child. You think the fault lies with you, but perhaps the failing was his. Tell me about him. He must belong to this club. The same club that owns this store you want to work for."

Zyah sat up slowly and pushed back her hair, facing her grandmother. "Yes, Torpedo Ink. He's a member. He has the same tree tattooed on his back that's on their jackets. I need the job, and hopefully he won't come in and bother me. If he does, I'll look for another job, but there just aren't that many around, and they offered the best wages for this area."

"You are procrastinating, and that's unlike you."

She was. Zyah traced one of the flowers in the quilt on her grandmother's bed. "I don't want to feel like I'm so shallow I fell for him because he's so beautiful, but he truly is. He's tall and has wide shoulders and a thick chest, with muscles that go on forever. His hair is longer than I ever thought I'd like, falling below his shoulders. It's thick and very unruly, light brown with sun streaks going all through it. I loved his eyes. He has the most striking blue eyes. They're an unusual shade of blue — icy blue and then dark royal blue, and very piercing, as if he can see right into your soul. He has a short beard and mustache, nicely trimmed. So yeah, gorgeous

88

man physically."

"You are not a shallow person, Zyah — I will never believe that."

Zyah gave her grandmother a small smile of thanks. "He's intelligent and loves music. He has an affinity for wood — for the earth. He's compassionate. His voice changed whenever he talked about his fellow Torpedo Ink members. He called them his brothers or sisters. I loved the way he talked about them. He clearly loves Blythe. You know her. Everyone does. She's a cousin to the Drake sisters, you know, Sea Haven's royalty."

Anat nodded. She'd lived in Sea Haven a long time. "Yes, I don't run in the Drakes' circles, but Inez and Lizz talk of them. Everyone does."

"Blythe is married to Czar, the president of Torpedo Ink, and Player told me that Blythe is kind of like a mother hen to all of the club members. It was the way he said it, not making fun of her like you might expect; his tone held absolute love and respect. He talked like Blythe walked on water. You just can't fake that."

Zyah rubbed at her arms, once again trying to remove the sensation of Player running his hands over her skin. Touching her. Creating flames licking at her. A hundred tongues of fire. She couldn't get him off her or out of her, no matter how hard she tried.

"I thought, when we talked all night and

laughed together, we were building a solid foundation. When we fell all over each other, I thought it meant something."

She shook her head, refusing to give in to the burn behind her eyes. This mistake was hers, and she always learned her lessons, accepted her responsibilities and didn't make the same mistake again, no matter how hard it was to avoid that same blunder.

"We were both exhausted in the early morning hours. He lay on the bed, and I went to lie down, just to sleep for a short while next to him. I wanted him to hold me. I wanted to feel his body curled around mine, but he shoved me off the bed. Pushed me away. Hard. He actually said he was done with me. He told me he never slept with women like me and handed me a wad of money. Said I'd earned it. It was a *lot* of money. He even told me to leave my number on the end table so he could give me a call sometime. Wasn't that just lovely?"

Humiliation turned her inside out. Color swept up her body all over again. Sadly, it was more than humiliation; disappointment in him, in her and the realization that she couldn't trust her greatest gift had overwhelmed her. The hurt had almost been unbearable.

"I gathered up my things and rushed out of there. He just rolled over and went to sleep. He didn't say another word to me. I looked

90

for Francine, but someone said she'd gone off with a man from the Trinity chapter early in the evening. She'd even deserted me. I was crying my eyes out and rushing for the door, and another Torpedo Ink member stopped me. He stepped right in front of me, blocking my way. He was really intimidating, but he asked me what was wrong, if someone had hurt me. I felt him, the way we can, and he was good inside. That part of him was protected, hard to see because he didn't want anyone to see it, but I knew he wanted to help me, and if I had said someone hurt me, he wouldn't have been very nice to them."

"These men from this club, the ones Inez likes so much, they are good men, then?" Anat asked.

"It is difficult to answer that, Mama Anat," Zyah said, wanting to be truthful. "Every single one of them that I came into contact with, including Player, had intense, dangerous layers covering the heart of them. I think these men could be either. It feels to me as if their intention is to do right, to be good men, but then *good* is relative, isn't it? I'm certain Player didn't intend to break my heart. He didn't know me. To him I was a woman he paid to have sex with. I played that part so perfectly."

"Zyah. Don't be bitter or fall into self-pity," Anat chided gently. "Those are wasted emotions. It is okay to be sad for what is lost.

91

What you missed. Your gift told you this man was the right one, and you acted on it, but he, for some reason, was wired wrong and didn't connect the same way. That wasn't your failing. Perhaps it wasn't even his. We don't know what this man has been through or why he didn't have the same feelings you did. You have to let that anger toward him go."

Zyah nodded. "It really isn't anger so much as embarrassment and sorrow that I feel I can't even trust my gift. My feelings were so strong. It felt so right to be with him. Nothing had ever felt that way before. When he said those things to me, it felt like he slapped me in the face. Hard. It hurt so bad and still does. I hear his voice over and over and can't seem to get it out of my head."

She could feel intense sorrow dripping down her soul. She'd been born with a priceless gift, one Anat had told her, from the time she was a little girl, had been passed down through her mother's family for generations. Anat was her mother's mother, and all of the women prior to Zyah had shared an affinity with the earth, a connection they felt through their bodies.

Zyah had made it a point to study science, to find a plausible explanation for her ability to feel a connection to others. The only thing that made the slightest bit of sense was that beneath the forest floor, mycelium acted like a wide network, distributing nutrients and other much-needed attributes to living plants and trees. At the same time, the mycelium knew to close off aid to the dead or dying or already decomposing plants it couldn't save in the forest. That was the short version, but it fit.

The human brain was very close to those same layers of threads of mycelium. She often wondered if she acted as that same wide network, a connection that was felt by her through the earth, her bare feet, or her hands in the air when she moved them in the graceful patterns taught to her by her grandmother and Amara, her mother. Their gift was a closely guarded secret, and no one outside their family was aware they could in any way help others through their dance or the sound of their voices.

Zyah found it strange that although she loved music, and had a way to pitch her voice to speak notes another person might need, she couldn't sing. She could dance with the best, and she found joy in it, but she didn't feel comfortable singing. Her gift was more about tuning to one person directly. She knew why her grandmother was always so amazing with her — she knew exactly what Zyah needed, as Zyah would know with her children and husband.

"My greatest fear, Mama Anat, is that I won't have my own family. I've always wanted a husband and children. You told me about my parents, how much they loved each other. I remember them and how they were always laughing together. You speak of your husband, and your voice and face go soft with love. I want that too, and I'm so afraid I'll never have it."

"This man may have been the right one but not at the right time. Another will come, Zyah, you just have to close yourself to this one and let your heart be open to another. It won't be easy."

"It isn't like I had him for weeks or months or even years. It was only a night. Not even twenty-four hours, yet it feels as if I had a long relationship with him and am grieving over the loss. I never want to hurt like that again," Zyah admitted. "I can't believe how far I let him in."

"It's the gift," her grandmother said. "I knew when you told me about the man you were dating some time ago that he wasn't right for you, because you weren't reacting with intense passion. You had to find that out for yourself. I couldn't tell you. This man, this Player from Torpedo Ink. He is dangerous to you now, Zyah. You'll be very susceptible to him. You have to stay away from him, because if you don't, you will continue to have great heartache. You know you won't be able to control what your heart or body desires."

Zyah knew that was true. She didn't want to think about him, much less see him. She shouldn't take the job at the grocery store because Torpedo Ink owned it, but there just weren't that many jobs close to Sea Haven, especially not with the salary they were offering. Caspar was only a couple of miles away, and she needed to be close to her grandmother. She wasn't healing as fast as Zyah thought she should be.

"How did physical therapy go?"

Anat winced. "Sometimes I don't think it's helping me, Zyah."

Zyah frowned. Her grandmother never complained. Never. She was always stoic. No matter the situation, she just fought her way through. It wasn't that she was complaining exactly, but she didn't sound like her normal cheerful, positive self.

"Why?"

Anat shook her head and smiled, but Zyah saw that for the first time, that sweet smile didn't reach her grandmother's eyes.

"I shouldn't have said that. It's just taking longer than I thought it would to recover. I need to have more patience." Anat's hand dropped to her leg and she rubbed along her thigh as if it ached.

Zyah considered how many times her grandmother might have done that while she was whining to her about Player. Anat had comforted her over and over, yet now that

Zyah thought it over, she had seen her grandmother rub her leg through the quilt on more than one occasion.

"We both liked the physical therapist. Terrie Frankle? She's from someplace in Washington, isn't she? A traveling therapist?" Zyah asked cautiously. "Do you still like her?"

"Very much. She's quite sweet. She loves to travel, and when the clinic was looking for someone, she jumped at the chance to come here. She had heard of Sea Haven already because she met Francine, Lizz's granddaughter, when she was traveling on a train to San Francisco to a job there a while back. She's been all over." Anat sounded very enthusiastic. "I like to listen to her stories of her travels while she works on me. It helps, so I concentrate on listening instead of feeling the pain."

Zyah didn't like the sound of that. "Should you be feeling pain? Do you tell Terrie that you're feeling pain?"

"I have," Anat admitted reluctantly. "She said a little pain is necessary, but it shouldn't be too much. I never know how much is too much." There was a little quiver in Anat's voice.

Zyah glanced at her watch. It was too late to call the doctor's office, but she was going to first thing in the morning. She wanted another X-ray of her grandmother's leg, just to see if it was healing correctly. She also wanted to talk to him about physical therapy and just how much her grandmother should be doing. It was so unlike Anat to say anything at all negative that the little she had said meant the pain was severe and she was really becoming distraught over the therapy. No one else knew her the way Zyah did.

"Mama Anat, you should have told me when the physical therapy began to get painful. I know you told Terrie, but I know you so much better than she does. The therapists expect patients to complain to them about pain. She has no idea how stoic you are. If you ask her if it's supposed to hurt, or say that it is painful, she just chalks it up to what every patient says. I know better, because I know you."

"You have so much to do. You've been out looking for jobs to pay the bills. I didn't want to worry you, Zyah." Again, Anat rubbed her thigh.

Zyah noted her hand was trembling. Her heart fluttered. "Maybe I should take you to the hospital tonight and get your leg X-rayed again. Does it hurt the way it did when you first broke it? Can you tell if the bone is fractured?" She tried not to sound anxious. "Either way, we're calling the doctor, tonight or tomorrow."

"I don't think it's that bad," Anat denied. "We can wait until tomorrow and call the doctor. I'm certain he'll say the pain is normal from the physical therapy."

Just the fact that Anat knew Zyah would call the doctor and she wasn't objecting meant her leg really hurt. Zyah was angry with herself and a little angry with Player all over again because she'd been so focused on her own shame and loss that she hadn't read her grandmother's distress and physical pain.

"Are you positive we can wait for tomorrow?"

"Absolutely. I don't want to go to the emergency room. I'd rather have you talk to the doctor first. You know I really dislike the emergency room."

Zyah knew that was the truth. Her grandmother would much rather clean her house, the entire yard and maybe her neighbor's house and yard before making a trip to the emergency room. She thought it was such a waste of time sitting there waiting to be seen.

"I can wait just as easy in the comfort of my home, and the doctor can make my appointments for tests," Anat said.

It didn't matter how many times Zyah explained to her that sometimes haste mattered, not even after she'd been rushed to the hospital after the attack. Anat had a major aversion to emergency rooms, hospitals in general, and now, it seemed, she wasn't going to be readily cooperative if it meant more tests.

Night had fallen outside, and inside the

bedroom, Anat had the lights blazing. That was the one striking difference Zyah noticed. Before the break-in and vicious assault, Anat rarely had more than one light on; now she preferred to have lights on throughout the house and even outside. She didn't sleep very well.

Zyah didn't like the idea of being away from her in the evenings, but Anat had insisted she help out her friend's granddaughter, Francine, although Francine had taken off with a man the first chance she got, so it would have been better if Zyah had just stayed home. Now, if she took the job in Healdsburg at the restaurant even two evenings a week, that would be leaving her grandmother alone, and clearly, she was frightened.

Zyah had money, but most of it was tied up in her retirement and deferred accounts. She could pull it with penalties, but she preferred not to if she could make enough money to keep her grandmother comfortable and pay the bills, not an easy task with the wages paid in the area. She'd always lived on the minimum it took to get by, sent her grandmother money and saved the rest for when she would need it. Maybe now was that time. Fortunately, she'd bought the house outright for Anat a few years earlier. They didn't have a monthly mortgage, and that helped.

"Last night, when you were gone, you asked if any of my friends from the Red Hat Society would come and stay with me," Anat ventured slowly.

Zyah heard the hesitancy in her voice. This was just as serious as the pain in her leg from her physical therapy. Zyah had to work at keeping her heart rate under strict control. Her grandmother would know the moment it was elevated. She pulled the privacy screen over the windows, not liking that the room was lit so bright and anyone outside could see them in the bedroom.

"Yes. You said Inez and her husband, Frank, came and played cards with you. I learned that Frank snores, but not very loud."

Anat laughed. "That's true. Inez and I both fell asleep a couple of times while playing gin. I was ahead."

"Of course you were." Zyah was patient, waiting for her grandmother to get to the point of the conversation. "There are very few people who can beat you when it comes to cards, Mama Anat. I always wondered if your gift included reading other people's cards."

Anat laughed, the notes sounding light in spite of the seriousness in her eyes. She rubbed her thigh again. "Someone came up on the back porch and tried the door. It was locked. You installed that fancy new lock just a few days before, but both Inez and I heard it slide open as if they had a key. Fortunately, you had put a chair under the doorknob. Inez went to check the door and the deadbolt was unlocked but the chair held. She called Jackson Deveau. She says he's like a son to her. He came right away and took a report."

Zyah could feel the color draining from her face. Her legs turned to rubber, and she sank into the armchair across from her grandmother before she fell down. "You didn't think I should have been told this *immediately*? Before I went to the job interviews? When I came back home this morning? Mama Anat, your safety is more important than *anything*. Why in the world didn't you tell me?"

"Because you wouldn't have gone on the interviews, and I know you have to work. It was taken care of. The deputy came. They're doing extra patrols." In spite of her brave words, a shiver went through her. "I'll admit, I'm afraid those men are going to come back. How would they already have a key to the new deadbolt? Jackson, he's the deputy, didn't have an answer for that, and neither did I."

"I can't take a job and be away from you, especially at night." There was no way she was going to be away in the evenings and leave her grandmother home by herself. As it was, she was going to make certain someone was always with Anat while she was at work. They would have to make do with the money from the grocery store if she got that job. If she didn't, she'd have to find something else that paid equally as well that was close. Maybe she should have taken the money Player had shoved at her. The hell with it — she'd pull money from some of her stocks.

"We'll figure it out, Zyah," Anat said, trying to pour confidence into her voice. "I talked to Inez, and she said whenever you were gone, one of the Red Hat ladies could be scheduled to stay here. She didn't know that you were applying for the grocery store job at the time. I didn't tell her because I didn't want to influence her. I didn't think that would be fair to the other applicants."

That was so like her grandmother. Everyone needed to achieve things on their own merits.

"I'm definitely not going to take the waitressing job at the belly dancing restaurant," Zyah said. "We'll just both go on diets. No more ice cream for me."

Anat laughed, the sound a little like gentle tinkling bells. "Since we're going to have to give up ice cream in the future, can we have some now? Before we go to sleep?"

Zyah wasn't certain how much sleep she was going to be getting, but ice cream sounded perfect to her. She couldn't help laughing with her grandmother, because when Anat laughed, everyone around her always joined in.

# FOUR

"You're absolutely positive," Czar demanded. "The two of you were sitting in the diner for how long before the Swords came in? You could have been made and not known it. In that time, they might have threatened Delia to gain her cooperation and burned her diner down to show her they meant business. She might have come here to kill Breezy."

Player looked around the meeting room at all his brothers and the two women, Alena and Lana. All of them were present for this important meeting. This was his family, the ones he could count on. They counted on one another. They'd lived through a horrific nightmare childhood together, and it had bonded them tighter than most blood families could ever hope to be. It had been Czar who had saved them all, kept them human and given them hope. He'd brought them this far, and they believed in him.

The president of Torpedo Ink waited for input from the other club members. Player had known Czar would be concerned that Delia Swanson, the woman who had owned the diner Breezy, Steele's wife, had gone into when she was alone and pregnant a couple of years earlier, might have been coerced into trying to harm her now. At that time, she'd given Breezy a job and put an apartment in her own name as well as given her a truck to drive so no one could trace her, to keep her safe.

"Not a chance," Master said. "I was careful. I spent all that time with Delia driving her back. I made her stay in the same motel room with me. You know I'm good at reading people. I slipped in questions, went at her various ways. No one is that good. She's shaken up, but glad to get out of there alive."

"She's in the apartment over the bar?" Czar continued.

Master nodded. "You said to take her there, and that's what I did. I told her to get settled, get some sleep and then, today or this evening, she could see Breezy. I figured we'd have the meeting, report and then Absinthe and Scarlet could run into her at the clubhouse while she's waiting for Steele to bring Breezy. They could chat with her and make doubly certain I'm right, but it's very clear to me that she cares for that girl and can't wait to see her again."

"It's just a genuine coincidence that she was already retiring and selling her diner when the Swords came knocking on her door?" Ink asked.

"I believe so," Master said. "The Ghosts were making their way toward Swords country, and the Swords were trying to track down Breezy. It sounded to me as if they were looking for her more to see whether she knew her old man, Bridges, and brother, Junk, had been killed than they thought she had anything to do with the massacre. It wasn't like Bridges wanted anyone to know what he was doing. He might have been president of the chapter, but he was stealing from the club."

"Code, what do you have on Delia Swanson?" Steele asked.

"She's sixty-six. Worked since she was fourteen. Married once, widowed. Her husband, Braxton Swanson, died five years into their marriage, an accident at his work. They never had children, and she never remarried. She bought the diner with the insurance money and worked her ass off to make that grow into a thriving business. A few parking tickets over the years, but for the most part, she has nothing on her record. She's clean, no affiliation whatsoever to any club."

"How did the Swords track Breezy to New Mexico?" Savage asked.

They looked at one another. Player's heart dropped. None of them had ever thought to ask that one simple question. How had Breezy's father and brother found her in New

Mexico? Code had looked for her, and he was the best at finding anyone. She'd gone completely off-grid. Ironically, it had been Steele who had taught her how. He hadn't thought she would ever be impossible for him to find.

Code sighed and glanced at Steele, clearly knowing he wasn't going to like the answer he'd come up with. "Breezy called one of the women in the Swords' club — Jerri, it looks like — back about a month after you kicked her out. Her father lived with Jerri for a few months when Breezy was around twelve. Jerri was pretty entrenched in another chapter of the club and was the old lady of one of the men by that time and so fairly protected against Bridges. My guess, when Bridges came looking for information, Jerri volunteered it rather than take a chance that she would get in trouble with him or the club. She knew the call had come from New Mexico under Delia Swanson's name. It wasn't that difficult for Bridges to find the diner. I'm guessing he only told a few of his best friends, the ones he felt he could blackmail or bribe or he knew were completely loyal to him, what he was doing."

Steele stood up, walked to the corner of the room and called his wife. It was necessary they verify everything. No one was going to take chances with Breezy's life, least of all Steele. He stood for a moment after he ended the call, back to the wall, his arm across his chest, head down briefly before returning to his seat.

"Yeah, when she realized she was really pregnant, she felt it was only right to tell me. She suspected, but didn't know for sure until after she was gone. She waited to take a test because she was trying to find a place to settle. When she knew, she wanted to get in touch with me, but I had blocked her. She called Jerri, knowing Jerri had a pulse on everyone in the club. She was told she wasn't allowed anywhere near the Swords, that she'd been blacklisted from the club and that Jerri would get in trouble for even talking to her. I'd had Breezy banned."

"Did she tell Jerri about the baby?" Czar persisted.

"No. Breezy apologized to Jerri, said she wasn't aware she'd been banned and hung up. That was the end of the conversation. She said she forgot about even calling her. She was really upset that I'd made it so permanent that she couldn't even reach out to me. When her father and brother showed up so much later, she didn't even connect the two events. They came looking for Breezy, to bring her back. They didn't know about the baby until they saw him and realized he was mine. That was when Bridges got the bright idea of making Breezy kill Czar and Jackson Deveau," Steele said. "He wanted to punish her."

"Did you tell her Delia was here?" Keys asked.

"Not a chance. If this goes sideways," Steele said, "Breezy would be heartbroken. She's had enough heartbreak in her life. Until Absinthe says Delia's on the up-and-up, she doesn't get anywhere near my woman or boy."

"As soon as the meeting's over, we'll bring Delia to the clubhouse. Bannister is having dinner with her at the bar right now. They're eating Alena's famous chicken. I think he's a little smitten," Reaper said. "Anya's watching her. You know how she is about Bannister. She's so protective over that old man, you'd think he's her fuckin' father."

"Poor Delia," Preacher commiserated. "She's probably the nicest woman on the face of the earth. She took Breezy in, gave her a job and a home, and everyone's treating her like she's got the plague."

"Fortunately," Lana said, "she has no idea. She thinks we're all being nice." Lana was one of the only two female survivors out of the eighteen who had made it out of the hellhole they'd been raised in. She was gorgeous. There was no denying the fact. Tall, beautiful figure, sleek black hair, shiny as a raven's wing, perfect bone structure — she was the type of woman who could stop traffic when she walked down the street.

"We are nice," Alena said, turning to glare at Destroyer. She was shorter than Lana by a couple of inches, with natural platinum hair and brilliant sapphire-blue eyes. "You didn't come by the restaurant last night to eat. You're Torpedo Ink. The brothers eat at the restaurant."

Destroyer shrugged. "Don't like you uncomfortable in your own place."

"Don't flatter yourself, hotshot. And don't piss me off. I cook it, you eat it, like everyone else."

"Afraid you might spit in my food."

A few snickers were hastily covered up when Alena turned that hot glare around the table. "Don't give me ideas." She gave a little sniff of disdain, managing to look haughty as only Alena or Lana could do, and turned her attention back to Czar. "Anything else on the agenda? I've got a restaurant to run."

"We've got to get this grocery store crap done once and for all. Who knew it was going to be such a big fuckin' deal to find a manager?" Czar said. "Although Blythe did warn me. So did Inez. We've got a few more applicants for the position, but Inez has only one she's willing to turn the store over to. She's just about done with running it, says she has to get back to Sea Haven. Frank, her husband, doesn't like running the store there without her. I can't blame him; this has taken far longer than we expected," Czar conceded.

"That's because Inez keeps shooting down every single person who tries for the job,"

Keys pointed out.

"True," Master agreed. "But in her defense, not a single one had any experience, and I don't think they knew how to do any math."

Code tossed the three files on the table. "Inez is right. The first two are total crap. One is a drug addict and has been in prison twice for theft. How he thinks he can hide that from us, I don't know. The second one looks good enough on paper, but she's gotten hurt on every job she's had within three weeks of taking the job and gone out on disability. A great con she's been running for years."

"Why the hesitation over the third?" Savage asked. He was a dangerous-looking man. One of their go-to get-it-done men.

Czar sighed. "She's so far overqualified she's completely out of our ballpark."

"I have to agree with Czar," Code said. "She went to school in Germany; her undergrad was international business. Her MBA with an emphasis in international retail management was paid for by her company while she did a retail marketing apprenticeship/mentorship with that company. They snapped her up, an international grocery chain, immediately after she graduated. She worked for them and traveled all over various countries. She's a freakin' genius and definitely knows what she's doing managing a chain of stores, let alone a little grocery store like ours."

"What the hell is she doing in Caspar?" Savage asked, suspicion underlining his tone.

"Her grandmother brought her to the United States when her parents, grandfather and uncle were killed in a boating accident out at sea. The grandmother, Anat Gamal — and that is her maiden name; they don't take the husband's name where they're from — was smart. She recognized that things were going south for women in her country and she contacted a friend of hers, Lizz Johnson, here in the States. They knew each other from school. Anat Gamal's family was very progressive, and she was sent to schools in both England and Germany. She met Johnson in Germany and they both attended school in England as well and were roommates. Johnson helped her and her granddaughter immigrate to the United States. That was seventeen years ago. They became citizens almost immediately."

Code looked around the table. "I have to say I really admire Anat Gamal. I'd like to meet her someday. She was smart getting out when she did. She didn't bring much with her, but she made a good life for her and her granddaughter in Los Angeles. They both worked their asses off."

Player found his heart beginning to pound hard, accelerating until he thought it might burst. Code refused to look his way. He

111

wasn't meeting his gaze no matter how much Player willed him to. He kept tapping the file he had on the applicant. It was fairly thick. Code always managed to dig deep really fast, using multiple computers to get what he wanted on whomever he was interested in.

"The younger Ms. Gamal was raised in Los Angeles, but like her grandmother, worked while she was in school, holding down several jobs and contributing to paying off the debt they owed to Lizz Johnson. Johnson gave Anat the money to get started. That debt was paid in full. I looked into Johnson's bank account and every penny was repaid."

"For fuck's sake, Code," Player burst out.

Code ignored him, but there was a faint grin on his face that told Player Anat Gamal was his private dancer's grandmother.

"When Anat's granddaughter went to Germany to college, Anat moved to Sea Haven. Lizz Johnson had retired to Sea Haven several years earlier and talked about it so much that Anat decided to retire there. The granddaughter's paycheck was extremely high, but her overhead was low. Her company paid for travel, living accommodations and just about any other expenses. Both she and her grandmother always lived frugally, so she bought her grandmother the home Anat is living in outright. It's a beautiful piece of property in Sea Haven, and they don't come cheap."

"If they have money, why is she so desperate for a job?" Alena asked.

"Most of the granddaughter's money is tied up, and she'd take hefty penalties to get it out. That said, she could do it and she'd still be well off. My guess is, she figures she can work and pay the bills and leave the money where it is. These women have been careful all their lives, and they'll continue to be. They don't mind hard work."

Player leaned back in his chair, running both hands through his hair repeatedly. It couldn't be that big of a coincidence. She couldn't just drop into his lap like this. "Code? Come on, man. Stop giving me a hard time. Is that Zyah? Is she the one applying for the job?"

Code flashed a grin at him. "The applicant is Zyah Gamal. She lives with her grandmother, Anat Gamal. She's unmarried and is twenty-seven years old. Smart as hell, Player, and far too good for you."

"You know this woman, Player?" Czar asked.

"Yes. Hell yes. She's mine." He claimed her without a qualm. "Doesn't know it yet and doesn't like me very much right now, but she's definitely mine."

Czar scowled at him. "What do you mean, she doesn't like you very much? That doesn't sound good to me."

"I might have screwed up with her," Player admitted.

"Might have?" Preacher echoed.

"Yeah, just a little," Maestro said, nudging Code. "Came in begging us to look at the security tape after the party. Wanted to see if his dream girl was real."

"Made her cry," Destroyer said. "She left in tears." He crossed his arms and leveled his gaze at Player.

"Can't have that," Savage said. "We need this woman to work that store. I'm not doin' that again."

Lana rolled her eyes. "You never actually worked in the store, Savage. You, Destroyer, Reaper or Maestro didn't ever pull a shift."

"Are you kidding me?" Alena burst out. She glared at Czar. "Are you kidding me, Czar?" she repeated, sounding outraged. "All of us had to pull a shift at that store. Why did they get a pass? It isn't like Savage is busy or anything. He just sits around sharpening his knife."

"I offered to cut up vegetables in your kitchen for you," Savage said. "Don't be jealous because some of us are manly men and we have to look pretty and be ready to defend you from the evils around you."

Alena flipped him off. "No one said the lot of you are in the least bit manly."

Savage flexed his muscles.

Lana laughed and punched him. "They did all the grunt work, Alena. Inez refused to have them scaring the customers in the front of the store where anyone might see them. They unloaded trucks and shelved everything in the middle of the night."

Alena looked from Savage to Reaper, Destroyer and then Maestro. "I can't see it in Maestro. He's so sweet. The others, yes, but Maestro? Why did Inez blackball him?"

"He gave her the death stare the moment she tried him on the register behind the counter," Lana explained and burst out laughing. "That was all it took. He was sent to do the grunt work with the rest of the scary boys."

"Let's reel it back in," Czar said. "I'm serious here, Player. We need this woman. The club needs this grocery store up and running in the community. We need to make it work. Inez has done her best, but she can't stay forever. We're trying to fit in here. What I really like about Zyah Gamal is the tie back to the community. Aside from the fact that she's more than qualified, the woman's grandmother is friends with Lizz Johnson, and she's a fixture in Sea Haven and a good friend of Inez's. You might claim her, and ordinarily I would say any brother who wants a woman, we all do what we can to help him out, but in this case, she's a real asset to the club. If you're not certain, Player, or you think she'll head for the hills, then you've got to stay away from her, because she's a huge benefit to us. Frankly, we need her."

"I have to see her again, because she seems too good to be true. If what I think happened really did, I'd be a fool to let her get away. I was so out of it. Too long without sleep, but I swear she was able to heal my brain after I tore it up keeping Master and me covered when the Swords walked into that diner. We had to have the illusion around us for hours. I was in a bad way by the time I got back. I was seeing caterpillars dropping loops of fog around Jackson Deveau's neck when he stopped me on the highway. The migraine was bad."

"Waterspouts and lobsters," Maestro affirmed. "Drinks rising in the air and pouring out by themselves. Women calling for the queen's maids."

Loud laughter burst around the table, just as Player knew it would. He forced himself to smile. "I was seeing the White Rabbit," Player added. "It was that bad. I was even afraid for Maestro, thinking he was about to become the White Rabbit, grow ears and everything."

"I had the truck keys," Maestro explained. "Not the pocket watch."

Again, there was laughter.

"I made a run for my room after taking a shower." Player smiled at Lana. "You had your special touch in the bathroom, that scent you like. It helped enough to get me down that hallway. It was moving, and the door was shrinking. Maestro had closed all the doors

116

leading to my room, thankfully." He gave them a little grin, like it was all a big joke, when it wasn't.

He was careful not to tell them that the pocket watch had gone from the White Rabbit's to Sorbacov's watch. All of them would remember that watch vividly. Sorbacov liked to pull it out and look at it while the children were being tortured, as if he were slowly marking the time. It was part of his cruel amusement. There were too many memories surrounding that watch, and when it began to intrude into Player's alternate world, the danger to everyone around increased significantly.

He kept playing to their amusement, yet at the same time wanting Czar to see that Zyah had really taken away his migraine and the crazy illusions that his fucked-up brain tricked him into believing and then projecting when he was that far gone.

"I got to my room, slammed the door and everything changed. She was inside dancing. Music was playing and candles were burning. She was exotic and beautiful. Every movement, every word she said, the sound of her voice, I could feel a difference in my head. I sprinted down that hallway thinking my head was going to shatter, just explode it hurt so damn bad, and then she was talking in this voice and every word felt like she was somehow mending my brain."

Player frowned. "I'm not saying it right. It was more than that. It wasn't an illusion. She really did it. She has a gift. We laughed and talked all night. We did a hell of a lot more than that, and I wasn't telling my body what to do either. But I was exhausted, and there at the end, I couldn't tell what was real and what wasn't. I'd somehow convinced myself the brothers had hired her for me. You drilled it into us never to let anyone stay. I kicked her out and, worse, gave her money, which she left on my nightstand. It was brutal when I woke up and began putting pieces together."

Czar swore and shook his head. "This isn't adding up. This woman is like some fucking miracle. Looking at the photo Code has of her — she's gorgeous. She has some fancy job that treats her like a rock star, gives her all kinds of money, and now you're saying she's gifted. What the hell is she doing taking a job in a small grocery store in Caspar that doesn't pay shit?"

"I don't care what brought her here," Player said. "She's here and I want her to stay. I'll figure out a way to make up for my stupidity."

"Because we have so much to offer a woman like that," Keys said.

Savage shook his head, his gaze fixed on Code. "There's more to this than you've said, right, Code? And you don't much like it."

Code nodded, his whiskey-colored eyes

intense. He wore his dark blond hair closely cropped, had a perpetual five-o'clock shadow and faint mustache. He didn't carry an ounce of fat on his body, but was all defined muscle without bulk. Czar had recognized very early the genius in him and had taken him under his wing and protected him as best he could from the hungry predators in the school when they were children.

"Yeah. It's not good. Zyah came home for a reason. Recently Anat's home was broken into and she was beaten severely, so much so that one leg, one arm and her ribs were broken, the leg in three places. The robbers might have killed her if a neighbor hadn't heard all the screaming and called the cops. That's why Zyah came home. To take care of her. She didn't just take a leave of absence, she quit that extremely lucrative job to come back and care for her grandmother." Code indicated the report. "It's all in there."

There was a sudden silence. Czar broke it. "What the fuck? Someone broke into that woman's home and beat her to the point she nearly died?"

Code nodded. "A second house was broken into two streets over from the Gamal house about three days after the attack on Anat. The occupants, an elderly couple, Benjamin and Phillis Gimble, were both beaten and robbed. Same exact MO."

"This is bullshit," Maestro swore.

Code kept going. "I started checking around and looked for similar robberies in other places. I believe there's a ring of thieves targeting the elderly. They scout them out, break in, beat and rob them and then move to another town. They target smaller towns where there's no police force and law enforcement is spread thin. Sea Haven meets those criteria."

"Damn it." Czar drummed his fingers on the table.

"It gets worse."

"Don't fuckin' tell me that," Czar snapped.

"The minute I realized this was Player's woman, I put everything I had on finding out as much as I could as fast as I could. Other than working on making certain Breezy was safe, and I am one hundred percent sure she is, I stayed up all night getting into police reports and looking into every corner I could in the time I had of finding out about Zyah and her grandmother's business."

"Just put it on the table," Czar said, sighing. Sprawling back.

Player leaned forward. He wasn't liking the look on Code's face.

"First let me say, Zyah's intelligent and aware. She began taking courses in Krav Maga in LA when she first came to the United States and continued training throughout her college years. Her company urged her to continue those courses due to

120

her extensive traveling, a woman alone in so many countries that can be hostile to women. She kept up her training, and I believe her company paid for it."

"Damn right that woman is intelligent," Storm said, flashing an admiring grin at his twin, Ice. "That company of hers really values her. They pay for everything."

*"Paid,"* Steele corrected. "Past tense. She quit to come home and look after her grandmother. Keep going, Code. What happened to put that frown on your face?"

"They came back. The thieves. Zyah changed the locks on the doors. She also put a chair under the doorknob at the back door before she left and told her grandmother to have company when she was gone. She didn't want her there alone. Inez and Frank were with her while Zyah came to the party here at the clubhouse. Apparently, Lizz asked Anat to have Zyah drive her granddaughter, Francine, so she'd have a sober driver. Francine has had two DUIs already. Zyah agreed but only if someone stayed with Anat while she was out. I know this because it's all in the police report. Someone unlocked the back door. They had an actual key. Zyah had just changed those locks. If she hadn't put that chair in place, I don't know what would have happened. Inez called the sheriff, but the robbers were gone by the time they got there. Anat was pretty shaken up, but she didn't

121

want Zyah told until after her job interviews. She was adamant about that. I got that right out of the notes Jackson wrote in his report."

"These women," Alena said, "are amazing. I want to meet them. I'm with Code, Player, you don't deserve her, but Zyah needs to be part of our club, so I'm all for you winning her back. And I want Anat to be part of us. I'm going to have to whip up something special and bring it to her. She's got to be the strongest woman I've ever heard of."

"Zyah has changed the locks again, according to the police reports, to the kind where you have to punch in an actual code," Code informed them. "She's not taking chances."

"What are we going to do about these thieves, Czar?" Destroyer asked. His voice was mild, very soft. Very quiet. Still, his tone carried a deadly note in it.

Czar sighed. "No matter what, whether Zyah works for us or not, whether she belongs to Player or not, we can't have a group of brutal robbers preying on the elderly in our neighborhood. Although getting involved with the cops watching could be risky. And some of the neighbors aren't going to like us watching at night if they spot us. We could be the ones accused. We'd have to take shifts, and Code would have to figure out who might become a target. That would stretch us pretty thin trying to cover them all. This is a fairly wealthy community to retire in."

"It doesn't matter if they have money or not," Savage said. "If they live in Sea Haven or even here in Caspar, the assholes are going to think they have money."

"If we take this on, we have to put everything else on hold. We have no idea how many homes we're going to have to watch," Steele said. "Player and Master risked a lot to bring back that intel on the Ghosts. We could lose them again if we don't act."

"That's true," Keys agreed, "but on the other hand, this group, whoever they are, aren't simply robbing these people, which would be bad enough — they're beating the crap out of them."

"They're escalating the attacks if they're the same ones," Code said. "It's my best guess as well as the computer's that it's them. The MO is too close in every case I've looked at."

"I just glanced over the file Code has here, and running the numbers, I have to say I'm with Code — the odds are good that these people are the same ones moving from small village or town to the next," Master said. "They always choose very small towns with no real law enforcement presence and hit hard and get out. They simply fade away. No one seems to have a clue who they are."

"This is bullshit," Destroyer snapped, his tone low, almost husky, as if his voice had been as scarred as his once-handsome face.

He crossed his arms over his chest. He was a very big man, and the look on his face was one of disgust. "If the club isn't going to take this on, I will anyway. I'm not leaving these old people to the wolves."

There was instant silence. Czar's piercing gaze swung to Destroyer. "That's not the way it works in this club. When you came to me and laid it on the line, I went out on a limb for you. I took your request to the others and laid it out to them, and they took you in on faith. On my belief in you."

Destroyer shook his head. "I spent a lot of years in prison, in solitary. Alone. When I wasn't alone, I was fighting for my life or my sanity. I don't know, Czar. It's not that I don't appreciate the chance you gave me, but —"

"Destroyer," Savage stopped him before he could say any more. He took off his cut and laid it on the table. "Have you ever really looked at this? Have you ever asked yourself what it meant? There were two hundred and eighty-seven children entering that school, if you want to call it a school. Count in you and your sister, that's two hundred and eighty-nine. Counting you, nineteen of us survived that hellhole."

Player was shocked that Savage was fighting for Destroyer to stay. Savage wasn't one who spent a lot of time arguing one side or the other on any issue. He had his opinion, expressed it succinctly and then waited for the others to discuss it. The club members really didn't know Destroyer that well. Only Czar knew much about him. He had been taken, like the rest of them, from his home and trained to be an asset for their government, but in another school to begin with. He had been brought to their school as a form of punishment. Or, more precisely, for Sorbacov's amusement.

He pitted Destroyer against Ice and Storm in a series of challenges Sorbacov's guests could watch and bet on while they "entertained" themselves with Alena and Destroyer's sister, Calina. The winner of the series of challenges would be able to leave the schools and return to the outside world — or at least that was Sorbacov's lie. Destroyer had won, and he and his sister had disappeared, never to be seen or heard from again, until he showed up as a member of the Trinity club asking to be patched over to Torpedo Ink. He didn't fit with the Trinity club. He didn't seem to fit anywhere.

"Czar is this tree trunk. He got us out, but he did more than that — he kept us from losing complete humanity. To get out of that place, to save ourselves, we had to do things even adults shouldn't have to do. Without him giving us a moral code, none of us would have survived intact," Savage continued.

Destroyer put both hands on the table, fingers splayed wide. He had big hands. His fingers were tattooed. His hands were clearly weapons. His arms, all the way to his shoulders and up his neck, were covered in tattoos — not the smooth artwork Ink did, but raw prison work done in cells with contraband. He had long hair he wore pulled back from his face and bound tightly in two-inch increments down his back.

"I'm not certain I ever got out of that prison," he said, his voice husky. At some point his vocal cords had been damaged. He had scars, but the tattoos swirling up his neck covered them unless one looked closely — and Destroyer wasn't a man to let anyone get that close to him.

"That's the point," Player added his two cents, trying to fight for the man. They all were drowning in their own ways. "We're better together. I'm not saying this right. I exist because we exist. I don't know how else to put it to you. That's how we get through."

"You've had one another since you were kids," Destroyer pointed out. "You went through all of it together. That had to have woven a tight bond."

"Or it could have done just the opposite," Steele said. "In many cases it did. So many children refused to join with others — with us. They were embarrassed, or they wanted to please Sorbacov, or the instructors, hoping for favors. Whatever the reasons, they went their own way and they didn't make it."

"I had no choice."

There was no bitterness in Destroyer's voice, and Player realized that was one of the reasons Czar had fought so hard for him. He accepted what happened and went on from there. None of them could change the past, but they'd had Czar and one another to keep going — what had Destroyer had?

"Yes, you did," Czar said, his tone low but firm, the way it was when he was making a point and wanted it to stick. "You always have a choice, and you know that. You stayed alive in that prison. Something kept you alive. Whatever it was, it was strong, and you made it out and it brought you here, to us. You came this far and you have to take that next step and let us in."

Destroyer shook his head. "I'm not ever going to be that man who tells someone what happened to me. You all shared that past. That gave you a tight bond."

"Stop using that as an excuse. You were there in that school. What happened to us, happened to you," Czar snapped. "What's really going on here? You didn't have to be in the same room with us, because those fuckers went after all of us. You lost your sister. You know what they did to her. Every one of us suffered losses. Too many of them."

Before Czar could continue, Alena put both hands on the table. "Let me, please, Czar." She waited for his nod of consent. "Destroyer, you wanted to be part of this club. One of us. It was huge to allow you in. We don't do that. I held a childish grudge against you and nearly held out because of it, but Czar reminded me that you suffered the same nightmare childhood and losses we did. You belong with us, but we live with a code."

Destroyer started to speak, but Savage shook his head and indicated for him to allow Alena to continue.

"This isn't easy for me to say. I have a difficult time with outsiders, and letting you in when I felt you betrayed me was one of the hardest things I've done. I'm working every single day to accept you wholly into our family. The thing is, you have to come all the way in. Yes, it's true that we lived together, so we have that advantage on you. You were taken to that prison and lived alone. It's difficult to merge with us, I know that. It must seem like so many rules and personalities. I'm getting to the point, I promise. I'm just working up the courage to make my confession."

"Alena," Czar said gently, "you don't have to."

"I do. He's a member of the club, and we all know one another's worst secrets. We all saw the terrible things done over and over. He didn't. He might know what happened. He might have experienced the same things, but he didn't see it happening to us the way we did. He doesn't get thrown out without me making an attempt to get him to understand. I was the one who behaved childishly, and I can stand up for a brother. We made him that when we gave him a Torpedo Ink cut."

"Alena." Destroyer's voice lowered another octave. "It's all right. I appreciate you standing up for me, but this thing is very personal to me."

"It's personal to all of us. We always talk out everything, give every side of it, look at every angle — that's our way. We vote, make a plan and then attack as an entire group, an entity. One. Torpedo Ink. You take on one of us, you take on all of us. It has to be that way. A long time ago, someone hurt Lana, really hurt her, and I couldn't stand it. I decided I was going to exact revenge."

Lana leaned toward Alena and covered her hand. "Baby, I love you so much." She whispered it so softly the declaration was barely audible.

Alena's blue eyes turned liquid, but she went on. "It had been drilled into me not to go off alone, or deviate from the plan, but I didn't care and I did it anyway. The consequences were extreme and taught me a lesson I'll carry on my soul the rest of my life. A young girl died as a result of my stupidity. We are safer and work better as a team. We have to be able to count on you at all times. And you have to know you can count on us."

Destroyer nodded. "You didn't have to tell me that, Alena. I know that wasn't easy for you. It's damn difficult to try to fit into a tight unit when you all have been together for so many years. I sometimes feel like I have nowhere to go."

"You're wearing the colors," Alena persisted. "They mean something. Make them mean something to you like they do to us."

"You said this was personal," Savage said. "Tell us why."

Destroyer looked around the table at the Torpedo Ink members, his brothers and two sisters, the ones wearing the same ink, bound together by something tighter, even, than blood. It occurred to Player that Destroyer said very little, and when he did, it was never about himself or his past. They all knew that, like theirs, his past wasn't good. He wouldn't have been in the schools if he hadn't been torn from his home. He would have suffered torture and rape; they knew his sister had. He had carried out the work of an assassin. They knew he had been sent to the worst prison possible when he was only fourteen years of age. How did one survive that and come out intact?

Destroyer curled his fingers into two tight fists. He had massive shoulders and arms. Every time he moved, muscles rippled ominously beneath his skin. Clearly, he fought his natural inclination, which was to just walk out and stay on his own.

Alena tried again. "All of us have hit a wall at some point, Destroyer, where we felt we couldn't keep going. It wasn't that long ago that it happened to me. We were in a huge fight and I ended up on the wrong side of a knife. The stab wounds were deep, and I knew they were bad, that there was no way I was going to make it through. I welcomed death. I was so damn tired of fighting for sanity every day. Lana was there. I remember her voice, looking up at her, hearing her call to me, telling me she needed me with her, and I knew I just couldn't keep going. It was all too much for me."

Player watched Destroyer carefully, as did the other members of Torpedo Ink. They knew Alena, knew just how difficult offering any part of herself up to a virtual stranger could be, but she was doing it in order to try to save him, to make up for the grudge she'd held against him. The club members saw past her tough exterior. That had been so hard-won. She was soft inside and needed to protect herself.

Her birth brothers, Ice and Storm, could barely contain themselves, but she had every right to put herself out there for a brother. Player was proud of her, but like Ice and Storm, and probably all the others, he wanted to wrap her up in his arms and carry her off before she exposed herself. Before she cut

131

herself open and bled for him. If Destroyer didn't see what she was giving him, he didn't deserve to wear their colors.

"You would never have sought out a club unless you were getting desperate. Unless, like I was, you were right there, saying, *Enough.* I was through waking up every morning to pain and memories I couldn't take in a world I didn't understand and could never fit into. When you didn't fit with that chapter, you came here, because you're like us. You see you in us. You have to take that leap, Destroyer, let down your guard with us, just like we're doing with you. Let us in. Give us something so we bond together, and you're part of us. We're all of us one. Part of these colors."

Player didn't take his gaze from Destroyer's eyes. The man looked like what he was — a brutal, dangerous man. He could be charismatic if he chose, with his dark, mesmerizing eyes, eyes that were fixed on Alena's face. There was despair there. Sadness. No way was Destroyer going to walk away from Alena's plea. He knew how difficult it was. He saw inside her to that soft, vulnerable part she protected, and the man was bracing himself to do something he'd never done in his life — share something that was real and painful and buried so deep no one knew how much it hurt to give it up.

Destroyer shook his head and ran his hands

through his hair again. "I've never really followed anyone in my life. Not since I lost my
grandmother, but Czar and I have a history.
If there's anyone I believe in, it's him. You lay
down an argument I can't exactly ignore,
Alena. All of you have. I appreciate you fighting for me." He managed a rueful smile that
didn't reach his eyes.

He sighed again. When he put one hand on
the table, he closed his fingers into a tight
fist. It was large, tattooed, scarred and had
seen many fights. "We lost our parents early.
Calina, my sister, didn't talk for a long time
after their accident." He ducked his head,
avoiding Alena's eyes. "It wasn't an accident.
My father started drinking more and more,
and when he did, he would get very angry
with everyone. He didn't like anyone looking
at my mother. She was very beautiful."

It was clear he didn't talk about his family
to anyone. He probably hadn't talked about
his parents since he was a child. He fell silent
and no one prompted him to speak. No one
became impatient with him. They simply
waited. All of them knew what loss was.
They'd all suffered enormous losses. It was
entirely up to Destroyer if he wanted to give
that piece of himself to the club.

"He flew into jealous rages, and he did that
night. He shot our mother and then tried to
shoot Calina, but I dragged her out of the
room and ran out of the house with her. I

133

wasn't very old myself, but I just kept running until I made it to my grandparents' house. They lived about three miles from us. He killed my mother and then himself. Calina was really just a baby, a toddler, and he shot our mother right in front of her — she had blood all over her. My grandparents took us in. They were good people. The best."

He did look up then, but this time at Czar. "I get crazy sometimes, in my head. What the hell is wrong with the world? When Sorbacov's men came for my grandfather because he was too outspoken against the new president's policy, the soldiers shot him, but they beat my grandmother to death, again, right in front of Calina. I tried to stop them, and they found that very amusing. I took a beating myself in front of her. She was practically in a catatonic state after that. I thought when Sorbacov and his son were dead and I was free, all the killing would end, all the brutality, but it follows me. What's the difference between someone who would kill a child and someone who would do the same to the elderly?"

Destroyer rubbed his fist in his palm in agitation. "A grandmother? They beat her? Robbed her? A woman with the guts to bring a ten-year-old girl to the United States and start a life? It's bullshit. It just triggered something in me."

"That's understandable, Destroyer," Czar

said. "I can safely say, it triggered something in all of us. We'll vote on it, but I don't think you have much to worry about."

Destroyer cast the first vote decisively in favor of watching over the elderly and finding out who was behind the robberies. It was unanimous, which didn't surprise Player in the least.

"You'll have to find out everything you can about the other robberies, Code," Czar said.

"I don't sleep so good," Destroyer confessed. "I can take the night watches, although if someone spots me, they'll probably be more afraid of me than the robbers."

"Not that I can imagine you letting anyone spot you," Czar said, "but we could have Inez smooth things over with her friends, let them know we're looking out for them. On the other hand, it might not be the best idea to risk it. Someone had the key to that lock at the Gamal house. That's someone who knows them."

"Best not to let anyone know so you don't get caught when you're on guard duty," Steele cautioned. "Are we finished here? I want to make certain my woman is safe so she can see her friend again."

"Not yet," Czar said. "One more thing. We can get to it fast, though, Steele. Code is overworked. He can't get everything done, no matter how many computers he uses. He can have dozens searching for what we want or need, but he still has to program them and monitor them. He's asked that we relieve him of the duty of treasurer. I propose we do so. Master is our resident wizard with numbers, and half the time he's working with Code anyway. He can manage everything, decide our investments, and Code will still maneuver accounts when needed. Are any opposed?"

Czar looked around the table. "That's it, then. Steele, you can have Delia escorted to the common room, and Absinthe, have Scarlet sit and visit with her. The two of you can vet her and make certain it's safe for Breezy. Once that's out of the way, we'll all breathe easier."

As they stood up, Alena touched the back of Destroyer's hand. "I'm really sorry about Calina. We talked when we were children. She was fragile, but I didn't realize . . ." She trailed off and turned her head away from him. "I feel bad that I judged you so harshly."

"You were fragile as well, Alena. You were a child. We all were." Destroyer shoved back the chair and spun around toward the door. "Thanks for fighting for me."

# FIVE

Player leaned against the wall of the empty building across from the grocery store, with most of his Torpedo Ink family hanging out with him. They'd come on the pretense of checking out the space in the building for Lana.

He glanced at her. At least he thought it was a pretense. Maybe not. He was so preoccupied with all the men crowding into the grocery store across the street that he wasn't paying enough attention to Lana's questions. She had declared her interest in deciding whether or not she wanted to set up a clothing store right there or somewhere else, or not at all.

Mostly, his brothers wanted to give him a bad time, not talk about space in buildings. Or, right at that moment, that was what it felt like to Player. Who knew there were even that many single men in the county who knew how to grocery shop? Or had heard about the new grocery store in Caspar? They certainly hadn't been shopping there when Inez was running it.

He knew his brothers were teasing him — that's what they did to one another to show support, most of the time. Just the fact that they were with him meant that what he wanted mattered, but his good mood had gone south when he saw the store was overrun by so many men. Some were actually shopping, or pretending to. Most were crowded around the counter where his woman — who didn't have a clue she was already claimed — was happily chatting away with them while she rang up groceries.

Even from a distance and through the very clean storefront window, Player could see she was fast and efficient. He could also see one of the men was leaning far too close to her. The fuckin' man was smooth too. A real snake. All melting charm. Probably didn't swear. Certainly didn't ride a Harley. Most likely owned the shiny black sports car parked right out front. Yeah, that was his ride. He was dressed in *GQ* clothing, not a hair out of place.

Player put a hand to his own wild hair. It was all over the place. It was long, and it fell past his shoulders in thick, out-of-control waves most of the time. It was light brown with what could pass for sun streaks but were really silver or gray. No one ever guessed that his childhood had put those strands of silver in his hair permanently. He rode a Harley, had a foul mouth and his colors were part of his soul. He was also a damn good shot with his gun. He could put a bullet right through that smiling mouth and take out those blinding white teeth.

"I thought you were here to be supportive, the way Ice was with Reaper when he was trying to win Anya. Or the way we all were with Ice when he was working to keep Soleil, but instead the lot of you are worthless. Go home." He glared at them. His brothers. Wearing the colors and laughing at his predicament.

Yeah. He'd screwed up. Definitely. He was willing to own his mistakes. He'd hurt Zyah. She'd been crying when she left the clubhouse. Everything Code had uncovered about her had been good. He'd been a first-class bastard — inadvertently, mistakenly, but he'd been one all the same. He was totally willing to admit it and make amends.

Someone snickered. It sounded suspiciously like Maestro, but when he turned his head, Maestro was glaring at the sports car clown. For certain, Keys smirked. That was going to get him a beatdown because Player's aggression toward perfect white teeth had to go somewhere.

"Alena and the rest of us gave you shit advice, Destroyer," Player declared righteously. "This is some serious bullshit going on right here. My woman's over there being hit on by every single man in the county and instead of trying to help me out, they're just giving me shit. This civilized crap Czar keeps throwin' at us is for the birds. I should shoot that asshole leaning on the counter flirtin' with her, most likely asking her out on a date with me standing right here. And while I'm at it, I should just shoot the lot of you too."

"Someone's in a bad mood," Lana said and blew Player a kiss. "You're right, not only is he flirting with her, but he *is* asking her out. His body language is blatant."

"He's into her," Storm agreed. "Totally into her, you can tell by the way he's looking at her. He's not seeing anyone but her."

"Why don't you just go inside?" Destroyer asked. "Talk to her."

"That would provoke her into going out with him even if she didn't want to go," Player said. "It's better to wait until the damn store clears out. What did Inez do? Put out a bulletin that an eligible woman would be mindin' the store today? A *seriously* beautiful one at that."

"You didn't think to stake your claim with Inez?" Alena asked. "Sheesh, Player. She's like the one person you should go to with this kind of thing. She's the resident match-maker. Don't go to Ice or Storm for advice. Or worse, consult the Internet yourself. You saw what happened to Reaper."

"Hey. I object," Ice said righteously, nudging his sister with his shoulder. "When are you going to let that go? It was a tiny little mistake anyone could make. A sex surrogate professionally trained didn't sound that far a cry from Tawny."

"Eww." Lana sniffed. "Ice, that's just disgusting. If you can't tell the difference, you don't have a brain in your head."

"I'm just saying if Player wants to win back his lady he has to think with his brain, not his dick," Alena insisted. "Consult the reigning queens around here. Go to Hannah Drake in Sea Haven. She has a shop everyone talks about. She makes these amazing concoctions. Kind of like Preacher does, but very potent and directed just toward your particular lady."

"I can make anything Hannah can make," Preacher objected. He gave Alena a sheepish grin. "Well. Maybe. I should make her a chemistry challenge. I'll visit her shop, Player, and see what kind of love potions she has. I can recreate anything she's got and make it stronger."

"You do that, brother," Lana teased. "I want a front-row seat when you do. But seriously, Player, Alena has a good idea."

Player glared at them. "Do you think I'm crazy? I know who Hannah Drake is. She helped us out a few years ago, and she's scary as all hell, not to mention she's Hannah

Drake *Harrington.* You know, married to the local sheriff, Jonas Harrington. I go near that woman and that thin veneer of his making nice with our club is going to come off."

"Is she supposed to be a witch or something?" Destroyer asked.

"If she is a witch, I think our advice to Reaper might have been safer than what you're giving to Player," Storm said piously.

There were several nods of agreement.

Alena rolled her eyes. "Destroyer, you weren't here, but the Drake sisters helped us when our club went up against the Swords. We were significantly outnumbered, and the Swords' president had major psychic talents. Fortunately, so do the Drake sisters. Sea Haven seems to draw talent to it. Hannah Drake is powerful, and I'm sure ignorant people would call her a witch because she has mad talents and is skilled in using them."

Lana tugged at Player's arm to draw him deeper into the empty space. "We wouldn't steer you wrong. Hannah's nice. I've met her numerous times. Also, if you do business with his wife, Jonas will probably like us even more. Just go into her place and look around. You don't actually have to talk to her if you don't want to. And you might not even need to. Who knows, maybe Zyah will totally forgive you."

Behind them, the snort of derision was loud. Player spun around to find that the oth-

142

ers had filed into the space behind them. He found himself smiling. He couldn't help himself. Big men, wearing their familiar colors, the tree with the solid trunk representing Czar, the man who had gotten them out alive and hopefully intact as human beings. The seventeen branches representing those left alive. Ink had said he would be adding an eighteenth branch soon to every one of their tatts if Destroyer stuck around. The ravens, resting in the branches or flying away, representing the ones they couldn't save. All the skulls piled high in the roots of the trees and lying around it, the dead, those he and the others had killed in order to escape or had tracked down and taken out to exact revenge for the deaths of the children in the school.

They wore that symbol on their cuts and on their skin, branded into their souls. They were bonded together, stitched together just as tightly as the lethal loom that they'd been tortured with, so many years ago, at that school. All of them bore those scars and woke with those nightmares.

He looked at Destroyer, wanting him to understand what was being offered to him. Willing him to take it, just as Alena and Savage had held it out to him. Czar had stood for him. Destroyer was covered in prison tattoo ink. He knew Destroyer still wasn't quite convinced he was where he should be, and somehow, like the others in Torpedo Ink,

Player felt compelled to convince him.

Player turned to Lana. "Babe, are you really serious about wanting to use this space for a shop?"

"Yes, but all of you were so busy worrying about Zyah and all the men fawning all over her you couldn't give me your opinion. I'm very serious. What do you think? Too big? Too small? Am I crazy to want to actually work? I hate being cooped up."

"If you want my real opinion, then I'm going to give it to you because you know I love you, honey," Player warned.

"Of course I want it, or I wouldn't be asking," Lana said, but she sounded wary.

The others wandered through the four rooms. There was the larger floor space with a single dressing room. A back room and a bathroom. The storefront looked out onto the street and gave a good view of the ocean. The back had a very nice enclosed, covered patio like most of the other businesses on the street, which were closed.

"I think the idea of you running a clothing store like the one you're talking about is unrealistic given your personality. You'll be bored out of your mind in a day. You would never have the shop open. Not ever. You already know that. What you should do is start up a business designing exclusive clothing for some of these kids Darby was telling us about, who can't afford shit and the other

144

kids are so fucking mean to. You could change their lives for them."

When the club came together for breakfast or barbecues, Darby, Czar's oldest adopted daughter, often talked about other teens she met that had difficult home lives. Sometimes Player found it difficult to listen to the stories she told about children who actually had parents. The parents didn't take care of them; instead they made alcohol or drugs their priority.

Alena spun around. She'd been staring out the window, keeping her eye on the grocery store, but she hurried across to them. "That's so brilliant, Player, why didn't I think of that? He's right, Lana. That's exactly what you should do. Design a few pieces of clothing. One of a kind. Sell them for a bazillion dollars so that everyone wants your label. You know they will. No one will be able to resist, just like with Ice's jewelry. Once your label is blowing everyone away, then have Darby bring these kids to you. You make their clothes for them and put your special whammy into them. It won't matter so much that they don't have the best home life. If they start hanging around your shop and talking to you while you measure them, sitting in your chairs or on the patio outside with Darby while you work, it really could be a good thing."

"Do you really think their parents are going

to let them hang around with a bunch of bikers?" Keys asked.

"I don't think we're talking about kids whose parents give two fucks," Player said.

"Player's right, Lana," Preacher said. "We go to Blythe and Czar's home nearly every weekend for breakfast or lunch in the afternoon with their kids. We teach survival class, and Darby or Kenny always brings up something about kids they know from hanging at the beach or down at the community school when they test, or when Airiana teaches them physics. Lana, you could really do some good."

Lana shook her head. She even took two steps back, as if the idea were terrifying, when she wasn't afraid of anything. "I don't know the first thing about kids. Blythe had a thing or two to say about the way we were handling survivor class, remember?"

"But she didn't stop us," Master pointed out. "One word from her and the show's over. We all know that. The kids know it. She looks at Czar and he just caves."

They all laughed — everyone, Player noticed, with the exception of Destroyer. He sent the man a small grin. "We sound like Blythe's a battle-ax. You've met her numerous times. She's really as sweet as she seems. It's just that . . . well . . . she's . . ." He trailed off again.

"Our heart, if we have one," Alena supplied.

"Everyone's in agreement, Lana," Ink said. He was leaning against the wall, quiet, the way he often was. Ink could be moody. "Player's onto something. You've got a gift. Help these kids out."

Her gaze jumped to his. "You really think I should?"

"Yeah, babe, I really think you should," Ink said. "Every damn time Darby, Kenny or that crazy kid Benito talks about those lost teens, I want Blythe and Czar to take them in. Just sittin' on your furniture will make them feel better, let alone wearin' something you make."

"You know if you make a few outfits and sell them to adults first, you'll be a huge hit and everyone will want your stuff," Alena said. "Just do it."

The others nodded in agreement.

Player indicated them all with a sweep of his hand. "This is why, Destroyer. Those colors you wear mean something. You were in that school with us. You lost just the way we lost. Let Ink put that shit right into your skin, the way we wear it in ours. You'll feel it."

"There's nowhere it can go," Destroyer said softly, his voice a husk of a sound, filled with something close to regret. "I've got ink all over me."

"Show me," Ink challenged.

The group went silent, all eyes moving from Lana to Destroyer. He stood for a long moment. Savage held out his hand, a casual gesture. Destroyer shrugged out of his vest and let Savage take it from him. The big man caught the hem of his T-shirt and pulled it over his head. His body was every bit as strong as he appeared to be, skin stretched tight over muscle.

Dark whorls and white slashes marred what should have been smooth skin, most wounds they all recognized — they had them as well. The shocking ones were the most recognizable, scars only Torpedo Ink members should have. No one from any other school had ever been subjected, as far as they knew, to the diabolical torture of the loom. That had been reserved for their school only. It had been hideous, and all of them still had nightmares.

How had Destroyer gotten those scars? They weren't just a few scars either. He had far more than any of them. They were all over his chest, but the stitches were torn as if his skin had literally been ripped off. He turned his back to allow Ink to see what he would have to work over. His back was very broad, and the scars there were much worse, long raised ridges making his skin look much like a road map. The worst had been made by the loom, long, hideous stitches weaving patterns in every direction. Again, those had been torn, ripped away as if he had been skinned alive.

Someone had crudely tried to tattoo various pictures around the scars, most depicting rank in the prison. It was clear Destroyer had risen fast in prison, but the artwork had to have hurt as it had been tatted along or over the ridges. The tattoos were done with whatever the prisoners could find to use.

No one said anything, but they all looked. Stared. More than ever, Player felt Destroyer belonged with Torpedo Ink. Czar had molded them into a family, one fiercely loyal to one another, and somehow Destroyer fit with them. The loom scars proved that. He was another strong thread in their tightly knit family.

Czar had told them Destroyer had completely damaged the loom and killed the weaver when his sister had been tortured, raped and murdered, but they hadn't seen the terrible evidence of the toll on his body. His skin had to have been pulled off both his chest and his back when he'd ripped his way out of the weave to get at his sister's killers.

Ink studied Destroyer's back, not looking at the black ink there but more at the ridges and whorls that were spread from his shoulders all the way to his buttocks. "Yeah, you want me to, I can work with this. I can make the tree kick-ass. The ravens are personal for each of us. They represent whoever you knew that didn't make it out. I can make them however you want, standing on a branch, wings out, in, flying, as many or as few as you prefer. Your tree can have eighteen branches. You've got the room, and it will help with covering this bad ink here." He ran his finger up along a particularly bad ridge.

Savage nodded, standing close to Ink, his eyes on the scarring the loom had made. "Yeah. It will look good. The skulls in the roots represent the ones we took out for those tortured, raped or killed. They could be an instructor inside the school or someone Sorbacov brought in and let enjoy us for his own fucking pleasure. You know what I'm talking about."

Destroyer took his shirt back and pulled it over his head, settling it back over his broad chest easily. "Yeah, I know."

Maestro took up the explanation. "The skulls lying on the ground are for missions for our country or pedophiles we've taken out. If you prefer, the kills for pedophiles can go under the tree, if you've got the room. Reaper and Savage pretty much have completely filled that space."

Savage handed Destroyer his cut and all of them watched him put it on.

"You belong with Torpedo Ink, Destroyer," Storm said. "It takes time getting used to having people at your back. Or getting into your business. But you belong. Those scars on your chest and back say so."

Lana nodded. "I don't know how Czar knows you so well, but if he's willing to fight for you, and all of us are, you have to be willing to fight to belong."

"Did you really think we were going to let some bastards come into our territory and hurt any of our people? Especially the old ones?" Savage asked.

Destroyer gave him a faint imitation of a smile. "You all talk too much."

Player burst out laughing. The rest of the club members followed suit. "Gotta agree with you there, brother. Not only do they talk too much, they aren't paying attention to the important things in life. We came here to figure out how to get my woman back for me. I don't hear any suggestions."

"I gave you a suggestion," Alena disagreed. "It was a very good one too. You were there when we fought the Swords. You know what the Drake women can do. They're all gifted. Heck, all the women Blythe claims as sisters are gifted. She is. We are. Hannah is no different. I'm telling you, if you're serious about wanting to get Zyah back, go to her shop and at least look around. See if she has something that might work for you."

Preacher gave Alena a mock scowl. "Are we talking some love potion? I can whip him up something. I'm the chemist in the family."

Lana threw her arms into the air. "Here we go again. Player, if you listen to them, you are *so* going to lose that woman."

"I say he just goes in and apologizes to her

151

like a man," Master declared. "Straight up. Tell her he was seventy-two hours without sleep and was delirious and out of his fuckin' mind. He's sorry and wants another chance. Women throw themselves at him. He's got charm, and he can grovel if he has to."

The others nodded their agreement.

"Did any of you bother to read the report Code printed out for us?" Lana demanded.

Player had. Every single word over and over. He had the damn thing memorized. He'd asked Code to keep digging. He wanted to know everything there was to know about Zyah.

"Code filled us in on the pertinent stuff," Ice pointed out.

Lana exchanged an eye roll with Alena. "Here's why Zyah's going to shut Player down fast," Lana said. "She isn't someone who hooks up ever. There's no evidence of it. Code couldn't find it, and he looked. She travels all the time, and she doesn't go club-bing. She doesn't invite men to her hotel room. She was in an exclusive relationship, and she didn't move in with the man or have him move in with her. That right there should tell you something about her."

Yeah. Player already got that part. He knew he'd screwed up royally. The rest of the club didn't want to get it. They were hoping it would be easy for him, but he knew better. The moment he remembered the look on her face when he handed her the money, he knew he was in trouble. It hadn't registered that morning, but it was in his memory bank. He had that image etched into his brain. He'd hurt her. Crushed her. Shattered her.

"So, she meets our brother and falls for him like a ton of bricks. He gets all down and dirty with her and she's thinking one thing and he's thinking something altogether different," Maestro said. "Or thinking *with* something altogether different."

Player sighed. He hadn't been thinking at all. His brain had short-circuited. "Shut the fuck up," he said, just because it was expected. "I was half out of it."

"Maybe," Keys said, "but your dick was working fine."

Another round of laughter went up at his expense. He couldn't deny what they were saying. His dick had worked. All on its own. Just thinking about her made him ache. Unfortunately, Lana was right. He was going to apologize, because he owed Zyah an apology, and maybe the universe was going to be benevolent to him and give him a pass, but he doubted it. He wasn't going to be that lucky. Not that she wouldn't be gracious. She'd be kind and give him some bullshit saccharine-sweet lie about how she hadn't given it a thought and not to worry. And she'd dismiss him.

"You sure you don't want me to fuck up

Mr. Charm for you?" Savage asked.

Player stared out the window at the man who was just now straightening up, his eyes still glued to Zyah. This time it was very clear he was staring at her tits. What an asshole. He was out for pussy. Hopefully, she was good enough to read that shit and not be dazzled by his appearance. He stank of money. His jeans were designer all the way.

"How much do you think he paid for those jeans?" Player asked.

"Five hundred, easy," Lana said. "Shirt is about three. That sweater? Close to a thousand. The boots? At least a thousand. He would be turning up his nose at your boots, Savage."

Savage looked down at his well-worn motorcycle boots. "What the hell's wrong with my boots, Lana?"

"I think you've worn through the soles."

"I have not. I'm not falling for that. You're tryin' to make me look."

Another round of laughter went up. Lana grinned at him and nudged Player with her hip. "Just so you know, there is an alternative to Hannah Drake. I heard a rumor that the Red Hat ladies in Sea Haven . . . well . . . I think that encompasses Caspar as well. I think a group of the Red Hat ladies sometimes help men get their women back when they've screwed up. Or if they want to plan a real romantic date. Something like that. Inez

154

told me about it. You know how she chatters. She's part of it. She was very enthusiastic. She said some men just aren't good at planning and they throw out ideas for them. Brainstorming, she called it. I thought it sounded kind of nice."

"Who in the hell are the Red Hat ladies?" Player demanded.

"I think it's officially called the Red Hat Society, but don't quote me," Lana said. "When you hit a certain age, you qualify to join. Women, I think. They get together and do whatever they want. Wear what they want, get crazy together. Just enjoy life. But the point is, they know stuff. Like Blythe does. They've lived and learned. We don't know shit, Player. That's the one thing we can all agree on. We don't have the least idea of what it is we're doing, especially when it comes to relationships. I'm just saying, if Zyah spits in your face like she should, maybe you can ask them for help." She shrugged. "Or not. It's up to you. On the other hand, when you go in and talk to her, maybe you'll decide she wasn't all you thought she was."

Zyah shifted her weight from one bare foot to the other on the tiled floor behind the counter, wishing she didn't have such a bad habit of removing her shoes whenever she wanted information on someone. Unexpected gifts from the universe could be curses as

155

well. She had been so certain she had found the man she fit with. Everything in her responded to him. Her body tuned to his. When she danced, the vibrations of the earth seemed to mold them into one, so they felt as if they shared the same skin.

Player had felt so fractured to her when he first entered the room. His color was nearly gray. Little beads of sweat dotted his forehead. His pulse was all over the place. She could tell his head was really hurting him. When her heart went crazy, tuning itself to his, attempting to slow his to normal, she was shocked at how strong her reaction was to him. She had to help him. She had no choice. Every single cell in her body reached for his. She'd been absolutely 100 percent certain he was the one destined to be her man. She'd been so wrong.

It hurt. Not only did she feel like a complete fool, but she was ashamed of the way she'd behaved with him. Clearly, he thought his fellow bikers had paid her to spend the night with him. Dancing. Fucking. She'd been making love to him. Giving herself to him. Being vulnerable. He'd been taking everything and not giving a damn. It was a hard lesson, but she'd learned it.

Now there was this man. Perry Randall. Flirting. Giving it his all. He was using all of his charm, trying to persuade her to go on a date, leaning on the counter, looking at her through his sunglasses that cost as much as his shoes had. She'd calculated several times how many homeless people she could feed with his clothes alone. Then shelter dogs. Then feral cats.

He was one of those men who was interested, but before he actually asked her out, he had to make certain he looked great, staring at himself in every mirror he passed by and fixing his hair as often as possible. He was definitely the type to ask himself if his friends would think she was hot. Once he'd convinced himself they would think she was gorgeous enough to belong on his arm and in his ride, then he would make his move on her and continue to do so, thinking she was playing hard to get if she said no, because who would ever refuse him? That was the kind of thing that always happened to her, no matter where she was in the world.

She sent Perry a vague smile and turned her attention to the next customer, engaging them in conversation, filing their image away, asking their name, introducing herself, and thanking them for coming in. She chattered away, making what appeared to be casual conversation, but every inquiry enabled her to find out if her customer was local, if they had a family and if they would be returning.

Inez had trained her for a week before leaving her on her own, and in that week, the pattern to the way grocery store customers had come in had been very specific. Morning shoppers were women dropping their children at school or on their way to work and picking up a quick bite. Afternoons brought the heavier shoppers, filling their carts with a week's worth of groceries. Evenings were those getting off work and picking up a few items to make a meal fast. Her first day alone hadn't been like that at all.

It was the weekend, but even that shouldn't have made all that much difference. It hadn't when Inez had been there. Today, there hadn't been a single block of time, not five full minutes, when she had a break. Inez had handled the store hours virtually alone, with only someone to stock shelves and give her required breaks. If this influx of customers continued, they would need to hire someone immediately, and finding reliable help seemed to be a major issue.

She glanced out the window. A long line of motorcycles had been parked there for what seemed the better part of an hour. Maybe over an hour. Player was there, across the street, and she knew she would have to face him. The idea turned her inside out. Her grandmother was absolutely right. She had to stay away from him, shut him out completely, or she would never be open to a real relationship.

Maybe something was wrong with her. Maybe it wasn't the men at all. The first man she'd really thought might be the one had turned out not even to be close. He'd had a lot to say about her shortcomings. She'd had a lot of time to think about those things he'd listed because they'd looped over and over in her head. She'd written them down. Listed them, determined to discover if they were true and work on them if that was so. She wanted to be a good partner. He claimed she didn't give anything of herself, and looking back, she was certain he was right — she hadn't.

Her gaze strayed to the clock more than once as the crowd thinned out. She wanted Perry gone, but she knew he wasn't going to leave. He was determined to outwait everyone and still try to talk her into going out with him, even though she'd politely declined three times. She was going straight home to her grandmother. She didn't want her alone for even five minutes, and there was a short period of time when she would have to be by herself in the house before Zyah's shift ended. She had to close, and that took time.

Her grandmother's latest X-rays hadn't been good. The doctor had to reset her bone, and that meant once again postponing physical therapy for her leg. Mama Anat had been so disappointed. She was anxious to get out of the wheelchair and be able to do for herself. Thankfully, Terrie Frankle, the physical therapist, was willing to help out with her

159

arm because she needed to speed up recovery and get the use back so she could be more independent.

Zyah had once again changed the locks and, with Inez's help, made out a schedule so her grandmother wasn't alone while she worked. Another house two blocks over had been robbed, and the couple occupying the cottage, beaten. Inez knew that couple as well. Gabe and Harmony Gleason were in their early seventies and, according to Inez, owned a gift shop in Sea Haven. They were very much part of the community. It seemed so senseless to Zyah for the robbers to beat the elderly when they had already turned over money and jewelry.

Torpedo Ink members began drifting in, one or two at a time five minutes before closing, picking up a few items and, when they came up to the counter, introducing themselves to her. Each of them gave Perry a hard look and then the once-over. It was intimidating as hell. By the third one, a big man with his head shaved and the coldest eyes she'd ever seen, Perry gave up and walked out to his hot car. He stood next to it for a few minutes, and when more of the bikers crowded onto the sidewalk just outside of the store, he drove away.

Few people knew the club owned the store. Inez was part owner, and her name was prominent when one looked it up. She co-owned with a company. One had to dig deep to find that Torpedo Ink owned the company. Perry had just left her alone with very scary men. He was afraid of them, but had no compunction about leaving her. Zyah managed the store, and she had been told Torpedo Ink co-owned with Inez. They had been very up front with her before offering her the job. They had also disclosed that the club members would be working in the back and stocking shelves and also watching over the store, as well as escorting anyone closing the store home, from a distance, but still, it was a policy and one they preferred she didn't talk about to anyone else.

Zyah didn't get bad vibes from the Torpedo Ink club members. They were courteous and simply introduced themselves and told her when they were on the schedule to work in the back or stock the shelves for her. They made certain she had their cell phone numbers in case of an emergency. She had always had a gift for remembering faces and names. This club took their jobs seriously. Alena and Lana, the two women, were friendly, although she got a very watchful vibe from them. They also were on the work schedule to help out in the store.

The last customer was gone, and she closed the register, hoping that Player stayed outside waiting for the rest of his club, too embarrassed to come inside, but she knew she wasn't going to get that lucky. He didn't seem like a man who was the kind to get embarrassed by his despicable actions. He was a . . . player. He played women. He'd warned her just by introducing himself. She was the fool for believing in her faulty gift — one that had only been in her family for hundreds of years. She was *not* going to cry again over her utter failure as a Gamal woman.

"You all right?"

History really did repeat itself. She would recognize that voice anywhere. It was low, husky, as if the vocal cords had been badly damaged at some point. He'd asked her the exact same question the night she'd run like a coward from Player's room, sobbing like a baby, feeling like he'd stabbed her through the heart. She closed her eyes briefly, hoping that would get rid of any leftover brightness in her eyes, and then forced herself to meet Destroyer's concerned gaze. He'd introduced himself as Destroyer that night. He wore that same look on his scarred, ruggedly handsome and terribly charismatic features.

Zyah had to admit there was something very compelling about all of the Torpedo Ink members. She sent him a faint, sheepish grin. "I just stubbed my toe. I'm not wearing shoes like I should be."

He didn't believe her, but he didn't call her on her lie. He glanced over his shoulder, and immediately Player stepped up to the counter.

"Zyah. I'm glad to finally find you. I've been searching for you since I woke up and realized what a complete ass I made of myself. I owe you an apology."

He sounded absolutely sincere. He looked absolutely sincere. Worse, he looked every bit as gorgeous and as perfect as she remembered. The wild hair, the tattoos and scars, the muscles on top of muscles. She could barely look at him. She had no choice or she would be the rudest person on the planet, and her grandmother would never abide rudeness no matter the circumstances.

She was extremely happy for the years of working in all the countries where the men weren't exactly thrilled taking orders from a woman. She'd had to learn to be a diplomat and keep an impersonal smile on her face no matter how she felt inside. Her heart could be pounding in absolute terror, she could be mad, sad or a combination of all three emotions, but her hands would remain rock steady and she could keep that smile going forever.

"No worries. I completely understand. There was every reason for you to misunderstand the situation. I appreciate that you didn't hold it against me when you realized I'd applied for this job." She sent him another smile and began to work in earnest. She had to get the job finished so she could go home.

Player didn't interrupt her, but he didn't

move away either. That meant he had more to say and she was going to have to listen to him whether she liked it or not. She heaved a sigh and forced herself to look up the moment she had made certain the till was right. "Is there something else I can do for you?"

Player leaned toward her. He smelled just the way she remembered. Masculine. Sensual. Just plain yummy. She was so far gone on him it was crazy. She busied herself again with receipts, keeping her head down so she didn't have to look into his amazing eyes.

"Zyah, I was seventy-two hours without sleep. That being said, you gave me the best night of my life. I fucked it up by being so tired I began mixing reality with fantasy. I didn't think you were real for a variety of reasons, the main one being I'd never been around anyone like you. I had no idea a woman like you existed or I could react the way I did. I'm damned sorry for the way I treated you and I'd like a chance to start over."

There it was. He was asking her to take a chance on letting him tear her heart out again. It wasn't his fault. He didn't know what he was asking. He wanted great sex. Their chemistry was off the charts. Right now, just looking at him, she could probably have a mini-orgasm if she let herself get close enough to smell him while she looked into his eyes. Seriously, that's how her body responded to his.

She pushed away from the counter a little desperately to put some more space between them. She had to get shoes on her feet so her silly wayward, *faulty,* misguided, unhelpful parlor trick of a gift wasn't feeling him and adding to the ferocious, almost desperate hunger rushing through her veins at his close proximity. The hell with that. She could find someone else to see to her sexual needs and not get her heart shredded.

Abruptly, she sank down on the little stool behind the counter and fished for her shoes. "I knew you were very tired, Player." Deliberately she said his name, reminding herself what kind of a man he was. "I was fine with leaving. I went to the party as a sober driver, and Francine hadn't texted me, but I went looking for her. As it turned it, she'd found a ride home, so it all worked out."

Player glanced over his shoulder and immediately Alena came up behind him, wrapping an arm around his waist as she leaned over the counter toward Zyah. Zyah honestly couldn't tell if she was a reinforcement for Player or if she had really come on her own, but the truth was, jealousy was a bitch and it reared its ugly head the moment Alena casually wrapped herself around Player.

"I forgot to ask. The club has a *huge* favor to ask of you, Zyah. It's big."

Zyah braced herself. Surely her job

165

wouldn't be contingent on dating Player. She wouldn't do it. If he had made that one of the requirements, she was out. Walking away. She didn't care if they needed the money. She would sell her stocks. Pull her retirement early. Whatever it took. It didn't matter.

She forced her gaze up to meet Alena's as she slid her foot into her shoe. "I'm listening."

"Naturally, before you were hired, Code did a background check on you, and he's very thorough. He found out about your grandmother, Anat. Not to mention, Inez talks about her all the time. She sounds like the coolest person ever born. So strong. We were all raised together. None of us ever had a grandmother. Well, Destroyer did, and his was awesome, but still, none of the rest of us."

The moment Alena said Mama Anat was cool and strong, the tension drained out of Zyah to be replaced by pride, because her grandmother was both those things and a million more.

"What I'm getting at is we'd like to meet her. Not all of us at the same time, but if you wouldn't have an objection and you don't think she'd be afraid of us, we'd really like to meet her," Alena continued.

Zyah frowned. "Why would she be afraid of you, other than if you all came at once? You could be a bit intimidating all together, I suppose." They were big men with a ton of muscle. Definitely intimidating.

"We look rough, scarred," Player supplied. "With a lot of tattoos."

Zyah ignored him. "Mama Anat would love to meet all of you. At the moment she's confined to bed or a wheelchair and she isn't happy she can't get around. She's normally very active and she loves company."

"Good," Alena said. "We heard what happened to your grandmother. I hope she's feeling better. I'm so glad you don't mind. We thought, since Czar insists any employee closing at night has an escort home, that person would be the best one to meet your grandmother each time. That way she knows you're safe on the way home and she'll be happy about that and won't mind them stopping in and saying hello." She looked suddenly anxious. "Unless you think it's too late for her to have visitors."

The grocery store officially locked the doors at seven and she was supposed to be out of there by seven-thirty. Eight at the latest. Her grandmother would love the company. Zyah nodded. "Mama Anat will definitely be up. She'll have music playing, and she'll want whoever she meets to drink tea or coffee and eat fresh-baked cookies or cake. If there isn't any, she'll expect me to whip something up."

"Can you bake?" Alena asked.

"It is a prerequisite in the Gamal household

167

to learn all domestic arts." She avoided looking at Player. In fact, she pretended he wasn't there.

"Player will be escorting you home tonight. He'll be the first to taste your baking, so I'll be anxious to hear what he has to say about whatever your grandmother offers him." Alena gave her a quick, genuine smile. "We're always very truthful with one another. I'm the chef at the restaurant just up the street, and I'm always looking for good help. You need extra work, give me a call. I'll see what you've got."

Zyah almost didn't hear the job offer, she was so busy panicking over the fact that Player would be following her home and then she'd have to introduce him to her grandmother. If she tried to come up with an excuse not to allow him into her house, she'd look less than gracious. Or worse, as if that one night had really mattered. Like it meant something and she was holding a grudge.

She forced herself to breathe slowly and then looked up with her trained smile. "I've heard from dozens of people that your restaurant is extraordinary. Getting reservations on weekends is apparently difficult. There's a waiting list. I promised my grandmother when she's able, I'll take her there. She's really looking forward to it." That was perfect. She didn't have to acknowledge Player one way or the other.

"You work for us, Zyah. There's always a table or two set aside for Torpedo Ink or anyone who works for us. Just call ahead and we'll have one ready," Alena promised. "I can't wait to meet your grandmother. She sounds incredible."

"She is. I know you'll really enjoy her," Zyah said. That much was true, and she knew her grandmother would welcome all of them.

# Six

"I did the best I could for you," Alena whispered, her arm slung around Player's neck as they watched Zyah get into her little car. It was a modest vehicle, nothing fancy. "I got you into the house. You're charming. Be sincere and charm the hell out of her grandmother. Pay attention to her. Give her your complete attention. That's going to be your only way in, because your girl has frozen you out."

"Thanks, Alena." Player brushed a kiss on her cheek. "Get home and get warm. It's turning cold on us. She's probably very happy I'm on my bike and she's in that nice warm car without me."

"My guess is she's trying not to cry and building that wall as high as she can. You want her, you're going to have to fight for her. She's not just going to roll over because you're cute."

He winced. "Don't be calling me cute. It aggravates the hell out of me."

170

"I know." Alena sounded smug.

"Who's on you tonight?" Alena looked around at her fellow club members. They waited patiently for her as she stood beside Player.

"Maestro. He left to go back to the clubhouse to get the truck and weapons. We'll be set up to watch over them for the night, and we'll be warm. Thanks for getting me into the house, Alena, I appreciate it," Player said. "Savage and Destroyer will join us later tonight."

She shrugged. "I like her. Lana likes her. Seal the deal, babe, bring her into the fold." She gave him her saucy grin and headed to her Harley.

Player immediately pulled out of the parking space. Zyah was long gone. She hadn't waited and he had known she wouldn't. She made it more than clear she wasn't going to make it easy on him. He could live with that. From everything Code had uncovered about her grandmother and Zyah, she was worth whatever fight it took to get her.

The Gamals earned money from working hard — a lot of money — and yet Zyah drove a very modest car, one that was good for the type of weather she would run into on the coast but that didn't cost much.

Instead of using the money the two women had worked so hard for, they had stashed it for retirement, or in savings. Zyah was willing to work two jobs — at the grocery store and at a restaurant where the waitresses were all belly dancers — to pay for her grandmother's extra care and her therapy.

Player was very grateful to Alena for offering extra work to Zyah closer to home. The last thing he wanted was for his woman to belly dance in front of a bunch of strangers and then drive home alone, not that he'd let that happen. He would have to find out from Code whether or not she had accepted the other job — because anyone who'd seen her dance was going to offer her the job.

Player knew the road between Caspar and Sea Haven. The motorcycle, even in the mist coming off the ocean, was easy enough to maneuver. He caught up with Zyah before she turned onto the street where the house she'd bought for her grandmother was located. The street was narrow like many of those in Sea Haven. Most houses were set off the road behind fences or hedges, with arbors of vines or climbing flowers.

He wasn't at all surprised that the Gamal house was a little different. It had the requisite white picket fence that seemed to line the road, adding charm to all the houses, but their property was unique in that it was a double-lot parcel. The house was a vintage Victorian, remodeled and beautifully kept, painted white with a red porch and accents. There was another building that appeared spacious, either a guesthouse or an art studio, as well as a double-car garage that was accessed from the back street.

Player followed Zyah around to a much narrower and less traveled road that was paved but was almost an alleyway. There were a few sparse houses, but mostly a long field of grass that separated the homes from the bluffs overlooking the ocean. As he parked across the street and walked over to the huge lot, he couldn't help but be impressed with the massive, elegant gardens that made up the large backyard.

There was no doubt in his mind why thieves had targeted the Gamals. Property in Sea Haven didn't come cheap no matter where it was situated, but if it had any kind of ocean view — and it was clear the Victorian at least had sweeping views of the bay from various points of the house, particularly the upper story — then the place was worth a fortune. He hadn't bothered to look to see what the original price had been when Zyah had bought it for her grandmother, but the value had gone up, not down.

Zyah drove her car into the garage. He heard her exit the car and close the door. She must have been irritated at him for standing there looking at the garden because the garage door began to descend. That seemed out of character and even a little petty of her. She had agreed to allow him to meet her grandmother. It didn't seem likely that she would force him to go around to the front door and knock when she could just bring him with her. Yeah, not at all like her. Definitely out of character. Zyah wasn't a petty person.

Pure instinct more than anything else galvanized him into action. He sprinted up the drive and threw himself under the garage door, rolling at the last moment. The sensor on the door did its job the moment the ray came in contact with his body, and the door reversed direction, slowly, laboriously, rising toward the ceiling.

He heard three voices almost simultaneously. A male on a radio, gruff but clearly warning those inside to get out, that *she* wasn't alone. A female inside, her voice distorted but adrenaline laced or very high, shouting, *Fuck her up — fuck her up bad.* And last, Zyah, warning him. *Player, look out.*

That told him they had a lookout and that Zyah had been specifically targeted. More, it was very personal to the female. He kept rolling toward Zyah, who was fighting with two men in ski masks. As he came to his feet, someone swung a baseball bat at his head. He caught the movement more by feel than by sight.

He blocked the baseball bat, went under it and struck hard, catching his assailant in the ribs, swung around and hit hard with an

174

elbow to the jaw. His opponent dropped like a stone and Player took a step toward Zyah. She was keeping the two men off of her with fists and feet. They seemed determined to drag her out of an open side door almost directly behind her. She was equally determined to remain in the garage. His mind catalogued the smooth way she fought, fluid, flowing like water, never stopping. Yeah, his woman could fight.

Snapping a front kick at the next man coming at him, catching him hard in the upper thigh with the ball of his foot, knowing from experience that would deaden his leg, Player continued straight at him, going for his throat. The man grunted and pulled a weapon, aiming and firing in the small confines of the garage. Player threw himself over the hood of Zyah's car, diving for the concrete. The burn of a bullet sheared off denim and skin as he landed, but it was the sound in the close confines of the garage that was the worst, his ears ringing with the blast, even though the gun had a silencer. Silencers were never as silent as most people thought, and with it so close, the blast hurt.

He landed hard and tried to roll toward Zyah, keeping his momentum going forward. Knowing the other side was using guns put an entirely different perspective on the fight. He came up, weapon in his fist, tracking the man closest to Zyah. He was grateful he'd had the foresight to use a silencer as well. Not all of his weapons had them, but each of the Torpedo Ink members carried them just in case.

Zyah was suddenly swung around, her body between him and his target just before he could take the shot. Player came up smoothly to get in a better position to aid her just as someone to his left shot him.

The bullet caught him on the left side of his head, blazing a groove from the back of his skull along the side to the front, and kept going straight, not slowing down in the least, hungry for more. It spun the man trying to drag Zyah out the door completely around, taking a chunk of skin with it as it tore through the garage wall and out into the street, where it lodged into the van waiting with door open.

Player went down hard, blood pouring down his skull and face and into his eyes, making it impossible to see a target. He didn't dare shoot, not with Zyah close. His stomach lurched, and for a moment the room went black. He hung on to consciousness through sheer will.

Where the hell was Maestro? How long did it take to get the fucking truck and a few weapons?

"Get to me," Player called to Zyah, wiping at the blood. He couldn't get to her. He could barely breathe through the pain in his head.

He could hear running.

"What the fuck are you thinking?" a voice yelled. "He's Torpedo Ink. You kill him, they'll never stop coming after us. We have to get out of here. Get the bitch and let's go."

"Zyah, call out now, right now." He needed to know where she was. He had the position of the other voice.

"Right here."

She was off to his left. Close. Protecting his hurt side. Her voice was strained. She knew they were trying to take her with them, and he was down, but hell if he was out. Stretched out on the concrete floor of the garage, cradling the gun in both hands, steady as a rock, completely blind, he fired at the first voice, the one warning the others that he was Torpedo Ink. Yeah, he was, and he'd trained blindfolded over and over, weeks, months, years of training, but they didn't know that, did they?

Someone screamed. High-pitched. Someone else grunted. Went down. "Shit. Shit. He's hit. We've got to get out of here."

He fired a second time at the second voice. Another loud grunt and a thud as a body hit the floor. The scream came again. There was the sound of dragging bodies, of running. Boots hitting the concrete. The roar of an engine. Silence.

"Don't move, Zyah," he whispered. His stomach lurched again. His head felt like it

177

was coming apart. Maybe it was, but she was going to be safe before it did. "We have to clear the garage. Make certain all of them are gone and they didn't leave any surprises behind."

He couldn't throw up. He couldn't lose consciousness. Everything was black already in his mind. Blood was so thick in his eyes he couldn't see. He wasn't certain he could cover her adequately if they had to move position, but he doubted if any of their attackers were left behind. The purpose seemed to be kidnapping her. His Torpedo Ink brothers would be there in a few minutes; he just had to hang on. Maestro was supposed to be right behind him. How much time had passed? He had no idea. Time always slowed down in a gun battle.

"I have to check on my grandmother," Zyah objected, but she went to her knees beside him, her hand on his head.

Her touch was gentle, trying to cup over the vicious wound, but it was very long, winding from the back of his scalp to the front. Player didn't move, didn't flinch. It hurt like hell, but he'd grown up in an environment where one never showed pain. Never. She pulled her blouse off and folded it into a wide band.

"Head wounds bleed profusely, Player. This one is terrible. I have to see how bad it is. I may need to call an ambulance."

"I'm alive. Hurts like a mother. And I don't do ambulances. Just be still for a moment. Hold your breath. Let me listen for movement. Breathing. Anything to give away an enemy."

He took the blouse from her with a shaky hand and wiped the blood from his eyes. She was right, it was streaming. More took its place. He sent a voice text to Steele. He needed the doc, and he damn well wasn't going to a hospital. He was counting on Maestro not being far behind him. Where the fuck was he? He was going down in another minute, and he wouldn't be able to control the situation.

"We're alone," Zyah said with confidence. "The garage is small and there aren't that many places to hide. I really have to check on my grandmother and then I'll be right back."

He glanced at his cell with blurred vision. The time. Shit. What seemed like forever to him had really only been a matter of minutes. The attack had lasted only three minutes, and then the men were gone. On the run. There was no waiting for his brothers to get there. Fortunately, the guns had silencers. No one had heard those little pops. Hopefully not her grandmother.

He had known all along he couldn't stall her very long. He would have gone to check on the grandmother immediately — it had to be done. His head felt like it had already exploded, had come apart at the seams and was leaking his brains all over the place. The least movement sent his stomach lurching alarmingly. Still, there was nothing else to do — he had to cover her. There was no way he could let her go alone.

Player had extraordinary abilities thanks to his psychic talent. He could control his brain for periods of time by shifting what was happening in real time to alternates, which meant he had to take himself as far from where he was as possible and still be there to protect her. He'd never felt so sick in his life. He knew the wound was bad and it was possible he might not even make it, but he had to protect Zyah and her grandmother until Maestro showed up.

He took a deep breath and let it out. "Let's go, then." At least the blood was out of his eyes and he could see. He felt like a fool with a blouse wrapped around his head. The devil only knew what he looked like, but he wasn't going to let her face whatever was in that house — good or bad — alone.

Zyah hesitated, shook her head and then turned toward the house. "You know you're stubborn as hell."

He couldn't deny that charge, so he concentrated on not vomiting all over her nearly immaculate garage. She hurried, walking upright, while he had to crawl. There was no way for him to get up on his feet. After she punched the code into the door and used her thumbprint on top of the code, she glanced over her shoulder and said something very unladylike under her breath.

"What are you doing? Player?"

His name was whispered right along with a curse word. He could barely distinguish between the two, but he was concentrating on dragging himself to the door without his head falling off.

"There's a trail of blood behind you wider than a river." She was back, crouching down to circle his waist with her arm. "This is silly. You can't even stand up."

Yeah, he got that. He clenched his teeth against the nausea, praying to the fucking devil he didn't throw up all over her. He went to his go-to place, trying to build bombs in his head, something he'd done since he was a child, to keep from losing his mind.

"I don't think it's a good idea for me to stand. What do you usually do when you enter the house? The first thing, Zyah?" He rested on the stairs while he asked. He wasn't even certain he was talking. Or making sense.

"I call out to her. Tell her I'm home."

"Do that, then, but don't go all the way inside. Does she answer you?"

"Yes, right away. She's always up waiting for me no matter the time."

"Pay attention to her voice. Does she sound the same? Under duress? Do you have a word or phrase you've worked out indicating one or both of you are in trouble?" He could barely think with the pounding in his skull. He had to speak through clenched teeth and hope she didn't notice.

"That would have been a good idea. But yes, I would know if she was under duress." She didn't wait but stepped inside the open door and called out cheerfully. "Mama Anat, I'm back."

"You ran late tonight." The relief in her grandmother's voice was evident. "I was worried, Zyah." Anxiety made her voice tremble.

"Are you alone? Did Lizz leave already?" Deliberately, Zyah helped Player crawl into the hallway and then turned on the water at the sink in the kitchen as if she were washing her hands.

"Lizz's granddaughter called earlier and needed a ride somewhere important. She waited as long as she could for you to get home. I told her I'd be all right. I have a sawed-off shotgun right here, sitting on my lap. She watched me load it before she left."

"Mama Anat, that is illegal here in the States." Zyah tried to keep the laughter out of her voice, but relief clearly was making her a little giddy. "You don't have a permit, or whatever it is you need."

"If the cops came, I was going to shove it under the bed. I had a plan."

Zyah kept her arm around Player, urging

him forward, but he balked at moving another inch. He didn't want to die in front of her grandmother. He could taste blood in his mouth. The edges of his mind were so dark now, he truly was afraid he was going to die before Maestro got there. Desperately, he worked on that alternate reality, trying to be meticulous about arranging his bomb, holding his brain together until he was alone and Zyah was safe.

"I don't want to scare her, looking like this." He couldn't get to his feet. He was still on his hands and knees, even with her arm around his waist. "The brothers will be here soon, and they'll deal with me."

"Who's that with you?" her grandmother asked, her voice sharp. Demanding.

"Zyah. Look at me. I can't meet her looking like this." Player was beginning to feel a little desperate. He wasn't going to make a good impression by vomiting all over her grandmother's floor, and that was about to happen. "Go in and let her see you. I'll be fine right here. She needs to know you're all right." He poured persuasion into his voice, knowing it wasn't right, but not caring. "Best not to say anything about all of this yet."

"He escorted me home, Mama Anat. He rolled over the hood of my car and hit his head on the concrete."

He was already looking around for a bathroom. He was going to be sick, and the moment she let go of him, he was going to topple over, straight to the floor. He was already on his knees, so he didn't have that far to fall.

The door between the kitchen and garage flew open and Maestro was there, his gun tracking, centered on Zyah as he took in Player's head and the blood-soaked blouse wrapped around his skull. There was blood all over his face and shirt and more on his shoulder and bicep. Even on his hands and knees, swaying, his vision going in and out, Player still made an effort to shove Zyah behind him.

"She's with me, Maestro," he bit out between his teeth. "They were after her."

"Zyah," Anat called out, her voice quivering. "Come to me now."

Zyah let go of Player and rushed out of the kitchen, ignoring Maestro and his weapon. Player would have hit the floor face-first if Maestro hadn't caught him.

"Going to get sick. Get me the hell out of here," he managed.

Maestro indicated a door just to his left and all but carried him. Movement rocked Player's head until he was certain his brain was going to explode into a million pieces. The image was starting to become difficult to keep at bay. His stomach lurched, thankfully disrupting the making of the bomb he had so meticulously learned as a child. He'd made them and dismantled them over and over until he could do it in his sleep.

The moment Maestro propelled him those last steps into the small bathroom, he found himself hugging the toilet and emptying the contents of his stomach repeatedly. Maestro thankfully took his gun and stood guard over him because he was incapable of guarding anything. He tried several times to indicate for his brother to check on the women and clear the house just to make certain everything was all right inside, but Maestro refused to leave him.

Within a matter of minutes, two more Torpedo Ink brothers crowded in, their broad shoulders filling the kitchen in complete silence, weapons drawn, faces grim. Savage meant business, and it showed in every deep line and the cold death in his eyes. Destroyer was with him, that same look etched into his menacing features.

"We're clear outside and only the two women are inside. Doc is here to look after Player," Savage assured Maestro.

Player had never been so relieved to hear anything in his life. He needed to warn them all that his brain was reacting in a confused, lethal way and everyone around him was going to be in danger. They needed to get him clear, not only of Zyah and her grandmother but of the club as well. Unexpectedly, before he could, everything went black.

Player woke to the sound of voices. He was very confused. Cold. Shivering. His head exploding with pain. He had no idea where he was. Or did he? A bedroom, definitely not his own. It hurt to breathe. To try to think.

When he dared to take a breath, he drew in combined exotic scents he recognized instantly. He knew the earth and all the various fragrances. Woods. Scents. Exotics and those closer to home. Very subtle, but definitely jasmine, a very distinctive cinnamic-honey background and a cassis-raspberry facet blending with the rich green floral mimosa he hadn't been able to get out of his mind since he'd woken up from what he'd been so certain was a dream. Being surrounded by that scent now just threw him right back into that same uncertainty. His dancer. Zyah. Was she real? Was anything in his life real? He honestly didn't know.

His head pounded. A jackhammer seemed to be drilling holes through his skull. He tried to surface all the way. His breath caught in his throat. He had to warn someone. Had to make certain they were going to get him away from everyone. He was dangerous when he had no control. Right then he definitely didn't know what the hell he was doing.

"Stop fighting."

He recognized Steele's voice the moment he came close, but he couldn't seem to pry his eyes open. Had they beaten the crap out of him again? Taken his skin off? Was the blood so thick his lids were sealed shut? He wanted to strike out. He didn't know.

"Settle down, Player. I'm right here. You're not going to hurt anyone." Steele's voice was reassuring. He was always calm in the middle of a crisis. "Maestro's right here. Savage and Destroyer are outside watching the place in case the assholes come back. You need to hold still and let me take a good look inside your head and see what's going on."

"Can you really do that? Look inside his head? Shouldn't you take him to a hospital and get an MRI?" A woman's voice. He expected a child's voice.

He was caught between the past and the present, but that had to be his dancer, Zyah, and her voice was filled with anxiety. Player couldn't help but like that. But what the hell was she doing down in the dungeon with them? That must be why her scent was everywhere. The fuckers had gotten her in spite of his trying to stop them. Or maybe he was out of his mind again. He had to let Steele take care of everything when he was so far gone.

"You're aware of certain psychic gifts, Zyah." Steele's voice was calm. Matter of fact. "I don't need an MRI to tell me what I need to know. If I have to do surgery, I can do the surgery here, repair his brain."

"Are you crazy?" Zyah's voice dripped with tears. "He's going to die. He's bad. I've seen his brain. I can look into his mind. I can't do surgery, but I can repair certain things. Even in a hospital, a brain surgeon might not be able to fix that damage. I had no idea it was that bad."

"Zyah, leave the room if you can't be quiet," Steele commanded.

No one disobeyed Steele when he talked in that voice. Firm. Low. Definitely all doctor. Player felt him then, inside his head. Moving shattered pieces around. The pain was excruciating.

"Let go, Player," Steele said.

Player tried to stay awake, to push at Steele, to tell him to take him away from all of them. He wasn't safe. Couldn't Steele see that? Steele only looked at his brain, not what was going on inside of it. He didn't see the damage inside, where he was so fucked up he kept going back and forth between his childhood and present day. Between danger and safety. He didn't know what really happened to him when illusion became reality.

Steele sighed with relief when Player succumbed to the pain of the terrible wound. Zyah gasped and moved closer as if she could bring him back.

"He's not dead. Move around to the other

side." Sweat broke out on Steele's forehead. He wasn't altogether certain he could save Player. He glanced at Savage. Met his eyes. Shook his head.

He wouldn't give up. He had a gift — an extraordinary one. He'd trained from the time he was a child with the best surgeons Sorbacov could provide for him to study under. He was a prodigy. He devoured books, and once the information was in his mind, his gift took over, allowing him to use his mind to heal. It had taken years to strengthen that talent, shape it into what it was today, allowing him to do surgery, to give Player the chance to live when he wouldn't have survived going to the hospital and undergoing brain surgery. No possible way would he have made it. Although the brain was an extraordinary thing and Player was an extraordinary man.

Steele fought for him for hours, working meticulously, healing him as he put him back together. He was aware, and a little shocked, that Zyah was right there with him, watching him, in Player's mind, which connected to him. How she'd gotten that way already, he had no idea, but he knew, from what Player had said about her, that she was talented.

It took the better part of the night to repair the damage to Player's brain. Steele had never attempted a surgery and healing of that magnitude before. It left him shaky and exhausted but triumphant. He was certain Player would heal very fast, especially if he continued to work on him daily.

Pain exploded through Player's head, bringing with it images of White Rabbits and caterpillars and lobsters on cyclones. He felt sick to his stomach and didn't want to open his eyes or move one inch in case he might vomit. He was aware of Steele close. Talking to him. Working on him. He felt warmth in his head.

"I want to take him home with me. We brought the van this time. I think we can get him down the stairs and transport him safely now. It's been a few days. I've got a much more sterile environment, and I have to work on healing him, although, already, I'm seeing an improvement." There was satisfaction in Steele's voice.

Player didn't feel like there was improvement. He didn't want to go to the doc's home, where his wife and child were, either. It was too dangerous, with his mind already spinning his illusions. He could see the bench and table in his mind where he built his bombs. That wasn't good. It was never good. Not if all those things were lining up. He couldn't open his eyes no matter how hard he tried to pry his lids apart.

"No." Zyah's protest was instant. Player recognized her voice. "That's not a good idea.

He has to stay here."

Player hadn't realized she was close. He didn't want her near him. Not when he wasn't in control.

"Stay still, Player," Steele ordered softly. "Let me take care of you."

Player subsided. He didn't dare go against Steele when he used his "doctor" voice. In any case, Player wasn't altogether certain what was really happening. He stayed still and listened, trying to put the pieces of the puzzle together.

"Explain why you think Player would be better off here with you instead of with me in my home," Steele continued as if nothing had interrupted them.

"I can't explain it any more than you can explain to me what you're doing right now," Zyah said. "Only that I have an absolutely strong reaction against you taking him from here." She hesitated. "Even when I don't want him here." There was honesty in her voice.

Zyah seemed to hesitate again, as if she were trying to decide what to say and how to say it. Player tried to focus on her, but even that small concentration put too much strain on him and pain exploded through him. Steele all but snarled at him, and he made an effort to keep very still and allow his brain to do the same.

Zyah's voice was decisive when she spoke.

"You have a tremendous gift, Steele. I've never seen anything like it. I doubt if Player would have survived without you, and I know he'll need your constant care for a while. Just the last few days have proven that. But I have a strong gift as well, and Player and I are connected in a very elemental way. Your talent works on the brain itself, repairing it. My gift works on the mind. I can only tell you that I believe with everything in me that if you take him away from me, we'll lose him. Something terrible will happen."

There was a long silence. Player willed Steele to say no. He couldn't stay there and endanger Zyah, not when he couldn't remember much beyond the caterpillar smoking and the lobsters riding the cyclones in the sea. Or the materials for making bombs laid out on the table for him to start work. He couldn't get past the pounding in his head to pry his eyelids open. Maybe the blood had sealed them shut permanently. He allowed himself to drift on the waves of pain as they rose and fell through his head.

The next time Player woke, he knew he was alone, but he had no idea where he was. He tried to figure it out, but the pain was too brutal. What had it been this time? What had they done to him? To his body? He couldn't remember. He didn't want to. Sweat beaded from his pores. He had no idea of time passing, but he rarely did. The pounding in his head prevented movement and thought. He just let the pain take him wherever it wanted to go.

Player wasn't like the others. They had useful talents. All of them did, whether they thought so or not. Lana didn't think she contributed much to their unit, their family — and they'd become one, thanks to Czar. Player knew better. Lana brought them all comfort. When it was at the bleakest hour, when there was no hope, Lana brought them out of the darkness. She found a way. The rest of them all had talents that counted, that contributed to their survival. What did he do for them? He skated the edge of danger all the time. The others just weren't aware of it as he was.

The knowledge had been growing in him ever since the unfortunate mushroom incident. That had provided endless laughter for his family. Player had laughed with them — on the outside. On the inside, he had grown very scared. He knew something was wrong with his brain, and that something was getting stronger, taking him over.

All of them had been so hungry. They were always hungry. Starving. Freezing cold and hungry. Held down in what they referred to as the dungeon, the basement of the school they all attended, they huddled together in a little pile of shivering bodies, leaking blood from open wounds and trying to stay alive. He wasn't certain why they bothered trying most of the time, but self-preservation was strong in all of them. Absinthe took turns with his older brother Demyan, or Transporter, reading *Alice's Adventures in Wonderland.* They did the voices, and that kept their minds off the ever-present hunger.

Where had that book come from? It hadn't been in the meager library of books they stole from. He tried to remember. Every time he did, like now, there was an explosion of pain accompanied by a memory of the long table with the pieces of the equipment laid out precisely, the way he always laid out the materials before he began building bombs. Behind him stood Sorbacov with his ever-present pocket watch, while Player hunched naked on the bench, trying to build the bomb fast to avoid the punishment — the whip tearing the flesh from his back if he didn't beat his last time.

Where had they gotten the book, *Alice's Adventures in Wonderland,* which was being read while they shivered with cold and hunger? Player couldn't remember, but he knew it was important.

Alena had managed to slip outside and make her way into the woods, where she gathered roots, nuts and mushrooms. She brought leaves, berries and cone nodules. She also brought bark and other supplies for their "medicine well." They had dug a hole and put in it the precious herbs, powders and barks she stole from the instructors or managed to get when she escaped through the narrow crack they'd widened just enough for her to slide through.

She was very small. They weren't given clothes down in the dungeon, because to their captors, they weren't human, so they greased her body as best they could, and she slid through the narrow crack and out into the forest in the dead of night to gather what she could to feed them and help Steele treat their wounds.

Alena knew plants, the ones they could eat and the ones that could be used for medicinal purposes. She had a natural instinct for them. Until the mushrooms. She was affectionately called Torch because she could start little fires when she concentrated. Czar had them all working to enhance and perfect their psychic skills — all but Player. Player didn't seem to have any psychic skills — at least any he'd admitted to the others yet. His was more of a parlor trick.

The pain pounded in his head, mixing with the sound of Absinthe's voice as he read *Alice's Adventures in Wonderland.* Player tried to concentrate on the story. It was wonderful, and he let the images build in his head, the caterpillar floating in the air, smoking, blowing those wonderful rings of smoke. He thought they would be a good thing to have if he could break through the walls of reality and drop those rings of smoke around the necks of the men who had flayed the skin from his body. The men who had beat some poor hapless girl because Player had controlled his body when she had tried so hard to arouse him. He'd been flayed while he aroused her and made her scream when she came. He hadn't made a sound when the fuckers beat him. But damn. His head was exploding.

Building the nooses from smoke, he crafted them carefully, sent them floating through the air, let them become smaller and smaller. The walls were faded enough so that there was nothing to stop his weapons from seeking their target. The smiling blue caterpillar floated on his little cloud pillow, blowing the rings, his smirk indicating he knew that each ring contained a thin little garrote that would slice through the neck of the men who had so savagely raped and beaten him.

His head was coming apart. Every time he moved, the smoke whirled around him faster and faster and the pounding in his skull got so much worse. He could see pieces of his brain flying out of him as he spun around like the Mad Hatter. The mushrooms. Alena's mushrooms were making him hallucinate.

Player tried to sit up, but that made things worse, his brain exploding, taking him right out of the dungeon so that he was no longer in Wonderland following his caterpillar. He was at a table constructing a bomb unlike any he'd ever seen before. Sorbacov was standing over him, with his inevitable pocket watch, the White Rabbit racing away as if late. Sorbacov peered over his shoulder, watching closely, as Player began to build the bomb with meticulous care.

"Player. Player, stop." Sorbacov caught at his arm and shook him hard. "Open your eyes and look at me. You have to stop."

He couldn't just stop. Not in the middle of putting together such an intricate piece of hardware. He was certain Sorbacov was shaking his arm. And his arm hurt nearly as bad as his head, which was really going to explode the moment the bomb was finished.

"Let go." He managed to get that out through clenched teeth. The sound of his own voice shocked him. He was hallucinating, sending out his silent smoky nooses to kill the enemy, taking down walls and building intricate bombs he'd never seen before. "Let go, Sorbacov." He tried his voice again, making it stronger.

"Maestro," his Torpedo Ink brother corrected. "You're having a dream."

The fog cleared. The walls shimmered and disappeared. The table he'd been bent over wavered and vanished along with Sorbacov. Had it really all been an illusion he was building in his head? Making a reality? His fucking head pounded so bad he was afraid he was going to vomit, and it wasn't his bed or his covers.

Player smelled her, his private dancer. So impossibly beautiful with her dark eyes and long flowing hair and that body of hers built for sin and pleasure. He was in her bedroom. In her home. Her grandmother was close by. Just downstairs. They were both close. Was she real or another one of his fucking illusions he'd made real? He just didn't know anymore, but he couldn't take any chances with her life.

"Get me out of here, Maestro. You have to get me out of here."

He struggled to sit up, but the moment he did, his head exploded. Completely shattered. He actually saw the pieces rushing away from his head like tiny wedges of broken shards of glass. They spun in the air just like in a damn movie, and floated in the air, his brains spilling out like mirror images. Great globs of blood blew into the air and swirled in slow circles.

"Geez, Player, what the fuck is happening?" Maestro whispered. "This isn't funny."

"What's going on in here? You're going to wake my grandmother."

Her voice. Soft like a summer breeze. Drifting into the room. Right into the gore of his scattered brains. There was no retrieving the rest of the pieces. It was far too late. Even with Maestro leaping up and trying to stand in front of him, how could he hide an exploding head?

"Leave the room," Zyah ordered softly. "If you want him to live, you have to leave the room right this minute."

"Don't listen to her," Player said, only nothing came out of his mouth. He couldn't talk with his brains floating away on the shards of glass. "It's too dangerous. I'm too dangerous."

He tried again to shout the warning. No one heard. No one listened or paid attention. He began to build a megaphone in his mind, or what was left of his mind. There was nothing. No brain cells — they had floated away. How could he talk? How could he think to form words? He wasn't making sense.

Maestro stood in front of him for another few seconds, staring straight into Zyah's eyes. "You hurt him, I'll fucking break your neck," he warned.

"Just get out and save the drama."

His sweet dancer didn't sound so sweet when she was throwing Maestro out of her bedroom. Maestro was as intimidating as they came — unless you were looking at Savage or Destroyer. Maybe Reaper, although if Anya was around . . .

"I'm standing right here by the door."

"Owww." His eyelids flew open, and he found himself staring into a pair of stormy, turbulent eyes. "Zyah, you have to leave. There's a bomb. I'm a bomb. It's going to go off again any minute. You're not safe. Your grandmother . . ."

Zyah wrapped a wide lavender scarf around his head, covering the long line of stitches Steele had put into his scalp. The scarf was soaked in something that wasn't in the least soothing and sweet the way his dancer should be. The liquid was some kind of astringent, something that seeped into his open brain and grew hotter and hotter until he was certain flames licked at what remained of his cells.

"Stop being a baby."

"I can see you have this under control," Maestro said and deserted him.

Player tried to push Zyah away. "My brain is scattered. Everywhere. In pieces. Can't you see? Like glass. I'm shattered. Like glass. I'm a bomb."

She put her head down close to his, hands framing his face, holding him still, looking into his eyes. "I'm a glassblower," she whispered. "No one is as good as I am at blowing glass. Just stay quiet and let me take care of this. I'll put you back together."

"Too dangerous. I have to get away from you."

She ignored his warning as she began to hum softly, her body swaying as she wrapped a makeshift bandage around his head, pulling more and more of the floating debris that were the scattered pieces of his brain back inside his skull.

He saw the table he'd been using to make the bomb. All the parts were laid out, and they shimmered beneath the glass and her fire. The parts looked different from his usual ones. His tools morphed into a set of tweezers in a variety of sizes, a crimp, a taglia and straight shears.

Zyah took her time, collecting the fragments floating around the room and, with the sound of her song, fitting them together, like a jigsaw puzzle. It should have been soothing, like the first night in her company, but this was anything but. Fire burned through his brain. Hot. Searing. Like the hottest blowtorch imaginable.

Player clenched his teeth and did his best to let the pain wash over him, but the blaze only seemed to grow hotter, licking along every pathway and nerve in his fractured mind. He felt that fire, each separate flame as it glowed through his mind. To really blow glass, the temperature had to be over one thousand Celsius, didn't it? This felt like well over a thousand degrees.

"Woman." He attempted to raise his arm and the same thing happened. A wildfire stormed from his head to his shoulder and roared down his bicep to his forearm. "I get that you're pissed as hell at me. You have every right to be, but aren't women supposed to have some built-in compassion? Empathy? What the hell?"

"Hell. Exactly. Hot like a fire. A healing one. It will seal all your brains back where they're supposed to be." She sounded a little smug, but she kept her voice low. Musical. Her body still moved in that flowing dance, arms out, hands graceful, mesmerizing. Her soothing song continued. Now her feet were moving on the floor, bare feet, calling out to the earth below with a patterned song. "Perhaps with a little help, you'll learn not to scatter your brains and bombs all over my bedroom."

She sang the words. *Sang* them. In that voice of hers, the one that penetrated all the way through the pieces scattered everywhere, pulling them to her as if she were gathering them into a long tube and heating the fragments as she blew air with the notes of her song right into them. She shaped them back into a whole entity with the sheer power of her voice and the movements of her body, generating the intense heat needed from below the ground, drawing it up from the earth with her bare feet.

He was shocked that she had the ability to override his fucked-up psychic gift. It was

202

useless. He was useless. Dangerous. The moment something went haywire, his brain went back to his childhood and the things he'd been taught — none of them good.

"*Concentrate* on where you are now, Player. You aren't there. You're here with me. You aren't a child locked away in a dungeon."

He closed his eyes and turned his face away, subsiding on the pillow. It didn't matter how bad the pain was. How hot the fire. She saw. She shared his mind with him. Even if she only caught glimpses of the boy with the skin flayed off his back, she saw what had been done to him, and shame washed through his mind. He didn't want to look at her. He didn't want her to see him.

She already knew too much. How his brain could build an alternate universe and trap others in it. Hurt them. Worse. Actually kill them. Now she knew what had been done to him when he was a child. No, more than a child. Beyond a child. A teen. She'd seen him building bombs. She knew what he was capable of. He had wanted to court this woman. Find a way to convince her he was worthy of her. That was laughable. What was he thinking? He had absolutely nothing to offer her. Nothing. Because he was nothing. The only fucking thing he had was the ink on his back, and that wouldn't mean a damn thing to her.

# SEVEN

Player should be dead. That was the truth. Had he gone to a hospital, there was no doubt in Zyah's mind, he would have died. Steele had saved his life — well, if he lived. That was still a question. He wasn't out of the woods. His club was well aware of it too, especially Steele. His club had no real idea of how dangerous he was. Player knew. In his delirium, when he semi-woke in the middle of the night, he continuously begged whoever was watching over him to take him away.

Steele came every day and worked at healing him. Zyah was astonished at how fast he was healing. The man was a true miracle worker — she said so every day. That didn't stop Player from feeling pain. Nothing stopped that pain. Nothing took it away. No matter what she did, he felt the pain. When it got to be too much, he woke, and his brain, already in pieces, would go back to his horrific childhood. She knew it was horrific, because she was so connected to him, she shared whatever memory or illusion he was in at the time — and all of them were horrific.

Zyah found herself sitting next to him on the bed, pushing back his damp hair with her fingers, trying not to cry. She didn't want to think the things he had in his head were true, that any child could have suffered what he had — but that nightmare world was far too detailed. It included every one of his brethren in Torpedo Ink, and they were all children in that same horrible place.

There were chains on the walls. Dried blood. Sometimes fresh blood. Sometimes the fresh blood was on the bodies of the children. On Player's body. She hated these nights and his memories. Her childhood had been all about love and warmth. Player's childhood and those of his Torpedo Ink club had been all about abuse and torture. The contrast between them was stark and raw.

She looked around her bedroom. Light spilled in from the large window. They were on the upper story facing the ocean, and the view was breathtaking. She could see the details just from the light coming in. She had several of her childhood memories right there in the room with her. Her mother's things sat on her dresser. A hairbrush and hand mirror. On the wall, a picture her grandfather had drawn himself and Anat had carefully hung for her in every home they had because Zyah had loved it too.

Her father had carefully crafted the beautiful frame. It was etched much like an ancient scroll, and because her father had been an astronomer, constellations, comets and stars adorned it. Every evening Zyah touched her fingers to her lips and then to the frame before she went to bed, making her feel closer to her father and grandfather.

Anat had similar treasures she kept in her bedroom. Things that had belonged to Amara, her daughter, that were personal. A lace shawl. Her anklet bells. Photographs. Her beloved husband, Horus's, monocle. He'd kept it on a chain because he lost them so often, he'd said. That had always made Anat laugh. That monocle was still on that chain, one of Anat's most treasured items.

What did Player have of his past but the scars on his body? Zyah had seen him naked the night they'd spent together and knew his body intimately. She knew every scar. Now she knew how he'd gotten them, and the knowledge sickened her.

She sat in the middle of the bed, her legs drawn up, arms hugging her legs, head resting on her knees, Player restless beside her. She slept in the guest room right next door, but each night she had to come in and put him back together. When the pain was so bad it woke him, he would hallucinate.

She made a sound of denial and hastily

covered her mouth, not wanting to disturb Player when she'd just gotten him back to sleep. It wasn't a hallucination. She wished it were. She knew Maestro and the others thought it was. They even laughed sometimes, or smirked.

Player's illusions always seemed to start with something to do with *Alice's Adventures in Wonderland.* The Torpedo Ink members thought it was funny and seemed to have good memories of that time in their childhood. That didn't in any way jive with how Player felt when the White Rabbit suddenly appeared or any of the other *Alice's Adventures in Wonderland* characters began to manifest in his mind.

Zyah's instincts told her that if Player had protected his fellow members from knowing that his illusions could become reality, then she shouldn't say anything to them either. She didn't understand what was going on, and until she did, she needed to stay silent and figure it all out.

One of the many problems was that the longer she was with Player, sitting with him, getting into his head and sharing his mind, even just to heal him, the stronger the connection between them became. She didn't want or need that. She didn't want to know about his past. She knew it humiliated him to have her know.

The good part about having Player in their home was that a member of Torpedo Ink was always there with him. Always. That meant her grandmother was protected night and day. She also knew that not only did someone stay inside the house with Player and Mama Anat, but someone was outside as well. That gave her great relief and allowed her to work at the grocery store without constant worry that someone would break into the house again and hurt her grandmother.

She didn't worry too much about Player during the day because Steele spent a great deal of time with him, healing his brain injury. As far as she was concerned, he couldn't heal it fast enough. Not because she was being selfish and wanted him gone — that wasn't it — but because seeing him in such terrible pain was horrific, and watching that throw him into his childhood nightmares was even worse. She couldn't share those things with her grandmother. She didn't have anyone she could talk to about it. The more time she spent with Player, the more he was finding his way into her heart — and that wasn't a good thing.

Zyah eased her legs off the bed, careful not to wake Player. This time had been particularly bad. It had only been a week since he'd been shot. She kept reminding herself that wasn't a long time to recover, but it felt like forever when she was so afraid for him. When she cared so much. Too much. She pressed her hand to her throbbing head as she made her way into the hallway. She had a headache now from crying.

"Zyah?" Savage's voice came out of the darkness.

She liked him. She knew she shouldn't. Violence swirled around him. He was covered in it. Sometimes it swallowed him. But there was — that voice. That genuine caring that couldn't be faked, not when she could read people when she was barefoot like she was. Savage cared. His eyes might be ice-cold and scary deadly, but he cared, whether he wanted anyone to know it or not. And the way he was with Anat — that couldn't be faked. He was always so unfailingly gentle.

"I'm all right. Sometimes he breaks my heart. He's in a lot of pain, and I can't take it away."

Savage saw a lot, and he seemed to have a really good bullshit meter. She had to be careful to be truthful, even though that wasn't the only reason she had cried.

He stepped close to her but didn't touch her. Those piercing blue eyes of his could chill her to the bone. They could also see far too much.

"We're used to pain, Zyah. He's going to get through this."

She nodded. "Thanks for being so good to Mama Anat. She really hates being confined to her bed. She can't get from the bed to the chair, and she said you put her in the chair yesterday so she was able to move around a little bit. That meant so much to her."

He shrugged, drawing back into the shadows. "It was no big thing. She wanted to make cookies and some other kinds of baked goods and needed to get into the kitchen. She's a little thing, so it was easy enough."

Zyah's eyebrow shot up. "She baked? With her broken arm?" Her grandmother hadn't said a word about baking. There hadn't been any baked goods in the house. Not one single cookie when she came home.

Savage was silent for a moment. Too long of a moment. She tipped her head back and moved closer to the shadows so she could see him, not letting him disappear. "She had you baking those cookies, didn't she?" Her grandmother could get anyone to do anything. She was pure magic. "She talked you into letting her walk you through the recipe, didn't she?"

Savage had one hip against the wall, his arms crossed over his chest as he regarded her coolly. He didn't answer, just kept looking at her like he might do her in if she persisted in the conversation. Zyah didn't know whether she could keep a straight face or whether she should even bother trying.

"I'll bet you had flour all over you," she taunted.

He didn't blink. He just continued to stare at her.

She grinned at him, quirking an eyebrow. "Did she make you wear an apron? She does that because she doesn't like a mess in her kitchen."

Savage didn't so much as change expression. As opponents went, he was good. Really good. Zyah could imagine her grandmother having great fun with him. There was no sound to warn her, but she knew they weren't alone in the hallway. Her neck hairs tingled, giving her a warning prickle. That had to be another member of Torpedo Ink, or Savage would have reacted. Savage and Destroyer were usually the two partners, so she took a stab at it.

"She has frilly aprons. You could have worn the one with the sunflowers and Destroyer the one with the bluebonnets all over it. You would have looked so cute, especially if you got flour all over the aprons. I'll have to ask Mama Anat if she happened to get pictures of you both. She loves to use the camera on her cell phone."

Mama Anat loved to use the camera, but more often than not, she had it pointed in the opposite direction or up at the ceiling or down at the floor.

Destroyer stepped around her. "This woman is trying to blackmail us with damaging photographs, Savage?"

"There's no proof," Savage denied.

"There's proof," Zyah said.

"Anat had the camera pointed toward herself," Savage said in his perfectly expressionless tone.

Zyah laughed quietly, always cognizant of Player asleep in the other room. She didn't want to wake him. It was *so* like her beloved grandmother to have her cell phone out and recording and the camera pointed in the wrong direction. But it also proved Zyah was right and Savage and Destroyer had baked cookies because Anat had asked them to. She would have given anything to see the two men following her grandmother's instructions.

"I knew you baked those cookies for her."

"What cookies?" Savage asked. "There aren't any cookies."

"Because you and Destroyer ate them all," Zyah accused. "I know darn well you did. Anat will try to cover for you, but she can't lie worth a darn."

"Go to bed," Savage ordered. "You have to work in the morning. You've worked on Player half the night already."

For the first time there was a hint of gratitude in his voice. Just a hint. Along with respect. Neither Savagen nor Destroyer gave much away, but that didn't matter to her. She always knew her grandmother was safe when they were watching over her. Now she knew they were pushovers just like everyone else around Anat. That really endeared them to her. She lifted a hand to both men and made her way to the next room, where she closed the door quietly and just let herself fall facedown onto the bed. She really was that tired.

"Seriously, Zyah, you should stop by the restaurant before you go home," Alena encouraged. "The boys are with your grandmother. It isn't like she's alone there."

She was draped at the end of the counter looking beautiful as only Alena could look in her casual blue jeans, tank and Torpedo Ink jacket. She didn't seem to notice the looks she got from the other customers as Zyah rang up their groceries, but Zyah did, and she had to hide her smile. Just the mere mention of "the boys" had the women's rapt attention, and Alena's good looks had the men's.

Zyah was a little shocked that it wasn't her grandmother she was the most concerned about. She knew Anat was safe with Torpedo Ink looking out for her. It was Player. She was worried that if he suddenly had one of his really bad episodes and she wasn't there, he could really hurt himself — or someone else. He mostly had them in the middle of the night. That was when the pain seemed to worsen. Or he couldn't stay on top of the pain because he was asleep and his past was

213

too close. Whatever the reason, she felt like she needed to be there for him.

"I could stop by for a few minutes, Alena, but not for long," she agreed. "Even if I call her and tell her I'm going to be late, Mama Anat gets nervous if I don't come right home."

She finished ringing up her customer and greeted the next one. She was a little dismayed to see it was Perry Randall. He was dividing his attention between Zyah and Alena, trying to decide who to bestow his brilliant white smile on. Zyah expected his teeth to have a white star with a little ringtone dinging when he finally flashed her the polished smile.

"Zyah." He said her name as if they were old friends. Instead of letting her pick up the bottle of water, he handed it to her to scan but then held on to it so he could look deep into her eyes. "You really need to reconsider and go out on a date with me."

Alena straightened slowly, drawing his attention. The bottle of water slipped from his nerveless fingers straight into Zyah's hand. She took advantage and rang the bottle up fast. It was just that Alena had been so artfully draped over the counter. Any man with eyes had to watch that slow-motion undulation of womanly curves. Zyah nearly burst out laughing but refrained as she waited for Perry to recover.

"That's impossible, Perry," Alena said. "Her man would get *very* upset with you. Trespassing on Torpedo Ink property can get you in big trouble." She gave Zyah a slow, lazy wink, ignoring the collective gasp from the various women standing in line behind Perry. "I'll see you at the restaurant tonight, then, Zyah."

Zyah gave her a small wave, shook her head and began checking out the next person. Perry barely shuffled forward a few steps to stare after Alena while she sauntered across the street to stop in front of the store directly across from the grocery. She stood there talking to Lana, the sun shining down on the two heads.

"Perry, can you move forward so I can keep working?" Zyah asked.

Perry didn't respond; he just kept staring at the two women across the street as if mesmerized.

Zyah rang up Mrs. Darden's items. She was next in line, and luckily, she didn't have many groceries. She was with another woman who looked very much like her. They exchanged rueful looks. Still, as Zyah put the items in the women's totes, they were trapped behind the counter. There was a line behind them and Perry in front of them.

"This is my sister, Jane," Mrs. Darden said. "She lives here in Caspar."

Zyah flashed her brightest, most welcoming

smile. "It's lovely to meet you, Jane."

Jane gave her a shy smile back. "I'm so thankful that the grocery store opened here in Caspar. Marie told me it would, but I knew Inez wouldn't keep it open if she didn't find someone she really trusted to run it for her. It can be difficult to get into Sea Haven for groceries. I know it isn't that far, but I walk, and it's much too far to walk."

"When we get up and running, I'll have to think about adding a delivery service," Zyah said. "That might be helpful."

"Oh, yes," Jane agreed, "especially when it's storming."

There were murmurings as the line became impatient.

"Perry, you really have to move," Zyah said, raising her voice slightly.

Perry glanced at her and then turned his attention back to the window, ignoring her and the fact that he was holding everyone up.

Mrs. Marie Darden was a very sweet woman, but she didn't have much patience. When Perry continued to stand in her way, staring at the empty street, she whacked him with a rolled-up magazine. "Move, young man. You're being incredibly rude. That's stalker mentality."

Perry whirled around, glaring. "You old biddy." He took a step toward her to close the gap between them, raising his fist. Zyah jumped onto the counter, trying to get across it so she could put herself between the man and the older woman.

"You touch that woman and you'll be picking your teeth up off the floor." The voice was ice-cold. Menacing. There was no doubt in anyone's mind the speaker meant what he said.

Zyah, sitting on the counter, looked up to see that Keys had come from the back room. He was staring at Perry Randall, ignoring the older women. "You put one hand on her and I'll take you apart."

"You touch me and you'll go to jail," Perry threatened, but he didn't make another move toward Mrs. Darden.

"There are good reasons to go to jail. I've got no problem going if I smash your teeth down your throat because you touched her. Get the fuck out of this store and stay out."

"You can't tell me to get out."

"Zyah?" Keys said, without looking at her.

"Perry, get out before I call the police," Zyah said, sliding back to the other side of the counter. "Don't come back. You don't get to threaten my customers."

Randall scowled at Mrs. Darden and then Zyah before stalking out. Applause broke out, which Keys ignored as he went back down the aisle to disappear into the back.

"Are you all right?" Zyah asked Marie Darden as she began ringing up the next customer in line.

217

"Yes, of course. That young man became that way because his parents taught him that he was entitled. He never had to take responsibility for anything he did. When he was a young boy he was spoiled beyond belief. He used to pull up Jack's flowers and laugh. His parents would act like it was Jack's fault. Such an obnoxious family."

"They're getting a little bit of that back now," Beatrice Golden said. She was a woman who lived in Caspar, and Zyah had met her the very first day she had come to work. "Their son refuses to help them at all. He doesn't work, you know. He lives off his trust fund. He lies around their guesthouse all day smoking pot. If they ask him for anything, he won't do it for them."

"How sad," Zyah said. "One would think he would at least have some respect for his parents." She put the groceries in Beatrice's tote.

Beatrice moved to one side along with Marie and Jane Darden to allow the next customer access to the space so Zyah could ring her up. Apparently, they were all going to continue talking.

"That young man, what was his name, that rescued Marie?" Chiffon, her next customer, asked. She was all of seventy but kept sending little glances toward the back of the store.

"Keys. He's Torpedo Ink. He was helping out today, putting stock in the back," Zyah supplied. He must have seen Perry holding things up on the monitor.

"He was very fast," Chiffon continued. "And so heroic, saying he'd go to jail for Marie."

"He did, didn't he?" Marie said.

"He's very good-looking, dear," Jane added. "You're single, aren't you?"

Zyah's fingers had been flashing over the keys, but she stumbled when she realized the ladies were in a conspiracy to hook her up with Keys now that they thought he was heroic and good-looking. Recovering, she gave them a small smile and a shake of her head. "You are all incorrigible."

The women laughed, in no way deterred or remorseful. Others in the line laughed or smiled as well. Caspar was a small town, and for the most part, those who resided there knew one another. This time of day, late afternoon, most of the shoppers were locals and retired.

"What is that young man's name again, dear?" Talia Barber asked. "I couldn't quite hear it." She made a face at the other women for talking so low.

Zyah knew Talia Barber lived two houses down from Jane. She owned a large piece of property with her husband, Lars. They had a main house they lived in, and had a second cottage they rented to a woman named Maggie Arnold, who, like them, was in her late sixties. They had a huge garden, mostly flowers, some very rare. Zyah had learned quite a bit about the garden from the Dardens.

"He's called Keys, and he's very nice. They all are, and they really have helped me. It's been kind of difficult finding help. They come in and stock shelves sometimes and unload the trucks when they come in for Inez. I really appreciate that."

"That's what Inez told us," Chiffon said. "Inez always knows everyone."

Zyah rang the next customers up faster, hoping to keep the line moving so the women would stop matchmaking and head home. Apparently, they had a quilting class to go to, which she wanted to tell her grandmother about. Anat liked to sew, and she might find something like that very fun. It seemed quite a few of the women either knew her or knew of her through Inez or Lizz.

The rest of the afternoon and evening passed in a long blur of work. Zyah enjoyed the various customers. She was getting to know the regulars and liked most of them. Like Sea Haven, Caspar was mainly a small town made up of retired people, but there were some younger families moving in. Real estate wasn't cheap. The views of the ocean were breathtaking, and many couples had bought homes specifically with the idea to retire there after working in cities.

Not everyone had tons of money. Many

people had homes they were trying to hang on to, with minimum-paying jobs. Some, Zyah could tell, were tired of fighting the usual drug and alcohol problems, while others were determined to beat the odds. There was a community center where people came together with all sorts of ideas, and she'd been invited to just about every kind of function there was. It surprised her that in such a small town, there were so many diverse activities for the very young as well as the very old.

She called her grandmother several times a day to check on her. Anat always sounded cheerful — sometimes tired, but always cheerful. When she asked about Player, he was always resting, with one of the Torpedo Ink members looking after him, and Steele had come by to see him twice a day religiously. She didn't know why, but she always felt a little twinge of jealousy, as if Steele were taking her place. She should have been grateful, but instead she felt as if she needed to rush home and claim the man for herself.

Night fell and she closed the store and made her way to the restaurant, Keys following her. She was used to the escort now and no longer resented any of the Torpedo Ink members shadowing her. She felt safer with their presence. She found it astonishing how quickly she'd adapted to the club.

The restaurant was on the smaller side, an intimate experience, not meant to feed a huge crowd. Alena had wanted to provide something special for her clientele. She didn't advertise. In fact, she'd been so nervous about her opening that she'd practically told the club not to let anyone else know the restaurant was opening its doors.

The building was rectangular, mostly made of glass, built up on the hillside so that it had the view on one side of the distant ocean and on the other of the climbing slope leading up to the highway. The slope was covered in wildflowers and lilac and lavender bushes, with stairs meandering through the overgrown shrubbery all the way up to the flat top.

Tables were scattered throughout the room, with space between giving the clients plenty of privacy for intimate conversations. The chairs were comfortable and inviting, the tables solid and carved by Player, Master, Maestro and Keys, all of whom owned a construction company together but, more importantly, had a deep affinity for woodworking and created beautiful, unique pieces of furniture.

The overhead chandeliers and wall sconces were simple but beautiful, tasteful handblown glass by Lissa, the wife of Casimir, one of the Torpedo Ink members. Lissa was famous for her artwork and sold it all over the world. Lana had sewn the tablecloths and napkins, white with gold threads running through them. Lana had also been the one to choose the chairs for the tables. Anya had helped with the inside design of the restaurant itself.

There was a second room, equally as beautifully appointed, held in reserve for members of Torpedo Ink and locals who were good customers and came in without a reservation. Alena tried to accommodate them if at all possible. The restaurant was small, but it was very upscale, and the prices reflected that. Zyah didn't know what she had been expecting, but when she went over the menu, she was a little surprised at what was offered.

She didn't recognize any of the three waitresses, although the youngest looked familiar to her, as if she'd seen her in passing. All three smiled at her and sent Keys a quick acknowledgment.

"I don't know them."

"Darby," Keys said, indicating the youngest waitress. "Czar's girl. Scarlet, Absinthe's wife. She's the one with all the red hair. And that's Soleil, Ice's wife. Everyone pitches in when it gets really busy. We're looking for help, but Alena's very picky." There was laughter in his voice. "She only serves wine here, not hard drinks, so no bartender." He kept walking, taking her back to the kitchen. "Alena really does need help. Eventually, she'll have a full bar, but at the moment, she just doesn't have the help she needs."

Zyah could see that. Every table was filled.

There was a line of hopefuls waiting. Word of mouth had spread fast. Alena had her two brothers, Ice and Storm, chopping vegetables for her, and it was clear they knew what they were doing. In one corner, a man she didn't recognize was putting the finishing touches on two plates right before he rang a bell and Lana collected the dishes.

"Thanks, Glitch."

Glitch turned to catch four more plates Alena put in front of him with four different meals on them. It was fascinating to watch the man finish off the plates. Each type of meal was treated to a different look, one that enhanced the beauty of the presentation.

Alena flashed her a smile. "Glitch is a genius. Who knew?"

Glitch didn't look up, but he smiled as he finished off the dishes and rang for Darby. He was very fast.

"Did you train for that somewhere?" Zyah asked.

Glitch shook his head as he started on three more Alena had put in front of him. "Watch a lot of cooking shows. They fascinate me."

Alena turned her head for a brief smile. "He's really good."

Glitch looked pleased but kept working fast. Zyah moved to a spot in the corner to better observe. She could see that the four of them, Ice, Storm, Glitch and Alena, worked smoothly together, but Alena definitely needed more help in her kitchen.

The back door swung open and a man stepped in, looking coolly confident. His gaze swept the room, smirking a little as he observed Ice and Storm chopping vegetables. He came boldly inside, his Diamondback colors sitting easily on his back. Ignoring the sudden tension in the room and the fact that the twins stopped chopping, he strode right up behind Alena as she was working and dropped a kiss on her neck. He acted as if he had every right to her, deliberately circling her waist with his arms and pulling her body into his possessively.

"Alena." He nuzzled her neck. "You've been working every damn night. This was supposed to be our night."

Zyah felt the instant tension in the room. She didn't need her shoes off, or her direct connection with the earth, to know that every one of the members of Torpedo Ink, with the exception of Alena, was immediately on edge — and this man not only knew it but wanted them to be. He was openly taunting them.

Keys very gently guided Zyah deeper into the corner of the kitchen and glided in front of her, shielding her with his body, as if there might be a fight, or he didn't want the other man to get a good look at her.

"Pierce." Alena's voice was soft with laughter. With something very close to affection. More than affection. "Honey. I'm working."

"Yeah. I see that. What are you supposed to be doing?" There was an edge of anger in Pierce's voice. Hurt.

Zyah's heart clenched. Pierce was trying to cover that hurt, but it was there, hidden beneath that arrogant surface of anger and deliberate taunting of the others. These were men and women bent on covering their feelings no matter the cost.

"This is the third time, Alena." He dropped his arms and stepped away from her just as she turned around, a look of dismay on her face.

"Our date. We had a date tonight. I'm so sorry, Pierce." Alena looked at him a little helplessly. She gestured toward the dishes she was working on. "I still don't have any help. I thought by now I'd find someone, but I haven't."

"You never prioritize any time for us. I've made the trip over here numerous times, but you won't do one little thing I ask of you. And you can't be bothered to remember when we have a date." He backed up toward the door, not looking at the others in the room, as if he were too humiliated to do so.

He was embarrassed, but not to the extent he was portraying to Alena. The hurt was very real, much more so than the humiliation. Pierce didn't strike Zyah as a man who cared what others thought of him. It would be so rude to slip off her shoes in a commercial kitchen, not to mention unsanitary, but Zyah's gift worked so much better when she was barefoot. She wanted to get an understanding of Pierce's true feelings for Alena and Torpedo Ink's feelings about Pierce. The *why* of it all. The underlying reasons for the hostility. And there was real hostility between Torpedo Ink and Pierce. It came from both sides.

Alena followed Pierce out the back door, closing it so they couldn't hear the rest of the conversation. Ice swore under his breath while Zyah stepped around Keys and calmly surveyed the various dishes still cooking on the burners. Someone had to keep an eye on things while Alena was trying to put out fires in her personal life.

Clearly, Alena found joy in her restaurant. Anyone could see that. Watching her expression while she cooked, while she put the assorted meals together, and feeling her energy made it very apparent: Alena not only loved what she did but she needed it as well. Zyah hoped Alena could make Pierce understand that she hadn't meant to forget their dates while she was trying to get her restaurant up and running. She was working hard, pouring herself into it.

Zyah certainly didn't have Alena's expertise, but she did have a certain understanding, thanks to Anat, of cooking times. She had good awareness of when foods were supposed to come off a grill or the heat. Instinctively, she pulled two of Alena's pans from the heat.

"Holy God in heaven," Storm said. "Zyah, do you have a death wish? Alena doesn't let anyone mess with her main dishes."

"They're going to burn," Zyah replied calmly, but her heart was pounding.

"Damn it," Ice exploded. "Who's on her out there?"

"Fatei, says she's otherwise occupied right now," Keys answered, letting Ice know another club member was watching her.

"Do you want me to let it burn?" Zyah asked. "This chicken was for someone. Where's the tag?" She found it and frowned, reading it.

"No," Storm said. "But she might kill us."

"Can you put it together like it's supposed to be?" Ice asked.

"I don't know how. Do you have a picture? Glitch? Can you?" Zyah asked. "I think it's chicken Kiev. They need to be drained immediately. I have to check that they're done and not overcooked." She did so carefully, checking for tenderness, willing each piece to be cooked all the way through but still be flaky. Thankfully they were, and they were filled with good richness inside. Definitely chicken Kiev, and a recipe she wanted, it looked so good.

Glitch shook his head. "It always comes to me fully prepared. The plate, I mean. She has

228

photographs of the finished dishes."

"Maybe there's a description on the menu. Give me the menu and I'll see what I can do. I'll need the photograph as well." Zyah wanted to run. She looked around, saw the nearest sink and washed her hands thoroughly while they scrambled to get the menu and photographs for her of the meal she needed to prepare fast.

Zyah worked as quickly as she could, trying not to hear her heart pounding, following the description on the menu and the picture. She added steamed green beans and carrots topped with fresh whipped butter. She added rice pilaf cooked in chicken broth, with a few sprigs of parsley. When she was satisfied she had the four dishes as close to perfection as possible, she sent them to Glitch to finish off and turned to look at the next tags. It was better than looking at either Storm's or Ice's face.

"You did good," Storm whispered. "Alena would hate it if her customers had to wait or if she burned something she couldn't repair. You did your best to help her out. That's all she's going to see. It's on her if she chose to try to keep that stupid relationship going."

"It's obviously not stupid to her," Zyah whispered back as she looked at the next tag. This one looked much simpler. Only two plates. Both were the same. She could handle these with more confidence. "Perhaps she wouldn't feel so alone if you got behind her a little more."

Storm didn't reply, and Zyah busied herself setting up the shredded beef with whiskey sauce, which was already prepared — she just had to make up the actual plates. That consisted of shredding the beef and putting it on a platter, adding the sauce on top of the meat, putting slices of fresh green apple and cheddar cheese on top. Around the sides she added the slices of avocado, lettuce leaf, thinly sliced beefsteak tomato, pickle spears, grainy mustard and thin slices of toast.

By the time she'd handed the plates off to Glitch, Alena had returned, rushing in and looking stressed, harried and guilty all at once. She avoided her brothers' gazes, hurrying to the sink to wash her hands and then to the stove.

Zyah stepped hastily aside, moving quickly to put herself in the corner out of the way again, twisting her fingers together. She could see Alena was upset and mortified.

"Did my chicken Kiev burn? Storm?" Alena turned to her brother. "My chicken? My shredded beef? What happened?"

"Zyah dealt with it," Storm said. "She did a pretty good job from what I saw too. Unless the customers drop dead, you might want to hire her."

Alena looked up, her gaze searching until it rested on Zyah. "Thank you. I really appreciate you stepping up. That's not happened before."

Zyah nodded. "No problem. But I really do have to get home. My grandmother gets very anxious if I'm too late. Since the robbery, she's been on edge."

"She does know that our brothers won't let anything happen to her, right?" Alena said. "There haven't been any other tries at getting into your house, have there?"

"No, I'm sure you would have heard about it," Zyah said. She was the one who was uneasy, not her grandmother. And it was mostly because she didn't like being away from Player at night. It was strange that he didn't seem to have the same kinds of episodes during the day that he had at night. He was in pain. He had the terrible migraines, but he didn't have the breaks with reality that he had when he went to sleep. She didn't want that to happen when she wasn't there.

"I'll walk you out," Alena said, falling into step with her. "I'm not like that. This restaurant really does matter to me. It does. It's just that Pierce does too, and I've put him off so many times lately to get this business up and running. He's been good about it . . ." She trailed off and rubbed the back of her neck, frowning as she said the last.

"Everyone's entitled to a bad day, Alena. I've certainly had my share," Zyah assured.

"Well, if you ever want a second job, it's

231

yours," Alena offered. "I mean it. I could use the help."

"Thanks. When I think my grandmother is safe, I'll take you up on it." She meant it too. She wasn't someone who liked to sit around the house all the time. She was used to working long hours. And she didn't want to brood about Player. It was going to hurt like hell when she had to let him go.

They were on the floor moving between tables now. The soft murmur of people talking, clearly enjoying their food and the atmosphere, appealed to Zyah's sense of harmony. Somehow, Alena's state of mind jarred the notes just a bit, so the melody was that bit off. Something wasn't quite right.

"See that man sitting over there in the corner?" Alena whispered. "The one with the little boy who looks to be about two?" She indicated a very handsome man who was leaning toward a little boy with a mop of dark hair, wiping gravy from the child's chin. "That man is trouble with a capital *T.* He comes in every week and sits at that table with his boy. And he's nice. I know. I had Code check him out. Like the real deal. A good guy. He takes care of that boy by himself. The mother's out of the picture. And he's a firefighter. Works for the fire department. EMT on top of it."

"Why is he trouble?" Zyah asked. They were at the double doors of the restaurant.

The doors were thick and beautifully carved. She touched the wood and instantly knew Player had been the one to carve the doors for Alena.

"Look at Darby. Be casual about it. She's Czar's oldest girl. He adores her. The club adores her. And she's looking at Mr. Firefighter. Mr. Dad. Mr. Super-Hot Guy."

Zyah glanced at Darby, and sure enough she was looking at the man with interest. More than interest. "How old is he?"

"Unfortunately, not very old. He's twenty-three. Had the kid when he was twenty-one. He's smart and was already in school for firefighter, EMT and paramedic. He continues with his schooling. And he's looking back at her. I can't blame him. She looks older than she is. She works hard and she likes children. But Czar would kill him for looking."

"You'd better give her that information," Zyah said. "That wouldn't be fair."

"I do so love a good Romeo and Juliet story." Alena sighed.

Zyah shook her head. She was afraid Alena might be taking that story a little too far herself.

# EIGHT

Zyah sat in the armchair across from the bed trying to puzzle out what was causing Player to continually have such horrific, traumatic nightmares when his brain was slowly repairing itself. They were four weeks in. Four weeks. He was so much better. During the day, he was up and talking with her grandmother. Entertaining her. He was pale but getting stronger every day. His balance was still a little off. It wasn't like he could go run races, but it was a brain injury.

Steele continued to come every day, but instead of twice a day, he was coming once a day. Zyah could tell the brain injury itself was mostly healed. Steele didn't want Player overdoing anything. He wanted him up and walking around, with his brothers supervising. He liked him with Anat, outside when they could sit for small blocks of time, nothing strenuous. Player was stronger, there was no doubt about it, but the nightmares and horrendous migraines were as bad as ever.

Zyah hadn't dared sleep in the guest room. She showered when she came home from work and just went straight to her bedroom, giving her grandfather's charcoal drawing her traditional hello and pressing a kiss to her father's intricate scrolled frame with two fingers before sliding into the chair beside the bed. Player always said the same thing.

"Not safe for you in here."

She always said the same thing right back to him. "Not safe for you without me."

He couldn't exactly argue with her. They stared at each other in the darkness. Why did he have to be so damn gorgeous? Why did she have to like him so much? When she was in his head, there was nothing of the smiling man he gave to her grandmother. With the things she saw in his head, she didn't understand how he could smile.

"Babe. Really. You gotta let them take me back to the clubhouse. Steele can take care of me."

"And what happens when you fall asleep, Player, and your mind starts with that weird illusion? It's happening every single night, and the effects are getting stronger. If we can't figure out what's happening soon, something bad is going to happen."

They had to talk about it. He didn't want to. He never wanted to bring his nightmares out into the open. He wanted to pretend illusions were illusions and nightmares were

235

nightmares, but that wasn't going to help either one of them.

"You're right, Zyah. Absolutely right, which is why I have to go. We can't take chances with Anat. I can't. I'm not willing to take a chance with either of your lives, and I have the feeling that's exactly what's going on here."

Player stretched his arms behind his head, locking his fingers beneath the thick mass of unruly hair she had the sudden urge to tame. He stared up at the ceiling, not at her, giving her the impression he didn't want to look at her.

"We're still going to talk about this," she said stubbornly. She hadn't gotten as far as she had in the business world by being a shrinking violet. "I'm in your head every night, Player. It isn't like I haven't seen what's there. Maybe it's real, maybe it isn't."

She knew it was real. No child thought up those kinds of horrors. That dark, dank basement with the rats and chains and too little food. With the pedophiles and bloody bodies. The torture, shivering and biting cold. The discipline and punishments, the turning of bodies into weapons. Most of all, learning to build bombs. She closed her eyes, grateful Player was staring at the ceiling. Let him think she thought his dreams were a child's nightmares.

"I have no idea why I keep having dreams

at night."

Zyah analyzed his tone. There was truth, but also a lie. "You often had nightmares even before you had a brain injury."

"Could you just not put it like that?"

She winced at the venom in his voice. He really didn't like the term *brain injury*. She'd noticed when Steele had used it a couple of times Player had gone quiet and not responded. He'd been very moody lately. She hated not being able to read him. He saved his sweetness for her grandmother. She wanted that sweetness for her, but then it was dangerous wanting that side of him. She was already too entangled with him. She didn't want to be wanted because they had off-the-charts chemistry — sex was great until it wasn't — or because she could fix his brain when he came apart. She wanted someone who loved her, not just needed her.

"I'm sorry, Zyah. I shouldn't be snapping at you. I need to be outside. Riding on my bike. Feeling the wind in my face. I don't know. I just feel like something bad is going to happen. And if it does, I don't want it to happen anywhere near you or your grandmother."

That was all true. She heard the sincerity in his voice. She could listen to his voice all night. Every night. She could lie in bed beside him, feeling the heat of his body, or sit, like she was now, and just feel him close to her and be happy with him in the same room. She didn't understand why he didn't feel the same way.

It wasn't about him being a player like she'd first thought. He was a good man. She knew that from being with him every single night. She was in his mind. She was connecting with him. He was holding back from her. Deliberately.

She got that he'd been shot, that the injury had been life-threatening, but they shared the same mind every night. Healing him the way she did, she had to give herself to him, surrender who she was to him. He saw her, saw into who she was, just as she could see him. He was rejecting the person she was, and that hurt.

No matter what her grandmother said, she felt her gift had to be faulty. The other women in her family had the gift. They found the men who felt the exact same way about them. She went barefoot in her home, connecting with the earth. Feeling vibrations. So certain. Every single time, it was always Player, and yet he never felt those same strong connections back. The physical, yes. Their chemistry was extremely strong, and he felt that, just as she did. He needed her, certainly. But a devastating connection that was forever, that would bind them together heart to heart, soul to soul — Player had no knowledge of such a thing, or at least he rejected that bond with her.

Zyah knew she should let him leave. Go to his brothers in Torpedo Ink. Let them take him to his clubhouse. Find a way to try to separate herself from him. She was already tangled with him so tightly she knew it would hurt for years to come when they separated. Something undefined, some powerful portent inside, told her if she let him go, he would die. She couldn't do that. She was always intelligent enough to listen to her instincts, and everything in her shouted to keep him close. She hoped it wasn't just her wanting to belong to him. Could she really be that lonely? She doubted it. She was independent. She knew she always would be, even if she found the perfect man.

"Zyah?"

"It's all right, Player. You don't have to talk to me. I'm here, so just try to get some sleep. Steele said the more you sleep, the faster you'll heal." She was tired of trying to connect with him on the same level. It wasn't going to happen. She had to face that.

She pulled her legs up and wrapped her arms around her knees, hugging herself tightly, staring at the artwork her grandfather had painstakingly drawn all those years ago for her grandmother. It was very different. Very unique. Black and white. Charcoal. Such beautiful, precise lines. Even his signature falcon had been drawn with those lines.

She couldn't believe how much time and care he must have taken to draw such a masterpiece for Anat. The piece was an abstract, lines, whorls, squiggles and what looked like bird wings. Thick shading and thinner ones. She sometimes traced them lovingly over the glass. She almost knew them by heart.

Her father's frame was equally as beautiful, a carved masterpiece, undeniably precious to her and every line memorized as well, that incredible scrollwork that looked as if it had been dug up from some ancient pyramid and was covered in the very stars above them. She often traced the various carvings, and now that she had seen the doors to Alena's restaurant and knew that Player had been the one to carve them, she thought he was the only one who might equal her father in his ability to capture such beauty in wood for her.

"I don't like going to sleep when you're upset."

"What's different about tonight than any other night? Let's just get you healed and out of here. Isn't that what we both want?" She was careful to keep the hurt out of her voice.

He didn't answer. She kept her head down, aware that, although it was very dark out, the light shining off the sea gave them both the ability to read expressions if they chose. She didn't want to chance him seeing her face. He made her feel vulnerable. Exposed. Every time she was with him — near him — she felt that way. She detested it when he felt so far from her. When she knew he wasn't feeling the same way and never would.

She stayed very quiet, going over in her mind the things she saw repeatedly in his nightmare, trying to ignore the childhood trauma. She concentrated on the beginning. *Alice's Adventures in Wonderland.* Something wasn't quite right there. It was as if the other children loved the story and the memories the hallucinogenic mushrooms brought them, but Player had a terrible aversion to the novel. He detested the recollection, which was odd because it happened repeatedly and he laughed with the others. He was so good at faking his amusement that those who knew him well believed him.

Zyah turned that over and over in her mind. She replayed the images of the various times she saw him do it in his dreams. The age changed, but the circumstances were often the same. There was some kind of intense trauma, a horrific torture of one or more of the others, and the reading would be asked for. At first, she could never get beyond the terrible things that had been done to the members of Torpedo Ink as children or teens, but eventually she forced herself to only look at Player's face. He despised when they asked for the reading of *Alice's Adventures in Wonderland.*

He never stopped Absinthe or Transporter or Absinthe's brother, Demyan, from reading the hated book, but he didn't look at the others while it was being read. Why didn't they notice? Because all of them had been beaten, tortured and used. They were all in such a terrible state and barely surviving. They were just children. *Alice's Adventures in Wonderland* was entertainment, and Player knew it. They had to get their minds off what was happening to them, to their bodies. His illusions of Alice, the White Rabbit, the Cheshire Cat, the Mad Hatter and the caterpillar were his way of contributing to his brothers and sisters, but the cost to him was much greater than any of them understood. Maybe even greater than he understood.

She rubbed her hand up and down her thigh, massaging her aching muscle. She really needed a long hot soak in a tub. That was one of the things she loved to do at night. Or sit in the hot tub on the lower deck out under the stars in the middle of the night. She didn't dare, not with Player waking every night in a cold sweat, out of his mind, the illusion turning to some strange reality she couldn't quite fathom but needed to figure out fast because last night, for the first time, she had actually heard the ticking of a clock. That hadn't been there before, not in all the four weeks of terrible nightmares and illusions.

Zyah glanced over at the bed. Player had drifted off. His body often went out fast, needing to rest and heal whether he wanted to or not. She glanced at her watch. He sometimes got a couple of hours of sleep before the nightmare took him. She hoped he would get at least that much. She knew from experience he was a very light sleeper, so she didn't make the mistake of standing up and pacing like she wanted to. Instead, she eased her legs out and stretched to give her muscles a much-needed break.

Once more, she concentrated on young Player's face while Absinthe read *Alice's Adventures in Wonderland* aloud to everyone. He stared down at his hands, even when the others clamored for the characters to run around the basement with them. They wanted entertainment. He wasn't proud in providing it for them. Why? It made him sick to do so. He squirmed, even though he kept a little half smile on his face. Guilt crossed his handsome features. Even then he'd already been so good-looking. What did he have to feel guilty about? He was every bit as tortured as the others. Beaten. Raped. The flesh torn from his body. Thin from lack of food.

The characters from the book suddenly joined them, acting out the scenes, making the others laugh, but Player's expression never changed from that dark, miserable little boy staring down at his hands with that enigmatic little half smile. He didn't think he was powerful, and yet he kept the characters acting out the scenes so easily, without looking or waving his hands toward them as a child might. Cards ran across the room to the delight of the others. Flamingos were held upside down to play croquet with.

Player's fingers began to move against his thigh in a familiar pattern. She had seen that pattern many, many times now. In his dreams and out of them. In his head he began to build things. Even while he created the illusion for his childhood sisters and brothers, he began to build the things that took him away from what was tearing him up inside.

Zyah sat up straight. Player detested the illusion of *Alice's Adventures in Wonderland* so much that he took himself away from it by doing something else. He occupied himself by doing things his brain was very familiar with. He built bombs. He had been forced at a young age to learn, and he was good at it. Very good. He had a mind for it, and his hands were steady. His eyes were excellent. His memory impeccable. He was fast. The pocket watch. The gold pocket watch. The one that went from the White Rabbit's very innocent golden pocket watch to the other one that suddenly appeared in the nightmare with the shadowy figure standing over the boy at the bench.

She forced herself to breathe evenly, afraid

the change in her breathing would wake Player. She knew she was getting close to some revelation. She just didn't know what it was. Who could be so twisted that they would do these things to children? She pressed her fingers to her lips and shook her head, wiping her mind blank. She couldn't think about that and help him. He needed help. He had to get through this. She had to get to a place where she understood what was actually happening to him to throw him from his nightmare into his illusion and then into an alternate reality that became his reality.

*So keep looking at that little boy down in that basement, Zyah. What do you see him doing while the others are watching the show he's giving them?* What did she see? He was tapping the rhythm on his thigh. Building the bomb in his head. Perfecting it. She saw the moment his head came up and alarm spread through him. What was it? What was different? What did he see that no one else did? They were still smiling. The *Alice's Adventures in Wonderland* characters were still cavorting around the room.

Zyah peered into the image until her eyes felt like they were bleeding. She looked everywhere and then looked again. Into the dark corners. The ceiling. She looked for the rabbit. The watch. Anything that was not part of the original story line that would have told a little boy that his illusion had gone from amusement into madness. Into the blurring of a line into possible reality.

She was connected to his mind. She had to stop trying to stay apart from him if she was going to find out the truth and let herself connect wholly with him, but if she did, it would just be that much harder to tear herself away from him.

She deserved better. She wasn't going to settle for a man who didn't love her. She didn't want to be needed because she had a gift that could shore him up when his gift harmed him. She didn't want to be wanted for sex. Okay, maybe that wasn't being quite as truthful. She pressed her hand to her forehead, trying to decide whether to continue to be a coward and just call herself that.

Player made a sound. The moment he did, she forgot about her dilemma and jumped up. From experience, she knew better than to touch him. He was already sweating, fighting the sheets.

Without warning, the silly rabbit appeared. She was used to him now, life-sized, just standing there, staring at his watch, pink nose wiggling. In front of him was the table. Before he had been shadowy, barely across from the bed, standing just in front of her grandfather's picture. That seemed such a sacrilege to her. Her grandfather and father had kept her safe for years, and now, when she needed their magic the most, it was failing her. Her gift was failing. Everything she counted on was failing.

A man sat on the bench with his back to her, as he did in all of Player's nightmares, still shadowy, still undefined, but she could make out wide shoulders. His head was down, and he concentrated on the various pieces of equipment in front of him. She had seen Player putting bombs together in his head enough times to know the likelihood was that whatever those individual tools, instruments and equipment were, put together, made up a bomb. The White Rabbit morphed into another man, one with a gold watch standing behind the man at work at the table.

The man working on the bomb was Player. Young or old, she would know him. His brown hair was wild and artfully kissed with white streaks. His back had the Torpedo Ink colors tatted into his skin, covering a multitude of scars and burns. The shadowy figure stared down at his pocket watch while he hunched over Player's shoulder.

Suddenly, Zyah heard the ticking of the clock loud in the room, just as she had heard the night before. Her heart jumped and then began to pound. "Player. Wake up. Wake up now."

The man with the pocket watch lifted his head as if he'd heard her. That was very frightening. Immediately, she began to dance, pushing her feet into the floor, calling up the magic of the earth. She gently extended her arms to bind Player to her, weaving them together, her voice singing softly to him to call him back to her. Fortunately, she had managed to forestall the nightmare before he was too far into it. By staying in the bedroom with him, she hadn't allowed whatever was gripping him so tight at night to take him down that path and fling him fully into another reality. If she didn't gather her courage and connect fully with him to see what he had discovered as a little boy when he had been so alarmed, she might lose him after all.

The shadowy figure abruptly disappeared, and then the bench with the man making the bomb disappeared as well. Player groaned and threw one arm over his eyes and swore in his native language. "Damn it, Zyah," he said finally.

She ignored him and went to the bathroom to get a cool washcloth for his head, just as she had every night for the past few nights. Kneeling beside him, she wiped off the little beads of sweat. "It wasn't as bad this time. You're getting better."

"Or you're just getting faster."

"I'm really good," Zyah said. "Dancing around the room, and you missed it."

He groaned. "That's not funny."

"It wasn't meant to be. I thought I was

really sexy when I danced. Most men think I'm sexy. You're the exception, it seems." She tried to tease him. Make it humorous when she'd been so afraid. The ticking of the clock had been terrifying.

He took his arm away from his eyes. Now they were piercing blue, icy daggers. "That's *really* not funny."

She wiped down his throat. "You're in a foul mood, but then you usually are when you're around me. You don't like me. You don't have to. I'm one of *those* girls. You apologized and all, but you didn't mean it. We fucked all night, over and over." She forced herself to say the words as crudely as possible, wanting them imprinted in her brain. "I get it. Some men think women who do that sort of thing are nasty girls or something. I don't know. Somehow, it's okay for the men but not for the women."

She avoided looking into his eyes when she said it because, honestly, just saying the sentiment aloud turned her stomach. Still, it was true. She'd come across so many men who thought that way. Not that she was promiscuous, far from it, but she didn't judge other women and didn't feel they should be judged. She wasn't even certain she believed that was the reason he didn't want to be around her. She hadn't found that in him. He didn't seem judgmental. She didn't know what the reason was. Only that he didn't want her. Maybe she just needed a reason, any reason. It was just that he kept pushing her away.

He caught her wrist. "Zyah. Look at me. You don't believe that."

She didn't answer him. She wasn't going to get into an argument. Actions spoke far louder than words, and so far, he could barely stand to look at her. "Let go. I have to get the washcloth cold again. You're burning up."

He swore again and pushed into a sitting position. She really avoided looking at him because he was all corded muscle. No one should have that kind of muscle. She remembered tracing every single one of them with her tongue. Ashamed, she turned away from him and slipped off the bed. Ordinarily, she hurried to the bathroom, so she could make his skin cooler, make him more comfortable. Now, she took her time, not wanting to get back to him so fast, needing a few moments to get herself back under control.

She could do this. She was strong. She repeated the mantra to herself over and over. She just had to get through a few more days. His brain injury was healed. It was just the nightmares. She had to find a way to stop the nightmares and the migraines. If she could do that . . . He was getting stronger, although as long as he was there, her grandmother was safe. She had to keep that in mind. Torpedo Ink stayed close because they stayed near Player.

Player had a pillow behind his head, but he was sitting up, sheet pulled up to his hips. She tried not to look at his body. He wore something, she saw the edging just above the single sheet covering him. It wasn't much, and one leg was out. She knew his body. Every inch of it. Still, she averted her eyes and handed him the washcloth rather than wipe his face, neck and chest the way she normally would have.

"I'll get a towel." She was suddenly aware of her own lack of clothing. What if he thought she was coming on to him? She always wore a racerback tank and little shorts. Long pants twisted around her legs and drove her nuts when she slept. Mostly, she slept in the nude. Not that she'd do that with Player in her bed, and anyway, she was sitting up in a chair most of the night now.

"Zyah." He tried to catch her wrist and missed. "For fuck's sake, sit down next to me. You have been every damn night. What you've been thinking is pure bullshit, and it doesn't even make sense. So, for the love of God, will you stop making my head hurt worse and get your sweet little ass over here before I have to get up and get you?"

She stood in the middle of the room frowning at him. "You are an ass. A complete and utter ass. I have no idea why I ever thought you were anything but an ass." She had to do something to save herself, because after seeing his childhood and spending every night with him for four straight weeks, she was so in love with him she couldn't stand herself.

He threw back the sheet and was out of the bed so fast she barely had time to turn to sprint for the door. She even squealed like a little girl, but muffled the sound with her hand just in case she woke her grandmother, which was unlikely since she was downstairs.

Player caught her around the waist, tossed her over his shoulder so she was upside down and marched back to the bed. She should have protested, should have done something, anything at all, to stop him, but a million butterflies took wing. Her sex clenched, wept with sheer need. She wanted him. She'd wanted him every time she thought about him. It was a sin. It was so wrong. He was her obsession.

He threw her easily right into the center of the mattress and came down on top of her before she could move, pinning her down. Zyah went very still. He might have had a brain injury, but Steele had somehow miraculously healed him. Now the rest of his body was working just fine. She knew because she felt every single inch of him hard and tight against her. She knew his body, all those defined muscles, the wide shoulders, the deep chest that went into that impressive rib cage and narrowed into his hips. His cock was beautiful. She knew because she'd worshipped him with her hands and mouth. With her body. She could still taste him. Feel him inside her.

At night, when she was alone, she still felt him sliding into her, pushing through her tight folds, his piercing blue gaze staring into hers like he was seeing into her soul. He'd been a miracle, a feast of pure pleasure she hadn't thought possible, and there was no forgetting the many ways he had taken her, shocking her at times but always giving her such pleasure, she had been more than willing to repeat the experience again and again with him.

He caught her wrists and held them down against the mattress. Even that, the way he shackled her wrists and pinned her, like a captive, his grip unbreakable yet so incredibly gentle she knew he wouldn't leave one single mark on her skin. She almost wanted him to. When they'd had one night together, he'd been wild, leaving marks of possession all over her with his hands and his teeth. He would go from gentle to rough. From sweet to wild. She loved every single second with him. He'd set up such an addiction that even now, knowing he held himself away from her, her heart beat wildly and her body went liquid with urgent hunger.

"I know I hurt you with the careless shit I said to you."

His blue eyes stared directly into hers, so

253

that it was impossible to look away no matter how much she wanted to. It didn't matter that she was hurt and even angry with him — he was always going to be that man she responded to. His eyes were no longer cold but fiery blue flames, fierce like the wild, turbulent, out-of-control lover she'd been with that first night.

She was over the things he'd said that morning. *So* over them, but she'd let him think that was the cause of her hurt. What would her excuse be now?

The intensity of that blue flame burned right through every shield she might have attempted to put up. Her body responded to that look. *She* responded. She couldn't just blame it on her body. She could feel the flames licking over her skin like a million heated tongues. He wasn't doing one single thing other than holding her down and staring into her eyes, yet she could feel his mouth moving over her bare skin. She tried to hold back a moan.

There was his voice. Like velvet. Brushing along every nerve ending. He knew how to use it. Compelling. Commanding. While he spoke to her, his thumb caressed the inside of her wrist right over her pounding pulse, sweeping back and forth in a mesmerizing rhythm that robbed her of her ability to breathe. At the same time, one of his legs slid in between hers, pushing them apart.

"I swear I had no idea what I was saying or doing that night. I was so damn tired, so many hours without sleep and I'd held an illusion for too long. You were the best thing that ever happened to me. You still are the best thing that ever happened to me."

He didn't wait for a reply. He simply took her mouth, and the earth itself spun so fast it fanned the flames rising between them. The fire burned hot, a whirlwind, a storm that rushed over her so that she had to have more. Needed more. She opened herself to him. Gave herself to him. There was no holding back. There hadn't been before, and there couldn't be now.

Player released her wrists and caught her tank, tugging at it. "Is this a favorite? Get rid of it, or it's gone. I need your tits, baby. I've been looking at them for weeks. Thinking about them. Dreaming about them." He dragged the tank over her head and tossed it away.

The sensation of the night air on her suddenly exposed breasts was shockingly sensual. The way the blue flames in his eyes leapt and burned over her added to the fire rushing through her veins and roaring between her legs.

His hands tore at her shorts next. "Don't want anything between us. Not anything. I wake up with the taste of you in my mouth, and go to sleep with you there." He ripped the shorts off her hips with one vicious jerk and discarded the scraps.

Zyah couldn't stop the soft little moan from escaping this time. Her hips jerked, and she felt her body slick with welcome for him. She had those same sensations every morning, every evening, and she was so grateful she wasn't alone. Right at that moment, it didn't matter if it was just sex or not, she was desperate for him.

"Sometimes I lie on this bed with the scent of you in my lungs and I can actually feel my cock sliding into your hot mouth or your tight little pussy and think I'm going to go insane if I don't have you again."

Those blue eyes burned right into hers until she felt as if he branded her soul. He wasn't saying anything she hadn't felt night after night. The memory of his cock stretching her lips, heavy on her tongue. His taste. Inside her. Deep. Even there, stretching her until she felt so full and taken. Until she felt as if he'd written his name inside her.

He lowered his head again, and his mouth was on her neck, his teeth nipping and then catching, so that her body shuddered as the fleeting pain somehow sent fire streaking through her. His tongue was velvet, his lips soft as he kissed the sting away. He kissed and nipped his way to her breast, his hands cupping the weight as he slid down her body.

"I love your tits, baby." His hands were

rough, squeezing and massaging.

She loved the way he touched her as if he couldn't get enough, as if he was in such a hurry to take every inch of her in. She caught at his hair, all that beautiful, messy, untamed hair that made him look like a fallen angel. Her nails slid down his back, long streaks of fire, to urge him on.

His mouth found the top of her right breast while his hands caressed underneath both breasts. His mouth was hot, lips velvet soft to match the gentle fingers stroking along the curves. Then his teeth nipped, and his fingers bit into her, kneading possessively. She arched into him, giving him more, wanting more. Those lightning strikes kept streaking like fiery arrows from her breasts to her clit, so that she clenched and clenched. Her hips bucked. Her sex wept.

"I love your mouth, Player," she whispered. "Your hands on me."

"My teeth. My cock. You fuckin' love my body, baby, the way I love yours."

She did. There was no denying that. He was nibbling at the sides of her breasts now. First one, then the other. Avoiding her nipples. She was dying for him to touch her there. To settle his mouth there. She had more than generous breasts. She remembered how much time he spent on them, worshipping them. He had even dribbled wax on them and slowly peeled it off. He'd wanted to eat off her breasts. He told her he wanted her to dance for him with nipple clamps on and that he'd have his brother, Ice, a jeweler, make her a beautiful set, one of a kind, with bells, just for her, to go with her anklet of bells.

She slid her hand down his body, trying to reach his cock, but he was too far. She could only dig her nails into his back and the tops of his hips to try to get him to where she wanted him to be.

He laughed softly against her breast, his breath warm. "Do you think you're going to gain control by digging your nails into me? I like that you want me, Zyah. I love that you're making that little keening mewl that says your sweet little pussy is hot as hell and slick for me. My cock is pressed against your thigh. You feel how hot it is? How hard? That's all yours. But you're going to wait until I take my time and claim every fuckin' inch of you."

She loved the way he did that. He talked to her like that, as if he owned her. As if her body belonged to him. He talked dirty. He was rough. He was gentle. She needed his kind of wild sex to feel alive. He brought out a side of her that, when they came together, made her truly complete. He made her feel beautiful and powerful. She loved being his.

"Well, let me have it." She leaned into him and bit his shoulder and then soothed the sting with her tongue. She loved his skin. The taste of him. "Do you know how good I could make you feel?" She didn't have to deliberately make her voice sultry; it was already that way — for him — for Player. Tempting him. Wanting him.

He retaliated, biting the left side of her breast and then the right, sending flaming arrows straight to her sex so that her hips bucked and she cried out. His tongue traced her areola, a long, slow sweep, very gentle. It felt so good she closed her eyes. He moved to her other breast, repeating that same sweet action, his tongue a wicked weapon, teasing her senses, drugging her until she couldn't think properly.

His tongue went to her right nipple, flicking, circling. She found herself holding her breath. Arching her back. Trying to push her breast into the heat of his mouth. His hand came up to cup her breast, his thumb and finger finding her left nipple while his tongue worked her right. She wasn't certain where to concentrate. His finger brushed her nipple. His thumb strummed as if it were a guitar string. Her belly tightened in anticipation. Liquid heat spilled between her legs.

"Player. Please. You're killing me."

He laughed softly. "You deserve it, woman. You've been killing me for days. Weeks."

He blew on her nipple. Then his mouth covered her breast and sucked hard. Really hard. He drew her flesh into that scorching-hot cavern, teeth scraping, tugging, biting

259

down until she wanted to scream with absolute desire, her hips bucking, one leg trying to steal out from under him to wrap around his thigh. His fingers caught her left nipple and pinched down slowly but kept going, taking her breath until she was arching up as high as she could, pushing into his hand and mouth at the same time. When he released her, he kissed his way from one breast to the other, the blue flames in his eyes nearly glowing as he surveyed the marks he'd left behind.

"You aren't going to scrub me off you so easily, Zyah," he said, satisfaction in his voice and in every line of his face.

Before she could respond, he bent his head to her left breast, repeating the same thing, exactly the same way, not hurrying. She thought she might come undone. Unravel. She was unraveling. She was so desperate to get off that she slid her hand down her body between them to try to give herself some relief.

Player caught her wrist. "Naughty girl. I'm going to have to punish you for that. You can just wait. I'm getting there. Put your hands on your breasts. I like to see you work your tits while I eat you. Then when you get wild and can't hold on to them, they bounce all over the place. It's a beautiful sight."

Player flicked her nipples with his tongue, bit gently down one more time and then kissed his way down her belly, sliding slowly between her legs, keeping his body wedged there so she couldn't close her thighs. His shoulders were wide, and it felt as if he were stretching her legs to capacity, although she knew better. The night air was cool, and she was so hot that the contrast fed the flames, adding to the roaring need coiling tighter and tighter.

He settled himself and lifted his head to look at her. His eyes. He stole her willpower — her heart — with those eyes of his.

"I've been starving for you." He stated it very simply and then bent his head to her right thigh.

His tongue was like velvet on her inner thigh. Up high, close to her heat. Close to where she so desperately needed him. She knew it wasn't going to be that simple. He wanted to make a statement. A claiming. She couldn't blame him. The first chance she had, she was going to do a little claiming of her own.

Zyah closed her eyes, crying out when his teeth marked her, when his mouth sucked at her tender skin, leaving behind a signature going up her inner thigh. It wasn't enough on her right thigh; he had to duplicate it on her left. Then his mouth was on her lips, his tongue tracing them, flicking and teasing, sipping at the taste of her. Circling her inflamed clit. He flattened his tongue and pressed hard. Circled again. Plunged his tongue deep.

Flicked. Strummed. Plunged.

She found herself hissing his name. Demanding. Trying to find purchase with her feet to push her body into his mouth. Nothing she did or said mattered. Player took his time. Then he suddenly shifted his body, catching her thighs and pressing her legs over his arms. His mouth covered her slit, and her world went red and orange. Fiery flames. No oxygen. He devoured her just like he'd said he would. He was relentless. Merciless. He was unashamedly greedy.

She sobbed through her first insane orgasm, spiraling out of control. She'd forgotten that, the power he could generate in her body. The waves that kept coming and coming when his mouth and tongue didn't stop. He added his fingers, stroking. Pushing deep. Sliding between her cheeks. Claiming every part of her for his own. Sending a second wave even more powerful than the first so that she was shattered and only he could save her.

Player lifted his head and wiped his face on her thighs, his eyes blazing like blue fire. He caught her legs. "Turn over, Zyah." It was a demand, nothing less.

He was at the end of the bed already, and he didn't wait for compliance. She couldn't move, the ripples taking her over, throwing her into another realm. He caught her ankles and rolled her over so that she was on her belly. Immediately, he was on her, catching her around the waist, yanking her up on her hands and knees.

"Player." She wailed his name. She loved him like this. Wild. Crazy. How many times had they been like this that first night?

He put his hand between her shoulder blades and she went down to her elbows.

"*Bog,* I love your ass." His hands shaped her cheeks. "You're so fuckin' beautiful, Zyah. There isn't a single spot on you that isn't gorgeous."

She felt the slide of his hair on her bottom and then his mouth, his tongue. She couldn't help tightening her muscles. His hand smacked her hard. "That's for trying to get yourself off instead of waiting for me." He smacked her again. "And that's for making me wait to taste you when you knew I had to be starving for you."

Her breath was coming in ragged gasps. She pushed back into him. "Player. Give me your cock."

"You don't deserve it yet." He bit her. Hard. He ignored her yelp and repeated the action on her other cheek. Then he lapped at her entrance, pushing her legs wider apart, his tongue trailing the mixture of hot cream up into the seam between her cheeks.

"Hold still for me, and I might decide you deserve my cock after all."

His fingers pushed into her slit and his thumb found the little forbidden star. He used both, watching his fingers disappear into her body while she cried out and nearly ground her forehead into the mattress. Player withdrew his fingers with a curse. She waited, breathing hard, hearing the tear of foil. Where had he gotten a condom? Without any warning, he slammed his heavy, thick cock into her body.

Zyah had come three times, and she was extremely slick. It was the only reason she was able to take the thick invasion as he wrapped his arm around her waist and began pounding into her. Over and over. Feral. Wild. That was Player. Nothing in her life had ever felt so good. Nothing. It was Player. It was always going to be Player. He was like a machine, the friction and scorching heat so intense she thought she might die.

Her lungs labored. There was no air. Breath didn't come. She grew dizzy, but he didn't stop. His arm was like a steel band. His cock a steel hammer. She never wanted him to stop. She needed him to, but she didn't want him to. Tension coiled and coiled, winding tighter and tighter. She pushed back helplessly into him, every bit as ferocious as he was. Needing his body just like this.

His hands transferred to her hips, and he was yanking her into him and shoving her away from him, pushing and pulling. It was a kind of madness. A kind of ecstasy. The fire was inside of her, burning through her body in such a brilliant, perfect way. The flames were outside her body, licking over her skin like a thousand hot tongues. He suddenly caught her hair in his hand and jerked her head back, forcing her back to arch, changing the angle of his penetration.

She muffled her cry as her body reacted, clamping down like a vise on his cock, surrounding all the white-hot steel with a silken fist. The waves crashing through her were powerful, a series of tsunamis threatening to overtake her and drive her out of her mind. Her entire body shuddered with pleasure. Every cell, every nerve ending, was so acutely aware of him, so connected and wrapped up with his body, that she felt not only her own crashing orgasm tearing through her but his as well.

His release was equally as powerful as hers. A hot, relentless, merciless crescendo that had his cock swelling, pushing tightly against her sensitive tissues until she felt his wild heartbeat. Every pulse through that heavy vein. Every violent jerk and blazing hot rope of seed filling the condom inside her silken channel triggering more powerful waves in her body. One orgasm rolled into another, and she went down to her belly, unable to support herself.

Player collapsed on top of her, arms around her, his cock jerking hard in her body, still connecting them. "*Bog,* woman, you are destined to kill me."

The whispered words against her neck penetrated the bliss Zyah floated in. The notes jarred. Rocked. Hit her like a punch in the gut. She groaned. Tears burned like the flames had in his eyes. She knew those blue flames were gone. If she looked at him, his eyes would once again be that intense ice blue that would already be distancing him from her.

Zyah kept her eyes closed, head turned away from Player's face. She couldn't look at him. What was wrong with her? What was wrong with both of them? Wild, dirty, crazy sex was total insanity, and not because it was addicting and heartbreaking. He would walk away unscathed. He'd already proven that. She, however, was going to be ripped to shreds. Still, they had no business acting like two wild animals when he was so injured. So okay, Steele had healed his injury. She got that. But his migraines were ferocious, and they were as bad as ever.

She worked at finding a way to breathe even while her body still rippled with aftershocks around his. Player's hand was in her hair, stroking caresses in that way that he had. She felt his breath on the nape of her neck. His lips moved from her neck to her shoulder. Goose bumps rose on her skin. She wore him there. She'd wear him forever. She'd feel him inside her, where she'd never get him out.

"Baby, I didn't hurt you, did I?" Player murmured. He slid his body off of hers, taking his weight. Taking his cock. Taking himself away from her. He knotted the condom so casually.

She swallowed her distress. She was a grown woman. She made her choices and took responsibility for them. "No, the sex was awesome, Player." She rolled off the other side of the bed, out of his reach, and caught up the blanket that was on the floor. Zyah wrapped the blanket around her shivering body. She was insane. Absolutely insane. Only Player could make her that way.

"Zyah, what the fuck are you doing? Come back to bed." Player sounded shocked.

"Absolutely not." She made every effort to be calm. Reasonable. Matter of fact. "We shouldn't have been having sex. You were shot four weeks ago, and I know Steele healed you, but you're still having migraines. I should have been watching out for you. We're definitely not doing that again."

"We're definitely doing that again." Not only did he sound amused, he sounded arrogant *and* smug. "And you got rid of my migraine. I think sex gets rid of them."

She would have kicked him if she'd been close enough, but she wasn't that silly. She had no willpower when it came to him. She couldn't get close again. He had every reason to be arrogant, amused and smug. "Yes, I noticed you had condoms ready and waiting." For some reason that hurt. It shouldn't have. She should have been happy that he cared enough to protect her. She thought he was more worried about protecting himself. He definitely distanced himself from her when it came to anything but sex.

"I'm going to take a bath." She didn't dare stay in the same room with him, not when he was looking at her with those tempting blue eyes.

She was feeling weak and vulnerable. Before he could say anything, she wrapped the blanket tighter around herself and walked out. Behind her, she could hear him swearing, but she didn't turn around — she didn't dare because tears were burning in her eyes, and she wasn't going to let him see how much it hurt to walk away from him.

# NINE

Zyah stood just outside the door to the living room, listening to the sound of voices. Her grandmother's laughter. She sounded young and worry free for the first time in the weeks since Zyah had been home. There was less pain in her voice. It was good to hear her sound so much more like herself. Player's voice. Low. That tone that got to Zyah somewhere deep inside she couldn't protect herself against. It was almost like she had some lock that kept everyone else out, but that tone penetrated like a key would, opening her up and making her very vulnerable to him.

She'd worked every day for the last few days and come home, two members of Torpedo Ink escorting her openly. Player remained at the house recuperating, Maestro staying close or one of the others replacing him. She knew one or more club members were somewhere in the shadows watching over them as well. She was okay with that because if they were watching over Player, they were keeping her grandmother safe, and that left her to work in peace.

Player. She heaved a sigh as she made the turn down the hallway to her bedroom. She wasn't certain what she was going to do about him. Rubbing her fingertips along her jean-clad thigh she pushed open the door to her bedroom, where he had been staying since he'd been shot, and stopped just inside to inhale his masculine scent. He'd been there over a month now. A full five weeks. She didn't know what she was going to do when he was gone.

The room was always clean. Not just clean. Perfect. He kept the bed made. There wasn't a wrinkle in the comforter. He was meticulous about the placement of the pillows on her bed, almost as if he'd taken a picture and knew the exact position she'd placed each of them in prior to his taking over the room. It was impossible because he'd been brought into her room unconscious, and he couldn't know where she'd kept the silly pillows.

She sighed as she looked around the room. Just because it was habit, and she needed comfort, she went to her grandfather's drawing and stood in front of it for a short time, looking at the beautiful lines and whorls, the delicate strokes and heavy slashes he had so lovingly and painstakingly drawn for Anat. Instead of feeling comforted, her heart ached more when she looked at it. The large intricately carved frame, so original, so thoughtful and perfectly surrounding the drawing with such love from her father, all for Anat on their anniversary, had always brought Zyah joy. She felt the love radiating from the gift to her grandmother from her grandfather and father. She knew over the years she'd built that up. This drawing was one of the few things she had — concrete evidence her family had existed. Right now, as she pressed a kiss to the pads of her fingers and then to the frame her father had made, she felt lonelier and more disconnected than ever.

She had always been a strong, confident woman, but she was losing that confidence in herself and in the gift that had been passed down from mother to daughter for hundreds of years. Zyah rubbed her temples, trying to clear her head. She was reluctant to join Player and Anat, knowing that if she did, Player wouldn't laugh so much anymore. Like Zyah was when she was around him, Player was stilted when he was around her.

It was different at night. She came in every night and took away the things that tried to spill out of his head. So many terrible memories haunting him, and with each one, he moved farther away from her. She detested that. She had become aware that part of the reason he distanced himself from her was that

271

he detested her ability to see what had been done to him as a child. No man wanted a woman knowing he'd been repeatedly raped and abused, subjected to the worst kinds of torture. He might want her to think they were nightmares, but they both knew she was looking into his real childhood memories.

She told herself a million times that she didn't want him to think that the terrible things done to him made him unworthy of a relationship, but she knew it was so much more than what he considered the humiliation of her knowing about his childhood. There was much more to his past than that. More that she had caught glimpses of and he had tried to hide from her.

The stark truth was, he had killed people. A lot of people. If the images in his head were anything to go by, he had done some pretty terrible things to them first. When the men had been waiting in her garage to kidnap her, he had gotten to her fast in spite of being wounded twice. And he'd hurt at least two of them pretty severely. One was very bad, and he'd done it with his bare hands.

She'd been fighting off the two trying to drag her out of the garage. She had skills, and they weren't trying to really hurt her — or kill her. That gave her an advantage Player didn't have. She'd tried to warn him, but she hadn't known there were so many in the garage lying in wait to try to kidnap her. For what? She had no idea what they were after. She had discussed it with her grandmother. The jewelry they'd had in the house was gone. The thieves had already taken it. What were they after?

Zyah forced her mind back to the pertinent facts, the ones she hadn't confided to her grandmother — or to anyone else. Player had already been shot, suffered a terrible brain injury, but even with that, even unable to see, he'd shot two men, just going off the sound of their voices. She saw them fall. They'd been dragged off by their friends, but they both were hurt, she could tell by the trail of blood left behind. Strangely, the garage, yard, sidewalk and asphalt didn't show one speck of blood an hour later, when she went outside. How had that happened?

Torpedo Ink had shown up. Player's family. His brothers and sisters. They'd come to ensure he was safe. Steele had performed a miracle on him, and then stitched that deep groove that went nearly halfway around Player's head before she had insisted he had to stay right there, that he couldn't leave. Because she had that strange premonition she sometimes got that told her she needed to be somewhere or something had to be done. She had good instincts, and in this case, she knew had she not acted on them, Player wouldn't have survived.

She sank down onto the bed, gripping the

wooden post, facing the window that over-looked the sea. It looked out over the grassy field and the bluffs, with the view of the ocean crashing over the rocks, throwing white foam into the air. Her life felt like it was spiraling out of control, when she'd always been completely in control. She'd thought that was her problem. Never once had she let loose. She hadn't known how — until that first night with Player.

Zyah had seen Anat working hard to get them out of debt and to provide a home for them. She had wanted to help her grand-mother. From a very young age, she had begun to do whatever she could to contribute. That had given her a serious view on life. She had become disciplined and very focused on becoming financially sound for her grand-mother and for her own future. She planned everything. Her job had allowed her to put her money in stocks and bonds. To put most of it toward retirement. She was even careful with her investments, not risking too much.

There had been so many nights she'd dreamt of letting loose. Of having friends and a partner. She could be that person she knew was inside her, waiting to break loose. "Player." She whispered his name aloud.

This agony had to end soon for both of them. He wasn't hurting because his heart ached for hers. Or his soul cried out for hers. He couldn't take her knowing what had been done to him as a child. She didn't blame him for that. But it still hurt when he stayed so distant from her. Since that night he'd initiated sex with her — and she wasn't putting that responsibility on him, because she'd been all in — he'd grown even more distant. That really hurt.

She knew that every minute spent with him at night, getting into his mind, connecting them together, made it that much more difficult for her to let go of him, and she was determined to see him through this. His injury was completely healed, yet his migraines had worsened, as had his nightmares. Steele couldn't explain it. They'd discussed the problem at length.

Every night, Player would have terrible relapses. The nightmares were so bad this last week that he'd gotten very little sleep. The illusions deepened until the reality they provoked grew stronger. She knew she would have to go back to the original *Alice's Adventures in Wonderland* moment when he first brought out the characters for his Torpedo Ink brethren to amuse them. She needed to study that scene again.

Zyah had known she'd been close to discovering something sinister, something only Player had been aware of in that room. She found it odd that even Czar, who seemed so sensitive to all of the other children and everything going on around him, wouldn't notice that Player detested *Alice's Adventures in Wonderland* or that something wasn't right in that horrible basement. But then, every one of those naked, brutalized children was freezing and starved.

She hadn't really looked at Czar's face. Had he known? She'd mostly looked at Player and listened to the other children. She hadn't wanted to see those little bodies with their ribs showing and sores everywhere. She hadn't wanted to see the skin torn from their backs. The conditions had been so horrific, Zyah hadn't wanted to look too closely. Did that make her a coward? She pressed her fingers tighter against her throbbing temples, hating to think she might be. She was still being a coward, trying to save herself by not looking deeper into Player's mind. It wasn't just the terrible things done to him and the others she would find there. She didn't want to see what he and the others had done to anyone else.

She lifted her chin. If she really was going to help Player, she had to stop being a baby and just do everything necessary. If that meant discovering criminal activity — which she already knew had occurred, though she thought it was honestly warranted — then too bad, she'd have to live with it.

"Zyah." Maestro stuck his head in the bedroom. "Need you downstairs. The cops are here. They want to see you, your grandmother and Player." His eyes met hers, and her heart fluttered at the warning there. "Be cautious, and think before you speak."

"I don't know what that means." But she did. She knew he didn't want her talking about the kidnapping attempt. Player had been shot aiding her. He'd shot two men to keep her from being taken. He wore a bandana wrapped around his head, hiding the raw evidence of the wound.

Maestro's eyes went liquid silver. Intense. "Zyah."

The Torpedo Ink members had a way of just saying her name that was a reprimand. Or an invitation to join them in laughter. The latter was extremely rare and only happened with a couple of them. Maestro was one of them.

She rolled her eyes and got up, following him down to the formal living room. She passed Player on the stairs. He touched her hand but kept going, disappearing into the bedroom. She caught a glimpse of his face, even though it was averted. He looked tired. She could feel pain beating at his head again.

"He's overdoing it again," she hissed to Maestro. "When I'm not here, you have to sit on him. He's recovering, but seriously, he isn't sleeping, and his migraines are getting worse. Hasn't Steele explained that to you? He needs to rest, Maestro."

"Yeah, he explained that to us. Someone

forgot to explain it to Player," Maestro said.

Zyah knew Player was pushing himself so he could leave. He barely spoke to her during the day. It was only when they were together at night that he responded to her, and then she was afraid it was because he thought she might give in to suggestions of her remaining in bed with him. She knew he wanted to have sex. Sometimes she lay next to him to ensure his nightmare stayed away. They just held hands while he drifted off, both afraid of his nightmares.

Savage and Destroyer were in the hall, back in the shadows. Both made her aware of their presence but remained where they were. They were the other two members of Torpedo Ink, aside from Maestro, who occasionally and unexpectedly made her laugh. She waited with the three club members until Player returned. He had put on his Torpedo Ink vest. When he walked past her, he gripped her hand and tugged, taking her with him. Once in the living room, he nodded his head at the two men standing near the window and took the love seat.

Zyah had no choice but to take the empty space beside Player, as he refused to relinquish her hand. She sat straight, trying not to look at Player, feeling the pain crashing through his head beating at her. She was a little shocked that no one else in the room could feel it. He looked almost gray to her.

Still, his thumb slid over her knuckles, rubbing back and forth as if she were his lifeline. With his other hand he tapped a rhythm on his thigh, never a good sign with him.

Her grandmother sat in her wheelchair looking regal, a thick pink blanket covering her legs. She inclined her head toward the two men as if bestowing benevolent gifts upon them as she waved them to the chairs opposite them.

"Do sit down, Jonas. You're so tall I'm going to get a kink in my neck if I have to keep looking up at you," Anat said, her warm smile in place. "There's fresh tea and cookies."

Jonas Harrington was the local sheriff and lived in Sea Haven, so when a call came in, it wasn't unusual for him to answer in person. Beside him was Jackson Deveau, his deputy. He also resided in Sea Haven. He was married to the youngest Drake sister, and lived with her in the famous Drake home overlooking the sea. Jonas always looked pleasant and friendly. Jackson was just the opposite. Zyah hadn't ever seen him look friendly.

"You have a beautiful home, Ms. Gamal," Jonas said as he sank into the armchair. "I could use a little pick-me-up about now." He reached for the teapot as if he'd been pouring tea all his life. "Would you like some as well?"

Anat nodded. "Call me Anat, please, Mr. Harrington. And I take it with milk."

"Doesn't everyone?" He grinned at her. "Jonas, then. What about you, Player? Tea? And you, Ms. Gamal?"

"Zyah," she corrected, keeping her voice soft and open when she felt completely closed off.

She glanced at Player. Worried. He was the one feeling so closed off. He had shut down and gathered everything he was, burying himself deep. He was surrounding himself with barbed-wire fences and the intricate bombs he was building in his head, even the new one he was so intrigued with. He did that when he was uncomfortable or the migraine was too severe. She knew him so well. His hand was on his thigh, hers pressed deep to his muscle, almost as if he didn't realize he was holding her hand now. He tapped that rhythm he'd been tapping since his childhood while he built his mythical bombs, which weren't always so mythical, in order to take away the pain roaring through his head.

"I'd love a cup of tea, thank you." Zyah tried not to be distracted. Even as she smiled at the sheriff, she felt a little desperate inside.

Maestro and Savage were in the room, and the two members of law enforcement had nodded a greeting to both. Savage seemed to just fade into the background. She always had a hard time remembering whether he was in the room or not once a conversation got started. She had no idea where Destroyer had

280

gone. Maestro was always quiet, but he made his presence known, one hip resting on the sideboard, his gaze fixed on Jackson Deveau as if the deputy was a threat to them. Neither man seemed aware that Player was creating a situation where all of them could be in danger. They never seemed aware of it.

As Jonas poured the milk into the tea, Zyah shifted her body closer to Player until their thighs were pressed tight. Deliberately and very slowly, she ran the pads of her fingers down his arm, feeling every muscle along the way. His gaze jumped to her face.

She smiled at him. Fluttered her eyelashes. "When I got home from work today, you forgot to say hello to me." She kept her voice soft. Intimate. Between the two of them, as if they were the only ones in the room.

It was difficult to look at him and not remember what it was like to kiss him. To feel his body moving in hers. To want to run her hands over his shoulders and down his back. To belong to him. To have him belong to her. She wanted to trace every line in his face with her fingers and rub the frown away, kissing him until he couldn't do anything but kiss her back and remember how good it was between them. She pressed those feelings into his mind.

She had to save him from himself. She was not only desperate to stop him from building the images that would cause illusions and then turn those illusions into an alternate deadly reality, but she couldn't stand for him to be in such pain. What was causing this terrible fracture of his mind? It wasn't the brain injury. Steele had healed that. For a moment, just as the sheriff set her tea on the little table beside the love seat, she was afraid she might cry, right there in front of everyone. She *had* to figure out how to help him. Nothing was making sense.

"What the hell is making that ticking noise?" Maestro demanded, his gaze swinging suspiciously toward Player. "I hear it every once in a while, mostly in the middle of the night, a clock ticking so damn loud I can't think. I want to smash the damn thing. Tell me I'm not crazy and everyone else can hear it."

Zyah blinked rapidly, trying to rid herself of the shimmering sight of the large White Rabbit thumping his foot on the top of a table behind Maestro. The rabbit was dressed in a suit, and he pulled out a gold pocket watch, shaking his head and glaring at Player. She was fairly sure that rabbit was still an illusion in Player's mind, but in another minute, it would escape into the room with the others.

Her grandmother spoke softly to Maestro, reassuring him he hadn't suddenly gone insane; she heard the sound of the clock as well but she had no idea where the timepiece was. He was welcome to look for it. Jonas chimed in and said maybe a battery was low, and the clock went off now and then somewhere in the house.

In sheer desperation, Zyah put one hand around the nape of Player's neck and with the other turned his head so he had no choice but to look at her again.

"Baby," she whispered softly, using her most intimate voice, opening her mind to his, allowing her healing warmth to flow into him. "I said you forgot to say hello to me. I missed you while I was at work." She framed his face with both hands and brought her lips to his, just rubbing gently. Exchanging breath. Breathing herself into him.

It was supposed to be just a brief moment, to bring him back. To get rid of the White Rabbit and his pocket watch. To remove all the bombs from Player's head. Just one small opening between them, but she had already poured too much of herself into his mind, given him so many pieces of her soul, that the moment she opened that conduit between them and her lips brushed his, the sheer intimacy between them became so much more. Raw sexual need swept through her veins like a tidal wave poured from her mind into his. There was no way her brain and her lips weren't communicating her desire for him, no matter how hard she tried to tamp it down in front of the others. She'd wanted to save him, save them all, but there was no way

283

to touch his mind without giving him everything.

His hands came up, sliding up her arms to capture her face, tilting her head to the exact angle he wanted, and he simply took over the way he did. Their chemistry erupted and exploded beyond anything she could have imagined. They weren't in bed. They were in her grandmother's parlor, but it didn't matter. He swept her away, just as he had that first night. Just as he had the week before. It was the same, so hot, so unexpected, as if they'd melted together, her arms winding around his neck because she couldn't do anything else.

"Seriously, Player?" Maestro snapped and slid his hip off the sideboard in disgust.

Player was the one to lift his head, his hands sliding from where they cupped her face to her shoulders, pulling her closer, then threading his fingers through one of her hands to bring it to his hip. He angled his body slightly, toward the others in the room, as if he was far more aware of them than he had been.

Jonas swung his gaze from Maestro to Player as if really noticing him for the first time. Anyone knowing Jonas knew better. "How exactly did you get hurt, Player?"

Zyah leaned her head against Player's shoulder and answered for him. "In the garage. He jumped over the hood of my car . . ." She frowned, looking at Player. "Who knows what he was doing? It just happened very fast. It terrified me."

She tilted her face toward his, and Player obliged her, kissing her again. This time it was slow and gentle, the burn smoldering, spreading fire through her veins until she wanted to cry. Until she couldn't think straight and there was no holding herself safe from him. Once again, it was Player who broke the kiss, as if he sensed she was losing too much of herself in the exchange or that, like her, he was giving too much of himself away.

She couldn't speak a single word. Not one. There was no way to get her mind and mouth to coordinate, but Player didn't seem to have the same problem — but then he never did. He tucked her closer to him and she didn't have the strength to pull away.

"Why are you here, Jonas?" he asked, threading his fingers through Zyah's and bringing her hand to his chest, rubbing her knuckles back and forth almost absently over his heart, although she didn't think he did anything without a reason.

Zyah expected the worst was coming. The sheriff hadn't come there for tea. She wanted to reach out to her grandmother as well. They'd had another good week. Player had been good for her grandmother. Torpedo Ink had. They'd all come to visit, one by one, just as they said they would. Each of the club members had brought Anat a small gift and made her laugh.

Zyah was more than grateful. Anat might not be able to do physical therapy on her leg yet, but she still had work on her arm, and therapy on her arm was fun now, not so demanding and painful with Player there, according to her grandmother. He played his guitar and sang to her. He made the time go by faster.

Zyah was a little jealous that she had never heard him sing or play. She knew he was in the Torpedo Ink band, and he had a voice that could move over her skin like the touch of his fingers, but she thought if he sang, the notes would dance over and through her. She wanted to experience the sensation — and yet he never sang to her.

Jonas Harrington sighed. "Fisherman pulled a couple of bodies just off of Pudding Creek sixteen days ago. Both men had died from gunshot wounds. Both were head shots, although neither died immediately. The shooter was on the ground, most likely lying down when he or she took the shots."

Player frowned. He exchanged a look with Maestro and then Zyah. She had tightened her fingers around his until her knuckles were white. He raised her hand to his mouth and brushed kisses over her knuckles before turning her wrist so he could pull the tips of her fingers into the heated cavern of his mouth. His mouth was hot. So hot her fingers caught fire. The flames seemed to spread out of control, rushing up her arm to her shoulder and neck. Heat took her fast, color turning her neck and face a soft pink she couldn't control.

"What has that to do with any of us?" Anat asked.

"One of them had a ring on his finger, Anat," Jonas said, his voice very gentle. "It was among the items listed as taken in the robbery of your home. One of the men had broken ribs. His cheekbone was broken as if he'd been in a fight. His opponent had to have been a very experienced fighter. Nearly five weeks ago, there were reports of a disturbance in a neighborhood close to yours, a vehicle taking off, sideswiping a fence just two blocks down, hitting a parked car before disappearing."

Maestro frowned at him. "Surely you were able to get paint from the fence and the car that was hit."

Player's eyebrow shot up. "Two blocks down, Jonas? That's pretty thin."

"Was it my husband's ring?" Anat asked.

"I believe so," Jonas confirmed, ignoring Maestro and Player. "The autopsies revealed that both men were alive for at least a few days before they succumbed to the bullet wounds. We checked with hospitals, clinics, local doctors and nurses, and no one remembered treating either of the men. Regardless, they would have had to report gunshot wounds."

"I certainly didn't beat these men up or shoot them," Anat declared firmly. "Although had they come into my house again, I might have, especially if I'd known they had my husband's ring." She made a face at Zyah. "My granddaughter has forbidden me to have a gun."

"That's because you might shoot me when I come in late at night. You're just a little bit bloodthirsty, Mama Anat."

Maestro laughed. "She always says that, and I don't believe her. Zyah's more likely to shoot someone than you are, Anat. My money's on her, Jonas. Arrest Zyah."

"If he arrests Zyah, you'll be running the store all by yourself," Player pointed out. "Czar will be so pissed he'll have you not only running the place but stocking it too."

"Yeah, I didn't think that one through. Zyah might mouth off, but she really couldn't shoot anyone," Maestro hastily backtracked. "She's too sweet. Doesn't have a mean bone in her body."

Raw passion had brought Player full force back to the present, all faculties functioning, but it was knowing Zyah was terribly upset that kept him from allowing his mind to retreat from the terrible pounding in his

288

head. He couldn't stand having her feel as if she were stripped completely naked and left alone and unprotected — completely and utterly vulnerable. He might know she had seen things too terrible for anyone to know about him, things he might kill someone else for knowing, but he wasn't leaving her to face whatever was going on alone.

"Player, do you have anything to say?" Jonas prompted. He pulled out two photographs and, shielding Anat from seeing the grisly sight of the remains, he shoved them under Player's nose. "You ever see these men before? The photographs won't help, but the artist's sketches might bring back a memory."

Player forced himself to look. He gripped Zyah's hand to keep himself anchored in the present. His brain would take one look at dead bodies pulled from the sea and have a field day with that whacked-out, fucked-up shit. If Jonas was going for shock value, he was on the right track. The pictures were truly gruesome. The remains had been in the sea for a couple of weeks, enough time for fish to find them. Waves had smashed the bodies against rocks, the shore, rolling them in sand. Crabs and other small creatures had invaded. There wasn't much to tell from the actual photographs, but a sketch artist had drawn the faces from bone structure, and the drawings were clipped to the photographs.

Zyah closed her eyes and pressed into

Player's shoulder as if for comfort. He glared at Jonas. "Take those things away. Get them away from Zyah." He wrapped his arms around her, anger stirring in him. "I've never seen either man." He hadn't. Not their faces. He wouldn't recognize them if he saw them on the street. He'd know them as enemies, because they'd feel that way to him, but he wouldn't physically recognize them. "There was no need to shove them under her nose like that."

"But I have seen them," Zyah said. She kept one hand over her mouth, muffling her voice. "They came into the store a few weeks ago. Inez was still training me; she might remember. They had another man with them. They laughed a lot and bought tons of groceries as if they were staying for a long while. I asked if they were local or just vacationing. That's pretty standard for me. The man with the very angular face answered me."

Jonas took the photographs from Player and passed them to Maestro. "Were they local, Zyah?" he prompted.

"No. They said they were on business but . . ." She trailed off and looked up at Player as if he would be able to help her out.

Player cupped the side of her face with one hand, his thumb sliding over her cheek and the fine bones that gave her such a classic, beautiful look. "What is it, baby?"

"They laughed when they said it. I know

this will sound silly, but sometimes I get a feeling when people are talking and I just know things. They were talking about very unpleasant business, and I had a bad feeling it had something to do with me or someone I knew. Even, possibly, the store. I took a good look at their faces because I wanted to remember them."

There was a small silence. Player leaned over her to reach the cup of tea. "Drink this, Zyah. Is there honey in it, Jonas? She likes honey in her tea, and that will help with the shock."

"I'm not in shock. It's just that those pictures were awful."

Again, she pressed into him. Player could feel her vulnerability and knew she would detest that the others would see her that way. He glanced up at Maestro, who immediately took the teacup from Zyah's trembling hand and added two teaspoons of honey off the tray, keeping his body between Zyah and the two cops. He took his time stirring the tea until Player nodded, and then he handed back the cup.

"Ms. Gamal," Jonas said, addressing Zyah's grandmother. "Anat," he hastily corrected himself. "There are a traveling band of robbers who target smaller towns and retired people, particularly ones who are grouped together. They seem to have inside information on those living in the town. They rob

291

and beat up the occupants of several of the homes and leave quickly. When they go, a body is usually discovered a few days later, one suspected to be the local informer. That person is a member of the family or a trusted neighbor of one of those robbed. The point is, the band hits fast, robs quickly and is gone. They don't stick around. So, the question is, why are they staying here? They've hit four homes. They came back to your home twice, and perhaps a third time."

Anat shook her head. "What do you mean, four? I know of only three, counting me. Phillis and Benjamin and Gabe and Harmony both got robbed. Who else?"

"Last night Lauren and Sean Barbery were robbed. Fortunately, a neighbor heard Lauren screaming and called it in fast. Jackson was able to get there before too much damage was done. But it doesn't explain why these thieves haven't moved on. They've never stayed so long in one place. And they've never hit a home more than once. Have they come back to your house again, Anat? After the second time? What are they looking for?"

Player could feel anger rushing through Zyah. He put his hand gently over hers. "Are you implying that Anat somehow knows these people, Harrington? How could she possibly answer that? Is she psychic? Are you psychic, Anat?"

"No, I'm not, Player, but I suppose Jonas

thinks these people tried to rob me more than once."

"You know they did," Jonas said. "They came here when Inez and Frank were here. I think they came back a month ago and met up with Torpedo Ink. I can't prove it, but I think it happened and they got the worse end of the fight. If that's true and they still haven't left town, what is keeping them here? What do you have that they want?"

"Blame it on the bikers," Maestro groused. "We've got broad shoulders. We can take it. But you know what? I'm friends with Hannah, your wife, and she isn't going to like you harassing us. And she likes Blythe. They're cousins. Did you know that? Cousins. As in family. Which makes us family."

Player tucked Zyah's hand over his thigh and let Maestro take Jonas's attention away from the two of them. Especially away from his head. If the two cops insisted on looking at what was under the bandages, he could be in trouble. His brain might be healed, but the outside flesh still looked as if a bullet had fucked him up. And Deveau hadn't taken his eyes off him. That was the trouble with Jackson. He was too good at his job.

"If you're family, Maestro, you've got to be at least ten billion times removed," Jonas snapped. "I'm investigating a murder, so let me get on with it."

"How do you know it's a murder? It could

have been self-defense. Or suicide. Isn't that jumping to conclusions? What kind of sheriff jumps to conclusions? You might be family, but you still have to do a decent job if you want to be reelected," Maestro pointed out in his most pious voice.

Zyah laughed. Anat joined her. Player couldn't help smiling. Maestro had given him enough time to orient himself firmly in the present, to know what was going on and how best to do damage control. Zyah had done her best to protect him. She knew damn well he'd shot both those men — and that he'd been the one to kill them. She'd taken that fact fairly calmly, just like she'd taken everything else about him.

He couldn't help himself, he had to indulge. He had managed to be sitting right next to her, thigh to thigh, her body tucked under his shoulder, and he sure as hell wasn't going to waste the opportunity. He wrapped a length of her thick, dark hair around his hand and closed his fingers, making a fist around it. Pure silk. He fucking loved her hair. He loved lying in bed with her, all that long hair sliding over his chest because he deliberately refused to wear a shirt, knowing she'd lie with him at night after his nightmares and he'd feel the silk of her hair and the satin of her skin, see the sweep of her long lashes.

"Are you paying attention, Player?" Jonas demanded.

"Not really," Player admitted. "I was looking at my woman. She's fuckin' beautiful. You, on the other hand, don't do much for me." He held up one hand in surrender. "Please restate, and I'll pay attention."

"The sheriff seems to think I'm holding out on him," Anat explained. "I don't have any more jewelry to steal, Jonas. There's not one more valuable item here in this house. I do have a safe, but it's empty. I haven't ever used it. I bought it with the idea I'd keep cash in it, but I just never did. Maybe they know about that and think there's something of value in it. You can have it if you'd like. Make a show of taking it out. Pretend it's very heavy, as if I have gold bars in it and you're taking them to a bank for me."

Jonas glanced at Jackson Deveau, and Player caught the nearly imperceptible nod the deputy gave the sheriff. Torpedo Ink had long suspected Jackson was a human lie detector, and Player was certain he'd just had confirmation. Deveau had just assured Jonas that Anat was telling the truth.

"I'm just trying to make certain you're safe, Anat. I don't understand why they keep coming here. Is it possible you talked about something expensive you owned when you were at lunch with friends? Remember, these thieves have an in with someone who knows all of you. You belong to the Red Hat Society. All of you have fun together, and you talk.

Could you have brought up something of value you have in your home to them?" Jonas asked.

Player had to admit, that was a good question. He exchanged a quick look with Zyah. It was true the thieves had returned three times. They'd made a grab for Anat's granddaughter. The why of it was a good question. Anat didn't know they'd done that, but they had.

Anat shook her head. "Horus, my husband, wasn't a man to buy me jewelry, because I didn't ever wear it. He made things with his own two hands for me. He wrote me poetry. Those were the things I treasured. My granddaughter is my greatest treasure. The ankle bells that were my mother's. The ones that were my Amara's — my daughter. They didn't get those, because they weren't kept in the jewelry box. They were angry that I had so little in the way of jewels. I had cash, which I gave to them. It was in a drawer in the kitchen. But there was nothing to tell my friends."

Player could have told them Anat would never risk her granddaughter's life even if she did have jewels, although they hadn't told the police that someone had attempted to kidnap Zyah. They hadn't because Player had shot two men. Now those men were dead.

As if Jonas could read his mind, the sheriff brought the subject back to the two dead men. "The robbers only have to *believe* there's something of value here, Anat. They have someone in town working with them. Someone who knows all of your friends. Someone you talk to and who has been inside this house."

"Please don't scare my grandmother," Zyah objected. She shifted as if she might get up. Player put a restraining hand on her thigh, so she reached out to take her grandmother's hand instead. "You have no idea how difficult it's been for her to try to feel safe in her own home after what happened to her. Those men broke into our home and robbed her. They *beat* her."

To Player's horror, there was a little sob in her voice. He immediately wrapped his arm around her head and turned her face into his chest.

"I know you're trying to help them, Jonas, but neither of these women has a clue why these men wanted to target them in the first place. They have no idea if they're still being targeted."

"I'm not making this up, Player," Jonas said quietly. "These men came back a second time, and if I'm right about what happened a few weeks ago, they targeted this house a third time. That means this gang is way off their normal pattern. If that's the case, something very big is making them risk getting caught when they wouldn't ordinarily take chances."

That gave Player pause. Jonas was right. Code had already given Torpedo Ink the information that this particular gang of thieves would always grab and move on to the next small town. They targeted a small group of elderly and got out fast before law enforcement even knew they were around. They didn't hit the same house twice, let alone try to kidnap a member of the household. That was way off the norm. They'd already hit four homes. They had come to Anat's house on three occasions. They hadn't returned because Torpedo Ink was there.

"Their violence has been escalating. They've always been willing to kill. They get rid of their insider once they leave," Jonas continued. "But they've never deviated from their pattern of hitting four or five houses and leaving town fast. That's how they never get caught."

"Maybe it isn't the same gang," Player ventured. He could feel Zyah tensing. She had spent so much time — too much time — healing his fractured mind that it was impossible for her to hide much from him. As far as Zyah knew, they had nothing of worth in their home that robbers would want.

Anat leaned so far forward in her wheelchair that Player actually put out a hand as if he could catch her if she fell. Maestro and Jackson did the same. She ignored them all, looking directly into the sheriff's eyes.

"I would never, *ever,* under any circumstances, risk my granddaughter's life. There is nothing in this world that I wouldn't give to a kidnapper, robber or killer to get her back. She is my entire world. She is my everything. I have nothing that I can think of that these people want. Whoever this insider is, this informant is, they know more about my household than I do."

Player felt his gut clench but kept the expressionless mask on his face in the ensuing silence. Jonas Harrington and Jackson Deveau would never miss a mistake like the one Anat had just made. The older woman sat back in her wheelchair, having made her point.

Anat sipped at her tea, looking regal. As far as Player was concerned, she was magnificent. He didn't remember having a grandmother. Or really, even, a mother. The weeks spent with Anat Gamal had been one of the best experiences of his life. She was intelligent, had a tremendous sense of humor and told him countless stories of places and occurrences in her past that were fascinating to him. She was a wealth of knowledge, and he did his best to learn from her.

When her friends came to visit, he tried to make himself scarce, but she never tried to hide his presence. She wasn't embarrassed to have a biker and his friends around. He just plain liked her, even though she'd just made a huge mistake and most likely, although inadvertently, thrown him under the bus.

"Kidnapper?" Jonas echoed, sitting up straight. He exchanged a brief look with his deputy. "Did someone attempt to kidnap your granddaughter? Is that what happened here a few weeks ago?"

Anat frowned. "What are you talking about? Nothing happened a few weeks ago. I was just reassuring you, I would *never* value anything more than I would my grand-daughter. There isn't anything in this house. There isn't, Jonas. I know you're worried. Player's worried. So is Zyah." She looked at Maestro and then into the shadows. "All of you are. I would tell you if I had anything worth them coming back for, but I don't." A little shiver went through her. "They scare me. I don't want them coming back."

"You don't have to be afraid, Anat," Destroyer's voice came out of the shadows. "We're here, and the sheriff has been doing extra patrols. No one is going to hurt you again."

# TEN

"I don't understand you, Player." Anat gave an exaggerated sigh. "You and my granddaughter seemed very close, kissing on the couch in front of the police, and now you barely speak to each other. I thought you'd worked everything out at last. You say you have to leave and yet you still seem to have such vicious headaches. I know this isn't the best thing for you. Did you have a fight? An argument? Couples get angry with each other. It's called passion. You have passion between you — anyone can see this."

"She kissed me in order to stop Jonas from asking questions, that was all." It was an honest answer, whether Player wanted it to be or not.

Anat had gotten so much stronger just in the weeks he'd been there. Her arm was definitely better, as were her spirits. Even her broken leg was better, according to the doctor, and would soon be ready again to try physical therapy. There was brightness back in her eyes and she smiled often. He hated to leave too, but it wasn't safe being around Zyah anymore. And it was extremely difficult to be in the same room and know he could never have her. He wanted her permanently, not for a quick fuck — and he couldn't even have that. His body was getting to the point he was afraid he might shatter.

Anat was silent for a moment and then she shook her head. "I promised myself I wouldn't interfere, but I'm old, Player, and I don't have time to wait around until the two of you figure it out. Zyah came home in tears some weeks ago, devastated by the behavior of a man she had been with. You, clearly, are that man."

Player took a breath. That hit him hard. Zyah crying. Devastated. He'd done that to her. Anat, a woman he respected and admired, knowing. That struck him deep. He pressed his palm hard over his heart. "That was me." He was responsible. "I'd been several days without sleep and for some reason when I don't sleep, I get confused. I always have. I can't think straight. Things get mixed up in my head, so reality and dreams mix together. I didn't think she was real. That isn't a good excuse. I went looking for her immediately and tried to apologize, but it was too late. I really hurt her, and then this happened." He touched the wrap on his head.

"What exactly did happen? I know what

Zyah told me happened that night, but clearly, there is much more to the story. I thought about it after Jonas left the other night. He was so certain you had something to do with those men the fishermen had pulled out of the sea. Did someone try to kidnap my granddaughter?" She asked the question directly, her eyes looking so much like Zyah's, boring straight into his.

He wanted to dismiss her. Walk away. But this was Zyah's grandmother. This was Anat Gamal, and he respected her too much to lie.

"Yes. They were waiting in the garage for her and they attacked her. I managed to get in under the door before it closed, but they came at me with a baseball bat and then a gun. I did roll over the hood of her car. Things happened very fast. Seconds. No more than two minutes. They ran. I never saw their faces, but there was a woman with them and she was yelling, wanting them to hurt Zyah. I felt she knew Zyah and that it was personal for her." He was hoping to distract Anat's attention from the two dead men Jonas had brought up.

"You and Zyah thought it best not to call the police?" There was no judgment. With Anat, he never found there was.

"Yes, I'm sorry, Anat. Torpedo Ink and the police don't always see eye to eye. We get blamed for a lot of things. We were escorting Zyah home. She works for us and it was late.

303

Czar heard about the robbery and what happened to you, so he told us that Zyah was to have someone escort her home every night that she worked late. Normally, there would have been two of us, but Maestro had returned to the club to pick up a couple of things before he caught up with us. That was why he was late getting here and arrived just when we came into your house."

"What really happened to your head?"

He took a deep breath. "I was shot."

Anat was silent for a moment, digesting the information. She shook her head. "I can't imagine what these people think I have. They took what little jewelry I kept. I live very simply. Zyah bought the house for me. She loved the views and thought it would be nice for both of us when she came home. She always talked of coming to live with me, although I didn't think she'd really come."

Player thought Anat sounded tired, and that alarmed him. It was still early, too early for Zyah to come home. He'd spent the day with Anat because, since he'd been there, no one had been scheduled to stay with her. He wasn't about to leave until her granddaughter was home and they both were safe, locked inside.

He knew the sheriff sent extra patrols, which didn't say much. They were stretched thin. Sea Haven didn't have a police department. They were under the sheriff's jurisdiction. It was only because both Jonas and Jackson lived in Sea Haven that the sheriff was around as much as he was. There were simply too many miles in the county to cover and not enough manpower. Torpedo Ink picked up the slack with Anat Gamal's home. They had someone watching it at all times.

As if she were reading his mind, Anat made a guess. "Torpedo Ink is watching over us, aren't they? Not just here in the house but outside as well."

"Yes, ma'am, they are. They'll continue to do so even after I'm gone, but you shouldn't tell anyone, including your friends, not even Inez."

She was silent a moment studying his face as if trying to read his reasons. "Your people are good people, Player," she said. "Very good people. Why are you leaving when you should be trying to make my stubborn granddaughter see that she is making a big mistake by not forgiving you?"

"She's forgiven me." He didn't want Anat to think Zyah was at fault. She wasn't. Not in any way.

Player detested these kinds of conversations. He was too restless to stay still in spite of the fact that when he moved around too much, it brought on a migraine. He had to admit, his head was much better — good enough for him to get on his bike and ride the hell away from temptation. He didn't have illusions when he was awake. Or nightmares.

"She's too damn good for a man like me." He told the truth. Straight up. What was the point of trying to beat around the bush? Anat had some kind of built-in radar for bullshit anyway. "She's a good woman."

Anat shook her head. "Hearing you talk this way makes me sad for you, Player. I thought you were more of a man than that. What you're saying to me is nothing but an excuse. An old one. Anyone can make such an excuse. Everyone has a past. Something bad that happened to shape who we are. Some more than others."

"You have no idea."

She waved her hand in the air dismissively. "In the end, it doesn't matter. It really doesn't because it is in the past. We can only choose to go forward. We can't change what's behind us. What was done to us by others, by our parents, by anyone. Even what we did. It is done. We have to live with it. Our responsibility is to move forward and do the best we can, be the best we can."

"Nothing is that simple."

"Of course it isn't, and yet it really is, Player. Life is very short. You have the choice to decide whether or not you're going to blame your past for refusing to take chances. You have to push yourself to become different, to change with the years and grow and

306

learn. No one says it's easy, but it's what people do. That's what we all do. At least most of us. We try. We work at it. We're never perfect and we make mistakes, but they're *our* mistakes and we own those mistakes, and then we have to let them go so we can move on and grow more. That's just life."

Player forced a smile even as he shook his head. "People have these maps their parents gave them. Or grandparents. Or someone. I don't have anything like that. I don't know the first thing about a relationship. Not one damn thing, Anat. That would be letting her in for a lifetime of hurt."

Anat sighed again. "Perhaps, Player, but then my Zyah knows quite a bit about relationships. She knows what love is, even if you don't. She is open to learning all the time. You've closed yourself off. Where you could have learned from her, you have shut yourself off from happiness. She should back away from the relationship, Player, and I was wrong to push to save it. I see something in you, just as she did. That matters little when you don't see it in yourself. Using your past as an excuse to stand still is still an excuse to be a coward, Player. I never would have believed that of you. No one can change your life but you. No one can save you but you."

Had anyone else called him a coward, Player might have resorted to violence, but he just stood there in shock, wincing at her condemnation. Absorbing every word.

The door between the garage and the kitchen opened and closed. "Mama Anat? I'm home, safe and sound. Savage and Destroyer escorted me home and scared everyone off just by looking at them." There was genuine amusement in Zyah's voice.

The sound of her laughter always opened up something soft and unexpected in Player he hadn't realized was in him. He'd thought every part of him was hard, completely closed off to anything human, but somehow Zyah had found a way into that one little piece that was still vulnerable.

"We're in here, Zyah. In the bedroom," Anat called, joy in her voice. "Perhaps you're right, Player. My Zyah deserves a man willing to fight for her. If you don't think she's worth fighting for, then you certainly are not that man."

Player opened his mouth to protest. Anat was deliberately misunderstanding him. Zyah was worth fighting for. He had never, not once, implied she wasn't. Zyah rushed into the room, graceful, her dancer's body flowing with energy, dark eyes bright, her hair thick and shiny even in the dimmer lights Anat had by the bedside.

"Did you have a good day, Mama Anat? It was so beautiful outside, I hope you were able to go out. Player, did you take her outside on the back patio?"

It was one of the few times Zyah addressed him directly unless they were sitting in bed with the lights off. The moment she did speak, the moment she looked at him, her eyes meeting his, he tasted her in his mouth. That perfect blend of subtle jasmine and a rich green floral mimosa. His tongue would forever know that very distinctive cinnamic-honey flavor edged with a cassis-raspberry facet. He wouldn't have even known what those flavors were had it not been for Alena's cooking abilities. She had schooled them all in various spices.

"We spent a couple of hours in the sun, although I made certain we were careful. She wanted to lie out in her bathing suit," Player said. "I told her it was too soon for that. And there was this man coming around, a Dwayne River. He showed up with an armload of flowers and suddenly she was all about suntanning in her altogether."

"Player!" Two spots of color appeared on Anat's cheeks. "I did not. I just said I didn't like tan lines. I wanted to put on a bathing suit. And only for an hour. We were out there longer, but I didn't stay in my suit the entire time."

"Mama Anat! You *did* go in your altogether." Zyah deliberately misunderstood, her eyes wide with laughter. "A few flowers from that man and you're back to being a cat woman. I told you sunbathing in the nude

309

was out for a while."

Anat made her trilling sound, the one Zyah loved from her childhood.

"Wait," Savage said, crowding into the bedroom behind her. He stuck his head in the room, keeping his body behind the door frame. "You really went out sunbathing in the nude because of some man named Dwayne River? Has Code looked into him? We need to have him investigated. He could be a total con man. Or a serial killer. Anat, you're too trusting. Beautiful women are always too trusting. Look at your granddaughter."

"That's true," Maestro agreed. "Zyah's way too trusting."

Anat laughed. "All of you are awful. Leave poor Dwayne alone. He's very nice. He visited me for a little while, but not while I was sunbathing. He makes me laugh. Not nearly the way all of you do. Serial killer?" She rolled her eyes.

"You never know," Savage said. "The nicest-looking men usually are the ones that fool you. The ones with bald heads and scars usually are good ones. They come around, and you should just feed them, Anat."

Zyah watched her grandmother's face light up again as she continued laughing. She really loved hearing that laugh. These men. Torpedo Ink. They charmed her. They should be the last ones to be charming, but they were. Both women could see past the dark, swirling violence surrounding them. Sometimes, as in Savage's case, it was so dark it was nearly impenetrable, but then suddenly, like now, there would be that small little path that led straight to his soul and they both could see the beauty of the man. It ran deep. No one else could see it. He couldn't see it. But they could. Zyah had come to care for the men. Anat had as well.

She looked up at Player's face, and her entire body stilled. Every cell in her body responded to him. His blue eyes were fixed on her. Piercing. Speculative. He was looking at her in a way he hadn't for the last few weeks. It was both exhilarating and frightening.

She forced her attention back to her grandmother and Savage. She couldn't let herself think about Player. Even if he changed his mind. What would be the point? He wanted sex. Off-the-charts sex, but that never lasted long, and she wanted to be loved. And he needed her. That wasn't the same thing as loving her. She knew what real love was. Player didn't.

"Did you really sunbathe, Anat? That might have been too long for you, all joking aside," Savage said. "I don't like the idea of you getting a sunburn or hurting your leg."

He sounded protective. That was one trait the members of Torpedo Ink — including

311

Player — seemed to have in common. Zyah liked them for that as well.

"I did sunbathe for an hour. The sun is very healing. Player made certain I didn't jar my leg. He's very strong."

Savage made a perfect replica of Anat's trilling sound. Perfect. It didn't sound like a mocking mimic. It sounded as if he had been born and bred in her village. "Don't tell him he's strong. He already thinks he's good-looking."

Anat sent Player her lovely grandmother smile. "He *is* good-looking."

Maestro groaned. "Now you've gone and done it. We won't hear the end of it."

Savage ignored the byplay. "I think it was smart to sunbathe. Anything to get that healing going. Did Player take off the bandage around his head? Maybe he'll get his brains back. Got any fresh cookies?" Savage added, getting to his main agenda.

"Since I was the one making the cookies," Player said, "no, there aren't any. At least for you. Stick around for a little while. I'm heading out for a ride."

He'd told Anat he was leaving. Now he wasn't so certain. With Zyah's scent surrounding him, with her taste in his mouth and breathing her into his lungs, it wasn't so easy to just walk away from her. He didn't dare look at the older woman. She would know she'd gotten to him with her reprimand

— and she had. He'd never quite looked at things the way she'd laid them out to him. He had a lot to think about, and he thought better on his bike.

Zyah whirled around to face him. She all but planted her body directly in front of his. "What do you mean you're going out for a ride?"

He shrugged casually, pressing his fingers deep into his thigh to keep from tucking stray strands of her dark, flyaway hair behind her ear. "I haven't been out for a while, and I need to ride. I get restless. I'll just be gone a short while."

"Steele said you shouldn't try it yet, Player. I heard you ask him last night." She lifted her chin at him, daring him to call her out for eavesdropping.

In the last few days, he'd offered to exchange rooms dozens of times, but she said it was too much trouble. Hell, he wanted — even needed — to get out of her bedroom; she was everywhere inside those walls. It was silly, really, to want to exchange rooms, since she came into the bedroom every night. She had to when he had nightmares, when the illusions started and then reality blended with illusion and he was building bombs he'd never seen before. It was just that things in that room that were sacred to her bothered him. Really bothered him.

He'd spent a great deal of time after he'd

313

taken Anat out in the sun, over two hours, just sitting on the bed, staring at the picture her grandfather had drawn for her grand-mother. It was truly a work of art. There was no question about it. The man had painstak-ingly drawn out every line, and it must have taken him months to complete the work.

Every time Player looked at the master-piece, it gave him a headache. The worst part about it was that he felt compelled to look. Zyah talked about it all the time. There was love in her voice when she did. She spoke about the love between Anat and her hus-band, Horus. There was the signature falcon rising from the drawing, and Zyah had explained that Horus meant "falcon" and that the bird was often drawn into his things.

Maybe it was because Zyah had such a his-tory of family that Player disliked the charcoal image so much. His own father had allowed Sorbacov to murder his mother right in front of him and sold his son to be used by pedo-philes and trained as an assassin.

Yeah, Player detested that charcoal draw-ing. He looked at it and saw something else. It actually hurt his eyes and made his head pound and feel like it was coming apart worse than ever. At times, he would rearrange those lines, the wings and whorls, making them into other, much more lethal things, because his mind was really fucked up like that. Worse, there was her father's beloved frame.

Player loved his Harley. He loved music. And he loved wood. He had an affinity for it. When he touched the surface of any type of wood, alive or not, he felt the roots going all the way to the earth, deep, connecting him. He could almost hear whispers of the past in the wood. He liked the stories the various types of wood told him. Touching the frame around the picture Zyah's grandfather had drawn, he'd expected to feel love along with the stories from the tree's native land. He didn't feel love at all in that frame, other than the places Zyah had touched. The frame felt sinister and threatening. Even more than the drawing, he found the frame disturbing, but he had no idea why.

"Player." Zyah's voice cut through his thoughts. "Steele said you shouldn't ride yet." She was insistent. "Your migraines are too severe and they come on too fast."

"Steele said it wasn't a good idea for me to ride, but he didn't say not to," he corrected as gently as possible.

She was upset, and that was the last thing he expected or wanted. He'd planned on leaving, but now he wanted the time to think. If she was this upset just at the thought of him riding his motorcycle, she was bound to really be upset if he left her house altogether. At least he hoped she would be.

"He said if a migraine came on, you could have balance issues." Her hands went to her hips. Her lips pressed together ominously.

The problem with her belligerent stance was, he found it sexy. Her voice was too smoky, far too sinful and sexy for her to sound as if she was lecturing him. Player also had a very vivid image in his head of those lips wrapped around his cock, which sent that part of his anatomy into a frenzy of activity. Shit. That wasn't good. Not with them being in her grandmother's room. He lifted a hand to Anat and slid back into the shadows, inching toward the door.

"A short ride, Zyah. I just need to clear my head a little." He began moving again, edging around her, trying to make certain there was no body contact. If he made it to the open road, he could decide if he was going to leave for good or not.

"Wait a minute. Destroyer, can you stay with my grandmother, make certain she's safe? I'm going with you, Player."

Player's heart stuttered. He put his hand over his chest and pressed hard. "Baby, you can't do that. You just got home from work and you're tired." He forced his voice to be gentle, to not dictate. She couldn't ride with him on the motorcycle. It was far too dangerous for either of them, and not in the way she was thinking. She'd resisted every time he'd tried to get her back in the bed with him, and he knew she was trying hard to save herself. He was trying just as hard to save her.

"No, Player." She glanced back at her grandmother, placed a hand on his chest and put pressure on him, so either he had to move backward or she would walk right into his arms.

Player had no problem with taking her into his arms, but not there. Not with her grandmother looking on, or Maestro or Savage, for that matter. What was between them was private and intimate in a way he didn't want anyone else to see. Their connection didn't just strip him naked and make him completely vulnerable, it did the same to Zyah as well. He wasn't allowing that, not even in front of his brothers. He let her walk him backward out of the room.

"What are you doing?" she demanded.

Her tone was low. Musical. It vibrated through his body, sending little electrical charges right through his veins straight to his groin. Her hand was still on his chest, and he doubted she was even aware of it, but he was. The heat of it seared him through the material of the tee he was wearing. Her head was thrown back, and more of that thick hair of hers had come loose, so untamable, just like she was.

"I need to breathe," he answered honestly. "My head is coming apart, and being so fuckin' close to you, breathing you in night

317

and day, is turning me inside out." He caught her hand and slid it down his body to the front of his jeans. "I've got to just take a breather, babe. Ride along the highway."

She should have pulled her hand away, but she didn't. She just looked straight into his eyes while her palm curled over his heavy erection. While she pressed harder and rubbed a caress over him.

"Don't you think it's doing the same thing to me? I'm breathing you in too." There was an ache in her voice. "Neither one of us knows why you're continuing to get migraines, Player, but you can't take chances. I don't know why you keep going back to building that bomb, but the last time, that bomb was too real. I saw it. It wasn't filled with some kind of soda, Player. It was real."

He had to think. Clear his head. He had to make choices, and one of them was to talk to Czar. He had to let him know the truth about his illusions and what happened when things went wrong. How they were going wrong now. Worse, he had to tell Czar about the things Zyah knew about him. About the club. About his brothers and sisters. He wanted to pound his fists into the wall until they bled. He wanted to pound his cock into Zyah's body until he stopped hurting so damned bad and he could think with a clear mind.

"You think I don't know that? How dangerous I am to you? To your grandmother? To my club? My head is so damn fucked up and I can't stop what's happening to me."

"*I* can," Zyah hissed, for the first time sounding angry. Not loud. Not belligerent. Her voice was still musical, but it took on the tones of an older instrument, a crumhorn. "Not Steele, none of your brothers or sisters. Not a doctor. They can't heal you or stop what's happening. I can do that. I've been doing it. You're almost there, and you're not going to mess it up."

She pulled her hand out from under his, away from his pulsing cock, and turned away from him, but not before he caught the glitter of liquid in her eyes. His heart stuttered.

"Zyah. I swear to you, I know my limitations. I wasn't going on some suicide run." Even to himself, his voice didn't sound sure, because he hadn't been so certain. He was a danger to her. To her grandmother, to everyone he cared about. He was the most fucked-up human being on the planet.

He'd learned to build bombs, several different types, but none like the one he'd been building over and over. He was getting good at putting that unknown bomb together. Fast too. He knew the parts now. The order. He was getting faster and faster while the shadowy figure timed him with that pocket watch.

She swung around to face him, and he shoved both hands through his hair and winced when he inadvertently touched the

319

long, deep, carved-out groove in his skull. "Damn it, Zyah, I don't know, I just have to think. I can do that on my bike."

"Fine. Then I'm going with you."

He took an aggressive step toward her, hooked her around the nape of her neck and used his thumb to press into her jaw, forcing her face upward. "We get on that machine together, and when we get off, I swear I'm going to fuck your brains out and you're going to let me."

"Fine, then. Let's do it. It's just sex. I can do just sex." She shoved at the wall of his chest without rocking him, turned and flounced up the stairs.

It was breathtaking, watching her walk away from him. The way her jeans clung to her hips and hugged her bottom. He was a damn fool to even consider putting her ass on the back of his bike. He'd made up his mind that he wasn't going to have anything to do with her, not after their last insanity in her bed, but he *had* to have her. And it was *never* just sex.

He'd been the one to push her away, over and over. She had tried to connect with him, but he'd been ashamed for her to see his past. He didn't want her to know about the many kills he'd made. She'd been so far into his mind, he was certain he hadn't managed to protect her from those things anyway. She'd been the one accepting and forgiving. Nonjudgmental. He'd been the one pushing her away, over and over.

He turned away from the stairs and picked up his jacket from the sideboard, shrugging into it. Anat had made some damn good points. Really damn good points. What was the standard he was judging himself by? His talent? It wasn't a talent, it was a fuckin' curse. Everyone else in his club had a psychic talent that contributed in a big way to their survival. He didn't. A couple of times, his talent had pulled them out of the fire, but then he'd nearly killed them all.

Building illusions and using them had been a disaster until he'd learned how to control that power. He'd kept quiet at first, afraid he was going insane, figuring he was useless when they had been children fighting for survival. He still felt that way. He glanced toward the stairs. Most people, if they did have psychic talents as Czar believed, never developed them. They still went after what they wanted. They still fought for happiness. He had one chance, and that one chance was that woman up those stairs.

Was he using his past as an excuse because he was afraid of failing with Zyah? Afraid of letting her down? Or was he afraid of failing himself? Being the one in the club who couldn't cut it yet again? Was Anat right? He had to take a good, hard look at himself. He never ducked a tough assignment. Never. He pulled his weight when it came to any kind of dangerous assignment. Hell no, he wasn't a coward.

Damn it all. Maybe when it came to personal shit he was. He never talked about his cursed gift to the others. Not even to Czar. He'd never admitted to them that illusion turned to ugly reality, and reality could kill. He was always afraid of being rejected by the others. Was that what he was doing to Zyah? Rejecting her before she could refuse him?

What was he doing standing there in the Gamal household with his colors inked on his skin, feeling them all the way to his bones, when he hadn't gone to Czar and told him the truth? Laid it right out in front of him. All of it. The White Rabbit with that pocket watch who persisted in turning into Sorbacov with his fucking gold watch. The ticking time bomb that was so real even Maestro and Anat heard it. They *heard* it. If Zyah hadn't stopped it by kissing him, connecting them so deeply, that bomb could have gone off.

He cursed under his breath in his native language. Anat was right. He was a fucking coward. Now not only could he lose his standing with the only family he'd ever known, but he could lose Zyah. Really lose her, as in she could be dead. He couldn't take that. He wouldn't be responsible for that. He needed time to think things through. He had to make certain she was safe, but also that

322

his family was safe. The ocean air would help. The open road and his bike would clear his mind. They had to. He couldn't make mistakes, not when lives were at stake.

Player felt Zyah's presence before she even appeared on the staircase. He turned slowly to look up to watch her descend. It was almost a compulsion. A need just to be in the room with her. To breathe her in, to see her like this, doing mundane, simple, everyday things. She flowed in silence down the stairs like the dancer she was, so gorgeous she took his breath away. Her beauty wasn't just skin deep.

He didn't think she was perfect for him because he found her curvy body sinful beyond temptation, a playground he could spend hours teasing and playing with, or even because she had a gift that could counter the mess of his own talent. She was unique. A soft-spoken woman unafraid of hard work, capable of unconditional love and loyal to a fault. She was worth fighting for, and he'd be a damn fool to let her slip away because he was afraid of failure.

She didn't smile at him when he reached out and pulled her close, standing her in front of him to inspect her gear. She wore a thick jacket and good gloves. She'd managed to tame her hair enough to twist it into a long, loose braid that was never going to hold with that thick mass, but with a helmet over it, she'd do fine. *Bog,* but she was drop-dead gorgeous.

A little half smile played around her full lips. She shook her head. "I am not. There're all kinds of things wrong with me."

"Did I say that out loud?" He probably had. Half the time he didn't know what the fuck he was doing around her. He caught the front of her jacket and tugged until she took a step closer to him. "You absolutely are. Believe me, I know what I'm talking about." He said that with all sincerity. "Are you dressed in layers under the jacket? It's going to be cold out there this time of night."

Her dark chocolate gaze slid over him, hot enough to melt a glacier. She was going to give him a heart attack for sure. He pressed the heel of his hand to his temple. It was hurting like a mother again. Pounding. When was it ever going to stop for good?

The only time his headache let up anymore was when Zyah was talking softly to him, usually in the middle of the night when he couldn't sleep because his damn head was going to explode and the ticking of the bomb was so loud the entire household could hear it. She would come and lie down on the bed beside him, take his hand and just talk to him.

"Stop thinking about it. You'll make it happen. I can already feel the illusion building. We're going for a ride on your motorcycle, and if you can't handle that, we'll walk outside for a while in the open air," Zyah declared.

"I'm sorry I'm putting you in such a bad position," he said, meaning it. Not meaning it. Rethinking his decision to leave. To give her up. He wasn't a coward. Her grandmother had given him a lot to think about. "I know every time you have to find the scattered pieces of my brain and glue them back together, it connects us more." He felt every single one of those ties binding them closer and closer.

Pulling on his gloves, he led the way outside and took his first real lungful of fresh night ocean air. He loved the sea. Living by it. The way it thundered at times, the waves racing toward the cliffs, spraying white water high into the air in sheer defiance of holding back. Water couldn't be held back. You could try, but it would always find a way to escape. He wanted that. Just to go out peacefully. Smoothly. A rhythm, because he loved that beat, but he'd just drift like that tide out there.

"Stop, Player. What is wrong with you tonight?" Zyah all but stomped her foot. "What happened tonight before I got home to put you in such a melancholy mood?" She caught at his arm and tugged at him until he stopped walking, pulling his gaze away from the ocean and back to her perfect, furious face. Her beauty caught at him every time.

325

"It's my head, Zyah, it just keeps coming apart no matter how many times you put it back together. I have this weird affiliation with *Alice's Adventures in Wonderland,* and I can accept that. I was reading that story when I was a little kid. We were starving. Freezing. I was fucked up. I'm not going to lie, you've seen enough of my memories to know what happened to me."

He shoved his hands in his jacket pockets and turned away from her, looking out to sea at the angry waves. Now he wanted to feel each of those waves pounding the bluffs, hammering at them the way he wanted to slam his fists into his enemies.

From her front yard, Anat's Victorian house faced several other homes, but her backyard had only a street between it and a very long strip of headlands. She had a gorgeous view. That piece of real estate was worth a fortune, which made it look as if she were very wealthy and probably brought her to the attention of the gang of thieves still looking to get something valuable they thought she had.

Zyah stepped close to him, so close he could feel her body heat and smell that fragrance that was unique to her alone. Her fingers slipped into the crook of his arm. She remained silent, allowing him to marshal his thoughts. He liked that about her. Their first night together, when they both had been so free with each other, talking and laughing as if they didn't have a care in the world, she had done that as well, waiting for him to speak, listening attentively.

"Player, tell me about that first time with *Alice's Adventures in Wonderland*. I know you detest those characters coming to life. You did when the other children loved it so much, yet you created it for them. I watched your face. I know you hated it. Tell me why."

They stood together in the dark, the roar of the sea traveling across the waving expanse of grass while he debated whether he was going to tell her the truth. She knew so much about him already, none of it good.

He shook his head. "I hate this, Zyah. I want so much for you to find something to like about me. The more you know, the more you'll loathe."

"That isn't true. You're in my head as much as I'm in yours, Player. You know I don't loathe you, or even dislike you. If anything, I have to struggle all the time to try to distance myself from you because you're the one holding back. You don't want me, Player, and I don't want to throw myself at you, but it's damned hard when I'm so connected."

She was so fucking honest with him. It was hard not to admire her. She was so much like her grandmother, and that was all good. And she came right out and called him on holding back.

"Don't think for one moment I don't want

you, Zyah." He knew by just looking at her she took his statement wrong — she thought he meant physically, but he was determined to tell her what she needed to hear. He also wasn't certain what he was going to do about their relationship, so he didn't try to explain to her what he really meant.

"Sorbacov was a man who never wanted to be the president. He liked being the power behind the throne. He enjoyed secrets and fear. He had so many secrets of his own. He had a perfect family. His wife and son. He didn't like women. He much preferred young boys. Very young boys. He also got off on torture and watching rape. He was highly intelligent, so he rose fast in politics, chose the perfect wife and a candidate to back and then became a very powerful man. He was smart enough to bide his time and keep his deviant proclivities under wraps until he could let them loose, and even then, he was extremely careful to make certain no one would live to tell."

Zyah started walking down the road, tugging on his arm, moving him around the bike. His head pounded like the waves battering at the bluffs. The road tilted a little toward the sea. The surf rose up, wild and calling to him. She didn't rush him to get to the part about *Alice's Adventures in Wonderland.* She just let him talk. Start where he needed to. He appreciated that in her.

"Sorbacov established four schools to train assets, meaning orphans, children of the murdered political opponents. In some cases, as in mine, Sorbacov saw me and liked the way I looked and wanted me for himself. My father was in his army and had his own depravities. I didn't find that out until much later. He sold me to Sorbacov. Sorbacov took me to the school. I was four."

Her arm tightened around his waist. "Player."

She said his name so softly, so intimately, he felt her in his mind, stroking him there. She made him feel as if he wasn't so alone, the way he'd felt he'd been for so damn long.

"They say you really can't remember anything that clearly at four, but I remember every detail. All of it. What we were all wearing. The weather. That watch of Sorbacov's. He took it out and looked at it when they were beating my mother as if it was boring him. Her screams. The blood. He was annoyed when some of her blood splattered on his shoes."

He tried to push the demons back, the ones escaping from the doors he kept closed and nailed shut in his mind. "I showed a unique ability for making bombs. It was insane, and no one could explain it. I tinkered with tools and could take apart and put things back together, and Sorbacov noticed. He brought in several instructors, and they would lay out

329

simple bombs at first, little ones, and he would stand behind me while I put them together. I didn't know what they were. It was fun. A puzzle."

He stopped walking and faced her, looking down at her, pleading for understanding. "We were raped every day, repeatedly. Beaten. Not just with fists. Forced to perform all kinds of acts. To sit at a bench and put together a puzzle was a respite; it took my brain somewhere else, away from pain, away from something so horrific I could barely keep from going insane."

Player had no idea why he expected Zyah's dark eyes to hold censure, but he did. He felt guilty enough for both of them. He always would. Instead, those dark chocolate eyes of hers, so beautiful, held compassion for a little boy; not just the little boy but the fucked-up man as well. He didn't deserve it, and she'd understand why in just a few more moments.

"Sorbacov was in a particularly sharing mood over the course of a week, and I was in a bad way. His friends weren't gentle, so much so that he even made them stop a couple of times and I found myself feeling grateful to him." He hated himself for that.

He stared at the crashing waves as they broke over the rocks just before they made it to the bluffs. He'd not had his fifth birthday, and he loathed himself for being grateful to Sorbacov, the man who'd had his mother beaten to death and who'd raped him and given him to his friends to rape, just because the man had told his friends to be more careful of him.

Player turned his face away from her, afraid that terrible burning sensation behind his eyes was something he would regret forever. "I was told to build a series of bombs over the next couple of weeks, and I was so happy. I could barely walk. Everything hurt, and I knew as long as I pleased him, built each one faster than the last, he wouldn't give me to his friends, even if he used me himself, which he did, every time I finished one of the bombs."

He swallowed down bile. "I made five bombs. He told me for my birthday, he was taking Czar and me to a party. It was a big deal. There was going to be all kinds of good food and cake and ice cream. I would just have to do a couple of things for him and then I could eat anything I wanted. I could even bring food home for the others."

They began walking again in silence, Player threading his fingers through Zyah's. He needed to feel close to her at least for these last few moments. They had crossed the street and were following the path that led through the grass of the headlands to the bluffs overlooking the ocean.

The sound of the sea rose up, and he realized he loved being close to it because it felt cleansing. The roar of the waves drowned out the voice of guilt in his head that told him he was never going to be good enough for the world Czar wanted them to fit into. He could never forgive himself for his sins, the sins he'd committed when he was five years old and kept committing for the sake of his own survival.

"I carried each of the bombs into the party wrapped like a gift and gave them to Czar. When all five were in, Sorbacov took me to a table and introduced me to a family. They were very nice. He said I was a friend of his family. He had told me to use my manners and to say exactly what I was told: My name, Gedeon Lazaroff, which is my real name. That I was a friend of the family, a friend of his son, Uri. Czar joined us at that table, and if I started to say anything I wasn't supposed to, he would grip my leg really hard."

Player realized he'd never told Zyah his name. "I should have told you that the first time I met you, that my name is Gedeon Lazaroff. I did tell your grandmother. I think she knows all of our names, but before anyone else, you should have been told."

She tilted her head up at him and smiled. Yeah. He should have told her. That meant something to her.

"Sorbacov sat at the table talking to the adults. There was a boy about twelve, and Czar talked with him, although I noticed

Czar was quiet and kind of stilted. Mostly, he looked after me. I talked to the girl. She was eight or nine, and she had a book." He took a deep breath. "*Alice's Adventures in Wonderland.* It was the coolest book I'd ever seen. She showed me all the pictures and read some of it to me. Sorbacov had told them all it was my birthday, and she was very excited for me. I really liked her. Her name was Irina."

He swallowed down bile again and stared at the white foam as it shot into the air. "Sorbacov got an urgent call, and we had to leave early. She gave me that book and wrote, 'Happy birthday from Irina.' I carried it out to the car. The driver pulled the car to the curb just up the block where we could still see the big hall. Sorbacov took out his pocket watch. I'll never forget that. The way he smirked when he looked at that watch."

His hand tightened around Zyah's. Again, he stood silently, working up the courage, although she had to know the rest.

"The explosions rocked the ground and our car, the bombs going off almost simultaneously. Dirt and debris filled the air. Rubble, bricks and cement hit the ground. We could see the flames glowing orange and black, and Sorbacov had the driver go back. He was smiling so big. He got out and started laughing. He made Czar and me get out and walk up to the ruins. We could see some of the bodies. I could see Irina's dress and part of her leg. Czar put his hand over my eyes and dragged me back to the car. He kept telling me not to cry. Over and over, he told me not to let Sorbacov see me cry."

"Player," she whispered and rubbed her head against his chest. "I'm so sorry. That must have been so terrible for you. How very traumatic."

That was the last thing he'd expected of her. "When we got back, the others took the food Czar gave them and Demyan, Absinthe's older brother, grabbed the book and began to read it. That day, Alena had slipped out of the dungeon. We called it that, but it was really a basement. She was so little and thin. Starved like the rest of us. She could slip through this crack and go out into the forest and harvest roots and berries and sometimes mushrooms. These mushrooms were different."

He gave her a faint grin. "All of us started having hallucinations, but all of mine had to do with what Irina had read from *Alice's Adventures in Wonderland.*" He rubbed at his pounding temples. "I started seeing the things in the story, all the different characters running around in the dungeon with us. Everyone thought it was so cool and funny. After that, they wanted me to do it every time things were at the very worst. That's how the *Alice's Adventures in Wonderland* characters came about, and that's why I detest them. That's why my brain always goes to making bombs. They saved me, and it's my go-to when I'm in a bad place."

"Player? What did you see that first time, when everyone else was laughing about the *Alice's Adventures in Wonderland* characters running around the room but you saw something that scared you? What was it?"

Her voice was music, moving through his mind like a breeze. Of course she would have noticed that when she'd been in his head. He glanced down at her, not answering her question. "You know the things you see in my head, you shouldn't know about, right? They can get you killed."

He hated telling her the truth of that. He really hated that it was the truth. She knew too much about the club. Their history. The fact that they were assassins. The fact that they hunted and killed pedophiles. They were all alive because they never left witnesses.

She looked up at him, her eyes dark with absolute trust. "I'm well aware."

"You ready to ride?"

She nodded.

"We need to go to Czar's. Tonight."

"It's late."

"I know, but we need to go. He has to know what's going on. You willing to go with me?"

"Is he going to take out a gun and shoot me?"

"If he tried that shit, I'd stop him." The moment the words were out of his mouth, he realized it was true. Anat Gamal was right, and Gedeon Lazaroff knew he'd just made a commitment. He was going to stay and fight for Zyah Gamal with everything and anything he had for as long as it took because she was worth it, and she was definitely the woman for him.

"Then let's go," Zyah said.

# ELEVEN

The moment Player was riding down the ribbon of Highway 1, Zyah's arms around his waist, her hands clasped together near his cock, his motorcycle roaring between his legs and the wind in his face, he felt alive. Totally, absolutely alive. He felt free. The world felt a completely different place on his bike. It always had.

After a lifetime spent in the freezing, rodent-filled torture chamber of a basement in his native country, a captive, a puppet forced to do a cruel master's bidding, riding in the open air with the blue of the sea throwing misty salt into the air on one side of him and wildflowers, trees and grasses of all colors on the other gave him a sense of absolute peace. He had never considered putting a woman on the back of his bike. He'd never wanted one there. If someone had asked him for a ride or touched his bike, he would have felt murderous. Zyah only added to that sense of perfection. Of well-being.

337

Her arms tightened around him as if she sensed what he was feeling — or thinking. And she probably was. They were that connected. He dropped his hand down to cover hers, just for a moment, needing to press her even closer. Her body moved with his, matching the smooth line of the motorcycle as it took the long, sweeping turns or the sharper, narrow ones. She never hesitated to follow his lead. They were in perfect sync, just the way they were in bed.

His Harley was a powerful machine, souped up, and eager to run when necessary. The machine rumbled between their legs, the vibration stirring already inflamed bodies. It was impossible to get near Zyah without wanting her. Having her on his bike made that need so urgent he could barely think. He felt her tits pressed against his back. It should have been impossible with the combined thicknesses of his jacket and hers between their skin, but he felt every movement, every bounce and jiggle. That just put extra stiffness in his already aching cock.

He swore she moaned. A soft sound in his mind. Intimate. Needy. Bordering on desperate. Just the way he was feeling. Now he could feel her thighs around his hips. Pressing into him. Her pussy tight against him, feeling hotter with every movement of the bike. For a brief time, it felt like agony, and then it wasn't. Then it was perfection. Beauty.

Just like Zyah. That's what she was to him.

To a man who had been trained to never have normal erections, finding Zyah was a miracle. A gift. Realizing she was much more to him than a sexual partner, one who would always inflame his body with just a thought or look, that sex alone wasn't enough for him and never would be, was enlightening — and equally shocking.

He had known he wanted her for himself. He just hadn't known it would be this — the feeling of wanting her for so many reasons. Knowing that his past didn't matter and that she was still there. Zyah was more than worth fighting for. More than worth putting himself on the line for. Anat Gamal was a very wise woman, and he vowed he was going to listen to her, no matter what.

Once he accepted the way Zyah made him feel, she became part of the experience of the night. Of being on his motorcycle. Of the ocean rising up toward the bluffs and stars overhead. It was clear and cold, the way it often could be on the coast. The wind was biting and capricious, whipping through the leaves of the trees and the long grasses, turning them a strange silvery color as they rushed past, just adding more magic to the jeweled blue of the sea.

Player didn't want the ride to end. There wasn't much distance between Sea Haven and the farm where Czar resided with his wife, Blythe, and their children. The farm was enormous, and Czar co-owned it with five other families. Each family had five acres to themselves, and the rest was planted with crops or groves of trees or rows of greenhouses. Two other members of Torpedo Ink owned the farm along with Czar, Blythe and the others.

He hesitated before he made the turn to the road leading to the farm. He really wanted to spend more time on the bike alone with Zyah, just having that experience, savoring it. He hadn't had too many great happenings in his life, and he wanted this one to last, but it was extremely late and it wasn't fair to Czar and Blythe to have to wait up long hours because he wanted to run the highway with his woman. Mostly, he was reluctant to betray Zyah to Czar. He was going to have to do that in order to protect the other members of his club, and he would have to make her fully understand the stakes before they went in.

The double gates loomed up in front of them. They were closed but not locked. Czar had made certain of that. He could control them electronically from his home, and when Player had texted him that he was coming with Zyah and it was important, Czar hadn't hesitated to tell him he'd be waiting up with his wife. He hadn't asked questions, he just said he'd be waiting. That was Czar. Always available to them. Always a constant.

The gates were a work of art. Lissa Prakenskii's work. She had gained fame as a glassblower, her chandeliers in demand throughout the United States and abroad, but she also did metalwork. Anything to do with fire and art. She was married to Casimir, one of the Torpedo Ink brothers. He was an actual blood brother to Czar, but not one of the original eighteen members. Player supposed he was going to have to get used to thinking in terms of nineteen, to include Destroyer. Destroyer had survived their school as well.

Player slowed the Harley and then brought it to a halt, indicating for Zyah to climb off. "We've got to talk." Another conversation he didn't want to have with her. One he didn't want to have with Czar, but there was no question. He had no choice. It was imperative that Zyah understand what could happen when he exposed his secret.

Zyah put her hand on his shoulder and slid off the bike, her movements graceful. Flowing. Just like always. She wasn't in the least affected by the experience of being on the back of the machine, and for a moment jealousy welled up. He'd wanted to be the first man to give her the experience of riding with the wind.

He studied her face as she turned back to him, watching him come to her right there at the ornate gate. Her hand gripped the beautifully twisted metal, and he realized she wasn't nearly as unaffected as she wanted to appear. Her fingers trembled just a little. He walked right up to her and removed her helmet, needing to see her expression clearly.

"What is it, Player?"

Did her voice tremble as well? Zyah didn't show weakness, but she was aware if they took this step, if they talked to Czar, there was no going back. She had seen too many things in his head to pretend.

He took a deep breath and then framed her face with his hands. That beautiful face. Those dark eyes. "I know you've seen inside my head. You know what kind of man I am. Look beyond the fucked-up one. See what kind of traits I have, Zyah. It's important you know."

Her long lashes fluttered. He let go of her reluctantly. She had to work it out on her own. There was too much between them, and she had to decide — now, before they went through those gates — if she could fully trust him. She didn't have to believe in him as her man. He'd rejected her so often over the last five weeks — he knew he might have a long road ahead of him to get her to look at him as anything but the man who had tossed her aside — but she had to know he would stand for her if he gave her his word.

Zyah moistened her lips with the tip of her tongue, and Player did his best not to groan.

Not to let his thoughts go south. This was too important to fuck it up with sex. Zyah was too important. She had to know she could count on him.

"Tell me what's happening here."

He reached for her free hand because she wasn't letting go of that gate. Even through the combined thicknesses of their gloves, he felt her tremble. He ran his thumb over the back of her hand. "I have no choice, Zyah. I have to tell Czar about the side effect of my psychic talent. He doesn't know. The rest of the club doesn't know. Not even the doc. You're very aware of that, or you wouldn't have been so insistent on staying so close to me."

He made certain to keep his tone strictly neutral. "This bomb isn't one I ever built before. I've never seen it. The ones I fall back on, I fill with harmless things, nothing lethal. This is very different and I can't seem to stop it. If you weren't there with me, something very bad could have happened. On top of that, the illusion has always been the same. Always. There's been the White Rabbit and then Sorbacov. Now I'm beginning to detect someone else in the shadows. Someone waiting I can't make out, but he's aware of me. And he's aware of you, baby. That makes this situation very, very dangerous."

Her dark chocolate eyes hadn't left his the entire time he gave her his truth.

She nodded slowly. "I've felt someone looking at us, like a big bloated spider in the corner." She gave a little shudder. "I hoped it was that horrid man you call Sorbacov."

Player hated to crush the little note of hope in her voice. "No, babe." He kept his voice as gentle as the fingers he used to tuck a stray strand of hair behind her ear. "Sorbacov is dead. That's why his figure is always blurred. He can't come back from the dead. The White Rabbit is an illusion, just like when I created him for my brothers and sisters to amuse them. Whatever or whoever is watching is beginning to blur illusion with reality."

"How?" Zyah challenged. "Why would reality start taking over the *Alice's Adventures in Wonderland* illusion? I'm right there with you, making sure you wake up and you're pulling out of it."

He had to be honest, because it didn't make sense to him either. "I don't know, baby. That's the problem. Nothing like this has ever happened before. I don't know if that bullet did more damage to my head than we thought . . . I just don't know."

"When you start dreaming, what's happening?"

He shrugged, his first instinct to shut down, but that wasn't fair to her. She'd come with him. Seen him through night after night. Now she was risking her life, prepared to walk into the lion's den with him. She had the right to ask any question and get the truth. She was everything he could want, standing with him. His warrior woman, nothing like him. Not hard. Not honed into a weapon. She was soft and gentle, a woman of the earth, but nevertheless his equal, a woman to walk beside him, everything he could ever want.

"It's always that first bombing, on my birthday. I despise birthdays. I've never celebrated one since." He confessed it fast. "Your grandmother has one coming up. Alena's been talking to her about it and asking what kind of cake and frosting she likes." He added the last, unable to stop himself from revealing the guilt and shame he felt in not being able to join in with the others looking forward to the celebration.

"Player." Zyah finally pried her fingers off the gate and slid her palm up the front of his jacket, over his chest and wildly beating heart. "Don't do that to yourself. Trauma can cause triggers. You're intelligent. You must know that. You can't beat yourself up because you have a very real one. You were five. You couldn't possibly have known what Sorbacov was planning to do. I would have done anything to keep from being raped and tortured."

"Each time I successfully built a practice bomb and beat my time before, he raped me. If I didn't beat the time, he whipped me until I couldn't breathe." His body shuddered before he could control it. That door in his mind had creaked open, the one he kept bolted closed for self-preservation. "None of the alternatives were very good."

She wrapped her arms around his waist and pressed her face against his chest.

"Don't pity me, Zyah, that's the last thing I want," he said gruffly, but he cupped the back of her head and held her to him. He didn't want her pity. He wanted a lot of other things from her, but not pity. He didn't feel sorry for himself. He'd done enough of that when he was a child. According to Anat, he might still be doing it, but he was determined to win Zyah. To be good enough for her. Soliciting pity wasn't going to cut it.

"It isn't pity when we're sharing the same mind and I need comfort, Player. You've lived with this a long time. I haven't," she reminded.

He hadn't thought of it like that. He plunged his fingers into the thick hair at the back of her scalp. She had that long braid, but the back of her head was covered in the thick, silky layers he loved so much.

"I don't understand where the bomb is coming from when I've never seen those materials before or the schematics. I've never built that bomb before, and I've gotten very good at building a good number of them. I have no choice. I have to take this to Czar. It's too dangerous not to. When I do, he'll know that you've been in my head, Zyah. There's no way to keep you out of it. The things you've seen about me, my childhood, the way I was raised and the things I did, the assassinations — those are all things not another living soul knows outside of the club members."

She tipped her head up to look at him. He had no choice; he had to let her, even when he didn't want to. Her eyes met his. She was a very intelligent woman. "Not even Blythe?"

"I don't know how much Czar tells his wife, but I doubt very much. He doesn't lie to her, though, so if she asks him, he'll give her the truth. It isn't the same as really knowing everything, the way you do, Zyah. You know our childhood. You know everything done to us. The way we were trained. The way we were used as assets for our country. The people we killed to stay alive."

"That's not exactly true, Player," she denied. "I know what happened to you. I know some of the things you did. I saw that the others were tortured and raped, but not the specifics, nor do I want to see. I never saw a single thing they did in order to survive. I see your memories, not theirs, and I'm grateful for that. As to what you had to do to survive in that place, I'm glad you had the strength to do it."

"I'm a killer, Zyah," he said quietly. "You can't very well deny that."

"You killed to survive. You killed for your country. That's considered reasonable under the circumstances, Player."

He refused to look away, staring down into her dark eyes, daring her to continue. He felt like he was falling. Drowning. A man could get lost there. She didn't say anything else, but she had to know the killing hadn't stopped once they'd gotten out from under Sorbacov. They had taken back kidnapped women. They had chased pedophiles. They weren't nice about it when they caught up with the ones they were looking for, and they didn't take prisoners.

"We're very careful, Zyah. We always make certain we don't make mistakes. Czar drilled that into us when we were kids. We're patient. We let our quarry walk away if we're not one hundred percent certain they're guilty. We make sure there are no innocents that can be harmed or are around to witness. We don't act until we know there aren't witnesses."

He felt her body tense. Her lashes fluttered and then veiled her eyes. The tip of her tongue moistened her lips and she tried to pull back. He locked his arms around her, refusing to relinquish his hold now that he'd told her the truth.

"Because you don't leave witnesses behind."

"We make certain there aren't any witnesses," he reiterated. "We're careful to ensure no one innocent is ever a witness."

"Unless they're like me and can see into your head."

He stroked a caress down the back of her hair. All that silky hair. Her braid was thick. He wrapped his hand around it, a peculiar, unfamiliar ache in his chest. "I don't think there's anyone like you in the world, baby." He couldn't keep the raw admiration out of his voice. The stark respect and desire. "The thing is this, I have to tell Czar the truth, and once I do, he could view you as a liability. Either way, I'm betraying you or the club."

"Player, how can you be betraying me if we're standing here together in front of these gates and you're laying it out for me? You're giving me this information because you know I can walk into that house and either text Jonas myself or ask Blythe to drive me straight to him. No one in the world will get me to believe that, even for her husband, she would commit murder or allow him to, not if she knew I was innocent."

His woman. Intelligent. He nodded slowly. "That, and I want you to be aware that if I tell you we have to leave now, you don't hesitate, you just come with me, no trying to argue, and we go. Your grandmother will be safe. The club would never hurt her. I have money stashed. I have ways to disappear, and I can put you somewhere safe while I try to fix this." He slid his gloved thumb along her cheek. "I'm sorry I got you into this. None of this is your doing. You were just trying to help me out and you landed yourself in the middle of a huge mess."

"Actually, *you* were helping *me* out. You kept me from getting kidnapped, remember? That's why you got shot. Come on, let's get this over with. You believe in this man. You've always looked up to him, and I did see his face when he was a child, watching over all of you, Player. He cares deeply. He's protective. He actually loves you."

"I know, baby, that's what I'm afraid of." Player reached out to run his fingers along her tightly woven braid, feeling the thick silk of it. Without warning, feelings welled up out of nowhere, intense, like a volcano. So unexpected. So powerful, shaking him.

"You know our relationship isn't about sex, Zyah."

Her long, thick lashes veiled the expression in her eyes, and she shook her head. "Don't. We have to do this thing with Czar and worry about everything else later. I mean it. I can only concentrate on one thing at a time right now."

He found himself smiling, his fingers on her stubborn little chin. Anat was so right. This woman was well worth fighting for, and he was going to fight with everything in him. He was a survivor. He'd fought every damn day of his life to survive. Being with Zyah meant surviving. Not because she would save

350

his sanity, or because he'd have the best damn sex in the world, but because she made him happy. It was really that simple. He was better with her. And he hoped she would be better with him. His campaign was starting immediately, and thankfully, he had an entire club that would back him.

Leaning down, he rubbed her lips softly with his. The contact was barely there, but he felt it all the way to his toes. She was potent. They were potent. She was perfect. His. Their chemistry was off the charts, and electricity instantly arced between them, a bright, hot connection so strong he thought he could see little sparks dancing off their skin. Zyah hesitated for the briefest of moments, and then her arms slid around his neck and her body leaned into his. She simply surrendered, giving herself to him, her lips parting, letting him in, while dynamite detonated between them.

He let the explosive chemistry catch them both on fire and then deliberately gentled the kiss, keeping the heat, the flames, but introducing tenderness, something he'd never known with another human being. That foreign emotion felt as necessary to him as breathing, adding to the fire of their kiss, turning it into something he'd never expected. The heat rushed through his veins and settled in his groin, but at the same time, it took over his body, moving through him to encompass his heart, embedding there, digging deep, deeper still, until he swore she was in his soul.

She gasped, her hands sliding to his chest, palms applying pressure to try to separate them. Obediently but with great reluctance, he lifted his lips and leaned his forehead against hers. "You felt it. I know you did."

"I don't want to talk about it. Let's just go and get this over with. You're getting tired. I am tired. I have to work tomorrow, and we're keeping Blythe and Czar up," she reminded.

Player gave in to the inevitable. He wasn't going to repair the damage he'd done in one night. He'd held her at arm's length due to his own stupidity. Now he had to make a confession to Czar and find a way to keep her, as well as his club, safe. Then, with Zyah, figure out just what was happening to him.

"Thanks for sticking with me," he said as they once again got on the Harley. "Very few people would have."

She wrapped her arms around him. "Very few people had Mama Anat as an example."

Player knew that much was true.

Czar answered the door, his gaze moving over them, taking both of them in, seeing too much. It didn't matter that Player had cultivated the mask that every club member had — no expression, flat, cold eyes — Czar knew him too well. He saw that he was stressed.

He could read possession and the protective way Player kept Zyah close beneath his shoulder. Worse, the way he held himself, ready for trouble. That told Czar more than Player wanted him to know, but then Czar was president of Torpedo Ink because he had earned their respect for a lot of reasons.

"Cold tonight. Blythe has something hot for you, Zyah," Czar greeted. "And a fire going in the other room. Let me take you to her."

Player started to protest. He didn't want them separated. Czar flashed him one look that stopped him cold. Zyah turned her face up to his. "A hot drink and a fire sound perfect, Player. And visiting with Blythe would be wonderful. I've heard so much about her. I'm sorry we came so late, Czar."

"No worries, we're used to the late hours," Czar assured her as he led the way through the house to a room a few doors down.

Player had been to the house numerous times. This was the designated music room. It had a piano for the children to learn to play, as well as several other instruments. Blythe rose immediately as they entered. Player went to her and bent to brush a kiss on her cheek.

"I'm sorry we disturbed you so late, Blythe. This is Zyah." He had his arm around her shoulders. "Zyah, Blythe. Blythe's the heart of our club, baby. None of us knows why she puts up with us, but as you can see, she does, even when we disturb her in the middle of the night."

Zyah flashed her gorgeous smile, and Player tightened his arm around her, proud of her. It took courage to be so gracious and calm knowing Czar was deliberately separating them.

"Blythe, I'm so happy to meet you." Zyah's tone was genuine. Happy. Perfection.

Player realized Zyah meant it. She had wanted to meet Blythe, and even under the tense circumstances, she was happy to do so.

"You are spoken so highly of by everyone who has met you, Zyah," Blythe answered. "Come get warm while the men talk or do whatever it is they do. I'll take good care of her, Player." She brushed his cheek with her soft lips.

He didn't want to leave Zyah. Anxiety hit him hard. He stood there in the middle of the music room, signs of Czar's family everywhere, still feeling an underlying threat to his woman.

She tilted her face up to his, her dark chocolate eyes unafraid. "Take your time, honey. I'll be enjoying myself, getting to know Blythe." She went up on her toes and skimmed his lips with her own.

His heart nearly stopped beating. She was reassuring him. It should have been the other way around. He managed to give her a faint grin. "You get the easy, fun half. I'm talking to Czar, and he's usually a grumpy bear."

"Only because you interrupted my night with my woman," Czar said. "Move it, Player." He indicated the door, giving Player no choice other than to leave Zyah.

Player led the way back to the great room with its vaulted ceiling and wide-open space, Czar keeping pace behind him like a silent wraith. It was significant that Czar closed and locked the door. In the Prakenskii household, few doors were closed and fewer were locked. They had an open-door policy, even to the club members. The children came and went, easily rushing in when the adults were visiting. They were always welcome, and Czar had taught them they were welcome.

"What's wrong, Player?" Czar said, seating himself in his favorite chair and waving Player to the chair across from him.

Player shook his head and began pacing across the room, adrenaline making it impossible to sit. Without Zyah to ground him, he realized the enormity of what he was doing. He glanced at the president of his club. Czar wasn't just the president of the club. He was the man who had saved them. He was the one they believed in. His word was law. For the first time Player was hesitant about laying everything on the line. He'd always trusted in Czar, but then he'd never had anything to lose before — not like Zyah. He'd come to

Czar's home to tell him everything, but now he wasn't so certain it was a good idea.

"You going to tell me why you're here or you just going to wear a hole in my wife's favorite carpet?" Czar asked.

"I don't know exactly how to start." That was the fucking truth. How was he supposed to tell this man he didn't belong? He might have betrayed them all. Czar had a family. Blythe. The children. Three daughters. Two sons. Steele had a son. It wasn't just the Torpedo Ink charter members at risk. It was all of them. The families.

He found, pacing back and forth on the very familiar carpet, that he knew those kids and Blythe had found their way into the circle that was his family — Torpedo Ink. He'd learned to feel for them when he thought himself incapable of feeling real emotions for anyone but his brothers and sisters. They were his as well. Now there was Zyah. Her grandmother. He was being overrun with emotion.

"Player." Czar's voice slipped into his low demand. "Brother. Talk to me now. You have something big on your mind. Tell me."

"I'm not like the rest of you," Player blurted out. "I never have been. All of you had such gifts, and you all made them count for something. Mine has been a fucked-up mess since the beginning. It's getting worse. Sometimes I think I'm going insane." He rubbed his pounding temples. He should have insisted Zyah stay with him. At least he could think straight if she was standing beside him. "This is bad, Czar. I've put your family in jeopardy. The club. Zyah. Everyone I care about."

"Take a damn breath, Player. You got shot in the head and shouldn't be on your feet this long. Steele said the injury was bad and you should be dead. Worse, he said he probably would have lost you. He told me the injury is healed but the migraines are worse than ever. Somehow, this woman has helped you with them, but he isn't certain what she's doing. I'm guessing a good part of this is wrapped up in Zyah. You need to give it to me one step at a time. Just sit in a fucking chair before you fall down, and start at the beginning. Start with the fucked-up mess."

Czar sounded the same. Calm. Reasonable. In command. Player took the required breath and dropped into the chair opposite his president, suddenly grateful to be off his feet. He hadn't realized how weak he felt.

He pressed a hand to his pounding head. "When we were kids, I recognized that all of you had psychic gifts. You had everyone practicing so they could contribute to our survival. I didn't think I had one. It felt like I was the lone screwup, the person that everyone else had to carry." He made the confession in a low voice.

Czar didn't say anything. He never did. He wasn't the type of man to interrupt unless it was for a good reason. He waited, giving Player the time to tell things his own way.

"Eventually, I realized I could create illusions. Small ones. It felt like a useless little parlor trick to me, and it was, in comparison to what everyone else could do. I've always hated casting illusions. What real good is it?"

Czar's eyebrow shot up. "Are you asking that question for real? You remember things a little differently than I do, Player," Czar said at his nod. "I remember you were nine years old and everything had gone to hell. Sorbacov was about to catch us red-handed. You threw a false image of a wall and door up, a perfect replica of the room, making it empty so we all could escape out the real door. You had to do that often. More than once. He never saw us. Never suspected. You were only nine and you held that illusion long enough for all of us to make it out. It wasn't easy. I remember waiting to be last. Sweat was beaded on your forehead, running down your face. I signaled to you to get through the door and let the illusion collapse."

Player nodded, his breath coming too fast. His chest hurt. He rubbed over his pounding heart. "But you didn't see the aftermath." His voice was very low. Ashamed. Guilt-ridden. I never told you what happens *after*."

Czar's gaze instantly locked onto his face.

"What happens after, Player?"

Player swallowed down bile. He wanted to look away from those piercing eyes. Czar could always see people for who they were. He could see into souls. Why hadn't he seen all the blood on Player's soul?

"If I hold the illusion too long, past the point where my brain can manage, reality begins to intrude. An alternate reality. In that case, I saw Sorbacov turn his head and look at us just before we went through the door. My head was pounding. We made it down to the dungeon. All of you were celebrating, but I was still locked into that place and I couldn't get out of it. It had happened to me before, more than once, and I knew it could be dangerous. I didn't want to bring him down there, to see everyone, even if it would be under slightly different circumstances."

Czar hitched forward, steepling his fingers, clearly trying to understand. "Keep going."

Player searched for the right words, trying to make Czar see the very real dangers. "Whatever is happening in the illusion is just an illusion, like the wall. But in the reality, that shit is the real deal. If Sorbacov is present, if someone has a gun, those things are real. That night, Sorbacov was angry that he didn't catch us in the act, and he was certain we were the ones who had killed that bloated pig of an instructor."

"He came down to the dungeon to check

on us," Czar said. "We knew he would. We had everything in place. Code had the cameras working, appearing as if nothing had interrupted them. I remember looking at you, and you were definitely stressed. Covered in sweat. Very unusual for you."

"Because the reality was something I could barely control."

Czar shook his head. "We knew he would come down to check on us."

"Think back, Czar. That's not true. Sorbacov wasn't supposed to be there that night. That's the reason you put the green light on killing Matrix." He scrubbed a hand over his face. "Matrix had a huge fight with the math teacher that morning. Every one of the other teachers knew about it. No one was going to blame a bunch of kids who were so torn up we could barely move. That's what you'd said to us."

It was Czar's turn to get up and pace across the room. "You're right. Sorbacov had a big meeting to go to that night. We targeted Matrix because he had already hurt so many of the girls in the school and he was looking at Alena and Lana. We knew it was only a matter of time before he went after them." Czar turned to look at him. "Why is it I didn't remember that, Player, when I never forget details?"

"It was very real, Czar. Sorbacov really did come down to confront us. Code really did fix the cameras to cover us. I made certain of it. I orchestrated it in my reality."

"That's why you kept Sorbacov's attention on you."

Player nodded slowly. "It was my fuckup and my mistake to fix. I could have gotten all of you killed."

"Instead, he took you to his rooms and returned you in the worst shape I'd ever seen you in," Czar said and slumped down in the chair, scrubbing both hands over his face.

There was a small silence. "I build bombs in my head when things get too crazy for me. It's a harmless pastime, like counting for other people," Player said. "At least, it started out that way. I've always done it. When Sorbacov would give me to his friends, I'd lose myself in my head by building the bombs. I'd just go there, and sometimes by the time I'd built several, it would be over. I wouldn't even remember how many he'd given me to or how many times someone beat me with a whip. I just built the bombs."

Czar waited, his piercing gaze once more jumping to Player's face.

"When this happened to me" — Player indicated the bandana covering the wound on his head — "my brain was really fractured. I started having nightmares. Then I have an illusion. *Alice's Adventures in Wonderland*. You know how much I despise that illusion and why. That's when the alternate reality creeps in. I am always sitting on that little bench Sorbacov would make me sit on when he'd lay the materials out on the table and press his pocket watch. At first it would be the White Rabbit there. Then Sorbacov. I'd be putting together the bomb. Only it wasn't a bomb I'd ever put together before. I didn't recognize the materials or the way it was supposed to be put together."

"Steele healed your injury."

"But the migraines have persisted. They've gotten worse, and so have the nightmares. With the nightmares come the illusions." He rubbed his forehead and met Czar's eyes, showing him it wasn't a joke. This was very real and dangerous. "The thing is, I see in patterns, Czar. I can look at things, at the materials, and I just know how they work. I began to build a bomb even though I'd never seen that type before. Sorbacov was always shadowy. At first, I was slow and didn't finish. Zyah would come in and stop the entire process. She has a tremendous talent, and she puts my mind back together, so to speak. She stays with me the rest of the night and the nightmare doesn't come back."

Czar frowned. "This happens every night?"

Player nodded. "Every damn night. In the beginning, it would happen sometimes during the day, but not anymore. But I'm faster at putting the bomb together. And it's too real. Others in the house can hear it ticking. I know it's real. Sometimes, lately, I can feel someone watching me. Zyah can feel them as well."

Czar sat back in the chair and regarded him over his steepled fingers. "How close are you to finishing the bomb?"

"Too damn close. I worry for everyone. And that's not all." He had to finish it. He glanced toward the door, hating the feeling he was betraying Zyah. "I would be dead if it wasn't for Zyah. She's been with me every night. She knows the threat, and she refused to let me leave. She says she has this gut feeling — and has had it all along — that she needs to be with me. Steele has the same feeling. But we're connected in this very strong way."

"Anyone can see that, Player." There was a trace of amusement in Czar's voice.

Player shook his head. "I wish it was just that. It's much more. Much more intimate. She's in my head. She has to be in order to chase out the bomb making."

Immediately, Czar's all-too-intelligent eyes narrowed, and Player's heart sank. He knew Czar would comprehend what he was saying. He went doggedly on.

"She sees my memories. My childhood. She knows the things I've done. I was straight with her, Czar, about what that could buy her, but even knowing, she came here with me."

There was silence. Outside, the wind blew,

a soft moaning sound that echoed through his heart. A branch slid across the side of the house.

"How much does she know?"

Just the quiet in Czar's voice told Player everything he needed to know.

"Our childhood. Our training. That we were used as assets for our country. No details on anyone but me. Obviously only my memories. But she knows we aren't saints even now." He wasn't going to lie. "She's mine, Czar, and I'll stand for her."

"Does she know that she's yours? Does she know what you standing for her means?"

Player shook his head. "I was up front with you about what an ass I was. I haven't exactly made the best impression on her since, but I'm not going to let her get away. She's the one. My only. I'm absolutely certain. If you want, I can take her away from here. She won't like it, but she'd go to protect Anat if she thought it necessary."

Czar shook his head. "You wrap it up fast, Player. I mean it. Get her to commit and make it solid. In the meantime, we have to figure this bomb thing out fast. I want you to keep her in bed with you. Write everything down, every detail, and compare notes. The two of you go over the notes and then bring them to me. If you think it's too dangerous for you to be in Anat's house, then we'll set you up in your home."

"I want to move out, but I don't know if I can persuade Zyah yet. She thinks her grandmother is still in danger from the gang of thieves. Code said, word is the cops don't think they've moved on, that they're just lying low. They haven't hit anyone since Jonas stopped by last week, but Code thinks the cops have it right."

Czar nodded. "That's what he said. No dead body left behind. Get Zyah's grandmother on your side when it comes to you and Zyah. She'll be your greatest asset," Czar added. "And Player, get it done fast. Zyah can't be left running around loose knowing about our club members."

Player didn't protest. Czar was giving him a reprieve.

"You should have told me about the byproduct with your gift."

"I felt like such a loser already."

"Because of the bombs."

"So many of them. Sorbacov took us to so many parties. After the first one, I knew what we were doing. I made them. Carried them in. You placed them. You covered for me when I couldn't put on a party face so many times." Player tried not to think about that five-year-old boy looking at the rubble and the bright party dress with blood splashed across it caught under the bricks and dirt.

"I shouldn't have let them read *Alice's Adventures in Wonderland.* I should have known what it was doing to you. You were always so willing to create the characters for them."

"It was the only thing I could contribute," Player said.

"That's such bullshit," Czar said. "You saved our butts so many times."

that he'd been just a child when he'd built
those bombs, thinking of them as no more a
way to cling into his mind and escape from
what was happening to his body once he
found out he didn't have worked. To admit
he'd kept building them. He'd kept carrying
them into the cities and — now insisted he
carry them. He'd done so when he was six.
When he was seven.

# TWELVE

Player should have headed straight back to the house, but he needed the wind in his face, Zyah's arms around him and the Harley between his legs. He'd asked her first if she minded a ride down the highway. She'd said she definitely wanted to ride, although she'd indicated that she wanted to talk to him where they couldn't be overheard. He needed the time to clear his head.

Czar had made it clear he expected Player to handle Zyah. To bring her into the fold. Zyah wasn't the kind of woman one just handled. He was going to have to prove himself to her. He had so many mountains to climb as far as she was concerned, it was laughable. He wasn't about to tell them all to Czar. He rubbed his palm over the back of her gloved hand. It was such an experience to ride the highway with her. A good one. He felt as if the wind washed him clean.

It wasn't as if Czar had excused him — there was no excuse. It didn't matter to him that he'd been five, a child, when he'd built those bombs, thinking of them as toys, as a way to climb into his mind and escape from what was happening to his body; once he found out, he could have stopped. He hadn't. He'd kept building them. He'd kept carrying them into the places Sorbacov insisted he carry them. He'd done so when he was six. When he was seven.

*Player.* In his mind, Zyah's voice sounded tender. Gentle. Just a brush, like fingertips skimming down his spine in the most intimate way. *You were a child. Stop condemning yourself.*

Her gloved hand opened against his jacket so that her palm cupped his abdomen, and she rubbed soothingly, giving him a feeling of being cherished. Player had never experienced that particular emotion and at first didn't identify it with an actual word, but when *cherished* crept into his mind, his entire body reacted. He didn't deserve her. He would never deserve her. No matter what Anat or anyone else said, no man deserved her.

*Sometimes you break my heart, Player. There was a time your mother must have cherished you. You don't want to remember because it hurts too much.*

His entire body flinched. Shuddered at the idea of even allowing that thought into his head. How did she get to be so damned smart? She was right. He refused to think about his mother. Not when he first was taken to what all members of the Torpedo Ink club referred to as the dungeon and not now. He rubbed his hand over hers and kicked their speed up a notch.

Her arms tightened around him. He felt the possession in her. The slow, smoldering burn. The ache was there for both of them. He knew, for him, it would never go away. Just looking at Zyah would put it there for him. Thinking of her could do it, but having her riding down the highway with him was going to ignite a blaze that rivaled anything he'd known.

She nuzzled her chin against his back. *Show me your house. Where you live. You made me a promise if I came with you tonight.*

His cock jerked hard. Every cell in his body was suddenly alive, aware. There was no way to miss the unashamed invitation in her voice. The way her tone slid along the walls of his mind like a temptress. His woman seducing him. She didn't have to work very hard.

*I did make you a promise, didn't I? I meant every fuckin' word.* Deliberately, he took one of her hands and moved it to the very front of his jeans, curling her palm over the thick monster of his cock. He held his hand over hers as he guided the Harley toward Caspar, finding the way toward his home. He ached for her in every way possible. If she came home with him, they would be alone. They would have a night together. She would need to work the next day, but he would have her alone, just like their first night. He could work with that. Neither one of them was going to get much sleep.

The house he'd bought suited him perfectly. He hoped Zyah would love it the way he did. It was out a little farther from the ocean than some of the other homes. He wanted to be closer to the trees. The house sat in the middle of three acres, which gave him privacy from neighbors, something important to him. He drove straight up the private drive, through the wealth of flowering trees and shrubs, to the sprawling single-story home. Every time he saw it, he was glad he'd bought it.

Aside from the main house, there was a two-car attached garage as well as an extremely enormous workshop with three garage bays, something he'd wanted, since he was always working with wood. Brick patios, a firepit, a greenhouse, fenced gardens and even a small fruit orchard had really sold him on the place. The chicken coop was empty at the moment, but someday he knew he would get chickens. He'd always wanted to have them. He didn't want to think too hard about his reasons why, afraid that might have something to do with his mother.

Player helped Zyah off the bike as the motion lights automatically came on around the house. He slowly got off, watching her as she wandered around the outside, looking at the things he thought were particularly beautiful in the front of his home. He loved plants. The colors and textures of them. The subtle differences in their leaves and structures even within the same varieties. Apparently, she did too, because she bent over one of his favorites, a lacy fern he'd planted near the front entryway.

She turned back to him as he pulled off his gloves and held out his hand to her. "Come in and see the inside." He couldn't keep the pride out of his voice. He knew most of the other members of Torpedo Ink had problems sleeping away from one another, a byproduct of the torture and rape of their childhood. They wanted eyes on one another. But Player always worried that he would somehow harm the others. He wanted distance from them in order to keep them safe.

Because he was alone so much, he took pride in his home and worked at making it as nice as he could. The band members came often to jam there, or practice. They wrote music and created songs. He had the workshop so they could build cabinets and furniture. Inside the house were two kitchens, a chef's dream, allowing him to cook for the

371

others or use the outside brick oven to feed them when they were over.

They took their boots off at the door, leaving them at the bench where he always left them. He had little places built in at the doorways for his shoes. He preferred to be barefoot in his house, to feel the wood under his feet. Zyah didn't object, removing her boots and socks as well. He appreciated it. His fellow Torpedo Ink members gave him a bad time about it and said he was a pain, but they usually removed their dirty boots before entering his home.

Zyah took his hand and he led her into the house. Strangely, he found that his heart was pounding. He hadn't realized how much it would matter to him that she like his home. It hadn't mattered at all that anyone else had.

There was gleaming wood flooring throughout the house. That was a good part of what he loved about it. Vaulted ceilings overhead. That always gave him the needed feeling of space — and he needed space. He had so many nights waking up with nightmares of that dungeon. Of being in chains. Of being confined.

There were archways, beautiful trim on the windows and custom cabinets built by a master crafter. He appreciated the work. The man had since passed, but Player would have talked with him for hours, and sometimes in the middle of the night he walked barefoot into the kitchen and dining room and had a conversation with the deceased man anyway, just to acknowledge his craftsmanship. Skylights provided natural lighting in many of the rooms, something Zyah couldn't see at night, but if she was there during the day, she would be able to appreciate the effects.

He let go of her hand so she could wander around on her own. The floor plan was mostly open, one room leading through to the next with the open archways. She moved slowly, looking into the more formal dining room with the gas fireplace built into the wall. She walked right up to the long table he'd built with his own hands. The thick slab of polished oak that gleamed as bright as the floor. The chairs were made of the same oak, but the high backs and seats were covered in thick square foam with black microfiber material Lana had sewn for him. He thought the effect was striking, and they were extremely comfortable.

"The table and chairs are beautiful," she said. "Truly beautiful."

"Thanks." His voice was gruffer than he intended.

She turned to him. "You made them."

He nodded. "Lana did the seat covers for me."

She ran her finger over the edge of the table. "This is incredible work, Player. Can you turn on the fireplace?"

The remote was on the long trim board above the fireplace that ran the length of the room. Flames sprang to life with one press of the button. Immediately, the atmosphere in the room changed. It had been beautiful before, but cold; now there was a warmth, a life, the flames flicking on the walls, dancing, throwing shadows as if for a show. Heat moved through him. He dimmed the lighting in the room until the fireplace was the main source of light, showing Zyah how the flames danced across the wood of the table, changing the color and making the top come to life.

Player came up behind her, unzipping her jacket as he leaned in, lips close to her ear. "What do you think? The fireplace gives the room an entirely different appeal, doesn't it?" He poured seduction into his voice.

She tipped her head back against his chest as he opened her jacket and tugged it off her arms, sweeping her gloves away with the jacket. "I like the way it looks right now. It's amazing."

"I made that table very sturdy. It doesn't move at all." His mouth wandered down her neck. Little kisses. Little nips. His tongue tasting her. Savoring her. All the while his hands were pulling the next layer of clothing off of her. A sweater this time. A thin one. He had to back off enough to pull it over her head. Her T-shirt was next. He got that off fast, leaving just her lacy bra. She wore the most beautiful underwear.

He kept her turned away from him, liking the way it felt to be fully dressed with her skin gleaming in the firelight, and that thin layer of lace, so delicate, stretched around the heavy, perfect tits he thought of far too often. He cupped the weight of them in his palms, his thumbs sliding over her nipples. As he did, he leaned forward and caught the lobe of her ear in his teeth, biting down. She moaned and pushed her bottom back into him.

"Unzip your jeans, Zyah." He whispered the words as he slid his hands around to unhook her bra, freeing her gorgeous breasts. As much as he liked her underwear, holding the soft mounds in his hands without anything in his way was much better. He bent his head to her shoulder, biting down on her neck, right where he remembered she couldn't resist. At the same time, his fingers traced her areolae and then cupped her breasts again, kneading and massaging gently, applying pressure and then becoming gentle.

"Push your jeans and panties off your hips." He poured velvet command into his voice, and she responded with another moan, pushing the blue jeans and underwear down her rounded hips and off her thighs as far as she could manage. She was so beautiful. The dancing flames played over her body with loving lights.

He removed his hands reluctantly so he could take off his jacket and sweater. "Baby, take your jeans all the way off and pull out the chair from the table. The one at the end so I can see your reflection on the wall."

She looked up at him, her gaze moving hungrily over him before she nodded and did as he told her. He removed his jacket and shirt but left his jeans on deliberately, only opening them to give his cock and balls relief. He went to her, taking her mouth, kissing her because it was essential in the way breathing was.

Her hand pushed at his jeans, wanting them farther off his hips so she could stroke his cock, cup and roll his balls. "I'm so hungry for you," she whispered. "That ride with the bike between my legs was wonderful and torture at the same time."

He caught her hand and moved it down her body, his eyes holding her gaze, refusing to allow her to look away. "I want to see how much you want me," he said, deliberately wicked. He curled her fingers into her slick entrance, coating them, and brought them up to his mouth. Her scent was that exotic mixture that made no sense but was all Zyah. He curled his tongue around her fingers and licked off every drop. Immediately, the taste set up a craving, and he almost laid her out on the table and feasted, but his cock was too thick and hard and he'd never last that long.

He spun her around and shoved her down over the tabletop. She cried out and gripped the table's edge on one side, pushing back with her bottom. He could barely manage to roll on the condom he had snagged from his jeans.

"Hurry, Player. I really need you right now."

The soft little entreaty nearly drove him out of his mind. He loved the way she looked as he forced her thighs farther apart. Her bare cheeks gleamed in the firelight. He rubbed them gently, his heart pounding right through his cock.

"You're the most beautiful woman in the world, Zyah." He didn't mean just her physical body, although he knew she would think that.

Her head was turned to one side, lying on the table he'd made, her eyes looking back at him, filled with dark hunger, with need. He ran his hand slowly and possessively from the nape of her neck to the seam of her cheeks meeting her thigh. Ignoring his own hunger, he lodged the overly sensitive crown of his cock in her slick entrance. She was tight, and he was broad. She clamped down on him, grasping, trying to pull him deeper into paradise. It was the most shockingly perfect feeling.

"Player." She gasped his name. Pushed

back hard with her hips.

He stayed where he was, allowing her to swallow an inch of his thick, broad length, so that he felt every tight, scorching-hot, silken muscle surrounding that inch like a greedy fist. He could feel her heart beating through his cock. It was insane and surreal. She took him to another world. He leaned forward, refusing to go fast, the way his body demanded. The way she demanded. When he leaned over her, he slid in another inch and she cried out. He wanted to do a little crying of his own.

Instead, he kissed his way from the nape of her neck down her spine. Slow kisses. Claiming her. From her neck to the small of her back. He meant each of those reverent kisses. He stayed still, watching the flames dance over her while deep inside her body her scorching flames surrounded his cock, threatening to burn him alive.

Bog, *baby.* He whispered it in his mind. Aching with his need of her. With things he could never say because he knew she wouldn't accept them yet. He'd done that, brought them to this place through his own carelessness. Now there were too many other things in their way. He recognized she would never believe he wanted her for her. For her beauty. He'd pushed her away over and over. He would have to find a way to make her believe him.

"Player." She wailed his name.

"Gedeon. You know my name."

Her lips pressed together and her lashes swept down. Deliberately he inched with excruciating slowness through her tight folds. Her body reluctantly gave way to his invasion. He felt every beautiful increment of her hot, narrow channel. It was unbelievably sexy. She clutched him in a silken fist, clamping down until it felt as if she were stroking him with a thousand tongues, gripping him with pulsing fingers, until she drove the breath from his lungs and the sanity from his mind.

He watched her breath catch. Turn ragged. Watched the beauty in her face heighten more. Her body took on a glow. Little urgent moans escaped her throat, sounds that only added to the vibrations playing up and down his cock. Her body shuddered with pleasure. With need.

"Player."

"Say my name." A long, slow withdrawal while her body tried desperately to hold on to his. The muscles were so tight, dragging over his sensitive shaft, the bundles of nerve endings just there at the vee at the broad head. He inched his way, trying to breathe, his lungs raw. She had so much power.

"Say it, Zyah. Gedeon. Say it for me. I need to hear you say it."

He rubbed her cheek when a sob of need escaped her throat. His fingers slid over her slick entrance where they joined. Circled her clit and flicked her gently. Very slowly he began to enter her again. It was a heady, sensual slide, watching himself disappear into his woman's body. He kept massaging her cheek gently. Then a little rougher. Sliding a finger across her clit. Circling. Flicking. Never varying the speed as he buried himself inside her.

"Player. Gedeon. I need you to move in me."

"I am moving in you." He caught her braid in his hand, wrapped the long length of it around his fist. Pulled her head so she was forced to arch her back. "How do you want me to move, baby? Because this feels like paradise to me."

"Hard. Fast. I need you to move faster and harder. Take me there." Her voice went back and forth from pleading to demanding.

He withdrew again slowly. Fire streaked up his spine. "You feel that? Fire. Flames. Burning from the inside out. Do you feel it the way I do?"

"Yes." Her breath hitched. "I can barely breathe."

He could barely think, let alone breathe. He leaned forward one more time and pressed a kiss to the small of her back and then caught at her hip, even as he kept her head where he wanted it. He surged forward. Lightning streaked through him. She cried out and pressed back into him hard. They came together, a frenzy of need. Of scorching heat.

Player wanted the feeling to last forever, but there was no way with the flames licking up his body, from his thighs to his groin. Fire danced over both of them, rolled them in a roaring conflagration until every nerve ending was alive and aware. Living for each other. He took her higher when she didn't think she could go. When her ragged pleas urged him on and yet begged him for release. He couldn't stop moving, his body taking on a life of its own, surging into hers, over and over.

Her body suddenly clamped down on his in a series of vicious, white-hot bites of sheer ecstasy. Surrounding his cock with a silken channel of a thousand tongues licking greedily, determined to take every drop from him. Fingers gripped and milked, squeezed down ferociously to jack every last rope of hot seed from his body. The sensation unleashed a volcano stored inside of him. His cock jerked over and over, hard, brutal, savage, unlike anything he'd ever experienced.

Zyah's sheath pulsed and rippled around him as he collapsed on top of her. He was lucky to keep his legs under him. He fought to find air and draw it into his lungs as he lay over her, eyes closed, savoring the feeling of near euphoria. He felt as if he'd been flung into some alternate universe, far out past the stars. It had been like that with her their first night together. Every single time.

Player breathed the scent of sex and Zyah into his lungs and found he loved the combination. He could live with that for the rest of his life. He felt lust for her like he'd never felt for another woman, but wrapped around that, intertwined with it, was something impossibly tender and overwhelming. He knew he was really falling in love with her. He didn't want to wear a glove. For the first time in his life, he didn't want anything between a woman and him. Not one single thing. He wanted there to be only Zyah and Player coming together.

When her body had settled, he pushed the hair from the nape of her neck and kissed her there gently before slowly straightening. "Are you all right? I got a little crazy there at the end."

"Mmm. Just fine." Zyah didn't move, and she didn't open her eyes. "I'm just going to lie right here and go to sleep."

He laughed softly. "There're three bedrooms in this house, baby. I think we can find you a much better place to sleep if you're tired." He kissed his way down her spine to her lower back before slowly and with great reluctance withdrawing. Just that movement triggered a reaction in her body. He felt it as he withdrew, and she smiled and moaned softly, shifting her hips.

"I like that."

"I'll bet you do." He knotted the condom. He hated the damn things now. They protected her but kept him from really feeling every inch of her, and he wanted that. "Baby, are you on birth control?"

"Yes."

"I'm clean. I haven't been near a bi . . . a woman in months. Years, really. Not inside her. I had blow jobs, but not inside her. I wouldn't lie to you. I detest using condoms with you. I'd much prefer to go without a glove. Think it over, will you?" He rubbed her bare cheeks.

"If you haven't been with a woman, why do you have condoms everywhere?"

"I don't know. Hopeful, maybe. I saw Reaper and Ice find their women. Steele, everyone knew it was Breezy, but then Absinthe found Scarlet. We all thought maybe there was a chance for the rest of us. I wanted to make certain my woman was protected. Now I kind of wish I hadn't done so much overthinking."

She laughed softly and his stomach had that peculiar reaction of a serious flip. *Bog,* he was bordering on sheer insanity when it came to her.

"I've been thinking about this room, Player. I think I'm really fond of it."

He helped her to stand straight. "I was hoping you'd give your approval of the dining room." He ran his finger from her collarbone to the tip of her breast. He liked to see the marks of his mouth and fingers on her skin.

A slow smile lit her eyes. "I *especially* love your dining room."

"Good, then. Let me show you the rest of the house. There are actually two kitchens inside the house. One outside. A smokehouse and a wine cellar. I like cooking, so it's my kind of house." He flashed a grin. "Considering I have a few fantasies of eating food off your body, I think it's fair to say we might need more than one kitchen."

"You do?" Her eyes widened. "Have a *few* fantasies? Not just one?"

He laughed as he beckoned her to follow him through to the kitchen. "You should know me better than that by now. I have all kinds of fantasies, my little innocent. We're going to need a weekend — or maybe a week — to show you a couple of kitchen fantasies."

She nodded. "If Inez ever approves of someone to give me some actual time off, I'm all over a weekend with you."

He stopped abruptly. "Lana is your backup."

She rolled her eyes. "Honey. Really? I love Lana. She's sweet, she really is, and I'm certain as a backup for a million other things, she's your bestie, but retail, commercial, anything with putting that woman in an actual store and making her stand behind a counter and deal with customers all day, not on your life. She'd decide it was the perfect day to watch the whales go by when it wasn't whale season, and you know it. She'd close the store."

He shrugged. "What's the big deal? We could close it down for the weekend." He kept her walking through to one of the kitchens where the center island, with its freestanding counter space, had given him all sorts of ideas when he was making meals long before he met Zyah. He knew what he would do if he was ever lucky enough to find a partner and share his house with her.

"You can't close a grocery store for a weekend. Customers depend on the store, *especially* over the weekend. Your club is very lucky you went into business with Inez and then you hired me. You'd go broke the first month without us."

He wrapped his arm around her. "That's probably true. See this island? It's just the right height to put you on when I get hungry while I'm working." He turned her to indicate the corner, where there was a small little table with two chairs. "And that's the perfect corner to put you in when you need to get on your hands and knees and wait for me to come over and see what I might want to do to punish you when you've been a very naughty girl like you so often are."

"I see." She laughed and pointed to the little bench with a thick cushion on it. "And that?"

"That's obvious. When I'm working, you can give me the blow job of the century. I recognize there's a lot of me, me, me in here, but chefs need a lot of encouragement while they work the long, thankless hours they work."

"I get that."

"Don't worry. I'll have plenty of ice cream, whipped cream, chocolate, and just about anything else I know you like stored in the fridge to keep your strength up."

"Nice. Very thoughtful."

"I'm a very thoughtful kind of man. Let's go take a shower. It will warm you up, and I can show you the master bedroom."

He led her through the other rooms and quickly down the hall to his room. He'd done the most work there. The master bedroom was the only one of the bedrooms that was really enormous. With the same wood floor, the walls had been white, the windows long, almost floor to ceiling, to give a view of the trees and shrubbery from two sides. The ceilings were vaulted, and the room stretched to add a sitting area and then grew to accommodate a master bath.

To Player, the room had seemed as if it were more suited to a woman than a man. He had changed the colors in the room from white to muted grays, beiges and blacks. He'd treated the master bath the same, adding in a Moroccan touch, with dark wood cabinets and black vessel sinks with wood countertops. The tub was a deep black bowl with all fixtures in gold. The shower was a masterpiece of gold and black, with heated stones and jets to rinse every part of a sore body after bending over for long hours of woodworking. Heated towels waited when he stepped out on heated tiles to dry off.

"Player. I love this. I really do."

He heard it in her voice. She really did like what he'd done with the room. It didn't matter that she was a woman, the colors still appealed to her. "I have privacy screens to keep the light out when I need to sleep in. I haven't ever used them, but I'm hoping someday I will." He flashed her a little smirk.

"It won't be tomorrow. I really have to work. But I'm okay with going to work without sleep. I already texted Mama Anat. She said Savage and Destroyer were staying with her. Maestro left when we did."

"Yeah, he followed us to Czar's. We usually run in pairs, and since this thing happened" — he touched his head — "Maestro's really been hovering."

She frowned and glanced out the window. "Is he around? I'm totally naked."

"First, babe, he wouldn't be looking. We grew up seeing naked bodies and others hav-

387

ing sex. It doesn't really faze us. That aside, no, he isn't out there. He's bunking down in the workroom. There's a bed there. He texted me when we first got here to let him know if we leave. By now, he's sound asleep. If it bothers you that he's on the property, I'll ask him to leave."

Zyah shook her head, wandering over to the bathroom. The doors were really black laser-carved screens. "These are cool. Did you make these?"

He watched the way her fingers slid over the inside of the shapes in what could only be described as little caresses. She made his heart ache when she did things like that. No one gave him those little recognitions. She probably wasn't even aware she was doing it, but to him, those gestures meant something. He came close to her, his hand on the small of her back, gently urging her forward so that she stepped inside.

The moment she did, automatic lights came on. Muted. He never had liked bright. He might rethink bright, a single spotlight over the bed to shine down on Zyah when he had her spread out, her long hair everywhere and her body undulating with heat and need. Or maybe he needed a room of mirrors to reflect every single expression on her face, every ripple of her body . . .

Zyah laughed and turned to him, her arms sliding up his chest, hands linking behind his neck, fingers teasing his hair. "You're becoming obsessed with my body."

"Baby, I'm way past obsessed. Water on. Isn't every man obsessed with your body?"

"Most definitely not." She turned at the sound of the water pouring down. Steam rose. The inside of the shower was all rock, smooth so it was easy to walk or sit on the stone bench, but it looked like one was walking into a large cavern. The rocks were various shades of brown, black, gray and white.

Once they stepped into the structure, water swept over them from various directions. Player pulled Zyah back to him, protecting her from one of the jets so he could adjust it better to her height. "Is the water too hot?"

She shook her head. "It's perfect. I like hot water."

They were compatible in every way. She was adventurous. Playful. She lifted her hands to her hair as the water cascaded down. Laughing. Uncaring that her hair was going to be soaked even in the tight braid she'd woven.

"Do you want me to take your braid out?" Truthfully, he wanted to take it out more than anything. He didn't get many chances to play with her hair.

"Not unless you have a blow-dryer in this house."

He grinned at her and reached for the end of that long, luxurious, very thick braid.

"Have you taken a look at my hair? I have one, I just don't use the thing. Lana got me one. Then Alena did because she thought I didn't like the first one."

Zyah's soft laughter made him happy. She drove away every demon just with that genuine sound. She let him wash and condition her hair and then her body. He took his time, using the gel to wash every inch of her. She took her turn, washing and conditioning his hair and then washing his body, paying attention to every nook and cranny. Zyah wasn't shy about the human body, and he liked that.

It did occur to him that she might not be the kind of woman who would ever enjoy the kind of parties Torpedo Ink had, where the men and women often had open sex. They tended to feel much freer when their brethren were around to protect them, when they had eyes watching to ensure no one could harm the ones they loved. They all felt a little vulnerable when they had sex without someone watching their back. Zyah most likely would have a difficult time understanding that. He was already going to be asking her to forgive too many sins and understand too many of his issues to add that one to the list right at this time. He'd put it on the back burner.

"Where'd you go, honey?" Zyah asked as they stepped out of the shower.

"Water off," he ordered. At once the water

went off. He handed her a warm towel to wrap her hair in and another one to dry her body off with. She smiled at him when she put her feet on the warm tiles. For just that smile alone, he was glad he'd spent the extra money to put in the heating.

"I'm sorry I got you into this, Zyah, and very grateful to you that you've stuck it out with me. I know you didn't have to. It's important that you know how much I appreciate you sticking with me, trying to sort out the bomb business as well as going to Czar."

She looked up at him, and then unexpectedly touched his mouth with the pads of her fingers, an intimate gesture, tracing his lips. "We're in this together, Player, all the way until the end. I'm not deserting you. And tonight is our night. Everyone else can go away for tonight. Agreed?"

Damn straight he agreed. A slow smile spread across his face until it almost hurt. "Agreed. Come on, I'll show you the living room. There are two. They sort of flow into each other. The large one, I suppose, was originally designed for entertaining, and the smaller one would be more intimate, for friends and family. Since I have rowdy friends and a lot of them, the larger of the two rooms, which would be more formal, is the one I use when they're over. I prefer the smaller of the two rooms, which is strange because I like wide open spaces."

"I have to dry my hair, crazy man."

"We'll dry it in the other room. Both have fireplaces. I'll bring the blow-dryer as well and the brush and comb."

"Are we just going to walk around naked?"

"Why not? If you put on clothes, I'm just going to keep taking them off of you, not that I mind, but you may as well be comfortable. There's a hot tub and an indoor heated saltwater lap pool at the other end of the house. I think the man who built the house used them for his therapy. Do you like to swim?"

"I do, but I don't like to rinse out my hair all the time. The doctor said water therapy would be good eventually for Mama Anat's leg."

Player nodded. "She mentioned that to me. I told her about the pool and said she could use it anytime she wanted to. I can give you a key."

"That's generous of you, Player."

He laughed. "The others will tell you, I'm such a generous man."

He pulled her through the kitchen to the living room, the one he particularly liked. Snatching up the remote, he flipped on the fireplace so the light would play through the room, illuminating it enough that she could see what he'd done with it. As with the dining room, he'd kept it simple. He didn't like clutter. The hardwood floor gleamed with the firelight spilling across it. He noticed Zyah pressing her bare feet instantly into the wood. She liked to do that the same way he did.

The hearth was made of gray stone, and he had utilized that color throughout the room. The chairs faced the stone fireplace built into the wall. The stones were great blocks of various sizes and textures of dark and light shades of gray. The only rug was on the floor in front of the fireplace, a thick gray-and-black mat of hand-knotted silk and wool. The chairs were wide and comfortable, both in black, which matched the carpet and the darkest of the stones. Over the fireplace was a picture framed in gold, a burst of color: a very large painting of a forest in vivid detail, done by an artist he particularly admired.

He sank down into his favorite chair, the one closest to the fireplace, where his acoustic guitar was near to his hand on a stand. He kept it there to play at night when he couldn't sleep, and he composed. He watched his woman walk around the room with that flowing grace she had, like a dancer, his private dancer. He wished she wore her anklet of bells. He had loved the sound of them as she'd moved around the room their first night together. Just that memory stirred his cock.

Zyah circled back to stand in front of him, the flames from the fireplace dancing over her body, licking at that secret place between her legs. "I can see why you love this room."

He caught her hips and urged her toward him, hungry for her taste. One hand skimmed down her hip, trailing to the inside of her thigh. "I'm suddenly so hungry, baby, you'll have to feed me before I starve."

She threw her head back. "You're supposed to be drying my hair."

"After. I need to build up my strength to be up for the task."

Her fingertips trailed over his cock, brushing fire over him. "You're up for something," she whispered, and stepped right into him, offering him everything.

# THIRTEEN

Player walked very slowly, moving casually down the sidewalk in Sea Haven, glancing into the store windows as he passed them by. He targeted one store in particular. The sign was clever, wooden, in the shape of a hat, although what the name had to do with a tea and organic bath and lotion shop, he didn't know. The Floating Hat sounded intriguing, but aside from cups in the windows looking like hats and the bells shaped like hats on the doors, the shop had nothing whatsoever to do with hats. What the hell did that even mean? Women. Always a mystery. Still, when he looked inside, the store felt inviting.

The space looked smallish from the outside, with bay windows on either side of the door facing the street. One window held the intriguing hat-shaped cups, an assortment of teas and stacked caddies of delicious-looking scones. The other window held lotions and bath products. Glancing into the windows, it was easy to see that the store was quite spacious, which was good, given that he had a difficult time with confined places. He could see at a glance that behind the counter there was at least one more room and another exit.

There were tables and chairs in one area. Most were for two people; some were for four. There was one larger table that could handle at least six. The tables were a distance apart from the other half of the store, creating a feeling of openness. He thought if Zyah and her grandmother really wanted to go there, he might make the sacrifice and take them.

Player walked on past to the end of the block, turned and made his way slowly back, trying to look as if he were just looking at the various stores. Coming up beside him, Preacher began whistling a tune off-key, making him wince. "Love Potion Number Nine" seemed to be a favorite lately with him whenever he was around Player and the subject of coming to Hannah's shop came up.

"What is that infernal racket you're making? You sound like a dying cow."

Preacher grinned at him. "Just wanted to get you in the mood."

Player flipped him off, glaring at him as he paced back up the sidewalk, carefully avoiding looking into the store he was weighing whether or not to go into. "Don't look, you moron, she'll notice," he hissed. "She's standing right by the window."

"It's your third time walking past her shop, Player. I think she's noticed," Preacher said, shoving a hand through his wealth of out-of-control curls, the bane of his life. "Our Torpedo Ink cuts kind of stand out, don't you think? And then there's Destroyer, sitting over there looking mournful with the bikes, and Lana and Alena across the street, grinning like apes, pretending they're shopping at the clothing store when really, they're making fun of you."

Player stopped walking and turned his head alertly to look for his Torpedo Ink sisters. "Why would they be making fun of me?"

"Because this was the dumbest idea on the planet, that's why. You need a love potion, I can make you one," Preacher assured. "You don't need to come here."

"I'm not looking for a love potion. Who the hell said I was looking for a love potion?" He gave Preacher his fiercest scowl. "Get the hell away from me. Go over and wait by the bikes with Destroyer. At least he's got the good sense to stay over there when he thinks we're doing stupid things."

Preacher grinned at him. "Not a chance. You're going into that shop, and I'm not letting you go in alone. Hannah Drake Harrington is one powerful witch. Someone has to save your worthless ass."

"She's not a witch. She's the wife of the local sheriff, and if you call her a witch, he's going to put a bullet right through your fuckin' heart. Seriously, Preacher, go away. This matters to me, and I don't want you to embarrass me."

Four little boys ran down the sidewalk across the street, nearly running right into Alena and Lana. "Hannah! Miss Hannah!" they called out in unison. They were all laughing. They looked to be around eight.

Player stopped to see what the woman would do. She couldn't fail to hear the raised voices. They sounded excited. Hopeful. Daring. All four boys stared at the shop with bright eyes. Preacher, Destroyer, Alena and Lana all paused as well, eyes on the door of the shop, as if they too waited for something huge to happen. Player had no idea what to expect, only that those four little boys were so excited, and whatever they wanted, they were so hopeful, he didn't want Hannah Drake Harrington to let them down.

The door opened slowly, the bells announcing her presence, setting those hats tinkling in warning. The boys went ramrod straight, mouths opening in suspense. Player found himself tense. There was a sudden silence as if everything on the street paused.

A breeze blew leaves down the street ever so gently. Suddenly, without any warning at all, the wind gusted, right over the four little boys, taking the baseball caps from their heads and throwing them capriciously into the air. The hats whirled just above the boys' heads, then traveled down the sidewalk, just out of reach, as the boys ran after them with outstretched hands, laughing. Player watched the boys run for a moment, realizing the wind wasn't really blowing that hard, yet the hats dipped and wheeled, like bats in the air, but at no time went near the street. The wind died down completely and the hats floated into the boys' hands. They caught them, put them on their heads, turned back toward the shop and waved. Player glanced back to the door, but it was closed, and Hannah Drake Harrington was back inside.

"What the hell was that?" he asked Preacher.

"I don't know," Preacher replied, "but you might want to rethink your opinion of the witch theory."

Player tapped a beat out on his thigh. He wanted to make things right with Zyah. He'd felt that shift in power the moment that door had opened and Hannah Harrington had stepped outside. It had been subtle, but it had been there, coming from the doorway of the Floating Hat. Maybe he'd come to the right place.

Abruptly, he made up his mind, turned his back on his Torpedo Ink brother and marched, ramrod stiff, a man going to his doom, back to the little shop sandwiched between the wine shop and the gift shop. The display windows looked harmless enough. Nothing out of the ordinary. Well, okay, a little girlie and froufrou.

He'd seen Hannah Harrington around town a few times. She was stunning. Breathtaking. She wasn't a witch despite that little display with the boys and their hats. He wasn't certain what that was, but he had his own talents. All of the members of Torpedo Ink did, and they knew that the Drake sisters did as well.

Hannah had been a model, the kind that graced the cover of every magazine and worked runways, in such demand that she could pick and choose which designer she worked for. She'd been considered the top model in the world, and everyone wanted her wearing their clothes. Tall, large blue eyes, high cheekbones, a generous mouth, with her signature long blond hair, which fell in natural spiral curls down her back, she had truly been one of the most beautiful women in the world until a madman attacked her with a knife and reportedly slashed her to ribbons.

The attack was caught on film, shown over and over on international television for weeks while she fought for her life and then retired to the small town of Sea Haven and the protection of her family and Jonas Harrington. Now she ran a small shop selling personal products made from organic materials she grew herself or purchased from the farm Blythe was part owner of.

Player had never actually been introduced to Hannah Drake Harrington, but he'd heard of her and he'd seen her a time or two walking down the street. She was a striking woman, very graceful, and she still walked like she was that model on a runway. There was always someone with her, usually one of her sisters but often her husband or Jackson Deveau, at least that was the report from Code when he'd asked about her. Player liked to be prepared.

He took a deep breath as he paused at the door. Was he really going to go through with this? Zyah was worth humiliating himself for. Hannah was no witch. She had strong psychic talents, no doubt about that, and she probably could wreak havoc on him, but he'd risk anything to try to find a way to get back in Zyah's good graces. He wasn't cheating by getting something stupid like a love potion. That might be a last resort, but he wouldn't mind a little advice on gifts. On things women liked. Surely in a shop like Hannah had, there would be special things that appealed to women. Things with special scents.

Player glanced back at Preacher, who was nearly on his heels. "What the hell. Go away, Preacher. I mean it. I'm going in, and I don't want you to get this woman upset at me. I'm already in enough trouble with Zyah. For all I know, they're best friends." He kept one hand on the door to prevent Preacher from opening it.

Movement inside caught his eye, and he turned away from Preacher's grinning face to see that Hannah had moved away from the window and was coming to the door again.

"Damn you, Preacher," he hissed and opened the door before the woman could get there. He had no choice now. Trying to look casual, he sauntered in. He did his best to close the door fast, but he heard the heavy, ornate wood hit Preacher's motorcycle boot. The little floating hats tinkled merrily, and Preacher joined him in the fragrant shop. The moment Player stepped inside, he felt a tremendous shift of power sweep over him. There was nothing subtle about that energy. It passed over and through him. He glanced uneasily at Preacher to see if he'd noticed. Yeah. He'd noticed.

Hannah smiled at them and then glanced over her shoulder. Another woman, leaning on the counter, straightened slowly. She was much smaller, with pale, delicate features and a wealth of black hair that could have overpowered her face had she not pulled it back. She was smiling as well, although Player could see she wasn't quite as genuine as Hannah. In fact, she picked up her cell phone. Player was pretty certain he knew who she was texting. He wasn't going to have very much time if he was really going to work up the courage to ask Hannah for help.

"What was that?" Preacher asked.

Hannah looked at him with a faint frown. Mild inquiry. "What was what?"

"Outside. With the boys," Preacher persisted.

Hannah smiled a sweet, vague smile that could have meant anything. "Aren't they darling? They come by regularly and say hello. May I help you find something, or did you just want to look around first?" Hannah's voice was musical.

There were very faint white lines running along her face. She could have concealed them with makeup, but she didn't. In Player's world, those scars were considered badges. He hoped she thought of them that way. She'd survived a vicious attack, and that meant something.

"I'd like to look around," Preacher said, giving up on any explanation.

"You're welcome to." Hannah gestured around the store, half turning away.

Player cleared his throat. "I might need a little help."

She turned back to him, that same smile in place. Now that he really looked at her closely, the smile wasn't so genuine. It just appeared that way. It was practiced, put in place to wear like makeup, but it didn't quite reach her eyes. Her fingers touched her wedding band, and then she grasped it like a talisman, twisting it back and forth.

For a moment, he considered that she was nervous because he was a biker. That happened all the time, but her eyes met his without flinching and he dismissed that idea. It was more likely that the attack on her had been so public, so ferocious and fast, that she still had problems facing strangers. That made her amazingly courageous to do what she was doing, although if the power he'd felt when he walked through the door was anything to go by, she had nothing to worry about.

"I blew it big-time with my woman." He just put it out there. He might as well get it over with. He glanced out the window at Lana and Alena. They were sitting on the sidewalk straight across from the shop and laughing together until he swore they were crying.

"I suppose you've come for a love potion. I really need to make one," Hannah said, sounding disappointed, again beginning to turn away from him.

"Why does everyone keep saying that to me?" he asked. "Do I really look that hopeless? I'll admit I was a jackass, but don't men buy women flowers and chocolate and shit?"

Hannah turned back, her blue gaze moving over his face. This time, her eyes seemed to see right through him in the way Czar's sometimes did. "Women don't want men to buy them shit," she said without a trace of a smile. "I'm Hannah."

"Player," he said. "And no, I didn't cheat on her, if that's what you think I did. And I wouldn't. Not ever."

"That's a relief. Tell me about her. What is it you love about her? What makes her so special?"

She walked over to a high table-and-chairs set sitting in the corner of the shop. It looked a little more delicate than anything he was used to. He'd seen outdoor furniture that was similar but built along much sturdier lines. She flashed a smile as she stepped onto one of the mauve-and-white-striped high-backed chairs. "They're really quite sturdy."

He wasn't quite as convinced, but he took her word for it. The chair, really a stool with a back on it, was surprisingly comfortable. The seat was thick and contoured to conform to one's bottom. "Who made these?" He could tell they hadn't been manufactured somewhere. Now that he was close and actually sitting in the chair, he could see the work was excellent. Someone had put a great deal of time and love into handcrafting the set for Hannah.

"His name was Pheldman. Casey Pheldman. He passed away a few years ago."

"He owned the house I bought," Player

said. He didn't bother to keep the admiration out of his voice. "I was so impressed with the craftsmanship. I haven't seen that kind of work very often. I really wish I could have met him. He was truly a gifted man."

"Yes, he was." Hannah's smile was much more genuine. "Would you care for coffee or tea while we talk?" She indicated a little teapot and coffee press. "No worries if you're in a hurry. I can make it very quickly."

"Coffee, then. Black."

He watched, fascinated, as she waved her hand toward the two pots and both seemed to start steaming at once. He frowned, looking around to see if there was a button she'd pushed.

"Now tell me about your Zyah. What do you think makes her so special?"

There was more than one person in his club who could use their voice to compel others to do as they wished. Player was one of them. His talent was subtle, not at all like Absinthe's or Master's or Maestro's, but he could still persuade others when he wanted something. Hannah was a force to be reckoned with. Player felt the need to answer her, and he knew she wasn't deliberately using her talent on him.

Player found himself wanting Hannah to know, mostly because he felt that the woman was gentle and kind. She wasn't the type to hurt anyone on purpose, ever. She was asking him because she genuinely wanted to help him — if he deserved it. He knew she was asking questions partially to make certain he wasn't a man who had in any way deliberately hurt his woman.

"Before I tell you about Zyah, I'm going to let you know right up front, she's nothing like me. I don't in any way deserve her. I don't. I never will. Still, she's the one, the only one for me, and I'll work every damn day of my life to make her happy. It's just that, if you're going to try to work out whether you think I'm a good man, I'll tell you I try to be. That I have a code I live by, but I fail more than I win."

She poured coffee into a mug. "That's refreshing to hear. The truth. You must really love this woman."

"I don't know what love is. I never had it. I want to know. When I'm with her, I feel things I don't feel for anyone else. I'd do anything for her. Anything. She's magic. She can take away demons with her laughter. Her smile. She doesn't judge people. She's like her grandmother in that way. She just accepts others. That doesn't make her a pushover. If that were the case, I wouldn't be in trouble." He rubbed the back of his neck, wondering why he was blurting out things to this woman he wouldn't say so readily to a stranger. In fact, he wouldn't be talking like this to a stranger. He took a sip of the coffee. It was excellent. More than excellent.

Those blue eyes moved over his face. She had feminine eyes, not at all like Czar's eyes, yet Player felt she saw in the same way he did, beyond skin and bones into one's black soul.

"You do carry demons, Player. They sit very heavy on your shoulders. I'm glad she takes them off for you. What did you do, if you don't mind me asking?"

He'd been afraid she would. He took a deep breath. This was the part he knew he'd have to man up for. He looked around the store. It would definitely appeal to women — and evidently did to Preacher as well. He had gathered up several items and taken them to the counter, where he was smelling them and putting them aside only to pick up others to do the same thing. Some he tore the packaging off, demanding to know the ingredients from the horrified clerk.

Player suppressed a groan. Preacher was going to get them kicked out of the shop before he could get what he needed, because he had the feeling Hannah could give him exactly the right gift to help him win back Zyah.

"I was overtired, too long without sleep. I wasn't doing well. I'd just met her and thought she was a dream. The best kind of a dream, but still a dream." He shook his head. "The things I said to her were insulting. Very insulting. I apologized, and she accepted. She's like that. But then . . ." He sighed. "We were so connected and she saw things about me I didn't want her to see. I was too embarrassed. It shouldn't have mattered. I just kept pushing her away. I can spend a lifetime apologizing, but actions speak much louder than words. I want to be that man of action, but I don't have a lot of experience when it comes to relationships. Neither do my friends. We're sort of winging it. I can't afford to do that with her. I don't want to make any more mistakes. I really hurt her. She fuckin' cried."

He forced himself to drink the coffee so he wouldn't make more of a fool of himself.

Hannah nodded. "I see. Tell me more about her. Anything at all. That will help me."

"She manages the grocery store in Caspar, and she has a great work ethic. I wanted to close the store down for the weekend, but she refused, even though she's exhausted, because she said people counted on the store being open on the weekends. Our club has always worked when we felt like it. We don't think about things like that. She's teaching me that we're responsible to others for those things."

Hannah nodded, sipping at her tea. Both pretended to ignore the growing heated exchange between the clerk and Preacher.

"She totally loves her grandmother. Zyah gave up an amazing, great-paying job to come here and take care of her after she was robbed and beaten."

Hannah gasped. "I read about those robberies. How terrible. Her grandmother was one of the victims?"

Player nodded. "Yeah. Zyah quit a lucrative job with an international food chain and came straight home to take care of her grandmother. She's that kind of woman. No regrets. She smells like this exotic combination of very subtle but definite jasmine, with a distinctive cinnamic-honey background." He looked up at her. "It's not perfume. I'm not kidding. It's her skin. I know I sound like an idiot, but we learned all this stuff from Alena, all the different types of herbs and spices. The citruses. When I get close to her or . . ." He trailed off. He wasn't about to start talking sex with Hannah.

"Is there more to her scent?"

He didn't want to sound like an idiot. He looked around the shop and dropped his voice almost to a whisper because unless you were a chef, you didn't talk like this. "Sort of a cassis-raspberry facet blending with rich green floral mimosa. All those scents blend together very subtly. I've got a really heightened sense of smell."

"And it isn't perfume?"

He shook his head.

"And she's on her feet all day?"

"She's a dancer. She likes to be barefoot.

She has an affinity with the earth. A gift. She feels things when she's barefoot. And she can heal when she's dancing."

"So, on top of everything else, she's gifted. She really is special, which means you are as well or you wouldn't have recognized that in her," Hannah murmured aloud. Her mind was already moving away from him and around her shop, clearly looking at the various things she had on her shelves.

Player hadn't meant to reveal anything about himself, and yet he'd given away quite a bit. He turned his attention to Preacher, who was usually one of the most easygoing of all the Torpedo Ink members. At least on the surface he seemed so. Right now, he seemed so furious, Player feared the shop might explode, blowing the walls from the inside out.

"I told you to stop tearing off the packaging. The ingredients are clearly marked on the *outside* of the packages," the clerk enunciated.

"And I told you, if you had the IQ of more than a donkey and could actually listen, that I would pay for all of these products, so it doesn't matter if I take off the packaging, that you haven't listed the amounts. I need the *exact* amounts. I know the ingredients you've put in. Well, not you. Clearly, you had nothing whatsoever to do with making these products because you can't tell me anything

411

at all about them."

"If you tear off the packaging on one more item, I'm calling the sheriff."

"You already called the sheriff the moment we walked into the store because we're wearing Torpedo Ink jackets and you're a fucking coward."

Player sighed. Preacher rarely swore. Most of them did, but he hadn't wanted to swear around Lana, and he had never really gotten into the habit. Player was going to have to defuse the situation before it really got out of hand.

"Don't you dare call me a coward. You can't possibly know I called the sheriff when you walked in. And give me that bath bomb right this minute."

There was a little scuffle. Preacher won, yanking the package. "I told you, I'm buying these things. You can't deny a paying customer. Go find something to do until the cops get here. You're annoying the holy hell out of me, and you're worthless as far as being a salesman."

"Probably because I'm a woman and *not* a man, you moron. Can't you tell the difference? A woman, for your information, has breasts and a vagina. A man has a penis."

Player nearly spewed coffee across the table. He was very thankful that Hannah had gone into the back room.

"Well, thank you very much for that enlightening information," Preacher said. "I'm glad you have an education in something. I should have known it would be in sex."

The clerk rolled her eyes. "That wasn't sex, you moron, that was anatomy. Get it right. And if you keep smelling that bath bomb, you perv, touching it with your nose, which, by the way, is now covered in a nice shade of shimmery purple, I'll have to charge you extra."

"Why would you have to charge me extra?"

"Makeup costs far more than bath products," the clerk answered smugly.

Hannah returned with a basket as Player was drinking the last of his coffee. The clerk was more than keeping up with Preacher. He had the feeling the woman was a stick of dynamite and if Preacher tore off any more packaging, she might really throw him out of the store. That would really be a show. Lana and Alena would never let Preacher hear the end of it.

"I put together a few things I think Zyah would really like, Player," Hannah said. "She's on her feet all day. You said she's a dancer and has an affinity with the earth. This particular lotion will appeal to her, the scent, the way it will feel on her skin and blend in with nature. In a way, it will amplify her awareness of the earth's call to her without her straining her talent. You massage it into her feet, ankles and calves very slowly, using a circular technique."

For a moment, Hannah looked uncomfortable. Her fingers went to her wedding ring and twisted it back and forth. "I would like to show you the technique. I'd need to touch your arm, if you wouldn't mind."

He shook his head and extended his arm to her, laying it across the high tabletop. "Of course not."

She took a deep breath. "You want to massage in a circular motion like this at first with a firm touch." She applied pressure. "Do you feel that? You don't want it to be too hard, but it has to penetrate in order for her to get relief and also to reach where her gift connects with yours. You always want to start out with this kind of pressure and the circular massage. I've written the instructions out for you and drawn a map of the foot, ankle and calf for you to follow, working your way up her leg. You want the lotion to absorb into her skin. That will bring tremendous relief to her."

Player nodded, shocked that Hannah had gone into so much detail for him. Her features were very intent. Serious. Clearly, she believed in what she was saying, and he believed it too. Just the fact that she said the lotion had to penetrate in order for Zyah to get relief but also for their gifts to connect. He'd never said a word to her about their connection. Not one word, yet she'd known.

"You want to work in a circular motion counterclockwise over the soles of her feet and then around her feet, just like in the diagram. Over the tops and then around her ankles and up her calves. Once you've done that, you switch from the lotion to this cream I put in the basket."

Hannah reached into the basket and brought out a large jar, holding it up for him. "I didn't have time to pretty up the packaging. If you want to come back, I can do that for you, make everything look really nice. I put all sorts of things in here for you, but the most important are the lotion and cream for her feet."

Player shook his head. "I'm just grateful you thought of something I could do for her."

"When you apply the cream, you use a completely different technique . . ."

Preacher nearly knocked over Player's chair, coming up behind him fast, his arms full of several items, which he immediately dumped on the table. Behind him, the clerk, looking like a furious little witch about to do incantations, rushed after him.

"Sorry, Player, but this is important." Preacher inserted his body between Player's high-backed chair and Hannah's. "You're the one who actually put all these together, right? You made these lotions and bath products."

"I'll throw him out for you, Hannah," the clerk declared. The declaration seemed ludicrous given she was half Preacher's size, but she looked more than determined.

Preacher put his hand on top of the clerk's head and held her at arm's length, ignoring her wild struggle to reach the items rolling off the table. Player went to catch them, but Hannah held up her hand, and they just seemed to stop in midroll. He blinked, a little shocked, uncertain of what had just happened.

"Pipe down," Preacher said to the clerk, not looking at her. "You are, right? You made this stuff. All of it. The ingredients are on the packaging but not the amounts. I have to know the amounts. You're amazing. You know that, right? Only a few people in the world can produce these kinds of products."

Hannah arched an eyebrow. "You haven't tried them yet."

"I can smell them. Taste them."

"He's wearing them on his nose," the clerk accused. "*And* he opened all the packaging. I told him not to, but he didn't listen at all."

Player looked at Preacher's face. He was wearing an expression he'd never seen before, almost fanatical, definitely passionate, and sure enough, the clerk was right, the end of his nose was a shade of purple that shimmered in the light. Player pulled out his cell phone and took a quick shot of Preacher's nose. Preacher didn't even notice. His total concentration was on Hannah.

"You're freaking her out, bro," Player said, putting his phone away. "He's harmless, Hannah. He's really into this kind of thing, and no one understands a word he says, so coming in here, he's probably in seventh heaven. You're some kind of goddess to him."

"Not some kind of goddess," Preacher denied. "*The* goddess. There's only a handful of people in the world that could do this without a company surrounding them, and I don't see a company around you. You do this solo, don't you? You grow everything, and you handpick your ingredients and then you make the lotion up or the cream or the candle for your store or your client."

The clerk relaxed, but Preacher seemed to forget he had his hand on her head. He remained, his arm outstretched, holding her in place while he stared at Hannah with admiration.

"Actually, Mr. . . ."

"Preacher. Call me Preacher."

The clerk made a rude noise, drawing Preacher's attention. "Of course you're called Preacher. I'll bet you preach to everyone."

Hannah took the opportunity to put her hands on Player's arm to show him the penetrating technique she wanted him to use with the cream. Not a circular motion this time but more of a deep tissue massage.

"Again, start with the soles of the feet. You might have to work up to a deeper massage if

417

it's too painful at first. I doubt that it will be. She has an affinity with the earth, so the aches are always going to be there. This will help with that tremendously. It will also establish an intimacy between the two of you if you can get her to allow you to do this for her after she's been working all day."

Preacher glared at the clerk, his fist closing even tighter in the thick wealth of black hair. "Someone needs to preach to you from the good book of manners. I'm trying to get some answers here — important ones, which you wouldn't know a thing about. Why you're working in this shop, I have no idea. You'd be better suited to the toy store down the street."

The clerk tried to kick him just as the door was flung open and Jonas burst in, gun drawn, a look of fury on his face. His blue gaze took in everything, including his wife's hands massaging Player's arm, the clerk kicking at Preacher and Preacher's hand buried deep in the clerk's hair. Player could imagine what it looked like with so many of the bath bombs, soaps, lotions and creams strewn across the table, along with the large basket. He shook his head and resigned himself to going to jail at the very least. The worst was, Jonas might really shoot him, since his wife had her hands all over him.

"What the hell is going on here?" Jonas demanded.

"Go away, Jonas," Preacher said. "I mean

it. The last thing I need is for you to come in here and make this more difficult. And take this horrid little fairy creature with you. If you don't, I'm going to have to tie her up and put her in the back room with a gag on her."

"Preacher, I swear I'm going to shoot you," Jonas said. "Let go of Sabelia right now, and Hannah, it would be best if you stop massaging Player's arm."

"Put the gun away," Hannah said.

"Go away," Preacher repeated simultaneously with Hannah.

Hannah burst out laughing, the sound filling the shop with genuine merriment. At once the mood seemed to change dramatically. The sun seemed to shine brighter.

"I'm not putting the gun away, Hannah, until you stop massaging Player's arm."

"I'm *working,*" she clarified. "What are you doing here?"

Player would have liked to pull his arm out from under Hannah's hands. That gun hadn't wavered, not one inch, steady as a rock, and it wasn't pointed at Preacher, which technically wasn't in the least bit fair. He was the one with his fist locked in the clerk, Sabelia's, hair. That should have gotten him the gun.

"Just what kind of work are you doing, Hannah?" Jonas demanded.

"*Jonas,*" Preacher hissed through gritted

teeth. "Leave now and take this . . . this *person* with you. You may not be aware, but your wife just happens to be a genius. A true genius. A fuckin' goddess. I need to talk to her without interruption. Take Player with you, even if you have to remove him at gunpoint. Take everyone, but just leave."

"He's crazy, Jonas," Sabelia informed Jonas in a haughty tone. She rubbed her scalp when Preacher released her. "Certifiably insane. Arrest him and put him in jail."

"For what?"

She wiggled her fingers. "For not recognizing the difference between sex education and anatomy, for one. And he thinks *I'm* the moron. He should be jailed for that alone."

Jonas holstered his gun, which Player thought was a good idea since the man was beginning to look harassed, not that he could blame him. He wanted to ask if it was always like that around his wife's shop. Hannah's blue eyes sparkled at her husband.

"What the hell are you talking about, Sabelia?" Jonas demanded and then held up his hand. "Don't tell me. I don't want to know. Hannah." He stopped. Shook his head. Turned and walked out.

Sabelia smothered a laugh with her fingertips over her mouth.

"Sex education and anatomy, Sabelia?" Hannah asked.

"Apparently, Preacher isn't aware of the

420

difference, so I was trying to educate him," Sabelia said, reaching around Preacher's body to try to collect the packaging that was strewn all over the table.

Preacher's hand slammed down over the paper, locking it in place. "I told you I was buying that. Don't touch it. I'm in a discussion here. Run along and find your broomstick. Sweep the shop or do whatever it is you normally do."

"Don't be rude to my help, Preacher, or you will be leaving," Hannah warned.

"She was rude to me, *and* she tried to have me arrested. She called Jonas just because I'm a biker. Not for any other reason. She deserves to have someone put her in her place."

Hannah looked at her employee. Sabelia met her eyes and then looked away. "I'll start cleaning the store, Hannah."

Hannah nodded. "I would like to finish with Player before we talk, Preacher. He's here for a specific reason, and I'm working with him. If you'd like to wait, I'll be happy to talk with you after we're done. You're welcome to sit at one of the tables and have a cup of coffee or tea."

"Try some tea, Preacher, something soothing," Player suggested.

Preacher glared at Player. "I don't suppose you —"

"No," Player cut him off, exasperated.

"I'm going to annoy the hell out of that little she-devil," Preacher said. "So you'd better make it fast, Player. Otherwise she'll call Jonas back here. If he catches his wife with her hands all over you again, he'll shoot you for sure."

He started back toward the main counter.

"Preacher." Player stopped him.

Preacher swung around, looking hopeful.

"Take your things. You may as well pay for them. And don't rile that girl up."

"You'd better not," Hannah echoed. "Just for your information, she's apprenticing."

Preacher looked horrified as he gathered up the various products and the wrapping.

"It would never have occurred to me to take on an apprentice, but she's special," Hannah said. "Instead of fighting with her, you might want to make peace with her."

Preacher grinned at her. "Having way too much fun getting her all riled up. She tried to kick me. Haven't had a woman try that ever that I can recall."

Player shook his head. "I'm sorry, Hannah. He really isn't crazy. In fact, usually Preacher's the one we can count on. It's just that" — he looked around the shop — "I love music and working with wood. He loves this kind of thing. He needs it. The rest of us don't have a clue what he does. He has his own chemistry shop, and we give him a bad time about it, but we don't have a prayer of understanding what he does in it or the things he whips up in it. I can't imagine what it would be like to meet someone like you after years of never talking to someone who could understand him."

He didn't want her to think Preacher was insane or that he might harm Sabelia. Preacher was a good man and much more stable than the rest of them — most of the time. He always held it together for Lana. Player glanced across the room at him now as he dumped the paper and products all over the countertop in front of Sabelia.

She made a face, glanced at Hannah and reached down to get a box.

"I'd prefer one of those really nice baskets like Hannah gave Player," Preacher said.

Sabelia regarded him with narrowed eyes, gritted her teeth, as if she knew he was deliberately trying to provoke her. "You have to pay extra for the baskets."

"Are you implying you don't think I have the money?"

"No, sir, I'm not implying that at all. I'm informing you of the extra cost just in case you weren't aware of it," Sabelia replied in a bit of a superior tone.

Hannah's head came up, and her fingers ceased moving on Player's arm.

"He's deliberately provoking her," Player said. "He can be a real ass sometimes. The fact that you said she's apprenticing under

423

you probably made him jealous. Who knows what the deal is, but don't embarrass her when he's already poking at her. I think she's handling herself quite well under the circumstances."

Hannah shook her head. "Once you work the cream in, using a deep tissue massage, let her rest for about fifteen minutes. Just keep her legs on your lap. At that point she should be feeling very good, all aches gone, and very connected to you. After fifteen minutes, offer her this drink."

She showed him two small glasses. They were beautiful. He recognized Lissa Prakenskii's work. They were small goblets with twisted stems, tiny hearts embedded in the stems and floating in between the layers of glass. He couldn't imagine how any glassblower, no matter how skilled, could produce that kind of work in something that small.

Hannah had included two bottles of a liquid in the woven basket. "This is nonalcoholic." She had a small bottle on the table he hadn't noticed. She measured a small portion into a glass and added water. "You just use two tablespoons and fill the glass. You can use sparkling water if she prefers." She handed him the drink.

Player forced himself to try it. He wasn't much on anything sweet, but Hannah had been really good to him, taking time to show him how to apply the lotion and cream. Even if it didn't work the way Hannah thought it would, Zyah would probably like the foot massage after standing on her feet all day. In any case, there was no harm in trying. He took a cautious drink. The beverage tasted . . . extraordinary.

"If Preacher gets ahold of this, he'll decide you're more than a goddess."

She smiled, clearly pleased. "Let's hope Zyah likes it. It's expensive, Player, because everything I do is made by hand, and it takes time to get everything right. I have to experiment."

He waved that away. "Believe me, I can tell without Preacher acting like a crazy man that you're well worth it. I really appreciate it, Hannah. Did you include a list of everything so I can reorder if she likes it?"

Hannah nodded as they both stood up. Preacher came hurrying toward them, nearly knocking Player down. "Are you finished?"

Hannah exchanged a slow smile with Player. "I believe we are. Sabelia will ring the purchases up for you, Player. Thanks for coming in."

"Preacher, don't keep her past closing time," Player cautioned.

"Don't worry," Sabelia said. "I'll make sure he leaves." She had followed him through the shop to put his packages on the floor beside the table.

"Thanks, Sabelia," Hannah said, forestalling any response from Preacher.

The shop door opened, and Alena and Lana sauntered in. Preacher frowned at them. "What do you two want?" he demanded.

"Tea," they replied in a perfect duet, and then laughed.

"I'm sure there's another tea shop somewhere," he groused.

"This is my business," Hannah reminded. "Sabelia will serve them while we talk."

Player left them to it. He hoped Lana and Alena would give Preacher some time with Hannah before they made him too crazy, but he wasn't going to wait around to find out.

# FOURTEEN

Some days were just longer than others. There was no getting around it. Of course, the fact that she hadn't slept the night before might have attributed to the hours dragging on forever. Zyah glanced out the large windows for the millionth time. The view should have gone a long way to making the job bearable on a day like this one. The ocean was particularly moody. The moon was out, shining over the water so that she could see the choppy waves, dark and angry, an ominous portent of something evil coming.

Dread had been building for the last hour. This was the store's late night. The locals came in to shop in a steady flow, peaking around seven and then tapering off at eight. She stayed open until nine. Only another hour and she could go home, see Mama Anat. She couldn't wait to see her. Her grandmother grounded her. No matter what was going on, no matter how chaotic, Anat made the world seem right. She needed her.

427

She also wanted to see Player. She missed him.

They both had slept for very brief periods of time, no more than half an hour, and maybe that was why he hadn't woken with a terrible nightmare. She called it a victory each time he managed to sleep and there was no traumatic dream. At her home she slept in the guest room and rushed to him if he woke, already wrapped in the illusion, the White Rabbit present most of the time. Or he would be covered in sweat, fighting in his sleep, trying to stop his attackers. She detested those nights the most. She caught too many glimpses of what had happened to that beautiful little boy.

He'd been such a sad child with his sorrowful blue eyes. She wanted to wrap him up in her arms and run, keep him safe. He'd had a mop of light brown hair, streaked with blond, not those white streaks like he had now. They looked like highlights he might have dyed in his hair, but she knew they were there naturally. He'd gotten them the hard way.

She glanced at her watch. Half an hour. She could start shutting things down. She hadn't had a customer in the last half hour. She was so lucky. The day had been crazy, with people streaming in steadily. Good for business. Over the last couple of weeks, she felt they were doing very well. Steady, returning customers. That, more than anything else, was what they needed to count on. She was getting a feel for what was needed. Many of those coming in had suggestions, and she took note of them so she could order and keep the right supplies on hand.

A bright pink Cadillac pulled up to the curb with a screech of brakes, jumped it and bumped off with a loud grating noise. Zara recognized the car immediately. It was Lizz Johnson's pride and joy. She made a show of driving it slowly up and down the main street of Sea Haven at least twice a week. She always drove it to Anat's house but called ahead to ensure she could park her beloved vehicle either right out front, where everyone could admire it, or in the driveway of the garage.

Francine, Lizz's granddaughter, leapt out of the driver's seat, doubled over with laughter. She slammed the door hard and came around the hood, still laughing, covering her mouth and shaking her head. She wore a tight skirt that molded to her slim hips and a low-cut blouse that framed her thin rib cage and showcased her set of breasts nicely. Her boots were knee-high, soft leather, a light tan, and worth a fortune. Zyah recognized the brand. Lizz definitely indulged her granddaughter in everything from clothes and shoes to jewelry and even allowing her to drive without her license. As she approached the door to the grocery store, she staggered for just a couple of steps, then recovered her balance, phone in hand, laughing as if it were funny. Clutching her purse, Francine made her way into the store.

"Zyah. Just the girl I'm looking for."

Princess to peasant. That was Francine, and no one was around to catch her act. She was that genuine. She really did think of herself as superior because Lizz had a fortune.

"Nice to see you, Francine. I see you have your license back. Congratulations. Mama Anat will be so happy for you. She was worried about how you would get around when the rains came."

Francine frowned and waved that subject off dismissively. Her driver's license was clearly of no consequence.

"I thought I'd take you to dinner tonight. I felt so bad that I went off with that loser biker. I shouldn't have done that without at least texting you and giving you the heads-up." Francine smiled, her white teeth dazzling against her red lipstick. She came closer to the counter so she could lean against it.

"I love your boots," Zyah said, not wanting to answer immediately. Francine's good moods could turn on a dime if she was thwarted in her plans, and Zyah had no intention of going to dinner with her. "They're absolutely gorgeous." Francine was very vain when it came to clothes, shoes, jewelry and even makeup.

Francine looked down at her boots, stuck the right one out to admire the soft leather and smirked at Zyah. "They're so comfortable too. I love everything Jimmy Choooo." She drew out the last name and then tossed her head laughing, bringing deliberate attention to her earrings and necklace.

Zyah's gaze was immediately riveted to the glittering star at Francine's throat. It was an amazing blue diamond and very, very real, as were the stars at her ears. That was part of Lizz's galaxy collection. Anat had told her about it and spoken of it in low tones, afraid of being overheard. What was Francine doing wearing a piece like that in public when there were known robbers preying on the elderly? Was she so selfish she would risk her grandmother to show off? Zyah was beginning to fear she would.

"You're wearing your grandmother's blue diamonds. I thought she kept those locked up in a safe at the bank."

Francine stuck her hip out. "I talked her into letting me wear them to the charity ball next month. I told her I had to try a couple of pieces with different outfits to see what would go best. It's such a shame to have such beautiful jewelry and then keep it in a vault somewhere and never even see it."

Zyah lowered her voice and looked around, although she knew the store was empty. She just wanted Francine to think she was entering into some kind of conspiracy with her. "Aren't you afraid those thieves might target you and your grandmother?"

Francine scowled. "I have a gun. I always carry a gun. Do you want to see it? You would never suspect I have one on me." Her body swayed, and she gripped the edge of the counter to keep from falling. Before Zyah could answer, she leaned closer, giggling. "You should carry a gun, Zyah. Someday you're going to need it." That made her laugh hysterically. She pulled her shirt up to show the tight band around her waist that had the gun holster with the gun fitted to her. "If anyone tries to take me in, I'll just shoot 'em."

"You mean rob you? Or your grandmother? Have you been worried they might? You haven't seen strangers hanging around your house, have you?" Zyah asked, suddenly feeling anxious. Francine wasn't making a lot of sense, but then she'd clearly had too much to drink. "Is that thing loaded?" Zyah glanced at the security camera. It made her feel a lot safer to know that there were two Torpedo Ink club members in the back. Someone was always watching.

"Of course." Francine dropped her shirt back into place, shook her head and then laid a finger across her lips, then looked around and beckoned Zyah closer. She waited until Zyah leaned across the counter. "I keep my grandmother safe. No worries about her. She might be an old bat sometimes, but I take care of her." There was love in her voice. "She takes care of me. No one is going to hurt her."

Zyah sighed. There was no way she was going to get to go home and take a hot bath and soak in the tub. She was going to have to go to dinner with Francine and make certain she didn't drive Lizz's precious Cadillac. She'd definitely had too much to drink. Zyah pulled out her cell phone and texted Player to arrange for someone to get Lizz's car and take it back to her. She would hate to have it left out all night sitting in front of the grocery store.

She found it strange that the first person she would turn to for help was Player, when Keys and Destroyer were in the back room, probably watching on the monitor.

"I think you should teach me to dance, Zyah." Francine began to undulate her body. "If I learned to belly dance, I could be beautiful and sexy like you. Then I wouldn't have to be such a whore." She giggled again.

Zyah froze. She was barefoot as usual and, although Francine had had too much to drink, she was still blurting out the truth as she saw it. "You *are* beautiful and sexy, Francine."

Francine shook her head. "No, I'm not. Not like you. My mother told me. She said, 'Francine, you'll never be like her. You might as well face it. You'll never be beautiful or sexy.

433

You were an ugly baby, an ugly child and you're ugly now. Be a whore and go after the money. Men are lying, cheating bastards anyway.' "

Every word was whispered, but Zyah felt as if they'd been carved deep into Francine's skin. Branded into her bones. What kind of mother would say those things to a child?

"Francine, that isn't true at all. Look at you. You're so beautiful. I don't have a clue how to wear makeup. I used to try to copy you all the time. And you have great fashion sense. I never could find the right clothes to suit me. I gave up a long time ago. When we were kids, my grandmother would always comment on what a beautiful child you were."

"She did?" Francine's voice wavered.

"Ask her. I heard it all the time. And it was true. I was always chubby and had to fight my weight. You were like this beautiful little doll. I can't imagine why your mother told you that, but it wasn't the truth. Surely Lizz tells you how gorgeous you really are."

Zyah poured sincerity into her voice. Francine had been a beautiful child. She'd gotten hard as an adult, and she drank far too much. The constant alcohol was beginning to show on her, but there was no question that she was beautiful.

"It would be fun to go to dinner with you, Francine. Thanks for asking. I'll just let Player know. He's with my grandmother right now.

I'll ask him to stay with her until I get back."

Francine frowned, tried to straighten and wobbled for a moment and then caught herself, waving her hand dismissively. "Why would Player be with your grandmother?"

Zyah winced at the belligerence in her tone. Francine had wanted to be with a member of Torpedo Ink. She was a naturally jealous woman, and she would want what she thought Zyah had. All the points Zyah had made with her were lost that quickly. She wasn't supposed to tell anyone that Torpedo Ink was looking out for Anat while she worked, or that they were there at night.

"We were going to go out tonight," she said. "I just texted him and said I wanted to go to dinner with you." She hoped that would be enough to placate Francine.

"Invite him to come with us," Francine said. "There's no reason for him to be bored out of his mind staying with an old lady who will just talk his ear off when he could be with the two of us. We can go to Alena's restaurant. He'd love to be with us; you know he would. Men like Player take on two women at once."

She leaned on the counter with both elbows and deliberately stared straight into Zyah's eyes. "Have you ever done that? Been with a woman and a man? Or been with two men? I'll bet Player's shared a woman. And I'll bet he's had more than two women plenty of

435

times. Ask him. I dare you. Text him right now and ask him. Ask him if he wants to party with the both of us tonight. We can go to his clubhouse."

Francine's face took on a greedy, almost obscene look of grasping glee. "You know how he got his name, right? Player? Did he ever tell you? Because I know how he did. Heidi told me. He took a bet one night from the others that he could do fifty women and they'd all call him back wanting more. They made the mistake of not making a rule that it had to be one woman at a time. He's that damn good, but you already know that, don't you?" She licked her lips, her eyes bright. "Come on, Zyah, you must have shared before. If you haven't, there's no hope in hell of keeping a man like that."

Zyah ignored the way her heart reacted. She knew Player wasn't like that. She'd been in his mind too many times, but she also had seen some of the parties in his head, those women all over him. Sometimes, like in that one little moment, it was difficult to push the images away. She kept her expression perfectly serene, a gift from the years of working overseas. She snapped her fingers.

"Let me have the car keys, Francine. I'll close the store and we'll head over to Crow 287. Player can stay with Mama Anat tonight. I don't like leaving her alone. You probably don't remember, but she was beaten pretty severely in that robbery, and she's nervous. He said no problem. He's got his guitar, so he's happy."

The door to the grocery store swung open, and Perry Randall sauntered in. Zyah tried not to react with a sigh, but the night was getting worse by the minute. Perry was dressed to go out, in slacks, a silk shirt, a dinner jacket. Nice shoes. His clothes cost more than her car. He dragged off his dark sunglasses, which, since it was already growing dark outside, he really didn't need, and his gaze immediately took in both women. He whistled.

"Why would I give you my keys?" Francine snapped, fury building in her eyes. "You're such a little prude, Zyah. You always were." She whirled around at the sound of the appreciative whistle, and at once the expression on her face changed. Color swept into her cheeks, and she pushed her blond hair back to show off the earrings.

"Ladies. I can see I'm in luck tonight," Perry greeted.

Francine tossed her head flirtatiously. "I think you are, Perry. It has been a hot minute since I've seen you, and you're looking fine."

"Not so bad yourself, Francine," Perry returned, winking. "Zyah. Came to take you out to dinner. You have to be closing, right?"

Francine spun around to glare at Zyah. "That's just great. You have *two* dates."

437

"I'm going to dinner with *you,* Francine," Zyah reminded. She was so tired she wanted to curl up on the floor and go to sleep right there. "Hand me your car keys. I'll drive."

"Fuck you, I'm not giving you my car keys. And I'm not going to dinner with you. You can go with Player and Perry." Francine stuck her chin in the air.

"I'm going home," Zyah said, "but you're not driving. Hand me the keys." She kept her voice even and quiet, knowing the battle was going to escalate now. Francine hadn't gotten her way. She was certain both Player and Perry were after Zyah. She was going to be as destructive as possible. "Perry, if you're looking for a dinner date, Francine is so gorgeous tonight. We were going out together, but I'm so tired I can't keep my eyes open."

Perry's insolent gaze, as it ran up and down Francine, set Zyah's teeth on edge. "You do look amazing, Francine," he agreed. "But I want a sure thing tonight. Seriously. The last time we went out, you bailed on me at the last minute. That wasn't cool."

Zyah could hardly believe what she'd just heard. She wanted to throw something at his head. Perry was an arrogant little ass.

"That wasn't my fault, and you know it, Perry. I got sick. I was sick." Francine sounded like a child defending herself.

Zyah was instantly angry, something very rare for her. She leaned across the counter.

"You have my phone number, Francine. You have the right to say no to anyone at any time for any reason. You call me and I'll come get you. Perry, you continue to amaze me with just how disgusting you truly can be."

"You still living with your parents, Perry?" Francine asked. "Because I'm living with my grandmother." Francine pulled her phone out and was texting. "I'm just letting her know I'll be late. Maybe you should tell your parents you'll be out most of the night — or all night." She sounded seductive.

Perry grinned at her. "I have my own house on the property. I don't stay in the main house with them. They would make me crazy. They whine at me." He switched his attention to Zyah. "I'm beginning to give up on you, babe. Francine may be right. You could be a prude. We could have had fun. Come on, Francine. Let's go."

"I'll meet you there." Francine glared at Zyah defiantly.

Zyah sighed. She was so tired she wanted to yell at both of them to just get out. "Hand over the car keys, Francine. I mean it. You've had too much to drink and your license was yanked for DUI already. You've got no business driving."

"What are you going to do about it?" Francine taunted.

Behind Perry and Francine, Destroyer and Keys emerged from the center aisle, almost as if they were ghosts. There was no sound, they just suddenly were there. Two very intimidating men.

"Give her the keys," Destroyer said, his voice low and harsh. "Do it now."

Francine whirled around so fast she nearly fell. Perry backed toward the door, his fingers closing convulsively around his sunglasses. "Give her the keys, Francine, and let's go," he said.

Francine fished in her purse, found the keys and flung them at Zyah. Hard. The keys struck Zyah just above her left breast, stinging her. Looking smug, giggling with satisfaction, Francine hurried to follow Perry out of the store as Zyah put her hand over the keys to keep them from falling to the floor.

"You all right?" Keys asked.

Zyah blinked back tears, turning to watch as Francine walked toward Perry's low-slung vehicle. She turned away more so that neither man could see she was emotional than for any other reason. She really didn't care to see that Perry didn't even bother to open the door for Francine. She already knew he was a first-class jerk. Francine could barely stand on her own, and when she bent to get into the car, she nearly crawled inside.

"Yeah, I'm just really tired. I want to go home and take a hot bath and go to bed."

"We don't do that shit, you know. None of us," Keys said, his voice very quiet.

Zyah turned back to him because he was very sober. Very sincere. Whatever he was trying to convey was important. And he was being truthful.

"I'm sorry?"

"We don't make bets like that bitch was telling you. That's not how Player got his name. She was making shit up. We aren't like that."

She flashed him a wan smile. "I'm well aware she is totally full of shit, Keys." Because she'd been in Player's mind too many times. She had no idea how he got his name, but she did know it wasn't the way Francine had told her he had.

"Come on, kid, get your shoes on and let's get the hell out of this place. Cash out. We'll do the rest."

"I can't leave Lizz's car here. I'll drive it to her house. I'll need a ride home after. I'd walk, but I'm too tired tonight."

Keys and Destroyer exchanged a long look. Destroyer shrugged. "No worries, we're following you anyway."

"I never thought I'd be driving a pink Cadillac," Zyah said as she went back to work.

"Better you than me," Keys muttered under his breath. "For a minute there, I was sweatin' it."

Destroyer raised an eyebrow. "I was looking forward to it. Kind of thought I'd look cool.

441

Thought maybe I'd ask the old lady if she needed someone to take it around the block once in a while."

Zyah burst out laughing. "You're kind of crazy."

"Yeah, you got that right," Keys said, but he flashed a small, appreciative smile at Destroyer. The two went about putting things away and locking up while she cashed out completely, taking the money to the back. Ordinarily, she might have put it in the heavy vault, but since the robberies, the money was turned over to her Torpedo Ink escorts, so she was never responsible for it. In the morning, they brought the money needed for start-up.

Just getting into the pink Cadillac should have made her smile. The car was polished and pristine, inside and out, just the way Lizz Johnson kept it. A dark dread crept over her, just as it had in the store, making her feel tired and depressed. She wanted Mama Anat. Just to lie on the bed with her the way she had when she was a child and be comforted by her.

Her grandmother would stroke her hair and make that wonderful trilling sound that vibrated through the room and then turned into a hum that filled her with joy. She would know the world was right. Balanced. That was what she needed. The world to stop being off-kilter. It felt that way. As if she'd walked

442

into a storm and the earth had spun wrong, shifting off its axis just enough to throw her off balance.

Once the Cadillac was safely tucked away in its home in the garage at the Johnson home, she gave the keys to Lizz at the door, trying her best to pretend not to see the tears as she hugged her. Francine had clearly taken the car without permission, although Lizz didn't admit it. Her shock was enough to give the truth away. Zyah debated for a moment whether or not to mention the jewelry, but she didn't want Lizz to have a heart attack if she discovered it missing. She casually brought it up, saying she thought Francine looked gorgeous on her date with Perry, wearing the blue diamond star necklace and earrings. Lizz paled visibly. She gripped her bathrobe tightly and then nodded, thanking Zyah, kissing her on both cheeks and telling her to give Anat her love.

Zyah had barely registered the sound of the approaching motorcycle during her conversation with Lizz, her heart was so heavy. She turned and he was there. Just standing there. Tall. Broad shoulders. Wild hair. Those blue eyes focused completely on her. She took one step into him, and he wrapped his arms around her. Home. Player felt like home to her. She closed her eyes and gave herself up to the feeling because she desperately needed comfort.

"Something's wrong, Player."

His hand cupped the back of her head, holding her to him, fingers massaging her scalp. "Let's get you home, baby. Hot bath. Relax. We'll talk it out. Figure out what's wrong together. We're getting good at that. Or you can sleep for a while. I'll stay awake and watch over you so nothing can go wrong. Either way, we'll figure it out."

His voice was magic. Soothing. He was so tuned to her. She wanted to just stay there in his arms, feeling safe, although her feet hurt. Maybe he could pick her up.

"Let's get you home. I brought you a jacket and gloves to wear." Player brushed a kiss on top of her head and then tucked her under his shoulder as they walked together to his motorcycle.

"Keys or Destroyer called you." She looked up at him. At his jaw. So strong. She needed him to be strong when she felt everything was dark and wrong. She touched his jaw, ran the pads of her fingers over the strong bones.

"They were worried about you. They worry, I worry. You should have called me, Zyah. I would have come to you."

"What would I have said? 'I have this bad feeling'? 'Francine upset me'? 'She brought this dark cloud and I can't shrug it off'?" She pressed her face against his chest again, borrowing his strength, because the lurching

444

inside her made her physically ill. "Something is really wrong, and I should know what it is. It was right there in front of me, Player. Right there. I had it and it slipped away from me. Francine slipped away too. For one moment I saw her. The girl she was back when we were children and her mother was alive. Her mother was so awful."

Player tipped her face up and brushed her eyes with kisses, her nose and then the corners of her mouth. "You're so beautiful, Zyah. Inside, where it counts. You hurt because you see the good in people. You see it in us the way Blythe does. You see with different eyes than most. I love you for that. One of the million things I love about you, but that particular trait stands out. I love you. I do. You don't have to accept that. Or hear that. But I don't think there's another woman on this earth that can measure up to you."

His voice was soft. A mere whisper of sound. Barely there. That declaration. She almost thought he hadn't said it. *I love you for that. I love you. I do.* He'd said it. His voice might have been low and tender, but it held honesty. She didn't have to be barefoot.

He terrified her. After pushing her away for so long, he'd just capitulated and wanted to be with her. Accepted her. He thought he loved her, but his reasons weren't really the right ones. Were they? She was so confused and mixed up. But right now she didn't care, she just wanted to be near him. And she wanted to go home, where she could see her grandmother was safe, because she felt edgy and a little scared.

"Who's with Mama Anat?"

Player shook out a heavy jacket, holding it so that she could put her arms in it. He zipped it up and handed her gloves. "Savage and Maestro. Trust me, no one will get near her with those two in the house, and you know there's always someone outside, unseen."

He swung onto the motorcycle with his casual, fluid grace. Every time she saw him do that, her stomach did a slow somersault. She put her hand on his shoulder and knew he could feel her trembling. She hadn't acknowledged his declaration. Had she hurt him? If she had, he hadn't showed it. He hadn't changed expression or treated her differently. When she put her arms around him, he locked her even tighter to him. She wanted to melt into him. She pressed her hands against his abdomen, all those muscles she knew were beneath his jacket and shirt. She knew if she took her glove off and slid her bare hand under his clothes, he wouldn't object. He'd probably just press her palm closer to his skin.

The bike roared between her legs. Player's body was warm. There was comfort in just riding with him, which she'd never thought would ever happen, being on the back of a Harley late at night. They didn't go fast because this was Sea Haven and it was late. Destroyer and Keys rode behind them. She realized that ever since she'd started working for them, she'd been absolutely safe. So had Anat. She knew Lizz was safe. Someone watched her house. Inez was safe. The Dardens were looked after. Torpedo Ink was stretched thin trying to watch over them, and she feared there were a few people who would be more afraid if they saw the bikers close in the middle of the night.

She waited as he put his Harley in the garage, lifting a hand to his brothers as they rode away. She almost hated to see the two men go. That dread in her hadn't left. It stayed right there, in the pit of her stomach. She actually pressed her hand there while she waited to walk into the house with Player.

"I need to see Mama Anat," she whispered. "She usually stays up waiting for me."

"I know, she'll be semi-awake. I played for her until Destroyer and Keys let me know you were upset. She was falling asleep then, but she resists until she knows you're inside. I should never have admitted to her that someone tried to kidnap you, but I didn't want to lie to her, and she asked me straight out."

"She would have known you were lying," Zyah assured. "She always knew when I

447

didn't tell the truth when I was a child growing up. I couldn't get away with anything. Not that I wanted to. I loved her so much that I couldn't bear to do anything that might disappoint or hurt her. I never could understand Francine and how wild she got when Lizz would be so worried about her. Lizz was so good to her, and Francine would just do these horrible things. The cops would pick her up and drag her home from parties and warn Lizz that they'd take her away, but that never stopped Francine."

Player helped her out of the jacket and hung it just inside the door, slipping the extra pair of gloves inside his pocket. He followed her down the hall to her grandmother's room. As always, there wasn't a whisper of sound when he walked, even in his motorcycle boots. How did he do that? His hand was on the small of her back. Warm. No, hot. She felt his palm like a brand.

"Zyah?" Anat called out as she stood in the doorway.

"I'm home, Mama Anat," she said. Love flooded her. Warmth. Just as she had known they would. She went straight to her grandmother, inhaling her scent. Jasmine. Lavender. The scent of love. "Are you all right? Did you look after all the bad boys today?"

Anat laughed softly, the sound so like beautiful music Zyah wanted to weep. She took her grandmother's hand as she brushed kisses on her cheek, needing to be close to her.

"They aren't so bad."

"They're very bad," Zyah corrected, "especially this one right here. Don't let their charm fool you." She jerked her thumb toward Player. "I'm going to take a long, hot bath. You go to sleep. I'm home safe now." She wished her heart didn't feel so heavy. Even now, surrounded by the two people she loved most in the world, her heart ached.

"I love you, girl."

"I love you too."

Player reached around her to take her hand and tug until she reluctantly let go of her grandmother's hand and let him lead her out of the bedroom. She just followed him up the stairs. That was how tired she was.

"I stopped by the Floating Hat in Sea Haven today and picked up some things for you," he said, his voice that same low, gentle, oh-so-casual sound that brushed through her mind with velvet strokes. "I think they'll be just the thing to help combat the fatigue tonight. Put your hair up, baby. I'll run your bath. Hannah, the owner, suggested some bath products when I told her you're on your feet all day. She gave me some lotions and creams for your feet and legs. We can try them when you get out."

He went on through to the bathroom, and she heard the water begin to fill the tub. He'd stopped by the Floating Hat? She couldn't imagine him walking into the shop, let alone talking to the proprietor and specifically asking her what would be helpful to someone standing and working long hours. That melted her heart. She had no idea what he'd come home with, and it really didn't matter, because it was the fact that he'd thought about her and wanted to do something for her. She was surprised that he'd even noticed or thought about it, especially with his head hurting so much all the time.

"I put this in the bathwater," Player said when she walked in, her robe wrapped securely around her. He handed her a tall, beautiful bottle of sparkling purple and blue crystals. "They dissolved and turned the water a pretty color. I hope they don't turn your skin that color."

It took willpower to force her gaze from his face to the water. Steam rose, but the water shimmered, a soft, inviting, almost magical pool of deep blue with a purple beneath it. Suddenly, she couldn't wait to sink into it. That water called to her, when she felt so exhausted and worn. When her heart was so filled with dread and unease.

"I recorded some music for you." This time there was less confidence in his voice. He sounded almost as if he half expected to be rejected, as if his offering couldn't be nearly as good as what he'd found at the Floating

Hat. Her heart gave a funny little lurch. "Just something to relax to when you're tired." He handed her an iPod. "I'll be in the other room. When you get out, I'll massage your feet for you. Hannah gave me this killer lotion and cream and showed me a couple of techniques."

She lay in the hot water, wondering at what was in the crystals he had put into the bath, because her sore muscles had never felt so good. Even the dread was dissipating a little bit, the deep blue of the water rippling, carrying her worries away with every little wave. The music was Player's guitar layered sound over sound and it was beautiful. Intricate. And oh so perfect. The sound blended seamlessly with the blues and purples of the water that surrounded her. She felt transported and let herself be carried away for just a little while.

She needed this. Her mind actually hurt after the long day, fighting her growing certainty that a dark shadow was looming over them and yet she couldn't find it. The long day after no sleep. Francine with her drunken jealousy and Perry with his entitlement. Player had gifted her with something unexpected and special. She closed her eyes and soaked in the music and blue water until the heat finally began to dissipate.

Player was waiting for Zyah on the bed in her room. Already, the hot bath had made her muscles feel loose and so relaxed she was almost a noodle. He indicated for her to lie back with her head on a low pillow of lavender and, to her shock, jasmine. The pillow had a place for her neck to fit, so she was completely surrounded by warmth.

"Another thing from the Floating Hat?"

"Yes. It's a combination of lavender and jasmine. I asked for both scents specifically because your grandmother always smells like them and I know they comfort you. I thought if you had a headache, the scents might help."

She could barely bring herself to look at him, veiling her eyes with her lashes, afraid she might burst into tears. Was he really that thoughtful? Had he been all along and she'd been so busy wrapped up in hurt she hadn't noticed?

He picked up her foot and began to pour lotion into his hands and then rubbed it into her left foot in a slow, circular massage. Her eyes nearly rolled back in her head. The lotion sank into the soles of her feet, where she'd thought nothing could ever take away the ache. Not only did his hands feel good, but the pressure was perfect. The lotion was heating up just right, somehow reacting with the crystals in the bathwater.

Zyah moaned. "I'm going to have an orgasm if you keep that up."

Player laughed. "Prepare to have several, then. I just learned how to do this, and I have to practice to get good. This is only my first time. She showed me on my arm for all of five minutes. You're always doing things for me, so it's my turn."

She was prepared to let him have his way. Definitely. She watched the concentration on his face as he massaged his way up and over her foot to her ankle and then her calf before picking up her right leg. He took his time, his movements unhurried.

"Lizz Johnson is extremely wealthy, Player. Really wealthy. Francine talked her into taking part of her jewelry collection out of the vault at the bank and bringing it to their home so it could be worn to a charity event later next month. In light of the fact that these robberies are taking place, it's so absolutely ridiculous and foolhardy, I can scarcely believe Lizz would do it, but Francine could always talk her into anything."

"Why would she do such a thing? Do you think Francine is involved?"

"No, she's just always been selfish and thoughtless. She likes to show off, and Lizz has always felt guilty because Moria, Francine's mother, was mentally ill, and Lizz's son refused to do anything to help her. He was like Perry. An entitled spoiled brat. He drank with Moria instead of trying to get her sober. Neither one of them seemed to care about Francine."

His hands on her foot were more than

magic, making her feel boneless. Even discussing a difficult subject was easier because she was floating.

"I've reached out to her over and over as often as I could at various times, but she always seemed to resent me. Tonight, when she came to the store, she was driving Lizz's Cadillac. The thing is, I know her license was suspended because she's had multiple DUIs. I also know Lizz prizes that Cadillac. It's her baby she takes out of the garage, drives around the block to show off and then puts back to bed, so to speak. Francine shouldn't have been driving it, and she was already on her way to being drunk. I was fairly certain she took it without permission."

Player put her leg down, reached lazily behind him and pulled a jar of cream to him. He once again picked up her feet and put them across his thighs. He didn't say anything but looked at her with his eyes, twin blue flames, silently telling her to keep going. The next thing she knew, he was using the cream and pressing deep into the soles of the feet with his fingers in a deep tissue massage. The entire time he watched her expression for her reaction to see if it was too hard or not hard enough. As far as she was concerned, he knew her intimately, because he applied the exact amount of pressure she needed.

"She was wearing the necklace and earrings to an extremely valuable set of jewels Lizz has. They're worth millions, more than just about anyone here would have in their homes, and like an idiot, Francine just walks out of the house unattended with them on. Then she goes out with Perry. That's how drunk she is, Player. I tried to stop her, but by that time she was so angry with me and she'd turned on me. I should have just called the cops and turned her in instead of thinking how Lizz would feel."

"What made her angry with you?" His voice was quiet. Washing over her so gently.

Instead of answering, she asked a question of her own. "How did you get the name Player?" Zyah hadn't known she was going to ask — the question just came out. In the darkness, between the two of them, for some reason, her inquiry sounded soft. Quiet. Intimate.

His gaze flicked to hers. Those blue eyes of his, so like ice at times. So like flames other times. Right now, alive with pain. With memories. She *felt* them moving through his mind. He could have locked them away, the way he did when his past escaped, but he kept massaging the cream into her feet, ankles and calves, creating a miracle of relief.

"Sometimes Alena or Lana would come back to the dungeon and they were so bad. So torn up."

His eyes met hers again and her heart nearly convulsed, there was so much pain

455

there. Zyah swore she caught the sheen of tears in all that blue before he looked down at her leg. His hands remained absolutely gentle, never wavering once. Never stopping. A part of her wanted to stop him, but it was so huge that he was going to share something voluntarily with her. She wasn't seeing it, snatching it like some peeping Tom from his mind. He was giving it to her, and she wanted that from him. She would treasure it.

"When they were little, they would call out for the 'Player.' I could make music out of just about anything. Turn the silliest things into instruments. My name, Gedeon, was sometimes hard for them when they were so hurt, so they called me Player."

Zyah swore he was shredding her heart in a whole new way. The raw pain in his voice was so real, it filled the room to capacity and was impossible to contain. The walls expanded and contracted and wept for him along with her.

"There was a time I couldn't bear to hear that name because it brought so many memories back, none of them good, but then I realized that Player had saved them, Lana and Alena, so many times during their childhood. When the worst of the pedophiles came, pretending to be instructors, the ones we knew would hurt them or possibly even kill them, I could cover their bodies in the illusion of sores so they wouldn't take them. And

456

when I was too ill myself to protect them that way, when they came back battered, I could be their Player and transport them from the dungeon on the wings of music for a short time."

"I think that all of you, growing up the way you had to, were lucky to find each other."

His fingers never stopped moving. "I never thought of it that way. I suppose we were. I always thought I was lucky that I didn't have siblings to be held over my head like some of the others did. Reaper and Savage. Preacher and Lana. Ice, Storm and Alena. Transporter and Mechanic. Sorbacov knew how to force them to do his bidding. Czar had six younger siblings. If he didn't toe the line, Sorbacov threatened them all the time." He ducked his head. "I think Czar took a lot of hits for me."

"What does that mean?"

"When I was younger and we had to go to the dinners and bring the bombs I built, I didn't want to go. I didn't want to engage with the other children at the parties. Czar spent most of the time trying to cover for me so Sorbacov wouldn't punish me after. He was afraid Sorbacov would kill me himself, or worse, give me to the kinds of men who enjoyed killing a kid for the pleasure of it."

His blue eyes had gone from heat to ice. "Babe, this was supposed to be a good night. We're not talking about this kind of shit. Let's talk about your grandmother and how great she did today. She's sick of being cooped up. I told her about the Floating Hat and said you and I could take her there for tea one afternoon and we'd go to Crow 287 for her birthday dinner. She really needs to get out of the house. We could invite some of her friends. Alena has a back room big enough, I think. If not, we can hold it at the clubhouse. She'd like that."

Zyah burst out laughing, because her grandmother would lord it over everyone that she'd had her birthday party at a biker clubhouse or in the back room of Alena's restaurant.

# FIFTEEN

Gedeon loved the silence in his mind when he built things, especially bombs. Everyone left him alone. He could sit quietly outside in a little corner of the garden where it was mostly overgrown with tall heather grasses surrounding the bench and table where Sorbacov would place all the pieces for him to put together. Next to the equipment would be a cold cup of water. The water was always clean, from the spring. It tasted good, and he'd learned to sip at it and make it last. He'd tried to save it and bring it back with him for the others, but Sorbacov never allowed that, so he didn't waste it.

On the other side of the table, lying across it, was the dreaded flogger. He hated that instrument. Sometimes, when he worked, Sorbacov would brush the leather strands over his back, up and down, almost as if he wanted to distract him. Gedeon would go deeper into his mind, hide himself there with the complicated calculations, with the way

459

things clicked into place for him, the trajectories and patterns that made sense to his brain.

Nothing about Sorbacov made sense. There was no logic to him and his depravities. As a child, Gedeon had tried to find ways to please him, but there was no real way to do so. Pleasing Sorbacov didn't earn rewards. Sorbacov liked to cause pain. He rewarded himself. Gedeon learned to read his moods, but that didn't always mean anything either. It was better to just disappear into his own mind and build as fast as he could, making each object more and more complex. Building each faster than the one he had before.

The air felt fresh and clean on his naked body. Sorbacov didn't give him clothes because he said he didn't have use for clothes unless he wanted him to have them. He didn't even notice he was shivering. He never minded the cold outside. The fresh air felt too much like freedom. He looked over the parts strewn on the table. The parts were completely different. He straightened, his heartbeat quickening. Something new. Something for his mind to work on.

Gedeon sat down on the cold slab, not even wincing. He didn't look around to see if Sorbacov or anyone else was in the gardens as he normally would have done. At seven, he knew better. Czar would have given him a lecture for that, and if Reaper was watching him, that would be reported back, but he doubted if any of the others could have gotten out in time to watch his back. It was rare. Sorbacov kept a pretty tight watch on them all now, especially Player. He didn't want to lose his prize bomb builder.

Gedeon surveyed the parts, automatically sorting through them in his mind. He laid them out swiftly, moving them almost without touching them, his hands a blur, fingers directing them where he needed them to go. There was satisfaction in watching them do his bidding, watching them come together.

A shadow fell across him, and he felt the brush of leather on his back, drawing him out of the tunnel, the place so deep no one could usually reach him. He wanted to scream at Sorbacov, and he turned quickly, a scowl of pure annoyance on his face. He *needed* to build the bomb. It didn't matter that it wasn't real; he had to figure it out. Why couldn't Sorbacov understand that?

Sorbacov yanked him off the bench, his face that mask of sheer brutal glee, the one all the children feared the most. That was the one he wore when he wanted to show his friends his absolute rule over everyone. He flung Player into the grass on his hands and knees and began to whip him mercilessly with the flogger, hard, brutal strokes, driving him forward, all the while laughing as Gedeon crawled like a wounded animal until he bumped into legs. A fist caught his hair and

461

yanked his head up. He found himself staring into mean, ugly eyes.

*Meet my friend, Gedeon. Open your mouth wide. He's rather big. But then, you're going to be taking good care of me, and he'll have to keep you from screaming while you do it.*

Harsh laughter rang in his ears for what seemed an eternity. He remembered pain. Terrible pain. So much of it. Then he was on the ground, unable to move. Curled in the fetal position. The flogger hitting him over and over until he got up and crawled back onto the bench, bleeding, unable to sit, so he knelt up at Sorbacov's insistence. Tears ran down his face, his throat swollen until he couldn't breathe, and his hands shaking so hard he couldn't pick up the cup of water.

Out of the corner of his eye he saw the White Rabbit. The animal was life-sized. As big as Sorbacov. Just standing right beside him, in a three-piece suit, pocket watch in hand, frowning down at it. Why wouldn't they all go away? He needed them gone. He wasn't going to make it this time if they didn't. He couldn't take another round with Sorbacov and his friends. He just couldn't, no matter what Czar said. He wasn't that strong. Nothing was worth it.

He tried rocking back and forth, looking at his bomb parts, ignoring the White Rabbit. Ignoring Sorbacov. Ignoring *everyone.* Tick-tock. The watch kept ticking. Did Sorbacov think he could concentrate when he hurt so bad? When he couldn't breathe? He made an effort to focus on the parts and began to put them together.

Sweat poured off his body, making his palms and fingers slippery. The White Rabbit took a sudden leap, and Sorbacov was there in the shadows instead . . . Behind him was something else. Something shadowy. Sinister. Another man. His breath caught in his throat and he began to fight. Not again. It wouldn't happen again. It couldn't.

Zyah shifted to her knees, rising above Player, calling to him softly, tears pouring down her face. Sharing his nightmares was pure hell. She didn't want to see those vignettes of his childhood. At the same time, she wondered how he could be the man he was — the kind, gentle one who had gone into a bath shop to get her lotion so he could massage her feet for her — after what he'd suffered as a child.

"Honey, open your eyes. Right now, open your eyes and look at me."

She could see the bench now, the one that little naked boy with all that wild hair sat at. He had already gone from a boy to a man. His back was to her, but she would know that broad back with those scars and that Torpedo Ink tattoo anywhere. That was her man. That was Player sitting at that bench.

The rabbit had morphed into a man right

in front of her. At first Zyah thought she was looking at the devil. A handsome man wearing a suit, with a graying neatly trimmed beard and mustache to match his thick head of gray-streaked black hair. It was the black eyebrows and piercing eyes as he stared at the pieces of bomb material laid out on the table in front of Player that made her think of the devil. The man didn't speak, but he held a pocket watch in his palm. It was gold, a vintage Russian pocket watch, quite unique.

She could see his features, although they were in the shadows. Murky. Player had told her that was because he was dead. He still gave her the creeps. He was so evil, she could almost believe that he could return to life.

A frisson of fear slid down Zyah's spine. It wasn't the first time she'd observed this scenario in Player's mind, and it wasn't the first time she felt as if someone else were actually in the room watching them. She looked around carefully. Every corner. The ceiling. Looking into the shadows. She remembered the way Player, as a child, that first time when he was creating the illusion of the *Alice's Adventures in Wonderland* characters for the other children, had looked so alertly and suspiciously around the basement, as if he knew something or someone was watching them.

Something was in the room with them, and she wanted Player one hundred percent aware, because whatever was staring out of the darkness seemed malevolent.

*Player. Look at me, now. I need you. Open your eyes and see me. No one else. Not your past. Not the bomb. Not Sorbacov or the White Rabbit. Someone is in the room with us. Look at me and then look around. They can't know we can communicate like this. Honey, please wake up.* She poured herself into him. Into his mind, flooding him with her.

There was a brief moment while her heart pounded and whatever seemed to be in the room with them stared at them like some bloated spider waiting for the moment it could pounce.

*I'm with you, baby.* He sounded rough, but he didn't suddenly open his eyes and look wildly around. He lifted a hand to her face, shaping her bone structure, as if reading her by Braille. He lifted his face to hers, brushing a kiss on her lips and then wrapping his arms around her tightly, his head on her shoulder.

Zyah felt his heart pounding, the aftermath of the nightmare. She felt his breath catch, but he didn't make a sound.

*The drawing. Your grandfather's drawing. I'm going to lie down, and I want you to sit back slowly against the headboard with me. Look at the picture. Just glance at it.*

Zyah didn't want him to let her go. First the White Rabbit had been standing in front of the picture, and then Sorbacov had been directly in front of it, where the White Rabbit had been. She felt his arms slide away from her, although one hand stayed in contact with her as he slowly started to sit up. She moved with him to the headboard, so they both faced the drawing her grandfather had made so lovingly for her grandmother.

The White Rabbit was completely gone, Player's illusion morphed into his alternate reality. Sorbacov's blurred image became so faded he wavered and was transparent. Where his face had been, in the center of the picture, eyes stared at the two of them, looking eerie, as if they actually peered out of the drawing itself, or through Sorbacov's wavering, ghostly body.

Zyah held her breath. Those eyes lifted to look around the room, at her. This was becoming far too real. The eyes wavered, grew transparent, just as Sorbacov had, and then slowly faded away. For a moment, she could have sworn, the frame on the picture rolled in a weird circle and then righted itself.

She gripped Player's arm, her nails digging into his skin. "That was insane. And very scary. I need a cup of tea. Or maybe a drink."

"Let's have a drink of whatever Hannah sent us and get out the notebooks. Each of us can write down what we remember and then compare notes. Czar said we'd figure it out faster that way, and we're going to have to figure this out."

"At least the bomb didn't start ticking."

"I hadn't started building it." Player pushed back his hair. "I hate that you have to go through this with me, Zyah. And I hate feeling Anat could be in danger. That *thing* staring at us was all too real, and it sure as fuck *felt* real."

"It was," Zyah confirmed in a low voice. She shivered as she reached into the drawer of the end table to remove the notebooks and pens she'd stashed there so they'd both have something to write in. "Something was in this room with us, Player — it wasn't the first time."

Was that the terrible dread she'd been feeling throughout the evening? She pressed one hand to her churning stomach. Had Sorbacov really been so evil that he'd found a way to come back from the dead? Was that even possible? She shivered again and moved closer to Player. His body was always hot. Always. Most of the time he felt like a furnace. She needed that heat right at that moment. Something evil had found its way into their home. A trace of its presence lingered behind.

"It's gone, Zyah. After you write down what you felt and saw, think back to the first time you felt the presence and write down anything you can remember about that night as well. Even what I was dreaming."

She leaned into him, rubbing her face against his shoulder. "I hate that anything like that creature might share knowledge that is just ours."

"He doesn't. He isn't part of my past." Player spoke with absolute conviction.

"He's not the other man who was there that day?" Zyah asked tentatively. Player rarely directly addressed his actual childhood with her, and she hesitated to bring it up unless he did. She'd seen enough that she didn't think talking about details unless he wanted or needed to was necessary. On the other hand, his past was entirely private, and no intruder should have any part of Player. He'd already had so much taken from him.

"No. That man is dead, Zyah. He would be like Sorbacov, a shadow, no more." He was writing in the notebook and didn't look up.

"You're certain he's dead?" she asked. "Sorbacov's friend? You know for a fact that he's dead?"

"Yes, baby. I know that for a fact."

She wasn't going to ask him how he knew it. "This was a shadow," she persisted. The room was dimly lit. There were shadows everywhere, and she didn't understand why Player wasn't as shaky as she was. She went still inside and turned her face up to Player's, her eyes on his. "Player. Look at me."

His gaze flicked from the notebook to her, and she flinched. The blue was a glacier.

Burning, yes, but so cold it was burning blue. Scary blue. She was looking at something in him that could be . . . deadly. Deliberately, she blinked, but that expression didn't go away.

"Player." She whispered his name in a kind of despair.

"I'm right here, baby."

She shook her head. "No, you're not. You're letting them drag you back there. You're letting them swallow you with their darkness. You were out of that."

He threaded his fingers through hers and pulled her fist to his chest, pressing their locked hands over his heart. "I've never been out of it, Zyah."

His voice was very quiet. Tender. That black velvet that whispered over her skin and broke her heart in so many ways. He brought their hands to his mouth and kissed her knuckles. The sensation caused her stomach to do a slow somersault. He rubbed his jaw along the back of her hand so she could feel the slight growth of his beard over her sensitive skin. At once, a thousand butterflies took wing. She was *so* susceptible to him.

"There's no getting out of what was done to me. They had me for years. You see glimpses and you're sick inside. I try to protect you, but when I'm asleep, I can't. I tried to walk away from you, give you up, but I'm not that strong. I'm so in love with you I

469

can't think straight. But you have to know, if you accept me, if you want me with you — in your life, in your bed — you have to have all of me. You have to know who you're going to bed with, Zyah. I don't want you waking up one morning and saying you had no idea."

She couldn't stop looking into his eyes. She could see what they'd shaped him into. That cold man capable of things she'd caught glimpses of later on. Not just the building of the bombs. The man who could lie on a floor and shoot a gun blindly and hit his target accurately. A boy, a teenager, sent out to kill grown men for his country, who did so without hesitation. He sat next to her, showing her he was still there, inside that gentle man who had massaged her feet and legs so thoughtfully when she was tired.

"What am I going to do with you, Player?" She honestly didn't know.

"That's the question, isn't it, baby?" He indicated her notebook. "Have you written down your impressions while they're still fresh? I'm about done. While you're writing, I'm going to make us a couple of those refreshing drinks. Hopefully, that will make us both feel a little better."

She didn't like him moving away from her, even just to slide out of the bed and pull the beautiful basket filled with items from the Floating Hat to him. Instead of writing down everything she'd observed, or thought she saw, she kept her eyes fixed on Player. That feeling in the pit of her stomach was still there, a dark dread that just wouldn't go away.

She didn't want to lose Player, and there was a deep fear that she could. She knew, from the little she'd seen of the glimpses into the members of Torpedo Ink's past, that they didn't like to take their eyes off one another. That was why they often traveled in pairs. Now she really understood. She felt as long as she could see Player, nothing could happen to him.

She watched him mix the liquid with water into the glasses and then come to her dressed only in loose-fitting drawstring pants that rode low on his hips. He looked disheveled after his nightmare. A little wild. He came around the bed to stand on her side in order to give her one of the tall, hand-blown goblets. It was beautiful, just like the man. Sometimes she felt overwhelmed with love for him — and fear for him.

"I'm not going anywhere, Zyah," he assured quietly.

She took a sip of the liquid. She'd never tasted anything so good. It wasn't too sweet. Or too tart. The drink actually cleared the clouds from her mind, and she was able to take a full breath for the first time since she'd felt the malevolence enter her space.

Player walked to the end of the bed to stand in front of her grandfather's drawing, staring at it. He was motionless as he sipped the drink. She didn't really understand what he expected to see. He was standing right where the White Rabbit, Sorbacov and, ultimately, the malevolent eyes of the intruder had been. Zyah sighed and began to write down her impressions of the night's events and then the time before when she'd first felt the presence of the intruder.

"I'm finished." Zyah put her empty flute on the bedside table.

Player slipped back into bed next to her and handed her his notebook, taking hers in exchange. She read his notes several times, frowning. Shocked. Not comprehending what he put down at first. His handwriting was impeccable. He didn't scribble, and each letter was precise, flawlessly slanted. No one had such perfect handwriting. It almost looked as if a machine had written the notes rather than a man.

"Player? You think this evil entity is *inside* my grandfather's drawing?" She couldn't keep the quiver from her voice. Even trying to concentrate on his handwriting and wondering how it had gotten so perfect couldn't prevent the absolute horror from recoiling in every single cell in her body.

She loved her grandfather's drawing. Every stroke, every line had been drawn with love. He had spent months on that carefully drawn artwork for her grandmother. And the frame?

472

Moving like some ancient scroll? Her father had done the same — taken months of care to create a masterpiece to frame the art for her grandfather's gift of love for Anat. How could Player think evil could intrude on love? It was impossible. *Impossible.*

"You believe you saw those eyes staring at us from in front of the drawing?" Player said. As usual, his voice was low. Where her voice had been all emotion, and she was still wanting to leap out of bed and pace or roll over and weep, he was very calm.

"Yes. They had to be. The White Rabbit was there like he always was, standing just over your shoulder. Then he was Sorbacov. I saw Sorbacov much clearer this time. His features. He was blurry and transparent, but I could see what he looked like. And right where his face was, where his eyes were, there was the other one."

She wrapped her arms around herself, shivering, remembering the way those eyes had looked at them. Too real. As if he could really see them. Identify them. She suddenly gasped. "Player. You didn't have a shirt on. You have a Torpedo Ink tattoo on your back. It's too large for anyone not to see it. He saw you and saw me. When you kissed me, he saw your back and the Torpedo Ink tattoo."

"I'm well aware of that."

Why did he have to be so pragmatic about it, as if it didn't matter at all? It mattered. If

473

that man was real and he was looking for Player, he now had a way to find him.

"His eyes were in the center of the drawing, Zyah, looking right at us. From *inside* the drawing. Think about it. Picture it in your mind." Again, his voice was very calm.

She shook her head, rejecting the idea. "You don't understand about that drawing, Player. Nothing evil could *ever* get inside anything created with such love. I just won't believe that. My grandfather loved Anat. It was in every single thing he did for and with her. My father loved my mother that same way. The person looking at us isn't capable of anything close to love, at least I don't believe he is."

"Have you ever really examined that drawing?"

She frowned at him. "What is that supposed to mean? It's been in my life always. It's hung in my room since I was a little girl. I begged Mama Anat for it. I know every line almost by heart. I think I could reproduce it, as well as the frame."

"Have you studied it from various angles?"

"I've looked at it from every angle." But had she? Growing up, she had just admired the drawing on her wall. Then she'd been at school and then off to college and overseas to her job. Since coming home, she'd spent more time with the artwork, but she hadn't really taken the time to study it from every angle. What was she expected to see?

"Do you know what anamorphosis art is?"

"I think so. The artist distorts the drawing or painting in some way, and the viewer uses a mirror or some device to see the true picture. Right?" She looked at her grandfather's very precise drawing. "But there's no distortion."

"My mind sees in patterns." For the first time he hesitated.

"We have to discuss this, even if you think it's going to upset me, Player." She knew she was going to be upset no matter what. That clarifying drink, so refreshing, had cleared her mind enough to give her the strength to continue. She needed to do this. It had to be done. She and Player had to figure it out once and for all in order to keep Anat safe as well as Player. Everyone, for that matter. She pressed her hand to her churning stomach. She loved her grandfather's picture. Had the eyes been staring at them from inside the picture? Was that even possible? No matter how terrible, they had to get at the truth.

Zyah tried to do what Player said and go back and pull the details out of her head — not what she *wanted* to see but what she'd really seen. Player covered her hand, and she realized she was gripping her thigh so hard her fingers were digging into her skin as she tried to recall the details. She'd been afraid the moment she saw the White Rabbit, even when she was aware she hadn't heard the ticking of the bomb. She could see the boy was no longer at the bench, but a man was bent over it, working. She would recognize him anywhere with his wild hair and distinctive tattoo.

The White Rabbit peered over his left shoulder, tapping his foot impatiently and staring down at his gold pocket watch. She tore her gaze from the watch to look above him. The rabbit's head was centered exactly in her grandfather's drawing, but in front of it. Relief flooded her. The White Rabbit began to fade, and there was the rather handsome older man looking a bit like the devil with his silver-streaked hair and beard, standing where the rabbit had been. Sorbacov wasn't as distinct as the white-furred creature. Much more blurred, even fully transparent in spots, his head in the exact spot the White Rabbit's had been, in the center of the drawing, but in front of it.

Zyah took a deep breath, filling her lungs with Player, before turning her gaze inward again. Instinctively, she tightened her fingers around Player's. He immediately brought her fingertips to his mouth and kissed them before pressing her palm to his thigh and just holding her hand there tightly. Those eyes staring so malevolently had really scared her, and conjuring them up again was terrifying, but they had to know. *She* had to know she

476

was right.

She forced herself to look at Sorbacov, his face. His eyes. He was staring down at Player so gleefully. Twice he switched his gaze to his watch. He was a man who loved power over all things. He rode on the waves of fear pouring off the children when he visited the "school" he'd created for his chosen victims. His eyes showed how depraved he was. Still, Zyah refused to turn away. She wanted to see that moment when he began to fade and the other took his place. The transformation was entirely unexpected.

Zyah swallowed and even leaned toward the apparition, even though it was all taking place in her mind, not in the bedroom. She saw Sorbacov fade even more, his facial features so thin she could see her grandfather's drawing distinctly behind him. The lines were etched into her memory, so she knew them and filled them in around his head, like a child's Etch A Sketch.

Weirdly, her eyes began to play tricks on her. The frame around the picture appeared to be rolling slowly and then picked up speed. She glanced back to look at Player. He was staring at the picture, his eyes very focused. They were holding hands, sitting close together, backs to the headboard, staring at her grandfather's drawing.

Her heart began to pound as she forced herself to look at Sorbacov. His head had completely faded away. Those malevolent eyes were staring at them, and they were all too real. Around the eyes was absolutely nothing but black. There were no lines. No charcoal drawings. The eyes did seem to be set back into the drawing, not out in front of it, as if the drawing itself were some kind of a tube.

"Player." She whispered his name, knowing the entity was gone, but still terrified. She needed the connection of her hand on his thigh, but raised the other one defensively to her throat. "What is that thing? Why is it here in my bedroom with us? It really does look like it's inside my grandfather's picture."

He suddenly gathered her into his arms and pulled her onto his lap. "Stop shaking. We'll figure this out. I can take you and your grandmother out of here and put you somewhere safe until we know what is going on."

Zyah buried her face in his throat. He was always so warm, his body comforting. "My instincts are very strong about this, Player, telling me we can't be separated. From the very beginning I felt we had to be together." At no time had that changed. If anything, her feeling had grown even stronger that they needed to stay together for safety.

"I believe this man has something to do with the bomb," Player said. "I just don't know what. I don't understand how he managed to get into this room. I had to have brought him here, but I don't recognize him. Can you sketch those eyes? It's possible Czar might recognize him from his eyes, but I sure as hell don't."

The eyes had been very dark brown. Zyah slid off his lap and reached for the notebook and pen so she could hastily sketch the eyes while she had them in her head so starkly. Very heavily lashed. There were lines around the outside corners of his eyes as if he'd seen a great deal of sun, but because the eyes sat right in the middle of an empty black hole, it was difficult to even see those. That was more of an impression.

"I think you're right, Player, but how would he know about the bomb? How could anyone know unless he saw you building them as a child?" She put the notebook down and rubbed her chin on her knee. "He would have had to know about not only your illusions but the fact that your illusions can morph into reality if you suffer a brain injury."

He shook his head. "It can happen if I hold an illusion too long."

"Not even your brothers and sisters knew that, right? Czar didn't know. You went there the other night to tell him. You were so upset that you'd held that information back from him. If none of them knew, who could have known? An instructor at the school? Did Sorbacov know? Could he have told someone?"

Player tilted his neck until he rested the

back of his head against the headboard. "That's a lot of questions, babe. I have no idea who could have known. Not one of the instructors. Certainly, none of the other students. My people had eyes on me, and they didn't catch on. The other kids didn't know me that well. They wouldn't have had a clue even if a life-sized bunny hopped through the room. Sorbacov is a different story. It's difficult to say what he knew. He had cameras planted everywhere. Once we began to kill . . ." He broke off and glanced at her.

Zyah pressed her lips together and then looked down at her hands. Player had lived a horrific life. They couldn't pretend he hadn't, and they couldn't tiptoe around it, not if they were going to be together in the way she needed to be with him. She wanted a total connection. A total sharing between them. She wasn't the kind of woman to be in a partial relationship. It was all or nothing for her. If he didn't feel the same way, she needed to know that now.

"I realize you and the others had no choice, Player. Not only do I believe you had no choice to do what you did, I think there was justice in it. I don't like the fact that you were children — babies, really — but there was no one else. If you were going to survive, how else were you going to do it? Ask nicely? I doubt if that would have gotten you any-where."

Player touched her face with gentle fingers, brushed across her lips and then down her chin. "I don't know how I got so lucky to meet someone like you. I don't like that you have to share what happened to me when I have nightmares — and I have them all the time. I don't normally build real bombs. I build bombs that don't work just to clear my mind. But you shouldn't have to see that world I grew up in, and if you stick with me, Zyah, it will continue to happen."

Zyah shrugged. "I like the intimacy of telepathic communication, which means being in your mind. I like knowing things about you that you don't share with others." Not even his Torpedo Ink brothers and sisters, but she didn't say that aloud. "If you're going to have a real relationship with me, and I'm not saying you are because I just don't know if I can trust this yet, I won't settle for second best. I won't settle for halfway. That means occasionally neither one of us is going to be comfortable."

"I said you shouldn't have to see the world I grew up in, baby, I didn't say I wasn't willing for you to see it. I think it's a little late to pretend I'm Prince Charming." He gave her a little half smile that tugged at the corners of her heart. "I'm willing to take you any way I can get you. One tiny piece of you at a time. And I'm not so proud I won't tell you so."

She lowered her lashes, veiling the expression in her eyes. He could read her so easily. That gift he'd given her. The basket was right there. So close. The contents exactly right for her and thoughtful. "You have to stop saying things like that."

Deliberately, she turned her attention back to her grandfather's drawing. "Do you really believe that you can see something in his drawing that I haven't, when I've looked at it for all these years? And my grandmother. If she knew, surely she would have said something to me."

"I've considered that," Player said. He slid from the bed again and walked over to where the picture was hung on the wall.

Zyah's heart accelerated, pounding hard. She hadn't wanted to believe her grandfather's art had anything to do with the entity that had been in her bedroom, but now that she wasn't certain, she didn't want Player anywhere near it. She jumped up and quickly turned on the light, dispelling the shadows, hopefully making it impossible for the thing — or person — to sneak back.

Player glanced at her over his shoulder. "He can't get back right now."

"How do you know?"

She came up to him, quite close, one arm sliding around his waist, not-so-subtly hinting. He reacted exactly the way she knew he would — he put his arm around her shoulders and pulled her to him, her front to his ribs,

482

tucking her close the way he so often did. She took a deep breath, inhaling him into her lungs, and then turned her head to look at the picture.

Every line, thin or thick, was so familiar to her. She knew them by heart. The frame, that beautifully rolled frame, carved with such loving detail into an intricate scroll of ancient time, complete with symbols. She'd traced every one of them a thousand times and pressed kisses onto her fingertips and then onto those etchings just to connect with her father. She moved her head from side to side, fast and then slow, to try to see if the lines in the drawing changed at all. Once or twice she thought they did, but nothing very significant, and it could have been an illusion, simply because Player had suggested it.

"What do you see when you look at the print?"

"I see the schematics for a bomb." He delivered the news softly. Gently. That same low voice he spoke with every day. Not like he was crushing her. Or would be crushing her grandmother if what he said was the truth.

She tried to pull away from him, but his arm tightened around her.

"Don't, Zyah. We want honesty between us. I don't have to be right. You asked me a question, and I answered you truthfully. I didn't want to. I could have lied to you. I know if

I'm right this is really fucked up. But my brain works out puzzles. I don't even consciously do it half the time. I stared at this drawing from the bed for hours when I first came here. It intrigued me. I couldn't look away. Sometimes I thought it was pulling me into it."

"Your mind automatically goes to putting together bombs when you're upset, Player," she pointed out, looking for a reasonable explanation. There were many. There *had* to be many. "You had a massive brain injury. It was natural for your brain to go to the one thing that's your fallback when you are severely injured and traumatized."

He didn't just dismiss her explanation out of hand. He considered it carefully. "That's reasonable, Zyah. I thought of that too. But it doesn't explain the fact that this bomb is one I'd never seen before. And it's very real. It works. Or that I studied the picture for hours from every angle while I was in this room and I could see it very differently. I've been here for weeks now. I know there has to be a device to read it somewhere. An object that the drawing is viewed through. Your grandfather was a genius to create this picture and have it be right out in the open and no one suspect."

Zyah did her best to have an open mind and process what he was telling her. Was it possible? "If my grandfather actually did what you're saying he did, that means he came up with the plans for building a new bomb, right?"

"He was a physicist, right?"

She was silent for a while, staring at the drawing that had suddenly taken on a sinister implication. She sighed. "I don't want to sleep in this room, Player. We should put a cover over this until we figure out what really is going on. Or better yet, get it out of the house."

"I agree. I think it's gotten to a very dangerous stage. I need to know who that man is. He isn't an entity from another world or another time period. That's a flesh-and-blood man from the here and now. He knows us. He looked right at us."

"Do you think he has anything to do with the robberies? Or the attempted kidnapping?" An icy shiver crept down her spine.

"No, I think this is entirely separate. I'd be surprised if he knows about the robberies or attempted kidnapping. He wants the bomb."

"I just don't understand how he got into the bedroom." She forced herself to look at the drawing again. She didn't want to touch it. Nothing about the entire matter made any sense to her. She knew about psychic gifts. She believed in them. She had experienced evidence of them. She'd even seen what the repercussions of talents going wrong could do just in Player with his brain injury and migraines. This was an entirely different level of psychic phenomenon, and it creeped her out.

Player was silent. She could tell he was studying the drawing carefully, his eyes moving over it line by line, quadrant by quadrant. There was no hurry. He did the same with the frame. "I would like to ask your grandmother if we could show this to Czar."

Zyah turned her face up to his, completely horrified. "You cannot take this drawing over to Czar's house, where Blythe and those children are. I was considering burning it."

Player's blue eyes warmed, crinkled around the edges. "Babe. Really? You're going to burn our mystery? I thought the clubhouse or my house, where no one is. Czar might be able to identify him. I caught a few more details than you did. You didn't read all of my notes. I also want to ask your grandmother a few questions. I think your grandfather had an item that was used to view the drawing through that would show the schematics of the bomb. It's far too intricate for anyone to just take a chance for someone like me to come along."

"I doubt there are very many people like you, Player." Zyah didn't think there was anyone like him. If that drawing really did have the plans for making a bomb, she doubted if anyone else ever would have seen it. "I'm not sleeping in here."

"We'll go in the guest room. Tomorrow, let's take your grandmother out. She's really tired of being cooped up. I can ask her if we can take the drawing to show Czar and the others and see if she'll talk about it. She'd like the Floating Hat. I'd also like to take her to Crow 287. She's so much stronger now, and if she stays inside much longer, she'll get depressed. You could call a few of her friends to meet us at the restaurant. Let's make this happen for her, Zyah."

There was an odd melting sensation in the region of her heart. He was making it impossible not to fall harder for him. He had been very caring of her grandmother even when his brain injury was at its most severe. Now he was so thoughtful in the midst of some man staring at them malevolently right in the room he'd been sleeping in.

"Let's take the picture off the wall, cover it and put it in the garage until we can get it out of here," Zyah decided. "We'll go to sleep in the guest room and figure the rest out in the morning. I'm so tired I can hardly stand up."

"I'll take care of the picture, baby. You crawl into bed. I'll be right back up."

That was Player. Always thinking about her. She was gratified he was no longer pushing her away. She didn't know why he'd suddenly made the decision to let her all the way in, but when she needed him the most, he was there for her. Still, she wanted to be a little cautious. Just a little, in case at the end of all of this he pulled back, or worse, he wanted her more for the wrong reasons than the right ones. She sighed. She was tired and she was overthinking. She did that and she had to stop.

# SIXTEEN

Player settled Anat's wheelchair right up to the table close to the window so she could look out onto the street of Sea Haven yet see everything taking place in the Floating Hat. She nearly glowed, her dark eyes bright. He knew Zyah would be like her as she aged. A woman always positive, always bringing the sun with her everywhere she went.

He recognized Sabelia, the clerk, immediately when she came to take their order. She was extremely sweet to Anat and Zyah, engaging them in conversation about various teas and scones. He realized, as he inhaled the fragrance in the shop, that he'd been looking forward to bringing the two women there, not dreading it.

Blythe was meeting them, which would make it easier for him to fade into the background and just enjoy watching Zyah make new friends. That was what he wanted for her. She hadn't had the time since she'd been back to connect with other women.

Anat told him Zyah stayed very close to her, rarely leaving her those first few days, and then she was working. Player wanted her to have her own circle of women friends and feel comfortable reaching out to them if she needed to. He knew he wasn't going to always be the easiest man to live with.

When Blythe walked in, she wasn't alone. Anya, Reaper's woman, was with her. Anya had long wavy dark hair and emerald-green eyes. She was tall like Blythe, and worked as a bartender with Preacher in Caspar at their very popular bar. No one knew how she'd managed to tame Reaper, but she had. She was definitely the center of Reaper's world.

Player made the introductions. "Anat, these are two of the women I consider family: Blythe, Czar's wife, and Anya, Reaper's woman. This is Anat and Zyah." Where Anya was tall and dark, Blythe was tall and blond.

"I know Blythe," Anat said. "Inez introduced us."

Blythe nodded. "We did meet. It was quite a while ago. You have a good memory, Anat. You came to one of the classes I was teaching on spinning yarn. And, of course, Zyah and I met the other night. It's so nice to see you again."

"Lovely to meet you, Anya," Zyah greeted. "Have you been here before?"

"I haven't," Anya admitted. "Blythe told us about it. I wanted to meet you, so I thought

490

this was the perfect opportunity to get to do both."

The women at once began to talk, laughing together as if they were good friends. Player found himself watching Zyah's face, the way her eyes lit up. He enjoyed hearing her genuine laughter. After the fear in her from the night before, he was grateful that he'd thought to bring them to Hannah's tea shop. There was something very magical about her shop. He couldn't say what it was, but he felt it and knew the women did as well.

"Before I leave you to it, ladies, I want to ask Blythe a quick question," he interrupted. "You know quite a bit about physical therapy, don't you? At least Czar told me you do."

She nodded. "I'm certified as a therapist. Hopefully, I can answer your question if you have one for me."

"Anat has been doing therapy on her arm, and she's been doing quite well. Before, she'd been doing therapy on her leg and it became very painful. When Zyah took her back in for more X-rays, they had to reset her leg. She'll have to start over again and is about to do so. When she'd told the therapist that it was hurting her to do the exercises, the therapist dismissed her concerns and told her a little pain was necessary. She's been going along all this time, doing great with her arm. I've stayed in the room with her. Lately, the therapist has been trying to get me to leave.

She insisted yesterday, and I finally did, but then Anat told me the exercises were very painful and the therapist said the same thing to her — that pain was necessary for improvement. I didn't like that she insisted I leave the room. Why would that be necessary when Anat always did the work with me there? And why is pain so necessary?"

Zyah leaned toward her grandmother. "You didn't tell me about this."

"I didn't want to worry you."

Zyah sighed. "You should have told me *immediately.* You should have called me when I was at work. And, Player, that therapist can't order you out of the room. If you feel something's wrong, don't leave her. The therapist can leave. We'll find someone else."

"Actually, Zyah's right, Player," Blythe agreed. "There is no need for Anat to hurt when she's doing her exercises. And certainly no reason for you to be out of the room, especially when you've been there all along and she's worked without a problem. I don't ever want to say anything against another therapist, but she doesn't seem the right fit for Anat."

"I have to agree with that," Player said. He smiled at the older woman. "You're always so sweet to everyone, Anat. It isn't that she'd get fired. She just wouldn't work for you specifically. There are a lot of other patients for her to work with. She travels, remember?

The clinic hired her to work with their overflow of patients. We'll find someone much more suited to you, especially now that you're going to start work on your leg again. Zyah can call your doctor for another reference."

"I really don't want that poor girl to lose her job, Player. She's very nice. She just gets so rough at times," Anat said. "She tells the most interesting stories. I really like her."

"You like everyone, Mama Anat," Zyah pointed out. "That's why everyone loves you so much." She covered her grandmother's hand with her own. "My grandfather was so crazy in love with her, he spent months drawing her a picture for their anniversary. Months. It was done in charcoal. When she left everything behind and came to the United States, she brought me and the picture."

Anat's laughter floated through the shop, tinkling gently like the bells at the door. Player loved the carefree sound.

"He did. He was such a brilliant man, and yet at his heart, he was a poet. An artist." There was such love in Anat's voice.

"Did he work for the government?" Player asked. "Zyah tells me he was a renowned physicist."

"He worked for them at first, but then he had a falling-out with them and quit his job. I was a little scared. In those days, it could get frightening to oppose the government, particularly if you were in the kind of position he was in. Thankfully, we were left alone. They came around occasionally to ask him back to work, but he always refused. He had friends who thought as he did, that the president was moving too far away from the needs of all the people. It was a time of conflict in my country, and he didn't want me involved. It was one of the few times when we didn't share everything."

Player didn't look at Zyah. Anat's husband had wanted to protect her — at least he hoped that was what he was doing. Player didn't want Horus's silence to be a betrayal.

"How wonderful that he gave you a charcoal drawing for your anniversary," Anya said. "That he even remembered you had an anniversary."

The women laughed, and Player made a mental note to remember the date he'd first laid eyes on Zyah. Anniversaries were important to women. If that was the case, he would have to get good at remembering them. He'd pass that information on to Reaper as well. Anya had laughed, but there was a little note in her voice that suggested she needed a little more care now and then. This shop was a gold mine for his Torpedo Ink brethren, whether they knew it or not. Preacher had recognized the genuine wisdom in Hannah.

A couple of years back, Torpedo Ink had worked with the Drake sisters and the women on the farm to end the stranglehold the Swords' international president had on human trafficking. The man was a billionaire and had a few very lethal psychic gifts of his own. With a club as big as the Swords at his disposal, he hadn't been easy to defeat, but with the combined efforts of the Drakes, Torpedo Ink and the women living on the farm with Blythe, and their psychic gifts, they had done it. Player had a great deal of respect for all of them. He knew the others in his club did as well. He hoped, like Preacher, they might avail themselves of some of Hannah's wisdom.

"Horus — that was my husband's name — always remembered every anniversary. He made me things." Anat's voice was soft with love.

"Was there something he had to look through to view the drawing?" Zyah asked casually. "Player says when he looks at it from different angles, he sees different things." She frowned. "What kind of drawing did you call it?"

"Anamorphic," he replied just as casually. Sabelia put a mug of coffee in front of him, and he looked up at her and smiled his thanks. "If you look at the picture through a special device, you see something different in the picture that no one can see just viewing it through the naked eye. Only a very brilliant artist could draw that kind of art."

"I've heard of that," Blythe said. "It isn't exactly the same as the 3D images, is it?"

"Not exactly."

Anat shook her head. "Horus didn't ever have me look through anything to view the picture. I could see it just fine, but he had to. His eyesight wasn't the best. He had to wear his monocle." She laughed merrily, that soft little trilling sound at the end. Her hands went around the hat teacup, warming themselves.

"You still have his monocle, don't you, Mama Anat?" Zyah asked. "It's one of your treasures, like mama's shawl."

Anat nodded. "I thought he looked so handsome whenever he would put that monocle on his eye. He always had it on a fine gold chain. I teased him about it all the time. Ken, Zyah's father, got him that chain. Ken was a marvelous man." She smiled at her granddaughter. "Quite brilliant as well. A renowned astronomer. They got on quite well. The two of them were always together. Ken made the frame for my Horus's anniversary gift to me, so of course, it means all the more."

Player's gut tightened. He couldn't look at Zyah. He knew Anat's sweet, guileless chatter about her beloved Horus and Zyah's father, Ken, would be heartbreaking to her. No doubt that monocle was the device needed to display the bomb. And her father with his

496

background in astronomy . . . Player hadn't told Zyah his theory on how the man had entered their bedroom. He didn't want to tell her.

The small bells in the shapes of hats tinkled merrily, inviting others inside. He looked up to see Breezy, wife of the vice president of Torpedo Ink, entering along with Soleil, Ice's wife, and Scarlet, Absinthe's wife. They came straight over to the table. No hesitation. He stood, making the introductions, knowing Anat was in her element. He wanted this for Zyah, but being surrounded by that many women was just a bit too much for him.

Alena and Lana sauntered in moments later, and Player started sweating. He glanced around the room. Sabelia was already adding tables and chairs to accommodate everyone. He helped her and then backed off when he spotted Hannah as she came out of the back room. She sent him a cheerful smile.

"Player. I was hoping you'd come back. I have another lotion I thought would be good for you to try." She waved to Blythe. "Ladies. Thank you all for coming. I'll be over in a few minutes. Is this your Zyah?"

"Yes." Player was pleased but not surprised that Hannah would be able to pick her out among all the women. "And this is Anat Gamal, her grandmother. This is Hannah Drake Harrington. She owns the shop."

"You made the lotion and cream Player

brought home," Zyah said. "I swear it was heaven after a long day on my feet. Thank you."

"He was the one who thought of it," Hannah said. "I was just happy to help. I hope you don't mind if I borrow him for a few minutes. I have something else to show him while you ladies visit. The peach scones turned out particularly excellent."

Zyah looked up at him, her eyes sparkling. In spite of the sadness she had to be feeling over the revelations about her grandfather, Hannah's shop was a good place to learn the truth. There was magic there, a feeling of well-being. Combined with the company of the women extending their friendship to her and Anat, it seemed impossible to feel anything but good.

"Thanks for the rescue," Player whispered as they made their way to the table in the corner on the other side of the room.

Hannah gave him her genuine smile. He knew the difference now. "You looked like you were having an excellent time, but you didn't feel that way. Although you seem genuinely happy for Zyah."

"She's new here and doesn't know too many people. Anat was robbed and beaten very severely. At the time, Zyah was in Europe, working there. She gave up her job and came home right away to stay with her grandmother and make her home permanently here. I want her to make friends. She's managing the store in Caspar and wants to take a second job at Crow 287."

"Alena's restaurant. I hear the food is amazing. Jonas has been promising to take me there, forever. I'm going to have to twist his arm. Joley and Ilya are back, and she'll go with me if Jonas persists in being a stick-in-the-mud. He loves to stay home at night. He says after working all day he just likes to put his feet up. Make that he doesn't want me to go out because I might do something rash."

Player tried not to laugh. "Do you do rash things?"

"Joley does rash things. Elle does them. I, however, do *not.*" She handed him the bottle of lotion she'd brought out from the back room and waved her hand at the little teapot sitting on the table. At once it began to sing.

Player tried not to notice when the teapot floated in the air and poured tea into her cup. A spoon whirled madly, stirring in honey. "You're not just a little annoyed with him right now, are you?" He wasn't mentioning anything at all to do with the tea.

"Now that you mention it, I might be." Her hair flew in every direction, blond spiral curls springing around her face.

She waved her hand toward something behind him. Player took a whiff of the lotion to keep from turning in his chair. Had he mentioned that Zyah had such a special

499

fragrance? Could Hannah have even managed to get that hint of cassis-raspberry facet? The blend of green floral mimosa. He was distracted until a plate of cookies floated to the table and landed beside her teacup. His coffee mug followed it.

"Why is it that men want their own way in all things?" she asked, her tone exquisitely mild, but her blue eyes turbulently stormy.

Player hoped this was one of those moments when a woman didn't really want an answer. She wanted someone to listen. He did his best to look very interested in all she had to say. Any woman who floated teapots in the air commanded his respect. Jonas Harrington, whether he carried a gun or not, was crazy to annoy this woman on any level.

The silence stretched between them until Player realized it was very possible Hannah required an answer. He cleared his throat. "You do realize I came to you because I totally fucked up my relationship with my woman, right? I don't have a clue why men do half the bullshit things we do, Hannah. I came here to learn from you, not to advise you. I'm trying to get the brothers to ask a few questions so they don't ruin what they have."

"You *so* deserve a cookie. They're really good too. Take two." Hannah beamed at him.

"You can't really turn Jonas into a toad, can you? I think Sabelia threatened Preacher

500

with turning him into one the other day."

Hannah inspected her fingernails. "I have considered it. It would certainly serve him right. He doesn't like toads, especially in his house or around his precious cars. He might just be having a bad day."

Player couldn't help grinning. "You really are a badass, aren't you?"

"Yep." She said it smugly.

"And a troublemaker."

"Sometimes. When it's called for. And it's called for. Do you like that scent? Do you think she will? It will really work well for massaging her body. And it's edible. When you massage this into her skin, you use a slightly different technique. Let me show you."

Player extended his arm to her, and Hannah poured some lotion from a small cup she had set aside on the table into her palms. "You have to rub it to activate it. Here, smell it now." She held her palm under his nose.

The fragrance reminded him of Zyah, but set off his addiction for her. He could taste her in his mouth. He had to work very hard to keep his body from reacting. The tea shop was filled with women, his lady included, *and* her grandmother, and he was having lustful thoughts triggered by the scent of lotion. Great. Just great. "That's amazing, Hannah. It smells just like Zyah. How did you manage to do that when you'd never met her?"

Hannah brought the lotion back to her nose

and used her hand to send the scent to her. "I got it right? I'm so glad. I made one for her to massage you with as well. Actually, I'll confess, it was a collaboration between Preacher and me. He really is talented. His gift is so strong. Sea Haven attracts many with various talents of different strengths, but truly, his is quite rare."

"You said Sabelia was apprenticing under you. Is she like Preacher?"

Hannah glanced up to look at Sabelia, who was waiting on two ladies at a table close to the large one where Zyah was. One of the two women was the physical therapist from out of town. She was having an animated conversation with a woman who looked to be about fifty. The two were laughing and seemed very relaxed. The older woman clearly knew Sabelia and had been in the shop often.

A shadow crossed Hannah's face. "No, Sabelia is more like me. Everyone has to choose their own path. We can't choose for them. I grew up in a loving environment. I don't know what I would have been like with the kinds of powers I had if I hadn't had a moral compass. Life has not been as kind to Sabelia. She has yet to choose her way. I can only hope that my genuine caring will influence her toward a better path."

She reached for his arm. "Let me show you the pressure you'll want to use on her back and down her body when you start. This has a cinnamic-honey background, and it will begin to heat, which, trust me, is what you want. You really will like the taste."

He already knew that. He had it in his mouth without bringing his arm up to his lips. The temptation was strong.

The bells jangled loudly, a burst of sound, and Player instinctively jerked his head up. Hannah stayed very relaxed, not turning around. Lana and Alena went on alert. Blythe put her hand over her mouth, hiding a smile. Player took the entire room in with one look. He didn't jerk his arm away from Hannah, but that was only because he was so disciplined. Jonas stalked across the room, fire in his eyes.

Jonas stood a foot from the table, fists on his hips, glaring at them. His gaze encompassed his wife and her delicate hands as they continued massaging Player's arm, Player sitting with his mug of coffee and the plate of cookies close to him, and then those fiery blue eyes swept back to his wife.

"This again, Hannah? What *exactly* is going on here?"

"What does it look like is going on, Jonas?"

Player winced at that tone. So very low and sweet. There was one tiny little note that should have been a warning to any male with half a brain to put the brakes on. Even though Jonas was the sheriff and technically it wasn't a bad thing for him to get taken down, Player wanted to warn the man. Hannah was no one to mess with. Jonas should know that.

"It looks to me like you're holding hands with that man, that's what it looks like."

"You'll need to turn that firearm in immediately. Clearly, you're going blind. I'll make an appointment for you with the eye doctor when I'm on my next break."

Her hands never stopped moving on Player's arm, her fingers working their way down his forearm and, honestly, it felt more than good, so he just relaxed and took a bite of cookie, beginning to enjoy himself.

Jonas glared at him. "I believe you've got your hands on my wife."

"She's right about your need for glasses, Jonas," Player said, waving the cookie around, making certain Jonas got a good whiff of the awesome aroma. "My hands are on the coffee mug and this really excellent cookie. Did you bake it, Hannah?"

"I did, Player."

Jonas made a sound of pure exasperation. "There are toads in my car, Hannah."

Player nearly spewed coffee across the table.

Hannah raised a casual eyebrow. "How is that my problem?"

"Woman, you know damn well you had something to do with putting them in my car. Get them out."

"I'm working, Jonas. I don't have time to

catch toads and put them in your car. I believe you've had problems with them in the past. It seems to me that you attract the toads to you."

Jonas leaned over her shoulder and reached for a cookie. The plate slid out of his reach, and sparks hit the ends of his fingers, zapping him. Player decided he needed to be back with the women at the large table, where it was safe. He stayed very still. There hadn't even been a surge of power, but the hair on the back of his neck stood up.

"Hannah. Princess. You're upset with me." Jonas's tone changed immediately. Gentled. Was conciliatory. "This is about last night, isn't it?"

She kept her face averted, but her fingers on Player's arm dug deeper. He wanted to find a way to gracefully remind both of them he was there so he could leave, but suddenly the two of them were locked into a tight intimate bubble where it was only the two of them.

"Hannah, I was out of line, but you know I lose my mind when I think you're in any kind of danger. That's the one thing I can't handle. That's no excuse for the way I acted." Jonas ran both hands through his hair. "I think better when I'm eating cookies, baby, you know I do."

Player was impressed. He was all about learning from the pros, and clearly Jonas was a pro. The plate of cookies floated straight to Jonas. He scooped up half the contents on the plate, smart enough to know if he blew it, he wouldn't get a second chance.

"I want this for us, Hannah, but not at the expense of your life. We have to be safe."

Hannah's fingers dug so hard into Player's muscle he was grateful he'd learned at a young age not to react.

"I'm not letting someone who wanted to hack me to pieces dictate whether or not I can have children, Jonas."

The pain in her voice alarmed Player. The sorrow. It went so deep he was afraid if she let it loose, everyone in that shop would drown in it.

"No one will dictate to us, Hannah," Jonas assured. "We just have to find a better way than last time. A safer way."

Player cleared his throat to remind them both that he was there. "Jonas, if she cries, I'm going to pull that gun out of the holster and shoot you right in front of all these women here. So better I just go over to the table where some of my crew is leaving. I can say good-bye and you can grovel like you should without a witness."

The love between the two of them was right out there where anyone could see. Unashamed. Strong. The way Czar and Blythe were. That was what Player wanted with Zyah.

Hannah let go of his arm immediately. "I'm so sorry, Player, you didn't need to get caught up in our drama."

"Anything to do with toads is always fascinating, Hannah," Player said lamely as he slid off the chair. He nailed the last remaining cookies for himself, figuring he'd earned them. "We'll be here for a while. Anat wanted to sample your luncheon special, so after the others leave, we'll be eating."

Hannah nodded. "That's good. I can show you after and maybe work a little with Zyah."

Player made his escape just as Soleil, Anya, Breezy and Scarlet left. Blythe and Zyah took Anat to the ladies' room, leaving him to join Alena and Lana. As he did, Terrie Frankle, the physical therapist, waved them over to her table.

"Player, this is Lucy Bellmont. I was telling her that your club owns quite a bit of the properties in Caspar. She's lived there most of her life. Lucy, this is Player. I met him at the Gamal house."

Player gave the Bellmont woman a smile, all the while wondering what Terrie wanted. Terrie was always unfailingly sweet to Anat, but the moment Terrie had insisted she wanted to be alone with the older woman and Anat had clearly been in pain after, he had changed his mind about the physical therapist. Now, watching her closely, he wasn't so certain anything about her was

507

genuine.

"This is Alena and Lana," he introduced his Torpedo Ink sisters and waited for Terrie to have her say.

"Lucy is interested in a job at the grocery store in Caspar, Player. I know Zyah works there and Inez has something to do with the store. Do you have any idea if Lucy should just go into the store and get an application or does she have to go into the one here in Sea Haven? That was what she was going to do."

Terrie liked to be in the know. Or was she trying to determine whether or not Torpedo Ink owned the store with Inez? It was a safe bet that they did, since they owned a good deal of the downtown properties, just as Terrie had pointed out.

"I think if you put in your application at either of the stores, Inez would be fine with it," Lana answered for him. "I happen to know she's working at the Caspar store today, so she might even interview you on the spot. Another woman was going there today in the hopes she had time to interview. They need a lot of help."

Lucy broke into a smile after looking a little strained, as if she hadn't been so happy that Terrie had asked Player for help. "Thank you."

"Inez really does own the store, then?" Terrie asked.

508

"That's the word on the street," Lana said. "Torpedo Ink has been helping her out with stocking until she can get it up and running. Good help isn't easy to find."

Player's gaze flicked to Terrie's face. She'd definitely been looking for information. "Enjoy your lunch, ladies." He stepped back to make room for Anat's wheelchair to get through the aisle back to her place.

"Did I miss anything important?" Anat asked.

Player leaned over and brushed a kiss on her cheek. "Only that I saved you a cookie and I refrained from shooting the sheriff. I think his wife put a bunch of toads in his car. That's a gift that could come in handy."

Sabelia cleared the empty hat cups from the table, pausing to agree. "I believe you're right, Player. I've been trying to perfect that one. I do need something to practice on. You wouldn't give me the make and model of the vehicle Preacher drives, would you?" She used her sweetest voice.

Lana swung around. "Is my brother deserving of toads in his personal truck?"

"Preacher is your brother?" Sabelia straightened to her full height, which was a little ridiculous next to Lana's tall figure. "I mean aside from being Torpedo Ink."

"Yes."

Sabelia flashed an impish smile. "He was extremely rude and called me a moron along with a wealth of other things. But I also was just as rude back, and he didn't get me fired, so we're even, and I don't know how to put toads in his truck unless I catch them, which I have no intention of doing. I just thought if I was going to practice something like that, he might be a good one to practice on. At least his vehicle."

"If you decide to pursue your craft, let me know. I'll do all I can to assist you," Lana said.

Sabelia laughed. Player thought the sound lifted some of the darker shadows talking with Terrie had given him. Sabelia's laughter had a similar tone to Hannah's when it was real.

Lana slipped into the seat across from Anat, intent on striking up a conversation with her and Blythe. Player didn't blame her. Anat was a gift, and just being close to her could brighten anyone's world. He wanted to be near Zyah. He looked around for her. Alena and Zyah stood by the window, looking out at the street. He joined them, crowding close to his woman, inhaling her scent, breathing away the last traces of gloom.

Zyah leaned into Player when he wrapped his arms around her waist. She loved the feel of his body against hers. His strength, and the way he was unflinchingly so possessive, so proud to let everyone know she was with him, made her feel inexplicably happy. She didn't need a man to be confident. She knew who she was, but being with Player brought her joy.

He had given Anat a wonderful time with so many visitors. Her grandmother was in her element when she was regaling others with tales of her past and her colorful homeland. She was a good listener as well, encouraging others to tell her everything about themselves. Those qualities made her popular among old and young alike.

Player and Zyah hadn't wanted to tire her out on her first real day out, so they had chosen to take her to the Floating Hat for tea and a luncheon. Blythe, Alena and Lana were going to join them. She didn't know if it was a coincidence, but it was wonderful that Breezy, Anya, Soleil and Scarlet had happened in for tea as well. Anat had really enjoyed meeting them.

Alena slung her arm around Zyah. "I could have used you at the restaurant last night — we were slammed." She nodded toward Jonas. "He had to come in last night because that little weasel Perry Randall wouldn't answer his cell phone."

"What was wrong? He was having dinner with Francine."

Suddenly, there it was, all over again: that terrible dread Zyah had been feeling from the night before. She'd thought the premonition was over her grandfather's drawing, but the feeling had hit her long before she'd gotten home. It had started right when Francine had driven up to the curb drunk in her grandmother's prized Cadillac. She found herself pressing her body closer into Player's.

"Perry's parents were robbed and attacked last night," Alena continued. She half turned to keep her body slightly at an angle away from Anat.

Player tightened his arms around Zyah's waist, and she was grateful for his support.

"Why did Jonas come looking for him so quickly? How bad was it?" Player asked Alena the question Zyah had wanted to ask but couldn't get the words out. She was terrified of the answer.

"His father is in a coma, Player. I don't think he's going to make it. And his mother isn't in much better condition. Honestly, from what I understand, Perry could lose both his parents. Jonas, of course, didn't tell Perry that, only that it was bad and Perry needed to get to the hospital. Blythe told me this morning when I asked. She's got con-nections at the hospital."

Zyah pressed her hand to her stomach, afraid she might vomit. Who in the world would beat older people to such an extent that they would put them in the hospital? Almost kill them?

"The thieves are escalating just the way Jonas said they were. I don't understand why they aren't leaving town the way they have every other place they've robbed," Player said.

"Did Perry go to the hospital right away?" Zyah asked. "He never seemed very close to his parents, and from what my grandmother implied once when she talked about him, he didn't treat them very well; he acted kind of mean to them. Still, I would hope he would have gone."

There was a part of her that wanted him to be the informant. The local man helping the robbers. She wanted him to be vile enough to serve his own parents up to the robbers in order to keep the cops from looking his way, not realizing the thieves would kill him before they left town.

Alena nodded. "He turned almost white. He looked shocked. The weird thing was, Francine didn't look so shocked. She must have been drunker than I thought, because it seemed to take a good while before it sank in that Perry's parents were in the hospital. She kept chattering away and acting like they had all the time in the world before they had to leave. She even had her phone out and was texting. She pouted because she was going to miss dessert. He finally got exasperated and told her to catch a ride home with someone else, that he had to go right then. She left with him, but it only seemed to sink in right before they left that something was wrong."

Zyah froze, everything in her going still. She had been missing something all along.

Francine was texting. She'd been angry when Zyah refused to have Player come to dinner with her. When Francine was angry, she always struck out verbally — which she had. She was already fairly drunk. The robbers had an inside person — someone close to the elderly community. No way would Francine ever condone hurting her grandmother. Would she anyone else? Francine might not like Zyah, but she did like Anat. Didn't she? And what about Lizz's other friends?

Surely the things going through her mind couldn't possibly be the truth. She didn't want to even consider such a possibility. Had Francine been trying to get Zyah out of the way, taking her to dinner so someone could get back into her grandmother's house? When she'd learned that Player was with her grandmother, had she insisted that he come to dinner with them in order to get him out of the house? Zyah didn't want to think those thoughts, but they wouldn't stop.

"What is it, baby?" Player asked, his lips against her ear.

She shook her head. She didn't want to voice her doubts out loud. Certainly not in the tearoom, where someone might overhear her. She could barely allow herself to consider that Francine would really set Anat up to be beaten and robbed. Not just Anat, but all of Lizz's friends in the community. Could she really sit at dinner with Perry, knowing his parents were being robbed? Would she go to a motel with him? Or worse, go to the guesthouse on his parents' property and have sex with him knowing his parents were being assaulted? The idea sickened Zyah. Was Francine really capable of that kind of behavior?

Then there was the woman in her garage. The one yelling, *Fuck her up, fuck her up.* The voice had been muffled by the ski mask over her head, and Zyah had been occupied trying to fight off two men, but thinking back, the high-pitched, eagerly gleeful sound could have been Francine when she was extremely drunk. Did Francine really hate her enough to have men kidnap her? Possibly kill her?

Zyah spun around, practically throwing herself into Player's arms, willing him not to ask her any questions.

"I didn't mean to upset you," Alena said.

"No, no, I'm all right. I just wish these people would be caught," Zyah said. "I don't understand why they went back to my grandmother's home. She never was one for jewelry. She loved to dance. Belly dance. It's part of the culture — in our family, I mean — so we have a few bracelets and anklets, but they aren't worth anything monetarily."

Player kept his arm around her, holding her in close to his body as they made their way to Anat's table, where Blythe and Lana talked animatedly with her. Zyah looked at Anat's hands. She never wore bracelets or bangles.

She didn't wear earrings either. She always said Horus preferred her not to, so she didn't. Now that Zyah thought about it, Horus actually had jewelry and Anat didn't. Horus gave her beautiful things he created with his two hands, and she treasured them, but he didn't give her jewels. So what did the thieves think Anat had?

She had a horrible suspicion she knew. What had Jonas asked Anat? At lunch had she ever talked about anything to her Red Hat Society friends? She always claimed she had a great treasure. Zyah was her great treasure. Anat really regarded her that way. It wasn't diamonds or gold. Zyah was her treasure.

Player waited for her to slip into a chair close to Anat, and then he sat beside her. His presence comforted her. More and more, she feared she was right about Francine. Francine was the traitor, the local who had given the thieves information on the elderly, what they had inside their homes and how to get in. Francine would have heard the gossip about Anat's treasure, and she would have passed that information on to the thieves, betraying Anat. Betraying Zyah. She glanced once at Terrie Frankle. She and Francine had some kind of connection. She traveled from place to place. She was in and out of people's homes. When Zyah had changed the locks on the doors the first time, she could have easily gotten a key to the dead bolt.

*Don't keep looking at her, baby. Talk to your grandmother and have a good time. We'll deal with all this later.*

Player. The voice of reason. She didn't know whether to cry her eyes out over Francine's betrayal, knowing how it was going to hurt Lizz, or stand up and punch Terrie Frankle right in the mouth for deliberately hurting her grandmother. Instead, she forced a smile onto her face and joined the conversation swirling around her.

# SEVENTEEN

Player stood in the shadows, watching Zyah and Alena moving through the aisles between tables. The restaurant was overflowing as usual. Crow 287 never lacked for business. For him, in that moment, Zyah was the epitome of courage. She moved with the grace of a dancer, flowing across the floor, stealing his breath. She was sheer magic to him, and he knew, if they spent a lifetime together, she always would be.

Zyah's thick hair hung in a braid down her back. She wore little makeup, enhancing only her eyes and long lashes and that lush mouth of hers. Dressed in her favorite pair of vintage jeans and a silk blouse the color of dark forest green, she wore boots that only completed her look of femininity. He wanted to scoop her up and rush her out of there, instead of watching Alena show her around as if convincing her she really should work there.

He could hear everything said through the tiny earpieces built by Transporter and

Mechanic. The two men made continuous improvements to the gear used on their hunt and takedown of pedophile rings. The earpieces would allow all of Torpedo Ink as well as Jonas to hear what was being said.

"I can't believe that Delia Swanson is going to work in a grocery store instead of a restaurant, where she's worked her entire life," Alena grumbled, glaring at Zyah.

Zyah flashed a triumphant grin. "It's not my fault she was sick of waitressing. Cooking. Running the entire operation. Or that Inez is that persuasive."

"Your store has two new employees in one day, and I'm still looking. I think you owe it to me to take the job."

"Alena." Player all but growled her name. "Zyah doesn't need a second job. She's on her feet all day as it is."

The two women made the circuit of the room right in front of the windows, Alena pointing various things out as they made their way toward the back room, where larger parties were often seated.

"I think I can decide for myself whether or not I need a second job," Zyah said.

Player fought down the flash of amusement and the wild reaction of his cock at the snippy belligerence in her voice. He also knew the shit-storm she had just ignited with his brethren, and it made him smile in spite of the gravity of the situation. His woman had no idea what that little outburst was going to set off.

Master was the first to weigh in with his opinion. "Are you kidding me? Are you taking that shit, Player? Your woman is out of control."

"What does he mean by that?" Zyah asked.

"Ignore them," Alena said. "That's what Lana and I do. Come on, honey. We need to parade around in front of the windows again before we go into the kitchen. Look really interested in how the tables are set up."

"A woman doesn't ignore her man, Alena," Keys pointed out. "And telling her to do that isn't a good idea. That could get her in real trouble."

Player thought the entire discussion was a good diversion when he knew Zyah was extremely nervous. He could feel the combination of laughter and feminine indignation, as if she couldn't quite make up her mind if she should believe a word they said.

"Real trouble?" Zyah echoed. "I think you're talking in Torpedo Ink code."

"That should earn her punishment," Maestro decreed. "I'm talking the real kind, Player, no joking around. She's already putting herself in a dangerous position, and now she's defiant."

"That's what comes of giving women choices," Savage chimed in.

"Giving women *choices,*" Zyah echoed, her

520

voice strangled. Outraged. But definitely amused at the same time. "Player, do you want to explain this conversation to me?"

"It means I've evolved and they haven't, baby. I have no intention of spanking that pretty little ass of yours, although it is a temptation."

She nearly whirled around right there on the floor of the restaurant to find where he was in the shadows, but fortunately, Alena slung an arm around her waist, preventing Zyah from giving them away.

Player didn't know if he really was that much more evolved. Not that he would ever want to dictate to Zyah, but he didn't want her to have a second job, as much as he wanted to help Alena out. When would they ever see each other? Even living together.

*Player?* At once Zyah connected to him on an intimate level. Mind to mind. Just the two of them. *What's wrong? I know they were just teasing to get me to relax.*

They were and they weren't. It was a running argument among the members, on how far one went to keep a partner in line, but that wasn't what had him worried. He had made up his mind to be truthful with her, and this subject bordered on something he wasn't so certain he knew the truth about.

*I realized I really don't want you to have a second job. I hadn't thought much about it before. A part of me is being selfish because I want to spend time with you. I work during the day, so the job at the store is fine. I had hoped the nights I play at the bar with the band you'd be there with me. And what happens if Anat gets to a point where she can't live alone? I've thought a lot about that. She can't go into a nursing home, Zyah. We won't know how they're treating her. If I hadn't become suspicious of that therapist or you hadn't insisted she get a second X-ray, she could have been really injured. If you have a second job, who would look after her? We could hire someone, but then we'd have to have cameras. I wouldn't mind staying home, but she would be uncomfortable with me taking her to the bathroom . . .*

*Player.*

With the way she said his name, brushing it so intimately along the walls of his mind, gently stroking each letter, each syllable, so lovingly, she took his soul.

*I don't want to be that man, putting my job ahead of yours.* He didn't. *I don't think I'm more important than you are, or that what I do should come before what you do.* He knew that much was true. But what was he thinking? Or saying? Or trying to say?

*Now that I'm really looking at myself and putting it in perspective, I don't want you to take a second job because I don't want to give up my music. It's part of who I am.* It was part of his soul. He *needed* music. *I have to play. But*

522

*maybe I don't have to play with the band in the bar at night. It's possible I could give those nights up to be here at the restaurant with you if this job means that much. I could chop vegetables for Alena. She needs the help.*

*Player, stop,* Zyah gently chided him. *You're overthinking everything. We've got time. Right now, I'm worried about Mama Anat. Are you certain they can't get to her?*

On some level he knew she was distracting him just as the Torpedo Ink members had been distracting her. Still, he caught the hint of genuine worry for her grandmother. He should have known she was worried about her grandmother, not herself. He wanted to kiss her, but he couldn't be seen with her. *Half of Torpedo Ink is with her. Jonas has Jackson Deveau watching over her as well. Just follow Alena's lead. Everything will be fine.*

Player was grateful the two of them had such an intimate connection they could talk mind to mind. They would have an advantage if something went wrong. He didn't like using her as bait to draw the thieves out, but he knew the robbers were getting desperate. Better to be ready for them, draw them out into the open, have them make their move on Torpedo Ink's terms, than have to scramble to keep Zyah and Anat safe.

Once Zyah laid out her concerns to him, that Francine was the local snitch, he was certain she was right. He already had his suspicions about Terrie Frankle working with the thieves. He had no real reason, other than she had access to every household where the robberies had taken place other than Perry's parents. He'd asked Jackson Deveau to check for him. The deputy had done so and confirmed Frankle had been the therapist for someone in each household.

Code had checked further to see if the therapist had worked in any of the other small towns where the robberies had occurred prior to Sea Haven. In every other case, Frankle had worked as a therapist. When she hadn't, a man by the name of Lester Gibbons worked as a traveling therapist. They alternated. While Code was following that trail, apparently Jackson had been doing the same thing. It hadn't taken much to convince Jonas and Jackson to let them give Frankle and the crew their shot at the Gamals.

*Destroyer is in the house with Anat. Lana is on the roof across the street, and she never misses. Jackson Deveau is right there to stop anything, and Czar has the other half of Torpedo Ink watching over her. I'm telling you, baby, she's safe. Just please stay close to Alena when you walk into the kitchen. We have no idea if they'll take the bait, but if they do, that's where it might happen.*

Zyah suddenly stopped right at the door of

the kitchen, pulling her phone from the pocket of her jeans and looking down at it. "Francine is calling me. She never calls. She always texts."

"Answer it," Steele commanded. He was used to running their operations, forgetting Jonas was also wired in.

"Act normal, Zyah," Jonas counseled.

Zyah kept the phone close to her ear so the extremely sensitive wire in her ear could pick up Francine's voice.

"You said to call if I needed you, Zyah. You have to come get me right now." There was a sob in Francine's voice. She sounded frantic — and genuine.

"What's wrong? Where are you?"

"I was so stupid wearing Gran's jewels. I was robbed. They beat me up. You have to come get me right now."

"Do you need an ambulance? Where are you? I can't come get you if I don't know where you are, Francine."

"Are you at home?"

"No, hon, I'm at Crow 287. I'm interviewing for another job, but it doesn't matter, I'll come get you. Just tell me where you are. I can send someone if I'm not close enough."

*"No!"* Francine wailed the denial so loud it hurt Player's ear. "It has to be only you. I don't want anyone to see me like this. I don't know what I'm going to tell Gran. I wasn't supposed to be wearing the jewelry. The

insurance won't cover it."

Francine sounded like she was babbling. The way she went from sobbing to talking almost crazy to then insisting that Zyah come alone puzzled Player. He found himself nearly believing the woman, that she'd been robbed and was terrified and wanted her friend to help her. That she couldn't get herself under control and didn't know how to face her grandmother. God only knew what had happened to her or how severely the thieves had hurt her. On the other hand, why was she insisting Zyah come alone?

"Francine." Zyah poured authority into her voice. "Honey, I need to know where you are. I'm coming to get you, but you have to tell me where you are. Do you need anything?"

"Promise me you'll come alone. You won't bring Player."

"Why do I need to come alone? Why is that so important?"

Francine shrieked unintelligibly into the phone, her words nothing but gibberish, crying so loud that if Player could have easily done so, he would have removed his earpiece. He was fairly certain all of them would have. Why would she specifically tell Zyah not to bring Player with her? That raised all kinds of red flags.

"Calm down, Francine. I can't understand anything you're saying."

"You have to come get me right now. Just

you. Please, Zyah. I know I haven't always been a very good friend, but I really need you. I'm at the headlands. You know where the blowhole is, right? Just there."

Zyah looked up, straight toward the shadows where Player was concealed, her expression sorrowful. That particular spot was on the bluffs, overlooking the ocean. Down from the headlands, in the town of Sea Haven, Zyah's grandmother lived on one street, and a street over, with the blowhole centered in between, was Francine's grandmother's home. Francine could easily walk to where she lived. In the time it would take for Zyah to drive from the restaurant in Caspar to the headlands in Sea Haven, Francine could easily be home.

Francine must have realized by Zyah's silence what she was thinking. "My clothes are torn, Zyah. I can't walk around looking like this. Someone might see me." She had lowered her voice as if someone might hear her.

Zyah's expression changed to one of horror. Player willed her to replay the sound of Francine's voice, not just hear the words every woman feared most. Alena touched Zyah's arm very gently. Zyah took a visible breath.

"Do you need me to bring you anything?"

"A coat if you have one."

"I do. I'll come right away." Zyah ended

the call before Francine could say anything else.

*Eyes are on you, baby. Take a deep breath. You can do this.*

*She was lying. At the end, she was lying. I don't know about her clothes, but she was lying about not being able to walk home.*

*I know.*

"She was lying," Zyah said aloud to the others. "I know her very well. I know her voice, the inflections. She wasn't telling the truth. She lives right down the road from where she says she is. She could walk from there. She's setting me up. She has to be the one who is helping all the thieves break into the neighborhood homes."

*Ink, do you have eyes on the spotter? We have to take him out the minute Zyah is in her car,* Steele commanded, using telepathic communication so Jonas was unaware.

They all heard the cry of an owl missing its prey. *I'm on him. Savage is moving in on him with me. We'll do the setup so Jonas will see we have no choice but to take him out.*

*Savage, don't get crazy with this one,* Steele cautioned. *Don't take a hit. Just make it look good so Jonas believes what we want him to believe.*

*Might not have a choice. Jonas has to believe this is real, Steele. I'll do my best.*

"I'm going to have to go alone in the car,"

Zyah said. "They have someone watching. I can feel them out there."

"No way are you going alone," Player said decisively. "Absolutely not."

"She's the bait," Jonas said. "That was the entire point of the setup. She doesn't go, we're not going to catch them. Your entire club is going to be surrounding her. Not to mention I'll be there."

"I'm going with her," Alena announced. "Come on, Zyah. We're going in my car. I brought the BMW. She rides like a dream. We'll go through the kitchen."

"You have a restaurant to run," Zyah protested.

"I brought in help for the night," Alena said, looking smug. "Delia and Bannister are cooking for me tonight while I'm gone. Delia has tons of experience. She'll handle things just fine while I'm with you. They aren't going to freak because you're with another woman."

"She's right about that," Jonas said. "They won't like it, but they won't see her as a threat. Don't wear your colors."

Alena gave a little sniff of absolute disdain as she let the kitchen door swing closed behind them, cutting off Player's view of his woman. His heart nearly stopped. He turned immediately and nearly sprinted down the hall to a small door built into the wall, the one that was an escape should they need it.

He exited the building that way. Jonas and Keys followed him out. Player moved around to the side of the building where the owl had called to them.

Running, they almost plowed into Savage and an assailant seemingly struggling. One appeared to have a knife and was stabbing it into the ribs of the other man.

"Savage," Player hissed.

Jonas shoved Player out of the way, weapon out, blazing fire, the bullet taking the assailant in the side of the head, spinning him around, dropping him to the ground, the knife falling from nerveless fingers. Jonas swore as he kept running toward the two men. Savage kicked the knife farther away, and then did the same with a gun, Player could see as they came up on the dead man.

"Thanks," Savage said, glancing at Jonas. He had one hand covering his side. Blood leaked between his fingers. "I saw the gun but not the knife."

"How bad?" Jonas went straight to him.

Savage backed away, his movement instinctive. "I've had a lot worse. He barely got me. I'll head out with Player and get this cleaned up by the time we get to Sea Haven."

"You'll need to stay here. I have to turn in my weapon. I can't just kill someone and not have witnesses."

"Take a few pictures, but do it fast. We're not having Alena and Zyah hanging out there by themselves. If you have to stay here with the body and wait for your people," Player said, "I'll need Savage with me to make certain the women are safe."

Jonas glanced down at his phone and swore. "Jackson just let me know that Terrie Frankle pulled up in front of Anat's house. She's going up to the front door now. Lift your shirt, Savage. Let me take some pictures. I'm going to need statements from all of you. Keys, Player, both of you as well as Savage."

"No problem," Player said. "But right now, I'm going after my woman. If Frankle is heading into Anat's house, you know these people are making their move."

Jonas swore. His hands were tied. It wasn't like he could leave a dead body lying on the ground. It was bad enough that his three key witnesses were leaving. "Get the hell out of here before anyone else gets here."

Anat unlocked the front door using her iPad, rolling back her chair to allow Terrie Frankle into her living room, greeting her with a smile. "Terrie. It's so late, honey. Is everything okay?"

Terrie nodded and looked around the room. The house was quiet, other than the sound of soft music playing. Anat always liked music playing in the background, even when they were working. The lights were muted, but as usual, when Zyah wasn't home, several of the rooms were lit: the living room and Anat's bedroom and sitting room. Terrie had driven past the house several times, both by the front of the house and down the narrow, less traveled street in back. The garage and back of the house and entire upstairs remained dark.

"Usually, you have someone staying with you until your granddaughter gets home, but when I drove by, it looked like you were alone. I was worried, so I thought I'd just stop for a minute and check on you. Is everything all right?" Terrie poured worry into her voice.

She'd taken acting classes, and they always came in so handy in these situations. The elderly were lonely and wanted company. They wanted to talk and share their stories. They wanted people to see them, and Terrie was good at making them believe she cared about them. Her partner, Lester Gibbons, was just as good. He was charming and good-looking. The women fell for him, and the men liked him. They made an excellent team. They were equally ruthless and had no compunction about killing if they needed to.

"That is so like you, dear," Anat said. "Inez was supposed to be here tonight, but some dear friends of hers are in the hospital, and she and Frank went to see them. I guess things aren't going so well with them, so they stayed there. Zyah will be home soon. She just texted me that she'll be here soon. She needed to stop by and see Francine."

Terrie didn't like that there was a text message from Zyah about Francine, but it wouldn't matter. Francine and Zyah would both be dead. Anat as well now. That little text message had sealed her fate. She winced at the idea of the mess that had occurred at the Randall estate. Francine was supposed to get Zyah to dinner, away from her grandmother's house, but Francine seemed to be so useless lately. She'd texted that Anat had visitors but that the Randall estate was ripe for the picking, and described just how to get in.

Francine had been right: the estate was a gold mine. Unfortunately, Gray Randall had tried to pull a gun on Lester, and Lester had gone crazy, the way he did when anyone thwarted him. He was already angry that they'd stayed in Sea Haven so long. They had rules. Those rules had kept them safe. They'd lost two members of their team, and their team was tight-knit.

"I heard something about that," Terrie said, her voice dripping with sympathy. "I never met them. Were they friends of yours?"

Lester had been smoldering with rage. He took it out on Randall, beating him, stomping him when he was down and then going back for more. When Randall's wife interfered, Lester became enraged all over again.

She had been hard-pressed to stop him. It had taken both Charlie, another team member, and Terrie to pull him away. Even then, Lester went back three times, with the alarms blaring and him swearing like a sailor. He'd even shoved her, something he'd never done before.

"Not really. The Randalls kept to themselves, although some of my friends knew them. Lizz, and Inez, of course," Anat said. "No one should have that happen to them."

Terrie had waited for Lester to get himself under control and suggested they cut and run, but he'd refused. Francine had insisted Anat was hiding a huge treasure in her home, the biggest anyone had. He was furious that the old lady had deceived them, and worse, Terrie hadn't discovered what she was hiding, so he blamed her as well that they were still in Sea Haven. The property was worth a fortune, and Francine had no reason to lie, so no matter how frugally it appeared they lived, the Gamals were most likely very wealthy.

"I agree, Anat: no one should have that happen to them. It could so easily have been avoided." Terrie kept her voice smooth. Gentle. It was time to come to an understanding. By now, Zyah should be in Lester's hands, or at least close. She pulled out her phone to check for messages.

Right now Ralph, another team member,

was following Zyah back to the headlands. His job had been to keep an eye on Francine, and he'd spotted the stupid bitch wearing jewelry worth a massive fortune when she was eating dinner with Perry Randall. She tried to lie to them and say it was costume — as if they wouldn't know the difference. Lester was so out of patience with her, he'd threatened her grandmother and told her to bring the jewelry to the blowhole. When she met him there, he beat her, took the jewelry and told her to call Zyah and get her there or his next visit was to the grandmother. It would be anyway. Francine admitted there was a lot more jewelry. They weren't leaving without it.

Terrie knew Lester was certain Anat would cave and give them the big treasure if they had a knife to Zyah's throat or if he started beating her.

Anat frowned. "I don't know what that means, Terrie. I must have missed something. I admit I didn't read much on what happened to the Randalls because it was too much like what happened to me and I still get very upset. Did they do something to provoke the thieves?"

Terrie rolled her eyes as she hastily texted. Her team member Randy was supposed to have joined her by now. He'd been in the car behind hers, patrolling. He was to make two rounds to ensure no one was near, and then she would let him in. They would spend whatever time with the old lady they needed.

Lester texted her that a car was parking at the headlands and that Ralph had texted him that two women, Zyah and her friend Alena, the owner of Crow 287, had come together. But no worries, the three men could handle them — just take care of the old lady. He hadn't been able to raise Ralph since, but they'd learned cell phone service was spotty in places on the coast, and he wasn't worried. He was going to do Francine immediately. He despised the whiny little bitch. Get it done so they could get to Francine's home, score everything in one night and get out. He sent her kiss emojis. The door opened behind her, and Randy strode in, grinning evilly at Anat.

"Bet you don't remember me without my mask," he greeted.

Anat rolled her wheelchair back toward the door to the hallway, her hand trembling. She made a little trilling sound with her pursed lips. "Terrie? What is this?" She kept rolling her chair until she was in the hallway.

Terrie followed with her partner. "Well, Anat. This is Randy, one of my partners. My other partners are with your granddaughter, so if you want to see her alive again, you'd better cooperate with us this time. Lester isn't nearly as nice as we are. He visited the Randalls the other night and things didn't go well. You don't want that happening to Zyah, do you?" She couldn't keep the laughter out of her voice.

Anat had backed her chair into her sitting room and slammed the door like a child. As if that would keep her safe. Or her granddaughter safe. Terrie stepped aside and Randy kicked the door open. He held a gun pointed at Anat's head, centered right between her eyes. He was right in front of the open window. The breeze fluttered the curtains, allowing the sea air to cleanse any fear from the room.

"Take the shot, take the shot," Jackson ordered in the ears of the Torpedo Ink members.

The bullet hit Randy in the temple, driving him away from the window and Anat, spinning him around and taking him down. Terrie screamed, diving toward the gun, scooping it up and popping up to take a shot at Anat.

A huge tattooed man came out of nowhere, wrapping his arms around Anat, taking her right out of the wheelchair to the floor, his body completely enveloping hers, taking the bullet meant for her as the rifle sounded a second time, and Terrie felt pain blossoming throughout her entire body and then went numb. She couldn't hold on to the gun, even though her brain told her she needed it. She was looking directly at the man who had taken Anat to the floor. He was enormous, all muscle. Terrifying. He looked at her as if she were already dead, and maybe she was.

"Anat, did I hurt you?" Destroyer spoke gently.

"No. My leg aches a bit, but you wrapped it so well. Are you hit?"

"It's nothing. No worries. Lana and Jackson took care of both of them. I don't want you looking at them. I'll get cleaners in here. I'm going to pick you up and take you into the bedroom. Jackson can hear me, so he knows you're alive and everything's all right. Both are down, Jackson. The male is dead, the female on her way out. Another minute."

"You hit?"

"It's nothing. Take care of Alena and Zyah. Lana, back them up. I've got this. Do we have anyone on Lizz?"

"Yes," Czar said. "She's covered."

"Lester plans on killing Francine," Jackson reminded. "We have to try to find a way to stop him. Do you have eyes on him? Or how many men he's got with him? I haven't spotted him yet."

*Francine knows Player killed those two men Jonas fished out of the ocean. She was in the garage the night they tried to kidnap Zyah. Sooner or later she'll tell out of spite or try to blackmail Zyah and him,* Czar reminded. *This isn't going to end well for Francine, no matter how much any of us would like it to.*

Player had managed to make his way to Sea Haven with the rest of his team to meet up with Czar's team, joining them just as the orders were given by Jackson for Lana to take the shot at Randy, and then she had to shoot at Terrie. They had choreographed ahead of time, over and over, as they did when they ran their own operations, to make certain they were prepared for every contingency. These thieves couldn't be left alive, not after Player had shot two of them and Jonas already suspected him.

Czar could be ruthless when it came to protecting his family. And his family was Torpedo Ink. Who was Player kidding? They all could be ruthless, and they would protect every family member — and that included Zyah and her grandmother.

"Trying to get eyes on him now," Ice reported. *The bastard is sitting about two hundred feet from Francine. He's got four men with him. They plan on boxing Zyah and Alena in.*

*They're expecting their lookout Ralph to show up as well,* Steele said. *Jonas had to stay with his body.*

Zyah and Alena got out of the car and made their way down the narrow path through the tall grass toward the bluff. The blowhole was about midway there, a small fence surrounding it to make people aware there was danger

539

and to stay away. The wind had come up just a bit, as it could on the coast, blowing in from the ocean, carrying both salt water and tendrils of fog with it.

Storm and Ice fed the fog, letting it thicken and darken, moving it toward the bluffs. Francine had been huddling on the ground, but as Zyah and Alena approached, she jumped up, a look of horror on her face.

"It was only supposed to be you, Zyah. Only you." She began backing up, shaking her head, her fingers covering her mouth, looking wildly around.

She hadn't been lying. Someone had beaten her severely. Her face was swollen and lumpy, eyes nearly closed. Her mouth was distorted. Her clothes were ripped nearly off. Zyah held out the coat to her, but Francine continued to back away, shaking her head.

"You don't understand." The words came out a moan. "You *had* to come alone."

"Why did she have to come alone?" Alena asked. "I'm a woman, honey. I understand these things. I'm not going to tell anyone. We'll get you home."

"No. No. They'll hurt my grandmother. They will. I'm sorry, Zyah, but it was you or my grandmother." Francine's sobs were loud, the sound carrying in the night air.

"Shut up, bitch. I'm so fucking sick of your whining. You were happy enough to take the money and watch all the old people get beat."

Lester's voice came from behind them.

"Stop," Francine whispered. She put her hands over her ears and kept backing up. "Don't tell them. Don't say it."

"Why? Don't you want them to know what you did? How you wanted us to fuck her up? You were right there yelling at us to fuck her up. To beat her until she couldn't stand up, until no one would be able to look at her face again. You laughed when her grandmother was beaten so badly and you told us we didn't get the treasure. That her grandmother hid the greatest treasure of all from us. *You* were the one giving us all the information on the families in this town, your neighbors, the people you grew up around. And you did it for money."

Lester continued to mock her as two men came up on the left side of Zyah and Alena and another two on the right. "And now you've brought these two women here so we can get the treasure. You know what we're still going to do, you little whiny bitch? We're going to take your grandmother's jewelry, all of it, tell her what you did and then beat her almost to death. We might leave her alive so she can think about you every damn day and how you betrayed her. First, though, I'm going to put a bullet in your fucking mouth because I can't take hearing your voice one more minute."

He raised his gun. Francine turned and ran.

541

Zyah yelled at her to drop to the ground. Three shots rang out simultaneously. The fog swirled thicker than ever. There was a thin wail that choked off midcry. Jackson was a marksman, and Lester had gone down immediately. He'd been hit by Jackson's rifle as well as Lana's and Preacher's.

The men on either side of the women tried to use them as shields, pulling weapons and firing into the night, one dragging at Zyah's arm to thrust her in front of him. Another clawed at Alena. Player ignored every command by Jackson, first sprinting and then somersaulting, coming up under the man holding on to Zyah, hitting him with both feet in the jaw, snapping his head back so hard, there was an audible crack.

Jackson swore and took the shot, taking out the man trying to pull Alena in front of him. Alena seemed to stagger backward, right into the man's partner, and both went down in a wild melee of arms and legs. The fog swallowed them so that it was impossible for the sharpshooters to cover them.

"Stupid little bitch. You messed with the wrong man."

"Stupid little bastard. You messed with the wrong woman." Alena had come down under him, but her legs were wrapped loosely around his neck. She tightened them and rolled, snapping his neck easily. "Idiot," she hissed. "I don't have time to play around.

I've got a restaurant to run."

She came out of the fog, staggering for Jackson's sake, took two more steps and then sank down, pressing a hand to her head where she'd let the nasty little worm kick her. She'd have a knot, but they had to look like they'd taken a beating, right? Jonas was too suspicious of them most of the time. She kept her hand pressed to her head, but looked toward the fog where Player was "fighting" with his opponent.

Twice the two men rolled out of the fog bank, struggling for the gun, just long enough so Jackson could see the furious battle. Zyah crawled toward Alena, helping her to her feet. She looked as if she was torn between helping Player, trying to go toward the bluffs to find Francine or helping Alena to the car. Reaper and Savage came up on either side of her, pointed toward the car and then started toward the bluff, disappearing into the fog.

Player was thankful it wasn't his job to make certain Francine had gone over the edge on her own. He just had to make it look good for Jackson before this last man was dispatched. Twice the man had tried to give up. The gun was in his hand, but Player controlled it completely. He was too strong, too powerful.

Each time Player took his assailant out of the fog bank, he gave Jackson a clearer shot, but he needed to make certain Jackson took that shot. He wasn't taking chances on anything else. Lana and Preacher were his backup. He was putting his life on the line to make certain this last man went down. He was also banking on the robber's instincts. He would have the gun at last and Player in his sights. Instincts should make him raise it even if he didn't pull the trigger. Player would dive to the ground, but that didn't ensure he wouldn't take a hit. Hopefully, it wouldn't be a head shot.

They rolled out of the fog together, came apart, Player "losing" his grip on the gun as they came to their feet. He dove into the fog as the robber lifted the gun. Again, shots rang out. Storm sent a gust of wind between the robber and Player as the gun lifted. The thief went down.

Zyah turned back from the car, screaming his name, running toward them until Keys and Maestro intervened, blocking her path.

"You alive, Player? You better call out if you are. Your woman is a little anxious. And Jonas needs your statement," Czar said. "He's a bit edgy right now."

"Fucking asshole nearly shot me," Player groused. *I'm fine, baby. Stay there with Alena. We'll go get your grandmother. She can't stay in the house. It's a crime scene. We'll arrange for her to stay with Lizz. I think Lizz is going to need her right now. Reaper and Savage told*

*Czar Francine fell over the bluffs.* He was grateful he could tell her the truth. They really did think she had fallen. She'd been backing up and, in the fog, perhaps hadn't seen how close she was. She'd been crying as well.

*I think she threw herself over the edge, Player. She was very distraught. She didn't want Lizz to know what she'd done. He kept taunting her.*

Player couldn't take the tears in her voice. He went to her immediately, wrapping his arms around her. "Jackson, tell Jonas I'm taking Anat and Zyah to Lizz. They're going to need one another. Then I'll come to him. You can talk to them at Lizz's."

Jackson started to protest but changed his mind and waited, just like Jonas, for the detectives to come to work the officer-involved shooting. They had asked for help and none was available, but they had filed step-by-step reports of their findings and what their fears were prior to their operation. They had contacted the department for additional manpower, but the deputies were scattered across the county, and they had relied on the law enforcement that was close to them, which was something they often had to do in an extremely rural area. Now both men had to wait for the detectives. Fortunately, there were plenty of witnesses.

# EIGHTEEN

Player watched Zyah wander around the master bedroom, barefoot like he was, in a sheer shirt that dropped to her knees. He found it sexy as hell. The shirt could have been a man's dress shirt but was transparent, showing off her luscious curves. She had them in abundance. Her tits moved with every graceful step and sway of her hips. Her ass was so perfect he wanted to take a bite out of it. Instead, he sat, sprawled in one of the chairs in front of the long row of flickering flames, eyes half-closed, just watching her. He could watch her forever.

She'd been wandering around the house without talking for some time. He didn't push her. He knew she was working things out in her head and she needed space. He gave her that. He didn't want to, fearing she might try to distance herself from him, but pushing her wasn't the answer either. He'd done what he could to show her she mattered to him. It wasn't always going to be easy. He knew that.

There were things about his club she was going to have to accept that would never be easy for her. He hadn't talked about those things yet either. But he figured, one thing at a time. He'd been the idiot keeping his distance from her when she'd given herself to him over and over. They were connected, and he knew she was willing to be with him, stay with him, but there was a little part of her that was holding back. That was on him.

Zyah turned suddenly, her dark eyes moving over him, taking in his bare chest and thin drawstring pants. Immediately, she walked straight over to him, waiting for him to widen his legs so she could kneel between his thighs and look up at him.

"I don't want you to want me because I can fix your mind when it's shattered, Player. Or because we have explosive chemistry. That's what I'm most afraid of. That the person I am will get lost in the things you need. I love the sex as much as you do. Maybe even more."

That wasn't possible, but he wasn't going to argue the point.

"But sex can sometimes disappear during times of sickness or pregnancy. Or children making you too tired. I don't know. Whatever. You can't make that an entire relationship. There has to be more. A foundation. And I don't want it to be because I'm some kind of nurse, repairing damage to your mind when

547

your illusions get out of hand. I want to be wanted for myself. I deserve that. I want to be seen for me."

He leaned toward her, looking down into her beloved face. Just looking into it made his heart clench in his chest. He framed her face with his hands, feeling how soft her skin was, running his thumbs over her high cheekbones and then along her jaw.

"Baby, do you honestly think I could know you and not love you for you? See you for you? How could I not? I'm in your mind. I see how you are with your grandmother. I see how you are with Alena. You're tired and you don't want that second job, but you're worried about her. You don't like to see her struggling."

He brushed his thumb over her lower lip, that lip that he loved so much. "Even Francine, for all her viciousness, her jealousy, the things she did to you, your grandmother and the others in Sea Haven, there is a part of you that felt sorry for her and wished you could have found a way to help her. You have such compassion in you. It's impossible not to love you for you. How can you be with me and not know that? Not feel that? Not be totally confident in that? Is it because I was so humiliated for you to know the things that happened to me when I was growing up? Because it wasn't just when I was a child. That shit continued through my teen years,

548

Zyah. That's difficult for a man to have to admit to his woman. Did I hurt you so much that you're finding it hard to forgive me?"

She was too compassionate for that. More than likely she had to come to terms with the fact that he killed so often. That he not only killed when he was young but was still doing it when he hunted — and found — pedophiles.

Her gaze never left his. Her mind was firmly in his. He felt her there, filling him when he'd always felt so alone.

"And you know there is no other woman for me. Right, baby? I don't cheat. I would never cheat on you, in spite of my name." He needed to reassure her even though she'd never asked for that reassurance.

"I'm well aware of that, after seeing your memories that you really didn't respond sexually to other women, that it wasn't something you just said. You meant it. I couldn't believe it at first because we were like crazy rabbits." She flashed a little smile. "We still are. It's always a marathon with us."

He was quite willing to begin a marathon anytime, but they had things that were too important on both sides to get out in the open. He needed to be just as fair. She was willing to be honest. He had to be just as honest.

"I love you, Zyah. That isn't going to change. I want you to be mine any way I can have you. I would prefer to marry you and have you live here with me. When your grandmother is ready and wants to move out of Sea Haven, we can have a place built on the property or put her closer in one of the rooms. But she isn't going into a care facility. That's my preference." He sat back in the chair, waiting to see what she would say.

She rubbed his thighs, her gaze still on his, still without flinching. "I love you too, Player. Very much. That isn't going to change. I want you to be mine any way I can have you. I am very traditional and would prefer marriage. I love the house. I definitely don't want my grandmother in a facility, so we can discuss what would be best when the time is right. I do feel worry in your mind, so I think you need to tell me what that's about."

That was the big problem with having a really intelligent woman and one that could read minds — at least his. Her hands were distracting, rubbing along his thigh, up close to his groin without actually touching where he needed to be touched. He reached out and slowly unbuttoned the first five buttons of her shirt. It was oversized, and the two edges parted easily, giving him access to the perfect globes of her tits. Her nipples peaked for him instantly. He needed to touch her while he talked to her. Feel her soft skin. Tell himself she would understand and not condemn him or the others.

"You just have to come out and say it, Player."

He took a deep breath. "I'm not certain how to start. We, meaning Torpedo Ink members, are so different. Everything about us is different, and people don't get us. Or understand us. To the outside world looking in, we're some kind of perverts. Really depraved people. Czar had this idea that we could start over here. Live differently. Find a way to fit in somehow. But we can't. Not really."

She stayed silent, but her hands were gentle on his thighs, and in his mind, he felt the stroke of her mind, as if somehow she was encouraging him to continue.

"I always felt different from the others. Guilty even. I had something that was valuable to Sorbacov. He had a type, little boys, so yeah, he raped me like he did the other boys. He liked to hurt kids and see them hurt. He especially liked to see girls hurt and then teens hurt. I got too old for him. He would bring his friends, ones who would torture, ones who were really sick and depraved, with extreme sexual practices, deviant practices. They killed so many. I escaped most of it because he wanted bombs built. He didn't dare take the chance that I would be harmed that badly. The others . . ." He broke off, shaking his head.

"Player, I saw what he did to you."

He nodded. "I know you did, baby, but it was nothing in comparison to what he did and had done to the others. It was difficult to be the odd man out, to know I wasn't subjected to that extreme the way they were. Sometimes I wondered if they thought I was a traitor."

"No way. They had to know you were loyal to them. I see them with you."

"I was a kid, Zyah. Kids think all sorts of mixed-up things."

He transferred his hands to her hair. All that silk. He loved her hair. He loved everything about her, especially her compassion. She had enough for both of them, which was a good thing, because he wasn't certain he had much left in him.

"We kept our eyes on one another at all times. We never had clothes. We had to watch out for one another. Seeing each other naked didn't exactly arouse interest. Then being trained the way we were in sexual practices. We were taught to have control over our bodies by performing on someone while someone else was beating us or using us brutally. The idea was to get the other person aroused while not being aroused. This was done in front of one another. If we could see one another we could keep each other from being killed."

He saw the dawning comprehension. "What you're saying is that when Torpedo Ink has parties together, just you, you have sex with your partners but with others in the room because you feel safer."

He nodded. "Most of the others feel so much less inhibited if they feel the partner they love is safe."

"You don't seem to have any inhibitions."

"Like I said, I was luckier than the others in that I wasn't as sexually tortured as they were. But I did get used to being with them. And looking out for them. Not to say I can't do without that, but it does separate me even more."

He felt her moving through his mind. How did he explain Torpedo Ink to her? He needed to try. He wrapped her hair around his fist.

"We aren't whole without one another. We try to be, but in order to survive, we had to become one person to get us out of there. We took pieces of one another and wove ourselves together. That's the only way I have to describe what we did. I need them. They need me. We all are trying to live our lives separate but together if that makes sense. We're trying to find a way to do what Czar would like us to do, but we're predators in a world we don't understand. We were kids, raising each other. Czar was our moral compass, and he still is."

She nodded. "I can see that. So what you're asking me is would I ever be willing to go to one of these parties and have sex with you where others might see us?"

"Not at the clubhouse. I wouldn't be comfortable with that, because there are other chapters now, people I don't know as well. But here at the house, if the others come over. Or on a run if we go and we're all together in a campground. How comfortable would you be around the others with me?"

"I don't honestly know, Player. Here at the house, when we're crazy, I doubt I'd even notice if someone was around, but I won't know until it happens. I would be very uncomfortable at the clubhouse, and I have no idea how I would feel on a run. I've never been on one. That's me being as honest as I can be."

Every time he thought he couldn't love her any more, she gave him something that made him realize she was branding deeper and deeper into his bones. She was in his soul. Wrapped around his heart. He didn't understand how she could possibly ever think that he didn't love her for herself. How could anyone not love Zyah once they knew her just for her? She was honest. She hadn't condemned him or his brothers and sisters. She hadn't said no. She had given him what she could, as honestly as she could.

"You do realize that no one can ever measure what someone else's life or the impact of their past is against anyone else. Each person is different. We're all born different. You escape into your mind, but your mind is very sensitive — that's why it can fragment when you build your illusions and hold them too long. You learned, over time, to become strong, but you were a little boy, working day and night to become strong. That took courage and discipline."

"I thought I was crazy. I thought I was so much less than everyone else. My psychic talent seemed so useless when everyone else had so much to contribute."

"And yet you could actually cover their bodies in the illusions of sores to keep the worst of the pedophiles from taking them," she pointed out.

He nodded. "That's true. I did. But they'd just take another child. I wasn't strong enough to cover everyone." He pressed his hand to his face, tried to scrub away the memories that seemed too close. "Sometimes, Zyah, if someone died, I felt as if I killed them myself. Just like every time Sorbacov forced me to go to one of his insane parties and carry in the bombs I made. I had to sit at the table and talk to people I knew were going to die. He would sit there laughing and talking with them, eating dinner and acting as if he were their friend. I built the bombs. I carried them into the party. Czar would cover for my silence, but most of the time, Sorbacov would be furious with me that I didn't engage with those at the table. I just couldn't."

"Because you were too sensitive."

"Twice, after one of the bombs went off, I tried to kill myself. The first time, Sorbacov saved my life. He and one of his friends used me repeatedly as punishment. I was nine. He beat me with a whip after, and I remember the two of them drinking wine and laughing. I crawled over to this pipe that was in the garden. It was jagged. I'd thought about that pipe so many times when Sorbacov would rip me away from building my bombs. I would just look at that pipe. Just stare at it and know someday I was going to use it."

Zyah closed her eyes and put her head down on his thigh. *Honey.* She whispered it, tears dripping in his mind.

His woman. The moment he felt her inside him, she pushed away the memories that were so close. Too close. He dropped his hands into the thick silk of her hair. "Baby, I don't know how I even went there. I didn't mean to. You don't need to hear that shit. There's no reason for it. You get enough just by fixing my mind when the migraines are so bad."

She stayed still, letting him have her hair, knowing he needed it. Knowing it was one of his favorite things. His fingers tunneled deep into the mass, loving the silk. Loving her.

"We're connected, Player. The two of us. It's always going to be the two of us. So there's a reason. You need to talk, I need to listen. And it goes both ways. Sometimes I'll need to talk and you'll need to listen. That's what couples do."

She lifted her head slowly. "I'm so in love with you, Player." Her dark eyes met his and then she stood up before he could react to her declaration. She walked toward the bed with her unhurried steps, the sway of her hips an invitation. The transparent shirt slid from her body and floated to the floor as she moved up to the bed.

Player got up slowly, loosening the drawstring so his pants fell from his hips. He stepped out of them and followed his woman. She was gorgeous. He would walk through fire for her. She walked around to the other side of the bed so she was facing him. She put her hands and knees on the bed, and then, deliberately slowly, she crawled across the mattress toward him. Hands and knees. Her eyes on him. Sexy. Her body undulating. Fluid. Almost like a cat's.

His gaze jumped to her full tits. He loved her breasts and the way they swayed and bounced with every movement. He was going to mark her tits, brand her with his mouth and teeth. He waited, his hand on his cock, as she took her time, stretching out, feet across the mattress toward the wall, legs wide apart. He wanted to see her inner thighs and that sweet little pussy of hers. He was going to brand those thighs as well. Mark them as his.

She lay back, her head off the bed, neck

back so her throat was stretched out. She looked back at him while her hand slid down her body, fingers moving over her left tit and down her belly. His gaze followed. His eyes darkened to lust as her fingers disappeared and she moved her hips, coating her fingers before bringing them out to show him.

"This is what happens when I think about having your cock in my mouth, Player," she whispered and brought her fingers up toward her lips. "I get so hot and slick for you."

"Is that what you want, baby? My cock in your mouth?" His cock was so fucking hard he thought he was going to shatter.

She licked her fingers. Her hair hung like a dark waterfall of silk. He stepped closer so he could feel the mass against his thighs. Her head was positioned at the perfect height. He ran the pads of his fingers over her throat as he circled his cock with his fist.

She brought her hand back to her pussy and curled her fingers deep. The sight was so sensual, sending little forks of lightning shooting right through his groin. He caught her wrist as she brought her hand up toward her face, turning her fingers to his mouth and sucking them clean. His cock jerked hard.

She reached back with her free hand and stroked his heavy balls. "I want your cock so much my mouth is watering, Player. I can taste you."

Dark fantasies shimmered through his

mind. Erotic images built with every second that passed as he looked down at her. He felt his heart beat through his cock, right into the palm of his fist, and it matched the beat of the pulse his fingers found in her throat. She was his, and she was offering heaven to him. Offering it her way.

The tip of her tongue slid around her lips, keeping them wet. For him. She swallowed against his hand, her eyes darkening even more with an erotic, carnal, very wanton invitation.

"I wonder which of us would get off first if you were in my throat, Player. Just thinking about having you that deep gets me so close I'm not certain I can hold out long enough to do the things I want to you." She whispered the invitation aloud, circling her clit, her knees falling apart.

She looked so sensuous, spread out on his bed, her head over the side, throat stretched out and down, hair falling like a dark silken waterfall. His lust rose fast and sharp, consuming him to the point he saw a red haze and thunder crashed and roared like a beast in his ears.

"I put my cock in your mouth like this, woman, I'm going to be going down your throat. You know that. There's no way I won't." It was a warning. He meant it too. He rubbed the crown of his cock around her lips, leaving a trail behind. Her tongue chased after the shiny liquid. That was sexy as hell. *She* was sexy as hell.

"Why do you think I'm lying like this, silly?" Her other hand joined the first one so both were caressing his balls.

The action lifted her tits. He loved the sight of her breasts, large and lush, her nipples hard and rigid for him. Her fingers were jiggling and stroking his balls until his seed boiled scorching hot, ready to explode whenever he was ready. He painted more of the pearly drops along her lips, watching her lick them off, just because it was so damn sexy.

"Baby, stop making me wait." She licked her lips again.

"I'm not certain I can stay in control," he warned, telling her the truth. "I could get rough." He watched her eyes. "You look so fucking hot, Zyah."

"Be rough, then. Just stay in my mind so you know I'm getting off on it."

"Keep your fingers in your pussy, baby. On your tits. You'll get off on it because you love to please me. And you're doing this for me." She was. He was in her mind and she wanted him in her mouth. Down her throat. She wanted to drive him wild, just like she was doing. She wanted him out of control, out of his mind. Not thinking. "You stop me if you get scared."

He was already feeling every one of those things. Out of control. Mindless. Her mouth was lush. Her lips gleamed at him. Wet. Her tongue had lapped at his seed. Chased after his cock. She looked at him with her dark eyes, and his cock went from steel to titanium.

"Open your mouth." He sounded harsh, guttural, even to his own ears. He didn't care. It was too good. "And keep working your pussy, baby. You get off too."

Her lips parted. He caught her jaw and pushed into that wet, hot haven, not giving her time to adjust, just going deep. The visual of her lips stretching around the girth of his cock was enough to drive his lust even higher. The feel of the heat of her mouth was incredible. The sight of her fingers pleasuring herself, curled into her pussy while her hips matched the rhythm of his, incited him even more. Every pump of his hips sent her tits swaying, adding to the visual, driving his craving higher.

"Suck hard. Harder." He could barely manage to get the command out as he thrust deeper and then withdrew.

Her tongue was wicked, her suction like a vacuum threatening to take the top of his head right off. He'd never felt like this before. He gave in to the feeling, a mindless pleasure, a euphoria of blazing heat. He could feel a volcano inside him churning. A mass of boiling, raging magma he'd suppressed for years. Not anymore. He thrust forward, held himself in that tight, restrictive tunnel, that paradise, watching her fingers bite deep into her pussy and her other fingers pinch her nipple. Then she suddenly began to shift her head as if she might fight. He looked down into her eyes for another long moment and then retreated, allowing breath before plunging deep again.

He never wanted this to end. It was sheer paradise. The sight of her lips stretching around his cock was so erotic, but the way, as he pushed deep, he could see the outline of his cock in her throat, that bulge, was even more so. When he did that, her fingers in her pussy were frantic, her hips bucking wildly. He loved watching her get off almost as much as he loved what was happening to him. That visual, as well as the feeling of her pleasure, compounded the erotic appeal of his cock moving in and out of her mouth, or just holding still in her throat, pulsing and throbbing deep.

"Suck," he demanded again, hoarsely watching. Fascinated. Fucking her mouth. Her throat. A thing of beauty. She was a thing of beauty. He controlled everything. She'd deliberately given that to him by putting herself in this position. She had to accept his demands, and he was demanding a lot. More lightning streaked up his spine, through his cock, and into his balls as she hollowed her cheeks and sucked hard. She lashed with her tongue, stabbed and trailed fire over his shaft.

Player roared with the fiery pleasure consuming him, the terrible rage boiling in his balls, so ready to explode. His hips kept plunging. "Suck harder. Fucking harder, Zyah. Take me deeper."

She choked, her body drawing up, but he refused to pull out, holding still. Staying deep. He soothed her in his mind. *Your cock, baby. Your man. Do this for me. Give this to me. Only you can do this. You've held your breath far longer than this.*

At once she settled, her mouth pulling at his cock, sucking at him, and he drew back to give her air, his hand stroking her hair. She couldn't quit now. She had to keep going. He bent his head to her tits, licked her nipples, sucked them and then bit gently before taking her mouth. Kissing her.

"Do you want to stop? I can fuck you, baby. You're slick. I can see you're dripping right now." He had to make the offer, but it was a strain. His cock roared for her throat. To finish what she'd started. "Anything we do is going to be perfect, Zyah. This was so good. Let me fuck you. You're close. I can see how close you are." He found he meant it after all. He loved her so much for giving him what she had, such a gift. He didn't need more. He might want it, but he didn't need it.

She shook her head slowly, her body doing a slow undulation there on the bed. "No, honey. I told you what I want. I panicked for one moment, but you steadied me. I want you just the way we were doing. Hurry."

His cock raged at him, felt like a monster out of control. He wanted to roar with hunger for her. "You have to be certain, baby. My cock is like a beast. I'm so on edge." He was. Dark with lust now. He wanted back in that haven she'd offered him.

"I'm absolutely certain. Give me back what's mine."

Zyah licked her lips, her eyes on his cock. She opened her mouth, and he didn't wait. He couldn't. There was no finesse. He circled the base of his cock with his fist and shoved half of it into her mouth. He wasn't going to last this time, and he knew it. She was already swallowing him down, lavishing attention, worshipping his cock. Hollowing her cheeks and sucking him like that vacuum he had felt surrounding him before but lashing him with more fiery heat than ever before. Her eyes were on his. Surrendering to him. Giving herself to him.

She fought off the need to breathe as he surged in and out of her mouth, down her throat. She controlled her gag reflex, her eyes going liquid, all while her tongue tried to tease, her mouth tried to work, but eventually there was no keeping up with his pumping. Her eyes held a dark lust as she struggled for him, controlling her fear.

Watching her deliberately swallow him

down, trying to take him deeper each time, magnified the ecstasy of the scorching-hot restrictive tunnel of her throat. It closed around him, silken and tight, a vise as she swallowed. He couldn't take his eyes off of her. Off of her lips, stretched so wide. Her dark eyes pure liquid now, filled with lust echoing his own. That delicate throat, distorted with his monster invading, swelling, cutting off her air. Thunder roared in his ears. His mind went to chaos, a haze of red that bordered on so out of control he barely knew what he was doing, only that his cock kept growing and she couldn't stop now.

"Don't stop. Swallow. Swallow me down. Take it now, baby. All of it. Every fucking drop." His hands went to her head, fisted in her hair as his cock swelled and swelled beyond anything he'd known. His cock began to jerk hard, over and over, erupting like a volcano, his seed boiling up like hot lava, exploding down her throat, long deep pulses, ejecting ropes of his hot seed. The pleasure bordered on pain but was a kind of ecstasy/ euphoria he'd never known.

He managed to get into his brain enough to realize she needed air, and he pulled back a scant inch or two to allow her to breathe, but his cock was still pulsing and he didn't have the strength to leave the warmth of her mouth. His shaft lay heavy on her tongue as they both gasped, trying to drag air into their lungs.

He felt her tongue curl around his cock. Gently. Her hips moved restlessly. Her fingers slid down to her pussy and curled inside again.

"Don't, baby. Wait for me to take care of you. Just give me a minute." He could barely stand, let alone get to the other side of the bed. And she needed water for her throat. He hadn't been gentle. He was still dizzy, unable to process what she'd done for him.

Zyah smiled, right around his cock. She shook her head. "Uh-uh." The vibration went right through his cock. *This was my gift to you. When you can find your strength, go to the hot tub. I'll follow in a few minutes. You're not taking this away from me. We have all night to make love together.*

"Then I'm going to watch."

Her eyes smiled at him. Her tongue leisurely bathed his cock while her fingers moved in her pussy and her hips rose and fell. Her tits swayed, drawing his attention. She was so incredibly sexy. Then his cock was free and her mouth was open and she made a soft little sound as a soft flush rushed over her body. His woman. Sexy as hell.

He managed to find his legs and get her a bottle of water. By the time he returned to the bed, she was sitting on the edge. He sat down next to her. Close. She drank the water slowly.

"Why did you do that for me? I feel as if that was very selfish on my part. And I was rough with you. Too rough."

She put her hand on his jaw so gently it turned his heart over. *I could have stopped you at any time. You needed it. You needed to be taken far away from where you were. And you needed to know that someone loves you that much, Player. I love you. I want to give you things no one else will give you without expecting anything back. It's my right to do that.*

He could barely breathe with his love for her. He hadn't known he was capable of emotion so overwhelming, so deep, that just looking at her could hurt. He looked at her for the longest time, unable to speak.

*Honey, go to the hot tub. I'll be right there.*

She tipped more water down her throat, and he looked away from her, worried she would see too much. The burning behind his eyes was unfamiliar. The lump in his throat. The way his heart hurt so fucking bad he didn't know if he could stand up without having a heart attack.

"Yeah. I'll get us some towels and lay them out for us. I keep towels for the pool and hot tub in the closet by the door." His voice didn't sound like his own. He managed to get to his feet and take a couple of steps from

567

her, but he couldn't just walk away. He turned back to look at her. He just stood there like an idiot, his heart beating too fast.

"I don't know what I would have done if you had walked away from me, Zyah. I know I never would have loved any other woman. I've never looked at another woman. Or wanted another woman. There's only been you. That's the fucking truth. I wouldn't hurt you for the world. Not physically and not emotionally. If I do, by some stupid mistake, please give me the chance to make up for it. Tell me straight up what I've done and let me fix it. Losing you would be like . . ." He trailed off, shaking his head. What could he say?

He turned and walked away from her before he made more of a fool out of himself. Why hadn't he taken more care with her? He rubbed at the shadow on his jaw. He'd never been like that before, so out of control. His mind turned the puzzle over and over. One moment he'd been upset, and the next all he'd been thinking about was sex. Not just sex. Wild, uninhibited, mindless, selfish, crazy sex.

He padded through the house to the opposite end, where the indoor heated saltwater swimming pool and hot tub were located. Just the brush of her mind against his set his nerve endings on fire. He unlocked the door to the spa room using his fingerprint and stepped inside.

Soft laughter flooded his mind. *I'm sure you'll figure it out.*

He felt that small stroke of her mind against his throughout his body, so much so that even though his cock was so thoroughly sated, it still stirred. He felt a spark of electricity dance along his thighs, travel up his balls to his groin and spread heat.

He realized Zyah had subtly fed his craving for her, weaving her fantasy for him. Then she'd driven his desire higher and higher. She had skillfully blended their lust together until the combined woven hunger raged into a dark, out-of-control, erotic raging fire.

Player laid out the towels and then, restless, dove into the pool, starting laps. The saltwater pool appealed to him, and along with the amazing craftsmanship the builder had displayed in every aspect from floors to cabinets, it had been a huge selling point. Everything about his house had appealed to him, but now, with Zyah in it, the house felt like a home.

He contemplated the idea of a home as he cut through the water with long, powerful strokes. All the members of Torpedo Ink gravitated toward Czar and Blythe's house for that feeling. Blythe represented home to them. Not the clubhouse. Blythe was their center. They all knew she was. Czar led them, but Blythe was their heart. She had taught them what a home was supposed to feel like and, really, what love was.

They gathered on weekends for breakfast or lunch or dinner. Loud, noisy barbecues that sometimes lasted most of the day, the children running around making them all laugh. Making them a part of a world they hadn't known before. Blythe accepted them. She'd been the first person to give them acceptance. They hadn't realized anyone outside of Torpedo Ink could do that — see them and invite them into their life with such complete lack of bias.

Czar had led them to Blythe. Blythe accepted them, and she took in the children others threw away. Children they brought to her knowing she would love what others didn't. They had come to believe in her the way they did Czar. Player realized it was because of that belief the club members had been able to accept Anya, Reaper's woman, into their lives. She had come first. Loving Reaper. Who knew that one of the scariest and damaged among them would find a woman who would take him as he was? Anya had managed to make their house overlooking the ocean, the one Reaper had bought just so he could defend and easily escape, into an inviting home.

Then there was Breezy. They all had known Breezy from before, when they rode with

Swords, undercover, determined to bring down a human trafficking ring. Steele's Breezy. She was easy to accept. Player considered Breezy's home. Of course, Steele had bought the mansion and had kept it practically sterile. Breezy had turned it into a home filled with laughter and love.

Ice had married Soleil in Vegas, a woman wealthy enough to have whatever she wanted in life, but she had eyes only for her man. She took cooking lessons so she could do the cooking, not have a chef. She loved to paint, and she was damn good. Ice was a jeweler, and together they designed beautiful artwork, but she was mostly devoted to her home — and always to Ice. Everything was about Ice. She'd created a home for him.

Absinthe had found Scarlet, a woman who looked the part of demure librarian but who could turn into a sex kitten or a kick-ass assassin at the blink of an eye. Scarlet had virtually transformed their home, removing any triggers that might throw Absinthe into the past. They were never far from each other, and the few times Player had been to their home, it had always felt warm and welcoming.

He'd recognized that characteristic in Anat's home immediately. He'd woken that first night with pain crashing through his head and Zyah's voice whispering to him soothingly. He'd inhaled her scent, breathing

571

her in, taking her into his lungs. He'd been in her bedroom, and she was everywhere, surrounding him. He'd felt like he was home. From that moment on, he'd known, just as he had the first time he'd laid eyes on her, that his world was about this woman.

Home wasn't about the structure they lived in. Not the houses they bought. Not for any of them. Home was about the women in their lives. Home for him was Zyah. It always would be. It wouldn't matter where they were, only that they were together.

He swam to the stairs and looked up. She was already there waiting for him, her dark hair piled on her head. She didn't have a stitch on.

"Come get in the hot tub with me. I want to feel the jets on my body." Her voice was husky, and the way she issued the invitation sounded like sin.

Player went to her immediately, removing the lid so that the steam rose. He took her hand to help her in. She settled into one of the deeper seats with a little sigh of happiness. He chose the one opposite her, wanting to see every expression on her face as he turned on the various jets so they would come at her body from all directions.

She gave another sigh and deliberately widened her legs so the bubbles would be directed straight to her pussy. "That feels amazing."

That was another thing about Zyah he loved. She wasn't in the least bit inhibited or embarrassed when it came to her sexuality. Watching her gave him tremendous pleasure. She always seemed to live in the moment, just enjoying whatever was given to her.

"I want to talk about what happened, baby," he said, moving his own body so that the jets could play over his groin, bathing his cock in the sensation of hundreds of tongues. Zyah's lashes lifted for a moment, her gaze moving over him and then dropping to watch his hand as he casually fisted his cock beneath the water. "I'm listening, although I have to say, I had no idea hot tubs could be so sinfully distracting."

Player chose his words very carefully. "You gave me the greatest gift today that a woman could give a man like me. I'll treasure it, Zyah, and never forget it."

The bubbles from the jets fizzed around his body, reminding him of the way her tongue had stroked over his skin. He did his best to shove down the memory and keep his cock under control, but there was so much steel in it he couldn't help a lazy slide of his hand as the bubbles gave the sensation of her mouth devouring him.

"The thing is, that was too dangerous to repeat. I was too rough with you. I didn't know what I was doing half the time. What you were doing felt so good, baby, and I was too far gone. I could have really hurt you. I'm not willing to take a chance like that with you."

Zyah's dark eyes moved over him. "You knew what you were doing. And I knew what I was doing. When I needed to stop for a minute, you stopped."

He had. True. But it could have gone either way. "I hesitated. You have no idea how close it was. I didn't want to stop. I knew you could take more. I knew you could hold your breath longer. I even reminded you. I remember that much. I was that far gone, Zyah, and that should tell you something right there."

He hadn't wanted to stop. Just talking about that moment where her mouth, her throat, had constricted his cock to the point of paradise and her eyes, all liquid for him, had looked up at him sent fire crashing through his body all over again. His cock jerked and pulsed with the memory.

"It tells me that you stopped and checked to make certain I was all right. You offered to stop. It wasn't just you, Player, it was me. I was feeding your emotions just as you were feeding mine. I wanted what happened. I took us there. I don't want you to feel guilty about it."

"You have a sore throat. Your voice is husky."

Zyah didn't deny it. "And hopefully, to-night, when we get really crazy in bed, I'll be deliciously sore other places as well."

Player lifted his head, his eyes meeting hers. She had to see him. Hear him. Understand what he was saying. "I'm not like that, Zyah. I'm not that man. I'm not a selfish bastard who takes his own pleasure and doesn't give a damn about his woman. In that moment I was thinking about myself, how I was feeling, my body, not you or your pleasure."

"No, Player, you weren't. You were very cognizant of me the entire time. More than I wanted you to be. That just proved to me more than ever that we were meant for each other." Zyah sound very complacent, even a little amused. "You were supposed to be wholly consumed with your own pleasure, that was the point, but you definitely were worried about me, and you liked how I looked all laid out in front of you."

That much was true. She'd looked so sinfully sexy laid out like an erotic offering. He'd never seen anything so sexy as her lips stretched so wide around his cock, or the way it had appeared like a monster in her throat. He had wrapped his palm around her throat to feel the way he invaded, the way she took him. Just the reminder had flames rushing through his veins.

"It's going to be one of those days, baby. I'm going to need you to stand up and bend over the side of the tub for me."

She raised an eyebrow as he rose. "Now?"

Deliberately she didn't move as he took the two steps to get to her.

"Right now." He reached for the mass of hair on top of her head.

Laughing, she rose from the water so it poured off of her. He caught her up, spun her around and pressed her body so it draped over the marble railing. Her breasts hung over the sides, dripping. His foot pushed her legs wider while his hand ensured she was slick and ready for him. She was. Hot. She pressed back with her bottom to entice him.

The sight of her naked body draped over the marble caught at him. She had the most beautiful ass. Everything about her was perfection to him. He loved her shape. Every curve. Her coloring. Her sense of fun. Every damn thing.

His cock jerked hard when she pushed her ass close and rubbed. He swatted her hard and laughed when she yelped and tried to turn her head. It was too late — he was slamming home, driving himself deep, letting the fire consume them both. He'd been sated earlier, so this time he was going to be able to hold out, take more time, feel the burn for a long, long time and give her multiple orgasms. Many, many. He had plans for the day. She didn't get many of them off, and she deserved to have the best day he could give her.

# NINETEEN

Czar stood for a long time studying from every angle the drawing Anat's husband had given her as an anniversary present. Player had hung it on the wall of the large shed farthest from his house. He'd kept the lighting bright throughout the shed, even spotlighting the drawing. He didn't want to take any chances that if the visitor appeared — and at some point, he wanted to draw him out — the man would be able to see enough to identify where they were. Already, Player feared he could find Zyah.

Czar wasn't the only member of Torpedo Ink present. Savage, Ink, Storm, Maestro and Mechanic were there as well. Player, like the others, wasn't happy that the president of their club had insisted he come. No one knew what they were dealing with, so they didn't want to risk Czar, Lana or Alena or any of the married men. Czar and Steele were deemed by the club far too valuable, although had they known the others had secretly met and had tried to keep them away, they would have been furious.

"No matter how I look at this thing, Player, I don't see anything but a very beautiful and complicated drawing." Czar turned to the others. "Any of you see anything different?"

Savage had draped himself by the door, but his gaze was fixed on the picture. He always looked casual and very relaxed. No one who knew him ever bought that pose. He was completely focused, ready to protect Czar should any threat suddenly come to him.

Player was grateful no one thought he was insane. They hadn't witnessed him putting the bomb together, nor had they seen the eyes watching from the center of the drawing, but they didn't question him. Maestro and Anat had heard the ticking of the clock, but that was the only real proof Player had to back his story, and it was thin. Zyah had added her testimony to his, handing her notes over to Czar, as well as her sketches, hoping Czar might identify the man from their past. He hadn't been able to.

"Sorry, Player," Savage said.

One by one, the others all studied the drawing just as thoroughly as Czar had. No one was able to see what was so clear to Player. It was frustrating.

Zyah fished around in her purse and pulled out a small box. Carefully she opened it and unwrapped a monocle, using almost a reverent touch. "Try this, Czar, but please be very careful. It means a great deal to my grandmother. It was my grandfather's, and he wore it all the time when he was working on this drawing."

Player had no idea she had asked Anat to borrow it. Instinctively, he knew Zyah would never have taken it from the house without permission. Her hand shook just a little as she handed it off to Czar. Clearly, she'd even asked Anat a few questions about the monocle.

Czar stood in front of the drawing and fitted the eyepiece over his right eye. His swift intake of breath was audible. "That fucker. What an anniversary present to give his wife. He put plans for a bomb in a drawing for her. First-class asshole."

Player glanced at Zyah's stricken expression. "Czar."

Czar followed his gaze. "Sorry, Zyah." Clearly, his anger hadn't been expelled, because he swore in his native language. *What kind of man does that to his woman?*

Zyah cleared her throat. "It's all right, Czar. I knew the plans for the bomb were there. I didn't want to know, but Player's been building it for weeks now. I had to accept the fact once he told me. I didn't know about my grandfather's monocle being the device to reveal the plans. And just to let you know — I'm a fairly strong telepath. I don't hear what

579

you're saying when it isn't directed to me, but I know you're saying something. You don't have to try to spare my feelings."

"Just the same," Savage said, taking the monocle from Czar. "There's no need to make you feel worse than you already do. Anat's going to have a very difficult time with this." He fitted the round piece to his eye and studied the drawing, whistling softly. "This man was a pro. This was made how many years ago?" He passed the monocle to Ink.

"You're not going to tell her, are you?" Maestro asked Zyah as Ink studied the drawing. "Does she have to know? She loves her husband. She talks about him all the time."

"Yes, I have to," Zyah said, her voice gentle. "We don't keep things from each other. I would never be able to face her again if I didn't tell her about this."

"Was she suspicious when you asked to borrow the picture?" Mechanic inquired, taking the device from Ink so he could study the plans for the bomb.

"No, we'd talked about showing the drawing to Czar when we were at the Floating Hat with Blythe," Zyah said. "I told her I'd take good care of it. She's very good at hearing lies, and I didn't tell her one. I borrowed the picture yesterday. I wrapped it up so carefully. Player and I brought it out here to the shed. I didn't tell her that."

She was watching Mechanic. Player moved closer to her, and she immediately put her hand on his leg. Her touch was light, but he knew she needed comfort. He covered her hand, applying pressure until her palm pressed into his muscle.

The two people who had studied the drawing the longest had been Savage and now Mechanic. Both had quite a lot of knowledge when it came to bombs. Mechanic looked at the drawing from every angle just as Savage had done. Player was interested in what they thought. This was no ordinary bomb, and the strange thing was, Player hadn't come across anything like it before.

"The device is definitely for a specific purpose," Mechanic murmured aloud. "Very detailed and different. I've never seen anything like it."

Savage joined him, taking the monocle. "I agree. The bomb looks like it would work, there's no question about that, but . . ." He trailed off and passed the device back to Mechanic.

Maestro was the only one who hadn't looked at the drawing. He heaved a sigh. "I don't know how you can do this, Zyah. Have you seen the proof yet?"

She shook her head. Player felt her press her hand deeper into the muscle of his leg. He knew she was torn.

"Your grandmother is one of the most

amazing women I've ever encountered." Maestro was utterly sincere. "If she'd have me, I'd marry her myself. That hound dog Dwayne River keeps sending her flowers and drops by the house to have tea with her. He doesn't even like tea."

Player could see that Maestro was trying to keep Zyah's attention on him rather than on the speculating the others were doing about the bomb. He knew it wouldn't work for long, even if she was distracted for a moment. Zyah was determined to get to the truth.

"Maestro," Savage said, without turning his head. "You don't like tea, and you've been deceiving Anat and drinking it with her by the gallon just to impress her."

A roar of laughter went up. Even Zyah had to laugh. "You do know it's impossible to deceive Mama Anat, Maestro. If you don't like tea, she would know it."

Maestro frowned. "How could she know?"

Zyah shrugged. "She just does. Same as I do. Player's never going to get away with anything because I'll always know when he's up to no good. Just remember that, honey, if you decide to run off with a hot little blonde. I'm very good with a gun."

Her fingers suddenly dug into Player's leg muscle very hard. His gut tightened into hard little knots. He looked down into her upturned face. Her dark eyes had gone liquid.

*Gedeon.* She whispered his name in his

mind. Brushing him with trepidation. With sorrow. Swamping him with fear. *Mama Anat.* Her voice dripped with tears at the dawning realization.

He didn't dare look at the members of his club. Like him, they had probably considered that Anat, having been married to Horus as long as she had, would have suspected, if not known. For certain, Czar would have considered it. And Savage had spent enough time with Anat to realize that she was too intelligent not to suspect.

Player sank onto the narrow wooden bench beside Zyah, locking his arms around her, uncaring what the others thought. He sent waves of soothing comfort into her mind. *Don't panic on me, Zyah. We don't know anything at this point. Anything at all. Everything is speculation. Until we know something as fact, we don't act on it or get upset over it.*

Czar had drilled that into them when they were children. It did no good to try to look ahead and fear what they didn't know for certain. They could only deal with their reality. That was what they needed to do right then. He stroked a hand down the back of her head. Czar looked at him sharply.

"I just owned right up to hating that poisonous brew," Savage declared, covering the silence. "Told Blythe. Then told Anat." He handed the monocle to Maestro. "This is a thing of beauty. Anat's man was a fucking genius, but I'm still not certain what part of the contents were designed for. Player, you must have figured that out when you were putting it together."

"At first, when I was working on it, I was doing so in my dreams. I was a child, building a bomb in my head when everything had gone wrong. When things get overwhelming for me, I retreat into my head and I build bombs." He despised admitting that to the others, but he did so matter-of-factly. "I look at it like puzzles in my head. I just fit the pieces together. I focus on that instead of what is going on around me."

"Yeah, I get that," Mechanic said. "I tend to do the same with engines."

"I do it with art, tattoos," Ink admitted. "Sometimes I bring wildlife into it."

"For me, it's the weather, the cloud formations," Storm said.

"Music," Maestro said.

"Best not to say what goes on in my mind when I need to escape, not with Zyah here," Savage said. "Suffice it to say, bombs are the better alternative."

Czar said nothing. He looked expectantly at Player, indicating for him to continue.

Player rubbed his hand up and down Zyah's arm. Both of them — maybe everyone in the shed — had realized, when Zyah had revealed that Anat had known Maestro was lying over the tea, that she most likely had to have known about her husband and his anniversary gift. If she could hear lies, and she'd lived with her husband all those years, how could she not know? Zyah was truly devastated. Player didn't know what to think, and he was determined to reserve judgment.

*You okay, baby? If you need to go up to the house for a break, I can handle this here. We won't go any further, other than trying to figure things out, without waiting for you.*

*I can handle it*, Zyah assured, cuddling closer into him. *I know my grandmother. She would never be involved in anything that would harm others. The idea just threw me for a moment.*

"The problem started when I was shot. I really hate to call it a brain injury." Player *despised* revealing that his brain had been torn up by that bullet. "Apparently, that bullet did a lot of damage. Steele worked his magic, but the trauma was very severe. The migraines started and refused to stop. I have nightmares nearly every night."

Now he really sounded like a pussy. He hadn't ever wanted to talk about this to his club. He'd felt so different from them, so apart, and this just seemed to make it worse, yet when he'd admitted he built bombs in his mind in order to stop himself from thinking about what was happening to his body when he was raped, the others shared they'd done

585

similar things. Player tightened his hold on Zyah. He'd sat next to her to comfort her, and now she was the one giving him the strength to tell the others what needed to be said.

"When I used to build illusions, playing around with *Alice's Adventures in Wonderland* and the characters for all of you when we were kids, if I did it too long, my brain couldn't handle it. I wasn't in full control of my talent then. I hadn't really built it up, and sometimes I'd get tired if I entertained you too long."

He rubbed at his temples, remembering the pounding ache that always told him he'd gone too far. "I'd get these terrible headaches. I learned to stop the moment I'd get blasted with one, but before I realized that was the warning sign, I discovered that my illusions could turn to an alternate reality very fast. The alternate was never good and would pull others into it."

Player glanced around the shed. The others were very quiet, very focused on him. "I often built the illusion of the wall with the door so we could all slip through. I did it dozens of times, but sometimes things would go wrong. We'd be in bad shape. The first few times, I was young and it was difficult for me. I wasn't strong enough."

He shook his head and glanced at Czar. Zyah tightened her fingers on his skin, her mind moving in his. "Remember when I was holding the illusion of the wall with the closed door so Sorbacov and his friends had no idea all of you were escaping out the real door? That time when we were all in such bad shape? Really bad shape. Every one of us. We could barely walk. They'd nearly killed Savage and Reaper. We thought they were dead. All of us were already in the dungeon, but we went back for them. We thought Sorbacov was gone. He and his friends came back."

Beads of sweat formed on Player's forehead. He felt them trickle down his face and wiped at them with the back of his hand. He couldn't look at Zyah. What if she couldn't accept him after he admitted this to her? What if Czar couldn't?

Maestro nodded. "We were trying to carry Savage and Reaper out. Savage was really bad. That's when they tore the skin off him and branded those words into his back. He was slippery with blood, and any place we touched him hurt like hell. He couldn't make a sound. Reaper had been cut and someone had played tic-tac-toe on his face with a knife. There wasn't a place on his body that wasn't bloody."

Mechanic kept his gaze fixed on Player's face. "You saved all of us that day. Alena was hurt, and I was carrying her. Ice was in bad shape. I think he'd been in the loom and they'd ripped him up. That was the day from hell. Czar, Transporter and Maestro took out one of the bastards who had tortured Savage while Demyan, Ink and Keys killed one of the ones that had gotten to Reaper. We had no idea Sorbacov and his friends were in the building."

"They left," Storm confirmed, "but came back for some reason."

"They'd left Savage and Reaper for dead. Even after we went back for them, we waited to move them down to the dungeon because it was so much warmer up above," Ink remembered. "It was a shit day. We were all in bad shape. No one had escaped being beaten and tortured. Steele tried to work on both Savage and Reaper in the hall upstairs, but he could barely see, he'd been beaten so badly. Czar, you had a broken arm. I don't know how you managed to get through the vents like you did. We wouldn't have survived if you hadn't thrown up that illusion and held it, Player. And you had been in the loom that day, hadn't you? With Ice?"

*What is the loom?*

Thankfully, Player hadn't had nightmares of being tortured in the loom and shared that with Zyah. *Later.* If ever. He rubbed his chest. *The scars on my chest and back.*

She touched him right over the worst ones. He didn't have them like some of the others did. Not like Destroyer. Destroyer had them the worst.

"We were all beat up that day," Player admitted tiredly. "I threw the illusion up as soon as Preacher told us Sorbacov and the others had returned and Czar started trying to get everyone down to the basement. The two instructors we killed were supposed to have gone with Sorbacov and the others to dinner. The bodies were found and the alarm went out."

He didn't want to tell them the rest. It hurt to even think about it. It hurt to have Zyah know about it. He thought it would be bad for his brothers to know. For Czar to know. But his woman. Zyah. She was so damned compassionate. So amazing. Moments like this one showed him why he didn't deserve her. He tried to wrap himself in her grandmother's words. He wasn't a coward. He wasn't backing away from their relationship. She would have to be the one to leave him.

"Sorbacov called his three favorite little snitches into his den the minute the alarm was sounded. His other friends were right outside in the big room just above the stairwell and hall where all of you were trying to get Savage and Reaper down the stairs. His friends at first were just talking, looking into his den while he grilled the kids, and then they got restless and began to pace around. They had their whips on them, still bloody from what they'd done to Savage. They were laughing about it and hoping Sorbacov would send one of his snitches to them to pass the time with."

Player wiped at the sweat. He glanced at the picture hanging on the wall. The frame around the drawing had changed. The etchings appeared much more prominent than they had before, more tubular, like an actual scroll. It wasn't rolling, but he could see the distinct curves that hadn't been there before. It was odd. He loosened his hold on Zyah and stood up, walking over to the drawing to get closer to the frame to keep his eyes on it while he explained to the others about his alternate reality.

"It took so long for all of you to get downstairs. Czar was trying to wait for me. I could see Sorbacov was getting enraged that the kids weren't giving him answers. He grew colder, like he gets. He pulled out that watch, that stupid pocket watch, and he came to the top of the stairs. I was already so damned shaky. My head hurt so bad. I could barely stand the pain. I could see the White Rabbit and knew it was going to be bad if you didn't get down there. Czar slipped through and I tried to hurry, but two of his friends grabbed one of the kids and I turned back."

He didn't want to admit the rest, not in front of Zyah. Not in front of the others. He didn't even like thinking about it. He shook his head, keeping his gaze fixed on the frame.

It seemed to be fading slowly back to just the etchings of scrolls and constellations.

"The scene morphed from holding the wall and door to scenes from *Alice's Adventures in Wonderland.* The doors were too small. The floors dropped away, and then knives rained from the ceiling. The fireplaces in Sorbacov's den and the big room suddenly had the irons glowing red hot, multiplying and attacking everyone in the room. The doorways became guillotines, and anyone trying to go through them was caught. I don't know what was in my head. Every book I read, every torture they'd put Reaper and Savage through, ran together and became real. All I know is it was a bloodbath. Four of Sorbacov's friends died along with two of the snitches. One of his friends was covered in burns."

He didn't look at Zyah. He couldn't. He didn't turn and look at the others. He forced himself to continue.

"I barely escaped through the door before it collapsed. Sorbacov came down almost right away to the basement. I was terrified I might have to try to throw up another illusion, and I knew it would collapse too fast. I was responsible for killing those people. I didn't mind Sorbacov's friends, they deserved it, but the kids . . ." He trailed off, shaking his head. "They were innocent, just trying to survive, the way we were."

"You saved our lives," Savage said. "That

day, Player, we all would have died."

"That's true," Czar agreed. "When Sorbacov came down, he was so certain it was us, until he saw what bad shape we were all in. He was positive none of us could have done anything to hurt anyone. He left without a word."

Player stared at the frame of the picture, trying to focus on it. The guilt of those deaths would never go away. Sorbacov had never spoken of the strange happenings that had occurred that night. No one had. Fortunately, Mechanic had disrupted the cameras so nothing had been caught on film. The mystery of the deaths had never been solved.

"Hell, Player, we were all lucky you were able to do what you did. You know it was a matter of time before he killed those kids," Ink said. "I'm sorry they died, but they were already dead the moment they started being his pets. None of those kids lasted very long. He was particularly cruel to them once he lulled them into a false sense of security."

That didn't make him any less responsible, no matter how true it was. He indicated the drawing, desperate to get to another topic. "Can any of you see the way the frame has changed? But it's already fading back to the original look."

Czar nodded. "I noticed it immediately. I was looking for something like that when you said the eyes staring at you had appeared in the middle of the drawing with total darkness around them. But actually, you drew something entirely different around the eyes than Zyah. She had total darkness. You didn't. You saw much more detail than she did. I think, Zyah, you were in shock that something like that could appear in your grandfather's drawing."

"I was." She gave a little shiver. "The eyes seemed really malevolent. And they looked around the room. I had the feeling he was trying to identify markers, ways to find us."

Czar raised his gaze from the frame to Player. "You must have a theory, Player. Do you want to share?"

Player glanced at Zyah and then sighed. He held out his hand to her, his heart pounding. He'd revealed a dark secret of his past, and now he was about to kick her in the teeth again. He waited. She put her hand in his without hesitation because she was Zyah. He should have known.

"I do. It sounds crazy, but then all of us have psychic abilities. The Drakes do. Czar, every one of your brothers do. The women living on your farm do. I believe that Zyah's grandfather did as well and so did her father. I think they came up with a way to create a portal. When they opened the portal, they could deliver a bomb precisely where they wanted it to go, close the portal and no one would be the wiser. Imagine handing the president a bomb and then closing the portal. The bomb would go off and no one would have a clue how it happened. You could target anyone in the world."

There was absolute silence. Czar moved first, studying the drawing again through the monocle and then the frame. "Your father was an astronomer, Zyah?"

"It's not possible," Zyah denied in a whisper, pulling her hand away from Player's. She rubbed her palm on her thigh as if removing his touch. "They wouldn't do this. And if Mama Anat knew, she would have destroyed it. It isn't possible."

"Even if it is possible that she knew, she might not destroy the drawing because it came from her husband," Maestro said. "Who is this man and how would he know, after all these years, about it? Why would he have waited this long to find the drawing if he did know? It isn't like Anat would have been that difficult to find. She didn't come to the United States under a different name."

"All good questions and ones I think we need Anat to answer," Czar said. "I'm going to ask Destroyer to see if Anat would be willing to travel here or if she would prefer us to go there. I'm reluctant to have this drawing anywhere near your home, Zyah."

"I feel the same," Player said.

Zyah shook her head. "I don't like any of this. Do you honestly believe that my father built some portal so a bomb could be sent to an enemy? How would they know his exact location? There are too many variables, not to mention it's all too sci-fi."

"You connect with me through the earth, Zyah. Ships found their way guided by stars. Are you telling me that you really think it would be impossible for your father to find a location he needed using the stars?"

"Maybe the location, but not the person on the other end. The stars would give him a wide view, not a narrow one, Player. You're talking about a specific location. Something would have to narrow that down, like GPS does. It would have to be even more precise." Zyah frowned, turning it over in her mind. "If it was even possible," she mused aloud.

"I think it is possible and your grandfather and father figured out how to do it," Player said. "Admittedly, there are pieces I can't figure out. The why of it. If your grandmother knew, she might be able to fill that in. And this man. Why would he suddenly be aware of us? Why didn't he come looking before?"

Again, there was silence in the shed while they all thought it over. "Suppose this man thought the drawing had been destroyed," Ink said. "There would have been no reason to come looking for Anat. In all this time there was no indication of bombs or portals. Nothing like this cropped up anywhere on the black market. No one attempted to sell it. He had no reason to think such a weapon existed."

"Okay, I'll go along with that reasoning," Player said. "So then my brain gets fucked up and I start seeing the White Rabbit and I'm building my bombs."

Czar nodded. "Every day you're in the room with this drawing and you're seeing the schematics for the bomb. You actually see it without the device, and your mind fixates on it."

Player had been in bed every night for five straight weeks staring at that drawing while his head was pounding out of his skull. "My head hurt like a mother. I couldn't escape the nightmares that triggered some of the worst migraines. My brain felt like it was coming apart. The bombs I normally built to try to counteract the pain weren't working, so my brain turned to one much more complicated and intriguing." He knew that was exactly what happened.

"This is making sense," Mechanic said.

"The pain was excruciating. At first I could barely lay out the various parts. Just moving made me sick. I know if it hadn't been for Steele and Zyah, I wouldn't have survived."

A murmur went around the shed, and all heads turned toward Czar for confirmation.

Czar nodded. "I was told, but there was nothing anyone could do. Steele did his best. Either he was going to be able to save him or he wasn't."

"Steele performed a miracle," Zyah said. "I watched him. I don't think anyone else could have saved him. He came twice a day for a couple of weeks after that and then once a day. He healed his brain injury, which was very severe, but the migraines persisted. Neither of us could understand why."

"We might have liked to have been with him," Ink said.

"A lot of visitors weren't going to help," Czar said.

"We could have taken shifts with Maestro and Savage in the house," Ink pointed out.

"We didn't want to upset Anat. She's very intelligent, and no one was letting on how grave his injury actually was," Czar said. "I understand you're all upset, and with good reason. I didn't go in other than once myself. Let's just get this done. He's alive and well, and he's got Zyah. Keep going, Player."

"Eventually, I could concentrate a little more, but then the nightmares grew worse. That brought the White Rabbit. The White Rabbit brought Sorbacov. That became a vicious circle. I got faster at laying out the parts and then beginning to understand and put them together. Each time I got further along."

"You didn't have this going on every single night?" Czar asked.

"Not after the fourth week. The bomb was becoming too real. Zyah realized it before I

597

did. The first two weeks I was pretty out of it and nothing could take away the pain. By that third week she was staying in the room, sitting up all night in a chair. By the fourth week she was stopping the nightmare almost before it began. We could both hear the ticking of a clock. Maestro heard it a few times. That was alarming. I knew then that my illusions, the White Rabbit and Sorbacov, were beginning to blur into the alternate reality of the bomb. That was scary being in Anat's house."

"We both felt that someone had been watching us at times," Zyah said. "We couldn't see anyone, but a couple of times when Player was making the bomb, I thought I could see something murky over Sorbacov's shoulder. It gave me the creeps. I thought it was someone from Player's past, like Sorbacov."

"They came to me," Czar said. "I told them to write down separately what they saw and felt the next time it happened."

Player indicated the drawing. "I knew the plans for the bomb were in the drawing. I had no idea about the portal."

"Who would?" Savage muttered. "That's insane."

"It was insane to see those eyes staring at us," Zyah said. "It was the creepiest thing ever, and I'm not altogether sure I can sleep in my bedroom ever again."

"I thought Czar might recognize him from my past, but he didn't," Player added.

"And you believe this man was actually somewhere else," Mechanic said, coming to stand beside Player to stare into the middle of the drawing, "looking through a portal at you? Because if that's so, was he summoned? How did he get there? How did you summon him?"

Player turned that over in his mind. It was a good question, and there was only one answer. "There has to be a portal on his side. It's possible he's connected to the bomb."

Czar nodded. "That's the only answer. He would have to be drawn to the bomb, and there has to be another portal. Zyah said she started noticing a shadowy figure behind Sorbacov in the dreams Player was having in his mind. Those became illusions and then alternate reality. It went White Rabbit, which was illusion, and then Sorbacov, which used to be the alternate reality. Is that correct, Player?"

Player nodded. "They both had a pocket watch on a chain. We all remember that fucking pocket watch of Sorbacov's. When I was building a bomb, he'd take it out and time me, acting like if I wasn't fast enough, he was going to punish me. I was never fast enough to suit him, but I could block him out most of the time by focusing on the bomb if it was new enough. Sometimes he brought a friend with him, and that's what threw Zyah off. She thought this man in the background was the friend Sorbacov kept bringing."

"Sorbacov is dead now, so it's impossible for him to be the alternate reality," Czar mused. "So is his 'friend.' The new man isn't dead. He's where the illusion crossed over. The bomb started ticking, and Maestro heard it."

"I think Anat said she heard it as well," Maestro said.

"We all did the day Jonas was there," Savage said. "But Zyah kissed you and it stopped."

"I was building the bomb in my head. I'd spent part of the day sitting on the bed, staring at that drawing. Before, I'd been in the bed staring at it. Just after Zyah got home, my head hurt so fucking bad I thought my brains were leaking out. I just needed the pain to stop for a few minutes. I went up the stairs and sat on the end of the bed, hoping it would stop before I had to go back downstairs and face the cops. I was staring at the drawing again. I couldn't look away. Sometimes I felt like it mesmerized me. It made my head hurt worse, and I began building the bomb to try to stop it."

Czar drummed his fingers on the wall. "Suppose the drawing triggered migraines in you, Player. You stared at the picture for hours. Your mind saw the plans for the bomb and put it all together. The longer you looked at it, the more your head hurt."

"It's possible," Player agreed. "I was out of it when I went downstairs and Jonas was there with Jackson. All I had was building that bomb or I was going to keel over."

"I think Zyah kissing you stopped it," Maestro said. "She brought the temperature up in that room by about a thousand degrees." He sent her a quick grin.

"He can kiss, what can I say," Zyah defended, but she didn't smile.

Player could see she was trying. He sank down on the bench beside her and slipped his arm around her shoulder. "Baby, I know this is hard. We aren't certain of anything yet. We don't know anyone's motives, and until we do, we can't judge anyone. I told you what Czar drilled into us when we were kids. There isn't any use worrying about something until we know the facts. We're figuring things out. That's all we're doing. Help us do that. I've spent time with Anat; so have Maestro and Savage. No way do any of us think she's capable of what this drawing would imply, so something else is at play here. We have to figure out what's going on to make certain everyone is safe and then decide what to do."

"Player," Czar said. "Look at the frame."

All of them immediately looked at the drawing spotlighted under the blazing lights. The etchings had once again subtly changed, moving to resemble an actual long scroll.

"Every time the two of you connect, the etchings change to that position," Czar said. "I've watched it do so over and over. When you move apart, it fades back to the original frame."

Zyah suddenly surged to her feet, pulling away from Player. "Remember when I said the stars would give a wide view for the portal? Well, if somehow it took both Mama Anat and Grandfather Horus to open the portal together, like we did, not that I know how we did it, and the portal gave the wide view of where the target was located, through her connection with the earth, Mama Anat would have been able to pinpoint the exact location." She looked at Player with pain-filled eyes. "You and I could do the same thing together. We have that same connection."

"She would never do it," Player said. "I'm telling you, baby, she wouldn't. You know she wouldn't. I don't care what the evidence says. She wouldn't do it."

Czar looked down at his cell phone. "Destroyer said Anat insisted on coming here. It's taken a while to get one of the vehicles for her to ride in that can transport her comfortably here. She'll be here soon."

Player went to Zyah, ignoring the way she tried to push him away. He wrapped her up in his arms. "Baby, I'm telling you, it's all going to be fine."

"I just hate this so much."

Savage took the monocle to the bench where the little box and wrapping paper were. Carefully wrapping it back the way Zyah had it, he put the device in the box. "I'm going to put this in your purse, Zyah, so nothing happens to it. I know it means a lot to Anat. If we have to destroy the drawing, I want her to have something she loves of her husband's."

"Thanks, Savage." Zyah sounded close to tears.

Czar stood in front of the drawing. "Kiss her, Player. Kiss Zyah."

Player frowned. Zyah ducked her head against his chest. "What are you thinking?"

"I think the portal is ready to be opened, and kissing her will open it. I mean really kissing her. Turn her around so he can't see her. You face this way. We'll spread out. Let him face us. He wants a confrontation."

"No," Zyah protested. "Wait for Mama Anat. She might know who he is. If she does, she can tell us how to handle him. If we say or do the wrong thing, it might put more people in jeopardy. All of you are so used to handling things on your own that you don't consider that it might be prudent to wait. You don't even know who this man is. We need information."

Player liked that she had included herself with them.

Czar nodded. "You're right, Zyah. I wanted

603

to see the portal work, and I'd like to see this man, but without real information, a name, a place, I can't put Code on tracking him. Once we know who he is, we can find him and eliminate any threat to Anat and you, but until we have that information, we're dead in the water. My curiosity got the better of me for once. Thanks for reining me in."

Player glanced at him. That was so unlike Czar, Player didn't believe a word of it. He'd deliberately forced Zyah to stop him. She had been the voice of reason for all of them. In doing so, she'd put faith in her grandmother's ability to sort everything out.

Savage handed Zyah her purse. "Put that somewhere safe. I have a feeling Anat's going to want to destroy this thing."

"If you wouldn't mind, Zyah, I'd like to take photos of the drawing," Player said. "It really is a masterpiece. It would be a shame to have it completely disappear. I'd get rid of the photographs eventually." He glanced at Ink.

Zyah frowned. "What would you do with them?"

"I thought I'd have the drawing tattooed on me. I think it would go pretty nicely over the loom scars on my chest. If it would freak you out, I wouldn't do it, but you love the drawing. I know your grandmother's explanation is going to vindicate your family. She will ask to destroy the drawing, and it will most likely be safer to do so."

"Take the photos, but if this all goes wrong, get rid of them immediately." She tucked the purse up on a shelf out of the way, just in case things got out of hand when they opened the portal after her grandmother got there.

Player knew, no matter what, Czar was going to have them open it. All of them were curious. He couldn't blame them. He would have been. They had no idea how very creepy it was. His main concern was the bomb. Did anyone else have the schematics for that bomb that could slip through the portal? If so, were there more portals and bombs? Could this man suddenly appear and slide a bomb into the shed where they were? It was difficult to believe someone else had the plans for the bomb because in all the years Anat had been in the United States, it would have shown up somewhere. At least, that was Player's hope.

"They're here," Czar announced.

Zyah dragged in air and reached for Player's hand, her eyes meeting his. Maestro hastily opened the door and waved to the others to move aside to give Destroyer plenty of room to roll Anat's chair into the shed.

# TWENTY

"Mama Anat," Zyah greeted, sounding as if she might burst into tears.

Anat looked around at all of them and then at the drawing under the powerful lights. "I was afraid of this." She gave a little sigh and looked at Player. "You have gifts, don't you? Who would have ever thought this could happen? I never even considered it. I thought my secret was safe."

She rolled her chair straight to the drawing and stared up at it. "Horus and Ken were both so brilliant, and their minds refused to rest. They were always dreaming up what-ifs. Could this be done? Nothing to them was impossible. They would talk about things until all hours of the night. I loved to hear them talk. So did your mother, Zyah. We'd sit around together and just imagine the improbable, the impossible, and how it could be done."

Her voice had taken on a dreamy quality. Loving. Sad. "I miss those times so much.

They really were so far ahead of their time. So beyond brilliant. We laughed so much together. Dreamt up so many crazy ideas. This one" — she gestured toward the drawing — "was in response to several things. The ban on belly dancing. Horus and Ken loved us belly dancing for them. Of course, in the privacy of our home, we continued to dance for them, but they were still very upset that something they considered beautiful was thought to be dirty. And the officials were always coming around with veiled threats. If Horus didn't go back to work for them building the bombs they wanted, there would be dire consequences. He had quit years earlier and they never let him rest."

"What did Horus do after he quit?" Czar prompted.

"He was independently wealthy," Anat said. "Which was a good thing. He was extremely interested in the force of gravity and properties of atom formation. He developed various theories and models to help explain it. He continually studied the very fundamental properties of atoms and molecules. He had so many interests, but he always came back to the evolution of the universe and atoms, molecules and gravity. He did present at the universities at times, but mostly, he experimented in his own laboratories. When Ken came along, they were so like-minded."

Player frowned, shaking his head, trying to

understand what she was saying. "This wasn't a project for the government? Or for some splinter faction protesting the government?"

"No, Horus didn't work for anyone. At times he presented his papers to the university. He lectured. But no, he refused to take money from anyone. He didn't need to. He didn't want anyone telling him what he should be working on. He wasn't . . . structured. He was a dreamer."

Anat indicated the drawing. "I shouldn't have kept it. We were going to destroy it, of course. We always destroyed anything that was dangerous." She stretched her arm up and touched the drawing with trembling fingertips. "I didn't think anyone would ever discover what it was. How could they? It took Horus and me to open it. Even Amara, my daughter, and Ken couldn't do it. So I thought it would be safe to keep it. I loved it so much, and I didn't have many things I could bring with me."

She dropped her arm and clasped her hands in her lap before looking up at her granddaughter. "I'm sorry, honey. I didn't think there was any reason to tell you. Clearly, there was. How did you find out?"

"I did," Player said. "I was in her bedroom all those weeks and I could see the drawing. I didn't need the device to see the plans for the bomb. I have this weird thing I do when I'm upset. Some people count; my brain puts together bombs."

Anat gasped, her eyes going wide. "Horus did that. He had . . . problems stemming from things that happened to him when he was a child. He said when he focused on building intricate bombs, new ones, different ones, he would have to concentrate completely; nothing would penetrate, and he wouldn't feel or hear anything going on around him. He learned to do that from an early age, so it was what he always did."

Player exchanged a long look with Zyah and then with Czar. "My mind must work along the same lines as your husband's did. In any case, I began building that bomb in my mind over and over. When Zyah and I were together, we accidentally opened the portal. Someone was on the other side watching us, and he was very unhappy with us."

"Amir." Anat whispered the name so softly, Player almost didn't catch it. "He would be furious. And scared. Confused." She looked at Zyah. "Amir was twenty when the explosion killed everyone aboard the yacht. You must remember him. You called him Uncle Amir. Everyone thought him dead. We wanted it that way. He barely survived. A fisherman found his body floating miles away and took him home. Amir convinced the fisherman someone had tried to kill him, so the man never told anyone he had found Amir."

"It wasn't an accident, then," Zyah said.

Anat shook her head. "Horus had enemies. He was too outspoken against the government at the time, and he refused to do the things they asked of him. I tried to talk to him. We all did. He was writing articles for the newspapers and stirring up the younger people. Horus had a brother twenty years younger than him. His brother and his wife were killed in an accident. His wife had no family, so we took their infant son, Amir."

"The man in the portal was Amir?" Player asked.

"It had to have been," Anat said. "There was only one other portal set up. Horus had a small estate in France. If we had to flee our country, we were to go there. He had property, money, identities for us if we needed them. The other portal was there. I sent Amir there. It was the only way I knew he would be safe. He would have a home, money and a life. I knew I could make a life for Zyah and me here in the States. No one would come after us. We were women and had nothing. If anything went wrong, I could contact Amir and send for money, but it was safer not to. I knew that there would be eyes on me for a long while. Not because of this project." She indicated the drawing. "No one knew about this but the five of us. But Horus's family was considered a threat, and that included Amir."

"You turned over all of Horus's money and

properties to Amir and came to the United States on borrowed money?" Czar asked.

"Most of Horus's money and property were confiscated — only what he had in France was left, and that was very little in comparison to what his wealth had been. I love Amir as a son. I raised him from infancy for twenty years. As a woman, I wasn't a threat to anyone, but he was. In France, with a new identity, he could marry, have a life. As long as we stayed away from each other, and there was no connection between us, there would be no threat to him."

"You sacrificed so much, Mama Anat," Zyah said.

Anat shook her head and indicated the drawing. "I should have destroyed this. It was the last I had of Horus and Ken. I loved them both so much, but I should have been able to part with it. Horus would have been so angry with me."

"Can Amir open the portal from his side?" Mechanic asked.

"No," Anat said. "The portal took two of us to open it, and it was always one-sided. Horus could talk to Amir through it, but Horus and I had to be together to open it. Player and Zyah must be together to open it. Amir must have been shocked when the portal opened and he started seeing through it. Probably shocked and rather horrified."

"The other portal has to be like this one is

611

— portable," Savage ventured.

Anat nodded. "Yes. The other is very small. I don't know how it got to be in France."

"Clearly, it meant enough to Amir to risk getting it from your home before he left and taking it with him when he was fleeing to France. How did he get to France?" Czar asked.

"We had friends," Anat said. "I had him smuggled out of the country, although I never revealed his identity to anyone."

"He took the portal, just as you took the drawing, because it was what Horus and Ken created," Savage said, his voice gentle. "You didn't do anything wrong, Anat. It's human to want to keep something because it holds memories for you."

Player exchanged a long look with Zyah. She knew things about the others that most people would never know, but she also saw moments like this one. Savage had so much good in him. Player, like all the members of Torpedo Ink, was terrified of losing him. Terrified he would ride over a cliff one day. Savage thought of himself as a monster, but seeing him with Anat, it was impossible to view him that way.

"Amir was so upset and didn't want to give up me or Zyah," Anat said. "He felt guilty at taking the money. And he was alone without us. He felt like, as the only man left in the family, it was his duty and right to protect us.

It was a hard time for us both. I insisted he couldn't contact me and that I couldn't contact him. I would do anything to keep him safe. As the years went by, he contacted me via email, and we were still careful, setting up a formal way to make certain we knew the other one was safe. He had a Facebook with pictures of his family. I did the same so I could share pictures of Zyah."

"Perhaps it's time to open the portal and talk with him," Player said. "We need to make certain he's on the same page." He had felt the absolute malevolence directed at Zyah and him. It was possible Amir hadn't recognized Zyah in the murkiness of the portal. Player had been the one facing him. There was no mistaking the waves of black anger pouring off the man in that portal. Player had known the stranger intended to find them and either kill them or use them for his own dark purposes.

"Yes." Anat couldn't suppress the eagerness in her voice. "Please do."

Czar waved the others back out of sight of the frame. "Leave Anat, Player and Zyah there for the moment. I want to be certain this man is going to cooperate with whatever Anat wants. Anat, can he pass anything through the portal to you?"

Anat frowned. "What do you mean?"

"Clearly, the bomb can be passed through the portal. Can Amir pass a bomb to us?"

"No, nothing can go from his side to our side. It's merely a means to communicate. The only thing that can go from our side out is the bomb. And the bomb is made to go through the portal. It was an experiment, like in the Jules Verne novels. The impossible that is improbable that becomes illusion and then reality."

Player looked over Anat's head to Czar. "Anat, did Horus have psychic talents? Was he able to build illusions and hold them?"

She nodded slowly. "Yes. He was very good at them, but if he held them too long, he would get terrible headaches and his illusions could become an alternate reality. That was very dangerous. He had to be careful. I know that sounds crazy, but it was our world. I could help him when that happened."

Zyah slipped her hand into Player's. "We understand, Mama Anat. We're going to open the portal now." She turned into Player's body, sliding her arms up his chest and winding them around his neck. "He was like you," she whispered. "That's why we can open it. He had a lot of your talents. And I have many of Mama Anat's."

Her mouth brushed over his lips. Little strokes of desire sending fiery darts through Player's bloodstream. It was difficult to keep his eyes open and focused on the frame, observing the way the etchings deepened into a full-blown scroll and then began to roll. He heard someone make a sound of shock, and then there was silence again.

Zyah's mouth moved on his. Her tongue traced the seam of his lips, and he opened, unable to do anything else. The tip of her tongue felt like a flame. The moment she kissed him, he was kissing her. The fire raced between them, hot and wild. No holding back. They always tried, but it seemed like a wildfire that just roared out of control.

Player tightened his arms around her but forced his eyes to stay open when he only wanted to keep his focus on his woman. The frame spun, moving faster and faster. The drawing itself receded into utter darkness, a black hole. The tension in the shed rose, stretched out until it felt as if any moment a hole could be torn in the atmosphere itself.

"Don't let go of each other," Anat counseled.

At first, it seemed, no one was on the other side.

"Be patient. If he isn't right there, the portal will summon him with a sound. If he's anywhere near, he'll come. He's most likely got it in his private den or somewhere the rest of his family won't see it," Anat said. "Please stay connected." There was eagerness in her voice she clearly tried to suppress. She hadn't seen Amir in seventeen years, other than in pictures on the Internet. This would be the closest she would come to him in person. "He goes by François Marcellus Sanchez. It's his legal name now."

A figure slowly began to take shape, the eyes first. He was a distance away, clearly guarding his identity.

"François," Anat called out to him. Her voice dripped with tears. "My son."

*"Maman?"* There was a wealth of emotion in the voice. The figure crept closer until a face with dark brown eyes was centered in the middle of the picture frame. He had dark hair, and as he got closer, they could see the web of scarring that ran along his face and neck, cutting along the dark shadow of his jaw.

Anat reached up with trembling fingers as if she could smooth those scars away. "François. I didn't think I would ever be able to talk to you. To see you."

"Seventeen years, *maman,*" he whispered. "I had made up my mind to come to you. I know I gave you my word that I wouldn't, but I feared I would lose you before I could see you again. Zyah grew up without knowing me. You were lost to me. She was lost to me."

"We're here," Anat assured.

"They don't care about us now. They don't even think about us," François said. "I want to get on a plane tomorrow and come to see you, and I intend to do just that." There was absolute conviction in his voice, as if she

616

might dare to contradict him. If she did, he was going to refuse to listen to her. "Someone opened the portal. I can see now, it must have been Zyah."

"She didn't know what she was doing. It was an accident. It scared her. You scared her. Her man, Player, is like my Horus," Anat explained. "They moved the drawing from my house in order to protect me, not realizing I knew what it was. Player was afraid the bomb might go off and kill me." She smiled affectionately at Player.

Player felt that smile right through him, like an arrow to his soul. Zyah's grandmother had taken the club, his family, into her home, into her heart, welcoming them in the way Blythe had. He tightened his hold on Zyah, feeling he was lucky to bring not only Zyah to his family, but Anat. For so long, he had felt unworthy of the others, apart from them. His mind defective and even dangerous to them because of his strange talent. Sharing Zyah and Anat had more than made up for any shortcomings he might have.

"I was recovering from a brain injury," Player explained. "The drawing was in front of me, and I could clearly see the plans for the bomb. My brain works on things like that, and it did. The next thing, Zyah and I saw you and you scared the crap out of us. We were terrified for Anat and had no idea what to think. I asked my family for help. They're very good at finding people. Fortunately, Zyah, my family and I all believe so much in Anat, that before we did anything, we asked her. She told us how this all came about. It's pretty incredible."

"Unbelievable is what you mean," François said. "The things Horus and Ken thought of and then proceeded to do were beyond this world. Out of a science fiction movie. If I tried to tell someone about them, people would think I was crazy." He hesitated. "What do you mean, your family? *Maman,* this kind of technology is extremely dangerous. If it fell into the wrong hands, it would be a disaster. No one else knew about this. It was kept a secret because it was so dangerous."

"Horus was well aware of that. He honestly didn't think it would work. None of us did. Ken and Amara tried first and couldn't open the portal. Ken was the one who had designed the portal, so naturally we thought they could open it. Even for Horus and Ken, the idea was too farfetched. You can imagine how shocked we were when it worked for us," Anat said.

"Zyah and — I'm sorry, I don't remember your name," François said.

"My family calls me Player," he supplied.

"Player, then. If it got out about this, any government or terrorist group would come after both of you in a heartbeat. You know that."

618

"I know. It was always meant to be destroyed. I just didn't think anyone else could ever open it or even read it," Anat admitted.

"Did you tell anyone about this?" François asked Player.

"Several of my family members know. They're here now," Player said. "I'm in a club. Czar, our president, is here. A few others. Mechanic, Savage, Destroyer, Ink, Storm."

Observing the absolute dismay on François's face as each man moved into sight and then out again, Anat tried to assure him. "These are good boys. I was robbed and beaten and they took care of me. Player was shot preventing Zyah from being kidnapped. They'll do whatever it takes to protect us, François. And I intend to destroy the drawing after talking to you. I don't want to, because I love it so much, but this has shown me that it is much too dangerous to have around. The club thinks it needs to be destroyed as well."

"I think it best, *maman.* I'm sorry that you'll lose Horus's drawing when it means so much to you, but I did buy a ticket, and I'm coming to see you. It isn't the same, but having your son back might help."

"It more than helps," Anat assured. "You have two beautiful daughters and a son of your own."

"I do. My wife is an incredible woman. I

can't wait for you to meet her. I haven't told them anything about why I'm traveling to the United States. I didn't know what was happening with the portal at the time I purchased the ticket, so I was traveling alone."

"When are you coming?" Anat asked, nearly holding her breath.

"I'm flying out tomorrow." Again, François's voice was very decisive.

Player glanced at Czar. That didn't give Code much time to find out very much about Anat's son. As far as the club was concerned, Anat was theirs. Their grandmother. That meant they took care of her. They protected her. She clearly loved this man. She'd raised him from the time he was an infant, and she'd done everything to protect him, but seventeen years had gone by and he hadn't reached out to her. He hadn't found a way to send her money or help. They had a code. It was different and they knew that, but still, it was the way they lived. Czar was already texting, filling Code in, telling him to put everything aside until they knew what they could about François.

"I can't wait to see you, François," Anat reiterated. "We will be destroying the drawing as soon as we close the portal, so we won't be able to contact each other this way."

"You have my contact information, correct?" François said.

She nodded. "And you have mine?"

"Yes. *Je t'aime, maman.*"

"I love you, François," Anat whispered. She glanced back at Zyah and Player. There were tears in her eyes.

Player released his hold on Zyah and put a little distance between them. At once the inside of the drawing began to color in. The process was slow, but it was impossible to see François. Where there had been darkness, light began to shine through, leaving the lines of charcoal to fill in. Player, watching, found it a fascinating procedure. Eventually, the drawing was just that again, an intricate, beautiful picture surrounded by an intriguing frame.

All of them stood behind Anat's wheelchair, staring at Horus's drawing for a long time. Destroyer leaned close to Anat. "You ready? Let's go out to the yard."

She nodded and reached back to pat his hand. "I guess I'm as ready as I'll ever be."

Zyah followed behind the chair and Player took the picture off the wall. He dreaded burning it almost as much as the women did. It really was priceless, but it was too dangerous to keep. He carried the framed picture out to the pit dug in the ground and lined with rocks, already waiting. The fuel, branches of dried oak and redwood, was stacked. Storm lit the tented smaller twigs, and Player waited for the larger branches to catch fire before putting the picture, face-

621

down, on top of it. He didn't wait, nor did he show it again to the women.

Zyah reached her hand out to Anat and then leaned close to her, circling her neck with her arm. Player stepped up beside her and wrapped his arm around her waist. Savage and Destroyer both pressed close to Anat to give her comfort while they all watched the picture burn. When it was completely consumed by the flames, Anat looked up at Destroyer.

"I'm tired. Would you mind taking me back to Lizz's house?"

"Not at all, Anat," Destroyer said.

"I'll go with you," Zyah volunteered.

Anat patted her hand. "Lizz loves you dearly, Zyah, but she isn't quite ready to see too much of you. She doesn't need reminders of Francine's treachery right now. You stay with Player. The two of you need time together. Let a couple of old women grieve together. Tomorrow François will be here and we'll have a fine celebration, although I don't know when I'll have my home back."

"We can use my home," Player said.

"Or mine," Czar said. "Or the clubhouse. You tell me what you want and it's yours, Anat. Alena will let us use the restaurant as well."

Anat blinked back tears. "You're all very good to me."

Player thought it was the other way around.

He drew Zyah close as they watched Destroyer put Anat in the van. The club helped him put out the fire, and then they left, leaving him alone with his woman.

Player sat on the edge of the bed, his pounding head in his hands. His body was covered in sweat. He was never going to be rid of the nightmares. Never. They'd lessened with Zyah sleeping beside him, but nothing was going to erase his past. Careful not to disturb her, he padded to the shower, hoping the hot water would relieve the terrible jackhammers threatening to rip his brain apart.

"Water on," he ordered. "Lights dim. Blue." He felt almost sick with pain.

Resting his forehead against the tile with his arms spread out, bracing himself with his hands on the walls of the shower, he let the water spray over his body from every direction. Above him, the multiple rows of shower heads rained down on him, providing a gentle rain that encompassed the entire large enclosure. Four of the side shower heads pulsed harder into his body, massaging his muscles. He hoped that would distract him from the pounding in his head.

"Honey. You should have woken me up." Zyah's arms slid around his waist. She pressed her breasts to his back. She was short enough that her soft mounds fit quite snugly into the curve of his back above his buttocks.

"I don't like that you don't wake me when you have nightmares. This isn't the first time."

Was there hurt in her voice? In her mind? He couldn't tell because it was all he could do to concentrate on keeping the pain from spilling over into her mind. He wasn't giving her that.

"Babe. Go back to bed. I'm all right."

She didn't move. Or speak. She stayed still, her arms wrapped around him, her face pressed to his back now, just as tightly as her tits. He could feel every breath she took.

"This happens. It's going to keep happening. We both knew it would." He dropped one hand over hers and rubbed back and forth, taking some solace from just having her close. "Can't get away from it. Don't like it touching you."

"You're not all right, Player. You hurt like hell. I can feel your headache and you're protecting me. It's like a battering ram. If you're protecting me, I can't imagine how bad it is for you. Why wouldn't you want my help?"

There was definitely hurt in her voice. His heart clenched hard in his chest. He couldn't cope with that right now.

"Babe. I love you, but I can't make things better for you when my head is coming apart the way it is." He tried to turn his head to look at her. That required opening his eyes. Thank heavens he'd called for blue lights or he wouldn't have been able to take it.

Zyah had stepped to the side of him, and her face was tilted up, looking up at him. Water ran over her from the many long rows of shower heads. Beads of water ran in rivulets over her shoulders and down the curves of her body.

"You aren't supposed to make things better for me, Player, I'm going to make them better for you." She raised her voice to a command. "Water off." Her chocolate eyes darkened, and she indicated for him to walk ahead of her. "Out."

If he could have managed, he would have smiled, but he obeyed her. His woman going all bossy on him could make him hard under the worst of circumstances. She rolled her eyes at him when he glanced back, his hand fisting his cock.

"Grab a towel instead of your cock and get on the bed. Lie down on your stomach." She toweled off and went to the cabinet where he'd put the many items he'd gotten from Hannah at the Floating Hat.

"You turn me on when you're so damn bossy, woman." He was telling the strict truth. He stretched out gingerly in the center of the bed. Just moving his head around hurt. That didn't seem to stop his wayward cock from reacting to her, though.

"I turn you on all the time. Just waking up turns you on," she said.

625

She moved into his line of vision, or rather part of her body did. He had his head turned toward her. He could see her narrow waist and generous hips. He loved the shape of her hips. The junction between her legs, those dark curls she'd shaved like a little landing strip that left her lips bare for him because he'd shaved her that way one day. She'd kept it for him. He liked to tease her with his mouth and tongue and teeth. Those little curls drove him nuts. But the bare lips and access to her clit made her all the more sensitive.

Zyah put one knee on the bed and crawled over him. Her hands, coated in lotion, began to massage the knots in his neck. She was quiet, working on the knots, letting the lotion do its magic along with her fingers. He was very conscious of her body straddling his. Her legs positioned on either side of his back, her pussy pressing into him.

All at once, when his guard slipped, she poured into his mind. Zyah. Soothing. Gentle. Just sliding in and filling him with her. Completing him. She found every one of the rips his past memories had put in his mind, mending them in the way she did. Zyah drove away the nightmares, replacing them with her sweetness, the way she loved him. The way she gave herself to him every single day.

He closed his eyes, surrendering to her

magic. It wasn't the lotion. It wasn't even her hands. It was Zyah and the way she took care of him. Already his house was filled with warmth. In the weeks she'd been living with him, she'd transformed the beautiful structure into the peaceful sanctuary he'd envisioned when he'd bought it.

Lizz had decided to move in with Anat, and the two women seemed to get along very well together. Lizz had the upstairs and Anat the downstairs. That decision had alleviated Zyah's worry that Anat would be alone if she moved out. Torpedo Ink still watched over Anat, taking turns as she did her physical therapy on her leg, but she was much more mobile now. Both Lizz and Anat frequently had dinner with Player and Zyah at Crow 287 or lunch at the Floating Hat. The little tea and bath and body shop had quickly become a favorite.

François had visited three times, bringing Anat such joy, Player couldn't help liking the man. The third visit, he'd brought his wife and children. That time, they'd all had a barbecue at Czar's so the children could play together. That had been a big hit, and Lizz had actually gone along. Zyah had really enjoyed getting to know her uncle and his family.

"Now that your head isn't pounding, Player, and I know you're feeling so much better," Zyah said, "I want you to tell me why you haven't been waking me up when you get these nightmares. They're coming frequently. You go off by yourself, play your music, or if they're particularly bad you head for the shower. Sometimes you go for a ride on your bike. I don't like being shut out, honey, so you're going to have to tell me why you're not waking me up immediately."

He'd been feeling relaxed. Just like that, tension shot through him. Instinctively, he knew she wasn't going to like the answer. It was a legitimate one, though.

He half turned, catching her around the waist, warning her so she had time to stretch her legs out, and then he rolled, tucking her under him. Her hair was wrapped in a warm towel, making her dark eyes larger, the lashes all the more noticeable. He traced her high cheekbones with his thumbs.

Wedging one knee between her legs, he nudged her until she accommodated him and he sank into his favorite place, cradling his body in her hips. She had a lush body, all curves, all feminine. Sometimes he wondered how he'd lived without her.

"Player." She'd perfected the art of the one-name inflection. Just like any club member, she could speak volumes with just one word. Low. Gentle. A brush of heat. A reprimand. Telling him to get on with it.

He bent his head and nipped her neck, then licked the spot soothingly, feeling her answering shiver. "I love you, Zyah. I want you for you, not because you can make my nightmares go away. Or because you can repair my brain when it's torn up. Or my mind when I'm all over the place."

"Player, honey —"

"Let me finish." He kissed his way down her throat to the curves of her breasts. "You were very casual about telling me you didn't want me to be with you for the great sex or because of your ability to repair my mind or take away the nightmares. You only said it once, and then you let it go. I thought about the times I wouldn't commit to you and you kept trying over and over, giving yourself to me full on. We had a connection. We knew each other through that connection. I knew what you were like. You knew what I was like. And then I was trying and you took me back, but I could feel it wasn't the same. There was a little part of you that held back. It wasn't like before, when you were all in. That very casual statement was the reason why."

Player shifted his body just enough to be able to kiss his way back up to her chin. To her lower lip. He used his teeth to tug on her lip just because it was so bitable. One hand slid between her legs just to make certain she was slick and hot for him. She was. He knew she would be. He had grown accustomed to the shifting of his heart now, the way it seemed to melt when he felt such love for her

629

overwhelming him.

"I realized no one would want to be wanted for their ability to repair damage to someone's brain, or to chase away nightmares."

Before she could protest, which he knew she would, he took her mouth. Slow. Gentle. Loving. Flames burned hot the way they did every time they kissed. Kissing ignited some deep well of fire in both of them so that a storm came together, no matter how gentle he wanted to be. He caught her legs, lifted them at the knees and urged her to wrap them around his hips as he lodged the head of his cock in her slick entrance.

She was so hot. Burning. Tight. He always wondered if he was going to make it into her, especially when he was like this, invading slowly. He loved looking into her eyes. Watching her as he joined them together. Her eyes always darkened more. Went wide. Dazed. A little shocked.

"Player." She breathed his name this time. Almost reverently.

He heard the love in her voice. Felt it in his mind. She swamped him with the emotion. He pushed deeper into that scorching-hot tunnel, one slow inch at a time.

"Never think that way, honey. I know you love me. I want you to wake me up."

Her breath came in the delicious little ragged musical pants he particularly loved to hear. He pushed deeper through those tight silken petals. Staring into her eyes when he took her this way always made him feel like he was looking into her soul and she was looking into his. It was incredibly intimate. Incredibly beautiful. He reached for her hands and threaded their fingers together as he rose over her, driving deeper, needing to be fully surrounded by her.

"I have complete confidence that you love me, Player." Her fingers tightened around his. Her legs tightened around his hips.

"I'll never get over the nightmares." He surged forward, burying himself those last few inches. "*Bog,* baby, you're so tight. I'm never certain I'm going to survive, it's so good."

He moved in her slow, withdrawing, feeling the friction dragging over his shaft, over his ultrasensitive crown. The breath left his lungs in a rush. His woman. His miracle. He pushed back just as slow, one inch at a time. She rose to meet him, her hips matching that slow rhythm, in complete harmony with him. Savoring each other. Worshipping.

"I know they're a part of you. I love *all* of you. I don't want to be shut out of any part of you, Player. I want all of you, including your nightmares. Including your past. You don't give that to anyone else. Only me."

Her hot tunnel surrounded him like a scorching-hot fist of living silk, squeezing and gripping until he thought his head might explode from the sheer pleasure. He couldn't keep that deliberate, measured pace that smoldered, a slow burn that built and built until the flames raced up his spine, threatening to consume him. He began to surge into her with harder, faster strokes. Forks of lightning streaked through his body, spreading through the fire until he could barely breathe.

*Player, tell me you're with me on this. It's important to me. I have to know you're with me, that you understand how important it is to me to be this connected to you always.*

He could read her so easily when their bodies were one. When their minds were. Their hearts were so connected, and he swore their souls somehow had been woven together. Yeah. He read her. She wanted that closeness, even if it meant seeing his past and the ugliness of the life he'd had as a child. Sharing the worst of him. Knowing the ugly things he did to escape. Knowing the things he did to bring down those who preyed on children. She was willing to live with his sins. How could he not love her? Worship her? Feel so fucking much for her he burned with it?

*I'm with you all the way, Zyah. If it's important to you, then it's important to me.*

*You give me your word of honor while we both can still think straight.*

*You've got it, baby.* He smiled down at her,

looking into her eyes as he gave her his word. And then he was lost in her body. Burning in the flames and loving every minute of it. Loving her with everything in him.

# TERMS ASSOCIATED WITH BIKER CLUBS

**1-percenters:** This is a term often used in association with outlaw bikers, as in "99 percent of clubs are law-abiding, but the other 1 percent are not." Sometimes the symbol is worn inside a diamond-shaped patch.

**3-piece patch or 3-piece:** This term is used for the configuration of a club's patch: the top piece, or rocker, with club name; a center patch that is the club's logo; and a bottom patch or rocker with the club's location, such as Sea Haven.

**Biker:** someone who rides a motorcycle

**Biker friendly:** a business that welcomes bikers

**Boneyard:** refers to a salvage yard

**Cage:** often refers to a car, van or truck (basically any vehicle not a motorcycle)

**Chapter:** the local unit of a larger club

**Chase vehicle:** a vehicle following riders on a run just in case of a breakdown

**Chopper:** customized bike

**Church:** club meeting

**Citizen:** someone not a biker

**Club:** could be any group of riders banding together (most friendly)

**Colors:** patches, logo, something worth fighting for because it represents who you are

**Cut:** vest or denim jackets with sleeves cut off with club colors on them; almost always worn, even over leather jackets

**Dome:** helmet

**Getting patched:** Moving up from prospect to full club member (you would receive the logo patch to wear with rockers). This must be earned, and is the only way to get respect from brothers.

**Hang-around:** anyone hanging around the club who might want to join

**Hog:** nickname for motorcycle, mostly associated with Harley-Davidson

**Independent:** a biker with no club affiliation

**Ink:** tattoo

**Ink slinger:** a tattoo artist

**Nomad:** club member who travels between chapters; goes where he's needed in his club

**Old lady:** Wife or woman who has been with a man for a long time. It is not considered disrespectful, nor does it have anything to do with how old one is.

**Patch holder:** member of a motorcycle club

**Patches:** sewn on vests or jackets, these can be many things with meanings or just for fun, even gotten from runs made

**Poser:** pretend biker

**Property of:** a patch displayed on a jacket, vest or sometimes a tattoo, meaning the woman (usually old lady or longtime girlfriend) is with the man and his club

**Prospect:** someone working toward becoming a fully patched club member

# RESOURCES

**Bikers Against Child Abuse (BACA)**
bacausa.com

**Advocates for Youth**
1325 G Street NW, Suite 980
Washington, D.C. 20005
1-202-419-3420
advocatesforyouth.org

**U.S. Department of Justice**
Project Safe Childhood
810 Seventh Street NW
Washington, D.C. 20531
AskDOJ@usdoj.gov
justice.gov/psc/index.html

**MaleSurvivor**
350 Central Park West, Ste 1H
New York, NY 10025
1-800-738-4181
malesurvivor.org

# ABOUT THE AUTHOR

**Christine Feehan** is the #1 *New York Times* bestselling author of the Carpathian series, the GhostWalker series, the Leopard series, the Shadow Riders series, and the Sea Haven novels, including the Drake Sisters series and the Sisters of the Heart series.

The employees of Thorndike Press hope you have enjoyed this Large Print book. All our Thorndike, Wheeler, and Kennebec Large Print titles are designed for easy reading, and all our books are made to last. Other Thorndike Press Large Print books are available at your library, through selected bookstores, or directly from us.

For information about titles, please call:
(800) 223-1244

or visit our website at:
gale.com/thorndike

To share your comments, please write:
Publisher
Thorndike Press
10 Water St., Suite 310
Waterville, ME 04901